'Shivery, creepy, melancholy, funny, fantastic and very real, the English folktale rises up again from the host of individual voices captured here. Neil Philip's classic collection offers us an overflowing cauldron of marvellous stories; this is a necessary book.'

Marina Warner

'Collections of folktales as good as this should be treated in two ways: first, they should be bound in gold and brought out on ceremonial occasions as national treasures; and second, they should be printed in editions of hundreds of thousands, at the public expense, and given away free to every young teacher and every new parent.'

Philip Pullman

'The generally admitted and admired glories of English literature rest on a much more neglected popular tradition of story-telling. This collection brings that tradition back to life, in a wonderfully accessible form, and demonstrates its splendid colour and variety of form, tone and message. It is also very helpfully annotated and edited, by a loving and erudite hand.'

Professor Ronald Hutton

'Some rare titles have a generational impact, opening up a folkloric landscape many of us have never stopped exploring. This book is one of them. It was a profound influence on me and Hookland.'

David Southwell

'This is the best collection of English folktales since Katharine Briggs's assemblage in four volumes, and perhaps the best ever in a single volume; here are tales poignant, strange, wonderful, and ancient, told by people usually shut out from history but here allowed to speak by Philip's exceptional and attentive scholarship. The general reader and the scholar should be equally glad to see this volume available once again.'

Professor Diane Purkiss

'Buckle up and prepare for close encounters with ghouls and boggarts, witches and merry-maids, talking cats and roaring bulls. These tales may be quintessentially English, but they are also part of a golden network of folklore that shows how violence can be vanquished, trauma healed, and justice secured. And where else will you find entertainments with as high a coefficient of weirdness as in this collection of tales, wild and whimsical?'

Professor Maria Tatar

'A book that inspires and informs, and opens hearts and minds to our story heritage.'

Professor Carolyne Larrington

'It has taken more than a century since Joseph Jacobs published his book of English tales for a complete collection of English folktales to be published. Thanks to Neil Philip we now have a superb anthology of more than one hundred extraordinary tales that reveal the exquisite nature of the English storytelling tradition. Philip's *Watkins Book of English Folktales* can be enjoyed by young and old. This is a dazzling book.'

Professor Jack Zipes

'As Job's children are restored to him, full of life and evergreen, this volume flashes its splendours and returns its golden fruits into our eager hands. Never was a better time for such a knowing, appreciative volume of our shared tales. Welcome to it; draw the benches up; tales older than centuries yet fresh as June fireflies are yours, to read, to share, to remember, to discover.'

Gregory Maguire

'This is a rare and wonderful treasure of a book: an expertly chosen selection of English folktales, that is highly readable, endlessly entertaining, and intellectually enlivened by the meticulous scholarship of Neil Philip. *The Watkins Book of English Folktales* offers unrivalled insights into the English imagination as it has taken shape in traditional storytelling over centuries. Here the reader will encounter the characters they might expect to find – Jack and the Beanstalk and The Three Little Pigs – along with the more unfamiliar denizens of popular English invention: the small-toothed dog, the one-eyed giant of Dalton Mill, and the terrible Mr Fox. For the cultural historian, there is also the enormous pleasure of Philip's notes, which identify the story variants, and track the narratives, as much as possible, though the mazy paths of oral and literary dissemination.

If by some mysterious goblin's spell I was condemned to give away all the books in my library but one, this is undoubtedly the book I would keep.'

Professor Andrew Teverson

This is a golden treasury of over one hundred English folktales captured in the form in which they were first collected in past centuries. Read these classic tales as they would have been told when storytelling was a living art – when the audience believed in boggarts and hobgoblins, local witches and will-o'-the-wisps, ghosts and giants, cunning foxes and royal frogs. Find 'Jack the Giantkiller', 'Tom Tit Tot' and other quintessentially English favourites, alongside interesting borrowings, such as an English version of the Grimms' 'Little Snow White' – as well as bedtime frighteners, including 'Captain Murderer', as told to Charles Dickens by his childhood nurse.

Neil Philip has provided a full introduction to the creation, collection and telling of traditional English tales, and source notes illustrate each story's journey from mouth to page. These tales rank among the finest English short stories of all time in their richness of metaphor and plot and their great verbal dash and daring.

Neil Philip was born in York in 1955. He now lives in Oxfordshire, where he divides his time between writing and research and his work as editorial director of a small publishing company. His consuming interest is folk narrative, but he has also written on children's literature and on English social history. His essays and reviews have appeared in numerous journals, including *The Times*, *The Times Educational Supplement*, *The Times Literary Supplement* and *Folklore*, of which he is a former reviews editor. Among his other books are *A Fine Anger: A Critical Introduction to the Work of Alan Garner* (1981), winner of the ChLA Literary Criticism Book Award; a country anthology, *Between Earth and Sky* (Penguin 1984); *The Tale of Sir Gawain* (1987), shortlisted for the Emil/Kurt Maschler Award; and *The Cinderella Story* (Penguin 1989). He has also edited *The Penguin Book of Scottish Folktales*. His *A New Treasury of Poetry* (1990), illustrated by John Lawrence, was hailed by *The Times* as 'among the great anthologies for the young'. He is currently editing *The New Oxford Book of Children's Verse*.

THE WATKINS BOOK OF

ENGLISH FOLKTALES

NEIL PHILIP

FOREWORD BY
NEIL GAIMAN

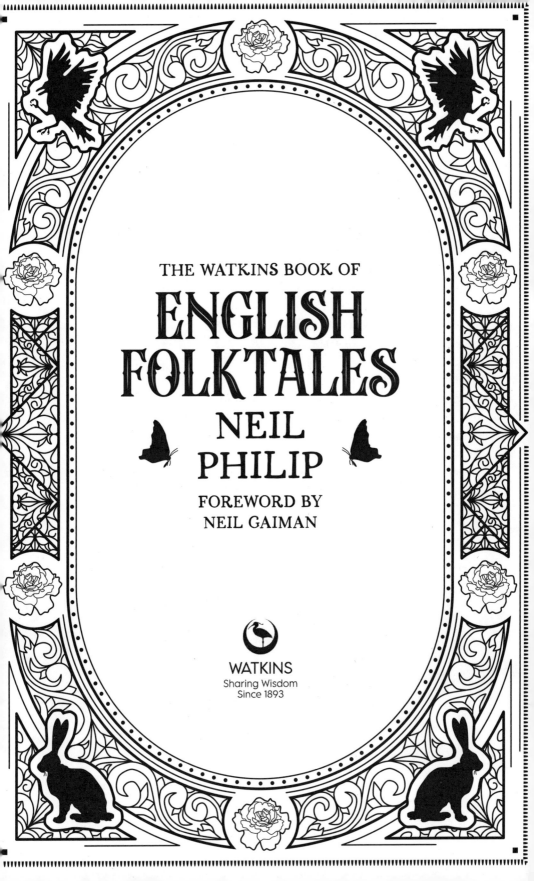

WATKINS
Sharing Wisdom
Since 1893

First published in 1992 as *The Penguin Book of English Folktales.*

This edition published in the UK and USA in 2022 by
Watkins, an imprint of Watkins Media Limited
Unit 11, Shepperton House
89–93 Shepperton Road
London
N1 3DF

enquiries@watkinspublishing.com

10 9 8 7 6 5 4 3

Designed and typeset by JCS Publishing Services Ltd.

Printed and bound in the United Kingdom by TJ Books Ltd.

A CIP record for this book is available from the British Library

ISBN: 978-1-78678-709-5 (Hardback)
ISBN: 978-1-78678-725-5 (eBook)

www.watkinspublishing.com

For Alan Garner

O, 'tis a precious apothegmaticall Pedant, who will finde matter
inough to dilate a whole daye of the first invention of Fy, fa, fum,
I smell the bloud of an Englishman.

Thomas Nashe
Have with you to Saffron-Walden 1596

Contents

CONTENTS

Acknowledgements

THE AUTHOR AND PUBLISHER would like to thank the owners of copyright material for their permission to reproduce the following stories:

J. M. Dent & Sons Ltd for 'The Grey Castle' from Dora Yates, *A Book of Gypsy Folk-Tales* (Phoenix House, 1948). The Estate of T. W. Thompson and the Brotherton Collection, Leeds University Library, for 'Lousy Jack and His Eleven Brothers', 'The Magic Knapsack', 'Sorrow and Love', 'The Frog Sweetheart' and 'Snow-White'. The Estate of T. W. Thompson and the Bodleian Library, Oxford, for 'Doctor Forster' and 'In a Haunted House'. The Estate of T. W. Thompson for 'Wanted, a Husband', 'The Tin Can at the Cow's Tail', 'Appy and the Conger Eel' and 'Fairies Down the Lane' from *Journal of the Gypsy Lore Society*. The Folklore Society for 'The Pear-Drum', 'The Lad who was Never Hungry' and 'The Parsons' Meeting' from *Folk-lore*. Random House Inc. for 'The Doctor and the Trapper' and 'The Railway Ticket' from William Wood, *A Sussex Farmer* (Jonathan Cape, 1938), and 'The First Smith' from G. E. C. Webb, *Gypsies: The Secret People* (Herbert Jenkins, 1960). The University of Salzburg for 'Four Jests of Sir Nicholas le Strange' from H. P. Lippincott (ed.), *'Merry Passages and Jeasts': A Manuscript Jestbook of Sir Nicholas le Strange (1603–55)* (1974). Beltons for 'Tommy Lindrum' from Ethel Rudkin, *Lincolnshire Folklore* (1936). Routledge for 'Dowser and Sam' from W. H. Barrett, *Tales of the Fens* (ed. Enid Porter, 1963).

Grateful acknowledgement is also made for permission to quote from the BBC Sound Archives, and from the manuscripts in the archives of the Folklore Society and the Centre for English Cultural Tradition and Language, University of Sheffield.

Every effort has been made to trace copyright owners, but this has not always proved possible. The publisher would be interested to hear from any copyright owners not here acknowledged.

Foreword

FOLK STORIES AND FAIRY tales came from somewhere else, not England. That was something I'd learned as a schoolboy.

The tales were still ours, of course: it didn't matter where they had originated, they were still performed on stage in Panto season by people who sounded like I did, and Cinderella, I knew, must be as English as they come, what with Baron Hardup and Buttons, and for that matter Aladdin and his Wonderful Lamp might have been set in ancient Beijing but the Widow Twankey was there to tell us, with a joke about eating fish and chips on the South Parade Pier, that ancient Beijing was incredibly local.

Still, proper folk stories were collected by the brothers Grimm, or by Charles Perrault. As I grew up, I'd find collections of folktales in books from all over the world – from Sweden to Alaska to the Philippines – and began to feel that I'd missed out by being English.

I had been raised in a country where stories mattered and had been told, and I knew that too many of those stories were lost, leaving something that was almost a fossil record behind. There were Jack tales, they were English, and I knew about them, and there were local monsters, and places in literature that spoke of the places that tales had been – Shakespeare's speeches about fairies, whether Puck or Queen Mab, implied a world of stories mostly lost to us; Dickens parodied local stories filled with Goblins, and I wanted to hear the originals.

I first read this book about thirty years ago. I had recently moved to the US, and missed the England I had left, and I found it in a local bookshop. I loved it, devoured it with delight. It felt alive. Here were stories I had never imagined existing that delighted and astonished me, alongside stories I knew, told in ways I hadn't encountered them before.

I read the Snow-White story, with three robbers instead of seven dwarfs, and it changed the inside of my head. G. K. Chesterton wrote, in *The Napoleon of Notting Hill*, that: 'If you look at a thing nine hundred and ninety-nine times, you are perfectly safe; if you look at it the thousandth time, you are in frightful danger of seeing it for the first time', and now I knew what he meant. I had read and heard and watched the story of Snow White all my life: one of the first books I remember owning had been a beautifully illustrated *Snow White and the Seven Dwarfs*. And yet the version that Neil Philip gave me here was dissonant enough, real enough, that I looked at the story for the thousandth time, and wrote a version of Snow White called 'Snow, Glass, Apples' in which the little princess was a vampire, her prince was a necrophile, and her stepmother was, perhaps, the heroine and the victim.

The retelling of Marie Clothilde Balfour's 'The Flyin' Childer' was a story I had never run into in any form before. It made a huge impression on me, and a few years later I retold it myself, in *Sandman*, illustrated by Charles Vess. It felt alive, in ways that I appreciated, a story shape I hadn't encountered, a story of murder and revenge, of a betrayed woman, of children who flew away. It was a strange, dark story and it delighted me.

The way that Lucy Clifford's (written, literary) story, 'The New Mother' transmuted into the orally collected story 'The Pear Drum' fascinated me, and reminded me that every story starts somewhere, and starts with someone making it up. Here was Dickens' hilarious take on Bluebeard, 'Captain Murderer' alongside the haunting tale of 'The Story of Mr Fox' (another story I would one day retell).

Neil Philip had researched assiduously and spread his net wide to create this collection. He had unearthed tales from all across England, stories that resonated, stories that were more than a fossil record of what was left behind but were a triumphant collection of stories that showed what English stories were – and that was something much more interesting than localized jokes in pantomimes. His commentaries on the stories were enlightening.

This is an important collection, and I was thrilled to learn that it would be available once again. But it's better than just an important book: it's a treasure-trove of living stories, and enormously fun to read.

Enjoy!

Neil Gaiman

Introduction to the 2022 Watkins Edition

THE ENGLISH FOLKTALE HAS entwined itself into English literature, from Chaucer and the Gawain Poet to George Peele, William Shakespeare, John Clare, Charles Dickens and Thomas Hardy. But by the time the original edition of this book came out in 1992, writers with an interest in the deep structure of English folklore, such as Alan Garner and Kevin Crossley-Holland, were regarded as outliers. What had folktales got to do with the worlds of Martin Amis or Julian Barnes or Craig Raine?

Thirty years later, things seem very different. There is a whole new generation of writers, many of them influenced by Garner, for whom the folktale is the bedrock of narrative. Philip Pullman, Emma Donoghue, Paul Kingsnorth and Zoë Gilbert are obvious examples.

Non-fiction writers such as Robert Macfarlane, Carolyne Larrington, Edward Parnell and Amy Jeffs have also begun to decode England's storied landscape in terms of its folktale heritage.

As I was writing and researching this book, there was a remarkable resurgence of oral storytelling in England, spearheaded by Ben Haggerty, Sally Pomme Clayton and Hugh Lupton. Under the auspices of the Crick-Crack Club and the Society for Storytelling, this has become a thriving scene, perhaps comparable to the growth of performance poetry, and the writers who have contributed to the lively History Press series of county-by-county folktale collections (a sample of which was published as *The Anthology of English Folk Tales* in 2016) are themselves storytellers, including Hugh Lupton, Kevan Manwaring, Sharon Jacksties and Maureen James.

The taking possession of folklore by storytellers rather than scholars has been part of what might be called a rewilding of the English folktale, in which narrators in both oral and written contexts have felt free to both absorb and recast their source material.

The most remarkable manifestation of this rewilding has been the creation by David Southwell of the ghost county of Hookland. Much of Hookland's folklore exists as tweets, a very modern way of telling folktales. He writes,

'When we explore place, we get the opportunity to interact with those myth circuits running in the earth, in the stone. Get ourselves dirty wading through folklore – that dark sediment of decomposing memory, disturbed by ritual, disturbed by our being in a place.'

Southwell's insistence that in Hookland 'nothing is made up, just remembered differently' prompted me to think again about the storyteller Ruth L. Tongue. She was a close friend of the great folklorist Katharine Briggs, and the pair collaborated on *Folktales of England* (1965), the English volume in Richard Dorson's influential Folktales of the World series. Unlike other books in the series, generally sourced from national archives, this volume relied very heavily on a single storyteller – Ruth Tongue herself. Tongue contributed forty-two stories, nearly half the book. My own *English Folktales* contains no stories from Tongue; I regarded her essentially as a fraud, with her vague attributions to unnamed sources and her put-on 'Mummerzet' dialect. But I see now that her pretence of being a folklore collector was simply a way of remembering differently, and that with her naturally vivid and expressive storytelling style she was in fact making a unique creative contribution to the English folktale. As Bob and Jacqueline Patten wrote, she 'drew no distinction between collection, recollection and recreation'.

Another collector whom I regarded with some suspicion was Marie Clothilde Balfour, a cousin (not aunt) of Robert Louis Stevenson. Her tales from the Lincolnshire fens in the 1880s were so different in tone and content from anything else collected in Lincolnshire, or indeed in England, that they seemed simply too good to be true. I highlight my doubts in the note to her story 'The Flyin' Childer', though I did choose to include both that and 'The Green Mist' in this book. Since then, a PhD thesis by Maureen James (author of *Lincolnshire Folk Tales* in the History Press series) has proved conclusively that the stories are genuine folk tradition, recorded by Clothilde Balfour as best she could. James has tentatively identified four of Balfour's storytellers, and explains the feverish nature of the stories as a result of 'regular and excessive consumption of opium': malaria was endemic in the fens, and widely self-managed with opium. If I had access to James's thesis at the time, I would probably have included a couple more of Balfour's laudanum-drenched fever-dreams, such as 'The Dead Moon' and 'Yallery Brown'.

One might think that all the stories that were ever going to be collected from English tradition had been already, but folklore has a habit of springing back to life. The most remarkable addition to the canon of faithfully recorded and transcribed English folktales was made in 1997 by Michael Wilson in his *Performance and Practice: Oral Narrative Traditions Among Teenagers in Britain and Ireland*, which contains, for instance, energetic versions of 'The Golden Arm' and 'Tom Tit Tot'. 'Tom Tit Tot' was collected from thirteen-year-old Eva Shannon, who heard it from her grandmother; it evidently derives ultimately from the text recorded by Anna Walter Thomas (included in this book), but the tale has taken on a new lease of life in the oral tradition.

There is also the case of the two-volume *Folktales of Newfoundland* by Herbert Halpert and J. D. A. Widdowson (1996). This monumental work shows folktales that have vanished from English tradition alive and well in Newfoundland. So, for instance, the tale type ATU 313 'The Magic Flight', which underpins 'Sir Gawain and the Green Knight', has only been collected twice in England, as 'Daughter Greengown', both times by T. W. Thompson from English gypsies (from Reuben Gray in 1914 and Taimi Boswell in 1915). *Folktales of Newfoundland* has versions from six different storytellers, all speaking in 'West Country English'. Wonders will never cease.

In short, the English folktale, far from being moribund, is alive and kicking.

Introduction

William Hone's *Every-Day Book*, that great nineteenth-century storehouse of the interesting and odd, contains an account written in 1826 of a festival of lying supposed to have been held each May Day at the village of Temple Sowerby in Westmorland with a hone or whetstone among the prizes. Hone's correspondent, 'C. T.', writes:

> There is an anecdote, very current in the place, of a late bishop of Carlisle
> passing through in his carriage on this day, when his attention being
> attracted by the group of persons assembled together, very naturally
> inquired the cause. His question was readily answered by a full statement
> of facts which brought from his lordship a severe lecture on the iniquity
> of such a proceeding; and at the conclusion, he said, 'For my part I never
> told a lie in my life.' This was immediately reported to the judges, upon
> which, without any dissent, the hone was awarded to his lordship, as most
> deserving of it.

This story about telling stories about telling stories about telling stories, with its unverifiable claims and its literary form, may stand at the head of any discussion of the complexities of the English folk narrative tradition.

Our picture of storytelling in England relies on fragmentary and often unsatisfactory evidence. Of all the major folk literatures, that of England is probably the scantiest. Why this should be is a complex question. It has much to do with what Joseph Jacobs, in the preface to his *English Fairy Tales* (1890), discerned as 'the lamentable gap between the governing and recording classes and the dumb working classes of this country – dumb to others but eloquent among themselves'. But it is also true that English society did not, except in special cases, provide the community of audience necessary to sustain a thriving storytelling tradition such as that described by J. F. Campbell in his classic *Popular Tales of the West Highlands* (1860), with semi-organized story sessions, 'the first tale by the good-man, and tales to daylight by the guest'. Storytelling in England has tended to be much more informal than this. Stories were told as the occasion arose, as a natural element of daily life, rather than recited to an audience. We might take as an image of English storytelling the excursion party in Albert Smith's sub-Dickensian novel *Christopher Tadpole* (1848). After 'the jolly man' has told a sensational story of an attempted robbery,

> such an impetus had been given to the narrative faculties of the van party that they all began to tell stories at once, of things that had happened to them. And after this they dropped down to anecdotes and witty sayings, and finally sang songs.

This scrappy and disorganized narrative tradition has never been easy to pin down or record.

It is true, too, that the English oral tradition was early destabilized by mass semi-literacy and the wide circulation of cheap reading-matter, offering the concept of a fixed text in place of the oral storyteller's creative reconstruction. Evidence of this process is clearly marshalled in Margaret Spufford's *Small Books and Pleasant Histories: Popular Fiction and its Readership in Seventeenth-Century England* (1981), which uses Pepys's collection of chapbooks to 'establish the nature of the world of the imagination, fiction and fantasy open to the unlettered reader of the seventeenth century, who had 2d. or 3d. to spend'.

Many of the best-known English tales, such as 'Jack and the Beanstalk' and 'Jack the Giant Killer', were first – and in some cases only – printed in chapbook form. Victor E. Neuburg notes in *The Penny Histories* (1968) that, 'the folklore sources of English chapbooks have never been examined.' A great deal of work remains to be done in this area. It is important to note here only that while many chapbooks printed stories from English tradition, or attenuated versions of medieval romances, the wide circulation of stories from Perrault in chapbook form from the mid-eighteenth century on soon established Perrault's 'Cinderella' and 'Bluebeard' as staple fare in the cottage as well as the nursery. The Northamptonshire poet John Clare – the son of an agricultural labourer and a labourer himself – recalls in *The Shepherd's Calendar* (1827, 'January: A Cottage Evening') stories told in his childhood (he was born in 1793). As well as tales of fairies and witches, and cautionary tales, Clare remembers versions of 'The Three Heads in the Well', 'Jack and the Beanstalk' and – significantly – 'Cinderella'. His twenty-line version of Cinderella quite clearly derives from Perrault, with its rat coachmen and pumpkin coach; equally clearly it has been modified by English oral tradition. It is, for instance, a glove not a shoe that Cinderella loses.

This section of Clare's *Shepherd's Calendar* is the most detailed and vivid description we possess of the tradition of oral storytelling in England: not only what was told, but the circumstances of telling. Clare describes only women as storytellers in the home setting:

> Things cleared away then down she sits
> And tells her tales by starts and fits
> Not willing to lose time or toil
> She knits or sues [sews] and talks the while.

The children 'cringe away to bed', fearful of the terrors they have heard about. Clare says (1824) of these stories: 'I hear them told to children still'; in his poem 'St Martin's Eve', of about the same date, he describes, interestingly, folktales being *read* to a rural audience, almost certainly from the chapbook *The History of the Four Kings* (see p. 39). Clare did attempt to record the folksong tradition of his neighbourhood (see George Deacon, *John Clare and the Folk Tradition*, 1973), but although according to Clare's first biographer Frederick Martin (1865) Clare's father not only knew 'above a hundred' ballads but also had a 'stock of ghost stories and fairy tales' that 'was quite inexhaustible', no stories survive.

Quite frequently singers will also have been storytellers. The singer Henry Burstow, some of whose songs were collected by Lucy Broadwood and Ralph Vaughan Williams, writes in his autobiography, *Reminiscences of Horsham* (1911), that, 'I inherited a tenacious memory, to which from babyhood upwards I committed particulars of numerous events and incidents, tales and songs.' Had English folktales ever been pursued with the same vigour as folk songs, we might now be able to study them with something like the same thoroughness and confidence. But the only folk-song collector also to collect stories was the Reverend Sabine Baring-Gould, who contributed sixteen stories as an appendix to William Henderson's *Notes on the Folk-Lore of the Northern Counties of England and the Borders* (1866). These include, for instance, 'The Rose-Tree', an English version of the story known as the Grimms' 'Juniper Tree'. Accompanying Baring-Gould's story-texts was an early attempt at classification of tales by means of 'story radicals'. Folklorists now use a classification system invented by the Finn Antti Aarne and developed by the American Stith Thompson, *The Types of the Folktale* (2nd revision, 1961). 'The Rose-Tree' is a version of Aarne–Thompson (AT) 720 'My Father Slew Me, My Mother Ate Me'. Besides the tale-type index of Aarne and Thompson, scholars also refer to small units of narrative by the numbers assigned to them in Thompson's *Motif-Index of Folk Literature* (revised edn, 1955). These indexes, and the others formed on their pattern, are indispensable for the comparative study of folktales. The best introduction to their use is Thompson's own study of *The Folktale* (1946). Ernest Baughman's *Type and Motif Index of the Folk-Tales of England and North America* (1966) applies their techniques to the English-language material, and is a very valuable tool.

It is important, though, to realize that these classification systems are tools, not ends in themselves. Developed to assist the Finnish 'historic-geographic' method of folktale research, which seeks to establish a 'life history' for each tale by tracking back from version to version, the Aarne–Thompson index has encouraged scholars to think of story as something that inheres in the plot rather than in the words, images and performance. It is foolish to imagine that the Platonic type is more important than the individual – possibly clumsy and muddled – variant: this is certainly never true for either teller or audience, who are the only significant parties to any storytelling transaction.

Best, perhaps, to speak not of a story but of a narration. For an orally transmitted tale is not a fixed thing, like a static printed text. It is fluid, changeable, alive. Each narration is a separate event.

If we record or report a spoken story, what we have on paper is evidence of storytelling, rather than the story itself. We do have such evidence for England, as Katharine Briggs's monumental *Dictionary of British Folk-Tales in the English Language* (1970–71), the central repository of texts, shows. But it is evidence which to be properly understood needs to be questioned and replaced in a context it is now almost impossible to supply, save by close reading of accounts such as John Clare's.

As a brief indication of the problems involved in assessing the texts of English folktale narrations, I will examine briefly the four stories in Joseph Jacobs's *English Fairy Tales* that he claims to have been, in their original texts, 'taken down from the mouths of the peasantry'. The first is 'Jack and his Golden Snuffbox' from Francis Hindes Groome's *In Gypsy Tents* (1880). Far from being an English peasant, the narrator of this story was a Welsh gypsy, John Roberts. Far from being taken down from his mouth, the story was written down by the narrator himself. Far from being told in English, Groome's text is translated from the narrator's Romany. Next Jacobs offers 'Tom Tit Tot' (see p. 97) and 'Cap o' Rushes' (see p. 106). While these are indeed remarkably lively and robust, they were written down by Anna Walter-Thomas from memories of the storytelling of her old nurse, over twenty years after the event; the original narrator is neither named nor described. Fourth, is the version of 'The Three Big Sillies' supplied to the *Folk-Lore Journal* in 1884 by Charlotte Burne (see p. 201), about which the only information given is that it was 'told in 1862 (and afterwards) by a nursemaid then aged sixteen, a native of Houghton, near

Stafford'. Again we have a twenty-year gap for time and folklore scholarship to efface memory. These four tales, remember, are the best that Joseph Jacobs, the leading authority of his day, could come up with in 1890 as 'English folk-tales that have been taken down from the lips of the peasantry'.

It is a matter for regret that Jacobs never published the scholarly study of the English folktale that he promised, and which he was uniquely qualified to write, and that the planned narrative volume of the Gommes' projected *Dictionary of British Folk-Lore* came to nothing. Instead, the English folktale had to wait for F. J. Norton, whose painstaking manuscript collection forms the basis of the Briggs *Dictionary*, for a properly diligent and informed survey. In the meantime, the man whom I consider the greatest of all English folktale collectors had embarked on and abandoned his work entirely in the dark, pleading vainly in the *Journal of the Gypsy Lore Society* for help from folklorists in his efforts to record and set in context the oral narratives of English gypsies.

The man was Thomas William Thompson (1888–1968), a Chemistry master at Repton who as an undergraduate at Cambridge first became interested in gypsy lore, language and genealogy, on which he soon became a leading expert. His later researches on Wordsworth have been edited and published by Robert Woof as *Wordsworth's Hawkshead* (1970), but his notes on gypsy lore remain largely unpublished in manuscript collections split between the Bodleian Library and the Brotherton Collection, Leeds. But he did publish some tales in the *Journal of the Gypsy Lore Society*, together with two key essays, 'English Gypsy Folk-Tales and Other Traditional Stories' (*JGLS*, new series, vol. 8, 1914–15) and 'The Gypsy Grays as Tale-Tellers' (*JGLS*, 3rd series, vol. 1, 1922).

This second essay is the most substantial and lucid essay ever written on the repertoire of a group of English narrators, their style and their attitude to their tales. In this essay, which as far as I can see has been all but ignored since it was published, Thompson gives a clear and vivid description of the varying storytelling styles of Eva Gray ('Doctor Forster', p. 145) and her brothers Reuben ('Wanted, a Husband', p. 171), Gus ('Sorrow and Love', p. 71), Shani and Josh.

Thompson was particular about hearing stories told more than once; about enquiring into sources; about establishing what parts of a text were 'fixed' and what parts subject to variation. His flexibility of mind about the subject he was investigating allowed him to consider, for instance, 'the possibility of latter-day invention of new stories':

My chance came when Eva declared one day that out of loneliness she had an evening or two earlier told herself a 'brand new tale'. 'I med it up myself from beginning to end,' she said; 'and it was a long 'un! But I sat up till I'd finished it: I couldn't give it up till I'd got everything to come right again.' What she had done, I discovered, was to invent a new plot, using incidents from *märchen* she already knew. 'I've med up many a new tale,' she said, 'when I hadn't nobody to talk to, and was feeling a bit down, but I never think nothing more about 'em, and if you was to ask me to tell you one I couldn't for the life o' me; they're all clean gone out'n my head. But the owld tales as I've know'd since I was no height, I can al'ays remember them.'

Thompson's interest in stylistics, performance, and how the individual storyteller builds, maintains and regards their repertoire, was far in advance of the conventional folklorists of the day: one can quite see why, with only Charlotte Burne's *Handbook of Folklore* (1914) to guide him, he felt lost. He outlined some of the problems facing him without sound recording equipment:

To induce tale-telling Gypsies to relate their stock of tales is easy; to listen so intently as not to miss a single word, and yet be memorizing fixed phrases, is difficult; to record afterwards, fully and accurately, what you have heard, is impossible. The human memory is a disgracefully inefficient instrument, of which the best that can be said is that its retentive power is reasonably high for a short time. To record tales, then, with something approaching completeness and correctness it is necessary that they should be set down within a very few days of their narration. In the case of the earlier tales in my collection, Noah Lock's, the majority of Gus Gray's, and a few of Eva's and Shanny's, I found it possible, firstly, to make notes, and, secondly, to write out the tales in rough from these, within the stipulated very few days. With the later tales, however, the best that I could do whilst my recollection of them was still reliable, was to make very detailed notes; notes which were on the average quite two-thirds as long as the tales themselves. In these notes I tried to do the following things, in particular:
(1) To set down accurately and in their right order the main incidents of the tales.
(2) To work in with these a good proportion of the wealth of detail with which the narrators embroidered their stories in most cases.
(3) To reproduce verbatim all phrases that appeared to have been memorized, or to the wording of which the tale-tellers attached importance.

(4) To report fully the drift of all monologues and dialogues put into the mouths of the characters, and as far as possible the actual words used whenever they seemed to be worth preserving. (3) and (4) overlap in some cases.

(5) To record the subject matter, and, when it could be recalled, the actual wording, of all striking descriptive passages.

(6) To indicate the nature of all repetitions and summaries.

(7) To note all formal beginnings and endings, all places where the narrators identified themselves with their stories, and all modernizations and topical allusions.

With such a programme of priorities, Thompson was able to do astonishing work, collecting many long stories in a single day from narrators such as Eva Gray or Taimi Boswell (see 'Lousy Jack and his Eleven Brothers', p. 33), and transcribing detailed summaries into numbered notebooks in his meticulous hand. His intention then to expand these summaries into full stories was never completely fulfilled; many of the expansions that do exist, sometimes in more than one version, were made in the 1960s, half a century after the stories were told. Nevertheless, coupled with the near-contemporary summaries (and sometimes near-contemporary expansions), and with Thompson's remarkably clear explanation of his working methods, these late texts are still of great value.

Very few collectors have left either such detailed accounts of their aims and methods, or such rich and well-ordered manuscripts. With many of the earlier collectors-cum-refurbishers of popular fictions (such as John Roby in his *Traditions of Lancashire*, 1829) we must painstakingly sift through pages of verbose and turgid prose for even a glimpse of a reflection of the original spoken story. As Katharine Briggs puts it, 'some of Roby's legends are so fantastically ornamented that we can hardly understand what is supposed to have happened in them.'

A similar case is that of Richard Blakeborough, whose posthumous collection *The Hand of Glory* (ed. J. Fairfax Blakeborough, 1924) is virtually unreadable. Blakeborough's voluminous manuscripts were scattered to the winds, but we may still hope that the notebook in which William Scorer, landlord of the Bedale Inn and one of Blakeborough's most valued informants, wrote down his stories, may turn up in some bookseller's back room, as the Blakeborough manuscripts now at the Centre for English Cultural Tradition and Language at Sheffield University did.

Of course T. W. Thompson is not the only collector whose work we can applaud. If I stress his contribution here, it is because his work has been so neglected; the standard history of folklore studies in Britain, Richard Dorson's *The British Folklorists* (1968), does not even mention him. Dorson does, however, give due attention to such key early collectors as Sidney Oldall Addy and Robert Hunt. Hunt has a claim to be the most diligent fieldworker of the nineteenth century. In 1829 he spent ten months in solid fieldwork in preparation for his *Popular Romances of the West of Cornwall* (1865), 'my purpose being to visit each relic of Old Cornwall, and to gather up every existing tale of its ancient people'. He writes, 'all the stories given in these volumes are the genuine household tales of the people. The only liberties which have been taken with them has been to alter them from the vernacular – in which they were for the most part related – into modern language.'

This liberty of Hunt's is one which no folklorist today would be allowed, but he did not abuse it, and the result is one of the most thorough and valuable surveys we possess of the storytelling of a single district. Its authenticity can be checked against another major work, William Bottrell's *Traditions and Hearthside Stories of West Cornwall* (1870–80).

Hunt and Bottrell were able to record the stories of the last of the wandering droll-tellers of West Cornwall, such as Billy Foss and Uncle Anthony James ('Droll of the Mermaid', p. 294). They also supply, in odd comments, a good deal of information about the way in which stories were told. Bottrell's first volume, for instance, opens with thirty-eight pages of close type relating the adventures of a hero called Tom, a story which is also given, in a variant text, by Hunt. We learn from his introduction that Bottrell heard this tale 'often' from 'an aged tinner of Lelant' (probably Jack Tregear, see 'Skillywidden', p. 274):

> It generally took him three or four winter's evenings to get through with the droll, because he would enter into very minute details, and indulge himself in glowing descriptions of the tin and other treasures found in the giant's castle; taking care, at the same time, to give the spoken parts literally as he had heard them from his ancestors.

The length of this story is not altogether unusual. T. W. Thompson heard of a noted storyteller, 'old Jimmy Smith, a migrant from Warwickshire way', of whom another informant, Johnny Smith, said:

> Last year when I was stopping at Lancaster wi' him, me and a lot more, he tellt us a tale about the Castle o' the Golden Phoenix, the Bottle o' Eversee Water, and the Three Sleeping Beauties, and believe me or not, it was fower o'clock when he finished and he begun at ten i' t' morning. But I could ha'

listened to him aw t' day, and I hev done afore now – many a time. He's got twenty tales as I've heeard, aye more 'an twenty, and ivvery yan teks t' best part of a day to tell it properly like, same as he does.

However, except for their chance survival among the English gypsies (as in Lowland Scotland among the Travellers), wonder tales, or *märchen*, have never been recorded in England in great numbers. George Peek's *The Old Wives' Tale* (1595) – a hectic conglomeration of folktale motifs – and certain references in Shakespeare suggest that *märchen* were once common in England, but by the nineteenth century they were already scarce, though some, such as 'Tom Tit Tot' (p. 97) and 'The Small-Tooth Dog' (p. 61) were recorded. It is worth noting that a good deal of the English narrative impulse went into verse, in ballads which were recited as well as sung.

As opposed to the paucity of *märchen*, England is very rich in local legends and stories of witches, ghosts, giants and fairies. A passage in the collection of folklore scraps known as *The Denham Tracts* (1892–5) preserves a marvellous list of supernatural beings, each of whom would have been the subject of stories and superstitions. This list, incidentally, is the source of Tolkien's 'hobbits':

ghosts, boggles, bloody-bones, spirits, demons, ignis fatui, brownies, bugbears, black dogs, spectres, shellycoats, scarecrows, witches, wizards, barguests, Robin-Goodfellows, hags, night-bats, scrags, breaknecks, fantasms, hobgoblins, hobhoulards, boggy-boes, dobbies, hobthrusts, fetches, kelpies, warlocks, mock-beggars, mum-pokers, Jemmy-burties, urchins, satyrs, pans, fauns, sirens, tritons, centaurs, calcars, nymphs, imps, incubusses, spoorns, men-in-the-oak, hellwains, fire-drakes, kit-a-can-sticks, Tom-tumblers, melch-dicks, larrs, kitty-witches, hobby-lanthorns, Dick-a-Tuesdays, Elf-fires, Gylburnt-tails, knockers, elves, raw-heads, Meg-with-the-wads, old-shocks, ouphs, pad-fooits, pixies, pictrees, giants, dwarfs, Tom-pokers, tutgots, snapdragons, sprets, spunks, conjurers, thurses, spurns, tantarrabobs, swaithes, tints, tod-lowries, Jack-in-the-Wads, mormos, changelings, redcaps, yeth-hounds, colt-pixies, Tom-thumbs, blackbugs, boggarts, scar-bugs, shag-foals, hodge-pochers, hob-thrushes, bugs, bull-beggars, bygorns, bolls, caddies, bomen, brags, wraithes, waffs, flay-boggarts, fiends, gallytrots, imps, gytrashes, patches, hob-and-lanthorns, gringes, boguests, bonelesses, Peg-powlers, pucks, fays, kidnappers, gally-beggars, hudskins, nickers, madcaps, trolls, robinets, friars' lanthorns, silkies, cauld-lads, death-hearses, goblins, hob-headlesses, buggaboes, kows, or cowes, nickies, nacks (necks), waiths, miffies, buckies, gholes, sylphs, guests, swarths, freiths, freits, gy-carlins (Gyre-carling), pigmies, chittifaces, nixies, Jinny-burnt-tails, dudmen, hell-hounds, dopple-gangers, boggleboes, bogies, redmen, portunes, grants, hobbits, hobgoblins, brown-men, cowies, dunnies, wirrikows, alholdes, mannikins, follets, korreds, lubberkins, cluricauns, kobolds, leprechauns, kors, mares, korreds, puckles, korigans, sylvans, succubuses, black-men, shadows, banshees, lianhanshees, clabbernappers, Gabriel-hounds, mawkins, doubles, corpse lights or candles, scrats, mahounds, trows, gnomes, sprites, fates, fiends, sybils, nick-nevins, white-women, fairies, thrummy-caps, cutties, and nisses, and apparitions of every shape, make, form, fashion, kind and description.

A manuscript now known as 'Naitby's Diary', in the Richard Blakeborough collections at the Centre for English Cultural Tradition and Language, Sheffield, reserves the following passage from the fly-leaf of a Bible dated, perhaps not reliably, 7 March 1680. The writer was concerned to uphold the Biblical accounts of giants:

. . . it is within the memory of our own fore-elders, that tales of long ago still remembered by them did set forth several as having mighty castles in these very dales . . . My own mother used of a night when we were about her knee to tell us despert wonderful tales about one Giant Gripgore o' Coverdale and of one Penhang o' Swaledale, he had his castle at the low end, while Penfang ruled all ower the top end. There was Oscar who had a magick castle close to Bainbrigg, and the Giant o' Penhill had his castle some two or three mile from the foot o' that mountain. Then there was a despert fierce monster of a Giant had his castle generally, that is when he recconed to be at home – on the very top of Addleborough – for he could shift it onny-where he minded in a crack, they called him Addleback, for it be said that where the mountain now stands there was once ower a great plain on which stood a prosperous town, but one night the folk of that town closed their iron gates again Addleback which was a despert daft trick for had the giant been so minded he could a bunched all the lot down with one kick, he took no heed o' what they did, but he went into Westmorland, pulled up a mountain by the roots, popped it on his back, and hugged it that way while he came to the town which had shut-ten its gates again him, and tossed the mountain right on the top on 'em while they slept, and that's how it came to be where it stands. It do be affirmed by some of our younger folk that on a certain night when the moon be full, it be on the eve of Saint Agnes, that the moans and groans of those underneath may yet be heard if the ear do be laid on a certain rock which jutteth out near to its summit. But this I do look upon as but a foolish vain conceit of the young and fanciful. And one Coates of Baimbridge calls to mind his hearing old folk clack in his younger days of a double-headed giant whose castle was builded at the top of Buckden Pike. It was likewise a magick castle, at least therein there was a magick room, into which anybody being putten did instant turn into whatsoever animal he was minded they should. This monster went by the name of Golden Club. It was a magick club whose end was tipped with a solid lump of gold weighing over two stones in weight. Now after these old dames do tell these tales the which they have in mind from their fore-elders, who is there bold enew in their brazen folly dare for to say the world hath never had giants . . .

The man from whose 'book of scraps' Blakeborough copied this passage, the Bedale schoolmaster David Naitby, attempted in 1817 to collect further information on these giants, but they were all forgotten. The man who began to tell stories of another Yorkshire giant was soon quieted by the firm expression by another of the company that, 'sike tales are nowt bud mak ups with no truth in 'em.' Elsewhere, though, Naitby records that an old cobbler told him several giant stories, 'too long to write down'. Farm labourer Fred Kitchen remembers, in *Brother to the Ox* (1940), hearing similar tales at the beginning of this century; the Yorkshire giants his workmate Tom described bear a certain similarity to the heroes of American tall tales.

The Naitby manuscript is in fact an indiscriminate mix of copyings from Naitby's scrapbook and a similar compilation by his friend, the Bedale cobbler Robert Hird. Hird's rough verse *Annals of Bedale* includes a vivid description of the types of story current in Yorkshire in his day. His description of superstitions about such creatures as 'bargests', ghostly beasts which often appear as black dogs, also encapsulates the rationalistic rejection of such stories that is mirrored in many nineteenth-century working-class autobiographies (for a discussion of these, see David Vincent, *Bread, Knowledge and Freedom*, 1981). Hird was born in 1768 and wrote, *c.* 1812, that as a child he was:

> Fear'd not by substance or of things in view,
> But of hobgoblin tales which were untrue:
> Told by the weak, the weak for to afright,
> In this old fools to children took delight
> To tell them tales, their parents did *them* tell:

Of spirits seen, where such a one did dwell.
Its different shapes: with confidence declare,
And say some person had been murder'd there.
To this my mother also was inclin'd,
Amongst th' rest in marvelous tales she join'd:
Of Barnardcastle bargest she oft told,
Which did people fright as round the streets it prowl'd:
Against such tales I with her did contend:
But all her bargest tales she did defend,
Nay worse than this, she always did declare
Dead unbaptized childer flew in th' air:
Not her alone, for my wife's Mother too,
Declares her father told her it was so:
Their whistling in the air had oft been heard,
And Gabriel's rackets: by these were call'd:
What priestcraft this: from whither did it spring?
Wisdom tells me that there is no such thing,
As frightful spirits on the road to see,
Fear is the Ghost that has laid hold on thee:
Which nonsense did instill when but a child:
Imagination paints: and eyes deceive:
Go touch the ghost you see: and then believe.

John Buckley's autobiography, *A Village Politician* (1897), shows similar stories being told in similar mood in the Chilterns in the early 1830s:

The old lady with whom I lodged used occasionally to relate stories about witches, ghosts, will-o'-wisps, warlocks and elfins that frightened me. She described their localities with accuracy, and her poor paralysed husband corroborated her stories in every particular.

Perhaps the best sample of typical witchcraft stories is that in J. C. Atkinson's *Forty Years in a Moorland Parish* (1891).

While localized legends about ghosts, witches and supernatural creatures and experiences undoubtedly form the largest category of oral narratives in the English tradition, both in the bulk of those recorded and in the frequency of their narration (and its persistence into the present day), there are also large numbers of humorous tales of various kinds. The following naive story of rural trickery seems to have become attached – like many such comic narratives – to local 'characters' all over the country. The Reverend E. Hinchliffe gives in his lively *Barthomley: In Letters from a Former Rector to his Eldest Son* (1856) an account of a local rogue, Samuel Lightfoot, a man with 'a vast fund of shrewd, dry wit, and many anecdotes, which he told with so much fluency and humour, that, in spite of all attempts to the contrary, it was impossible to help laughing'. One story Hinchliffe tells is that:

> Samuel, in consequence of spending all he had at the public house, found himself one day, without the pecuniary means of providing himself with a dinner; he went to his work as usual, and hit upon the following expedient to satisfy his appetite, which began to crave for food at twelve o'clock: An old sow was in the farmyard, and at her he rushed, feigning to be in a violent passion, and, with loud and dreadful imprecations, pursued her about the yard; the mistress of the house, hearing the noise, came to the door, and called to Samuel, 'What's the matter?' 'What's the matter!' re-echoed he, 'Why, the old sow has eaten my dinner, and I'll kill her if there's never another pig in England.' 'No, don't Samuel,' said the good woman, 'let her alone, and I will give you a dinner.' Samuel's plan thus proved successful, and, without any further exhibition of anger, he sat down to a hearty and plentiful meal.

Bob Copper writes in *A Song for Every Season* (1971) of a casual labourer called John:

> He played a sharp trick on Grand-dad one day. He had been working with a stack-building gang at Court Farm and when they stopped for dinner he sat down with the rest although he had nothing to eat. Presently he saw Grand-dad walking up through the farmyard so he picked up his prong and started hitting out at one of the farm cats that always appeared at mealtimes to pick up anything there was to be had in the way of scraps. He chased it, swiping madly at its bristling, furry hide until it jumped up and disappeared over the churchyard wall. 'Whoa, there! Hold on a bit,' came Brasser's resounding voice, 'don't hurt the cat, John.' 'Hurt'n, Mr Copper,' said John, 'I'll kill the bugger, 'e's ate all my dinner.' 'O damn,' sympathized Grand-dad, 'that's bad. You doddle up to the cottage and see Mrs Copper. She'll see you don't go hungry.' John went along and Granny gave him a lovely plate of hot meat-pie and vegetables – and a pot of beer. It was probably the best meal he had had for years.

And in *The Heart of England* (1906), Edward Thomas writes of an old man he supposedly encounters on his travels:

> He was still in his prime, a big man of fifty, and though he had been threshing all morning – 'it is a good many ups and downs of the flail to a pound of pork', he says – he had eaten no food and he had none by him and there was none in the house. Presently hunger so far mastered him that he stopped work and took a walk round the farmyard. There he saw a fat pig lying on his side, heavy and making bacon rapidly. In a short time he had laid his plans: lifting up his flail he began to thresh the pig, and shouting above its screams: 'Son of a fool, I'll teach you to eat my dinner.' Nor did he cease to beat the pig and to upbraid it for stealing his dinner until the farmer came out and, pitying his case, sent him out a dish of roast pork to make amends.

Hinchliffe, Copper and Thomas are good examples of one type of printed source in which one can find English folktales – miscellaneous volumes of memoirs, reminiscences, diaries, local history, oral history and topography.

The Briggs *Dictionary* is brimming with excellent stories culled from that most gossipy of autobiographers, Augustus Hare; Victorian clergymen's memoirs are loaded with folklore of all kinds (and all degrees of reliability). In the Reverend Edward Boys Ellman's *Recollections of a Sussex Parson* (1912; written 1889), for instance, a number of chapters are headed simply 'Anecdotes'.

Jokes, shaggy dog stories, numskull tales and other comic anecdotes are, like ghost stories, still widely told today. Other types of narrative, such as personal-experience tales, are now studied by folklorists alongside *märchen* and legends. In addition, many scholars are collecting and studying the macabre stories told as having 'happened to a friend', which are commonly known as modern urban legends, although I prefer the more accurate term rumour legends. These gruesome little anecdotes have a very wide circulation, and are remarkable for the way in which they slip in and out of print. They can frequently be found not only in the popular press but also in novels and short stories, in films and on television. The oral, written and mass-communication versions seem to co-exist quite happily and refresh rather than stunt each other.

Folktale collectors in recent years have brought a new sense of scientific strictness to their task but have not, in England, added significantly to the body of available narrative. Jim Carroll has collected stories from Travellers, and lodged his tapes with the National Sound Archive; Bob Patten has collected stories in Somerset; Kingsley Palmer has conducted thorough research in Wessex, published in rather bitty and unsatisfactory form in *Oral*

Folk-Tales of Wessex (1973); John Widdowson's 'Some Folk-tales and Legends from Northern England' (*Lore and Language*, 2, iv, Jan. 1976) prints a number of lively texts collected in Yorkshire between 1959 and 1969, including, for instance, a version of AT111a 'A Drunkard's Promise' that compares interestingly with that printed in M. C. F. Morris's *Yorkshire Folk-Talk* (1892) and another printed in *The Yorkshire Dalesman* (1, ii, 1939).

The two most significant narrators to come to light in England this century have been the Fenland storyteller W. H. Barrett and the Somerset singer and storyteller Ruth L. Tongue. Both of these pose problems for the folklorist. W. H. Barrett – like folksinger Henry Burstow – deliberately collected stories as a young man: his early manuscripts were, sadly, destroyed by flood in the First World War. In 1963, encouraged and edited by Enid Porter of the Cambridge Folk Museum, Barrett published *Tales from the Fens*, which was followed by *More Tales from the Fens* (1964), *A Penman's Story* (1965) and *East Anglian Folklore and Other Tales* (1976). His stories are down-to-earth local historical traditions, with no hint of the wonder-tale, and no echo of the macabre and violent stories recorded in the Lincolnshire fens in the nineteenth century by Marie Clothilde Balfour. Unfortunately Barrett wrote down his stories – like Robert Hunt, translating from the vernacular into standard English – and we do not know what sort of editorial processes were involved in arriving at the printed texts. He did record a few stories for the Briggs and Tongue *Folktales of England*, and these are close to the printed versions; but the transcribed interview material at the back of Barrett and Garrod's *East Anglian Folklore and Other Tales* shows him to have been a speaker of rather more pungent force than he revealed to Katharine Briggs.

The case of Ruth Tongue is even more interesting. The many stories recorded from her in Briggs and Tongue's *Folktales of England*, and in her *Somerset Folklore* (1965) and *Forgotten Folk Tales of the English Counties* (1970), reveal her to be an exceptionally gifted storyteller, with a rare delicacy of touch and verbal control. But her own creative involvement in the material is undoubtedly high. While her stories have a superficial air of having been collected rather than retold (she credits named informants, though the date of the 'collection' is frequently over half a century prior to publication), the shaping of the narratives is Ruth Tongue's. When storytelling she forsook her own educated diction and vocabulary for Somerset dialect, and some may feel that this, combined with her inventive powers, means that her stories are not truly 'traditional'. But folklore collectors have often in the past underestimated the storyteller's creative role, imagining each tale passed down with fidelity by 'tradition', corrupting with each change, and Ruth Tongue's, though an extreme case, may not be so unusual as is thought. Her fluid and robust narrative technique deserves close study, both for its possible roots in tradition and its own idiosyncratic expression of the storytelling impulse. While by no means a reliable unchecked source, Ruth Tongue was undoubtedly familiar with, and transmitted in her own form, a large body of folklore material unnoticed by academic researchers. Most of all, she shared with her collaborator Katharine Briggs the 'delight' in popular tales that motivated Robert Hunt's collecting in Cornwall.

There is always a tension between the inherited and the invented in oral storytelling. Brendan Behan's autobiographical *Borstal Boy* (1958) includes an intriguing account of storytelling in an English borstal *c.* 1940. The young convicts, who had inherited no tales, drew their material from the cinema:

> One would say, 'Tell us a picture,' and the other would begin at eight in the morning, and maybe go on half the time till the break at ten o'clock telling it.
>
> A lot of the blokes went in for this telling pictures, and if a crowd was working near him, they would all work in silence listening to a bloke a few yards away, if the story was a good one.

One wonders what formal qualities these narrations may have shared with those of the London tramps reported by Henry Mayhew, or the storytelling transportees recalled by William Henry Barker in 'Transported for Life' (*Household Words*, 1852).

Making up stories has always been as much part of the oral narrative tradition as retelling folktales. Often these may have been ephemeral tales of local and passing interest, soon forgotten. Occasionally, a good story may be remembered and enter the tradition. To take storytelling for children: parents and nannies feeding the child's never-ending hunger for story have always created new narratives as well as transmitting ones they themselves were told or found in books. Sometimes these have been entirely individual, such as the bedtime stories for his son Alastair that grew into Kenneth Grahame's *The Wind in the Willows* (1908); but often new stories were created out of the 'building blocks' of traditional motifs. Several of the stories in Addy's *Household Tales with Other Traditional Remains: Collected in the Counties of York, Lincoln, Derby and Nottingham* (1895) have a flavour of this. Flora Thompson, author of *Lark Rise to Candleford*, describes her mother's storytelling repertoire, which was probably fairly typical.

> Some of them were short stories, begun and finished in an evening, fairy stories and animal stories, stories of good and bad children, the good

ones rewarded and the bad ones punished, according to the convention of the day. A few of these were part of the stock-in-trade of all tellers of stories to children, but far more were of her own invention, for she said it was easier to make up a tale than to try to remember one. The children liked her own stories best. 'Something out of your own head, Mother,' they would beg, and she would wrinkle up her brow and pretend to think hard, then begin, 'Once upon a time.'

. . . Then there were serial stories that went on in nightly instalments for weeks, or perhaps months, for nobody wanted them to end and the teller's invention never flagged.

Parents and guardians of the young have always been among the most active storytellers. Parents not only made up new tales and passed on old ones, but also – as Flora Thompson's mother did – transmitted family legends: stories about ancestors or ancestry that serve to define the family's sense of itself as a family. Nannies, as Jonathon Gathorne-Hardy notes in his section on 'Terror by Story-telling: The Nanny as Bard' in *The Rise and Fall of the British Nanny* (1972), seem to have specialized in 'frighteners': writers as diverse as Charles Dickens and George Sturt record such stories as told to them by nursemaids (see pp. 162, 210, 353).

But the contexts of storytelling are by no means limited to the nursery. Stories have been told wherever people gather: in the home, in the office, in the field, in the pub. Nor are all types of story appropriate to children. Bawdy, suggestive or downright obscene jokes and anecdotes have always circulated among the male section of the population. Aubrey gives two examples (p. 230) attached to the life of Sir Walter Raleigh in his *Brief Lives* (written *c.* 1670). In *My Father and Myself* (1968), J. R. Ackerley writes:

It was when I returned home after the [First World] war, at the age of twenty-two, that I was judged old and worldly enough to share in this kind of entertainment which my father and his associates enjoyed – the telling of 'yarns', as he called them. He loved these yarns and would chuckle and chortle over them like the 'naughty boy' my mother sometimes called him, spinning them out, as time went on, to interminable lengths to delay, for as long as possible, the familiar or foreseen conclusion, savouring the smutty joke with relish as he savoured his old brandy. To my young mind these yarns were seldom good and never single; one of them always reminded him or his cronies of another; they seemed to adhere together in their sexual fluid like flies in treacle, and whenever I lunched with him,

Stockley and his other colleagues in his office dining-room in Bow Street, the yarn-spinning, once it had started, which it generally did the moment we sat down to table, would go on almost non-stop, each dirty story being instantly capped by an even dirtier one from someone else.

Flora Thompson refers in her account of rural life in North Oxfordshire in the late nineteenth century to 'men's tales', which 'kept strictly to the fields and never repeated elsewhere, formed a kind of rustic Decameron'. It is worth noting, however, that the seventeenth-century jest collection of Sir Nicholas le Strange contains a large number of obscene jokes narrated by women (see p. 235).

The most extensive repertoires of obscene yarns undoubtedly belong to salesmen, whose jobs require adeptness at both breaking the ice and keeping the conversation flowing in awkward semi-work, semi-social situations. Occupation has always had a bearing on storytelling. Travelling tradesmen and craftsmen tended to have a stock of tales with which to entertain clients and repay hospitality. Edward Ellman records, in his *Recollections of a Sussex Parson*, of the Sussex coach drivers of the 1830s that, 'many of the drivers were very noted for their anecdotes. George Simcox, the driver of the Lewes coach, was especially so, and the box-seat was always sought after for the sake of his amusing conversation.'

The social or domestic occasions for storytelling can often be guessed where they are not recorded. It is less easy, given the compromised nature of so many of the written texts, to make any definitive statements about the formal and aesthetic qualities of English storytelling as a whole, or the narrative styles of individual storytellers.

Some general statements about folktale stylistics can be made. As a rule, oral storytellers eschew analysis of character or motive: though the story may pack a powerful emotional charge, the narrative confines itself to action rather than reflection. The narrative tends to proceed not by strict logical sequence of cause and effect but by a dream-like unfolding of what Joseph Jacobs termed 'bright trains of images'. The tales are tightly structured, and the lack of narrative embellishment allows this structure to act as a self-correcting mechanism in retelling: it is hard to forget any part of the story because each part is necessary to the whole. All the above is particularly true of *märchen*. In *märchen*, also, we find characteristic verbal formulae of opening and closure, setting off the tale from the mundane world. The social investigator Henry Mayhew recorded – in a tantalizing passage in volume III of his *London Labour and the London Poor* (1861) – versions of AT 1525 'The Master Thief' and AT 1940 'The Extraordinary Names' in the casual ward of a London workhouse. He was told that some told stories very interesting; some were not fit to be heard; but they made one laugh sometimes. I've read 'Jack Shephard' through, in three volumes; and I used to tell stories out of that sometimes. We all told in our turns. We generally began – 'Once upon a time, and a very good time it was, though it was neither in your time, nor my time, nor nobody else's time.' The best man in the story is always called Jack.

Robert Graves reports in *Goodbye to All That* (1929) that his father's invariable opening phrase was, 'And so the old gardener blew his nose on a red pocket-handkerchief.'

In the notes to *More English Fairy Tales* (1894), Joseph Jacobs writes,

We have the rhyming formula:

> Once upon a time when pigs spoke rhyme,
> And monkeys chewed tobacco,
> And hens took snuff to make them tough,
> And ducks went quack, quack, quack, Oh!

on which I have variants not so refined.

The F. J. Norton manuscripts contain an uncredited formula that runs:

> Once upon a time
> when pigs drank wine
> and bricklayers had no mortar
> I caught a little bird
> and made him drop a turd
> and mixed it up with water.

Traditional story endings include many along the lines of one given in Halliwell's *Nursery Rhymes of England* (1842):

> My story's ended.
> My spoon is bended:
> If you don't like it,
> Go to the next door,
> And get it mended.

Addy's South Yorkshire version runs:

> My tale's ended,
> T' door sneck's bended;
> I went into t' garden
> To get a bit of thyme;
> I've telled my tale,
> Thee tell thine.

The narrator may also demand, as in a version of this formula in Northall's *English Folk-Rhymes* (1892),

> A piece of pudden',
> For telling a good un;
> A piece of pie,
> For telling a lie.

or may, more prosaically but just as effectively, simply say, like a Somerset woman reported by Thomas Keightley in his *Tales and Popular Fictions* (1834), 'and I came away.'

There is of course a whole class of tales – the 'Unfinished Tales', AT2250–99 – that consist solely of opening and closing formulae. These were told to tease, or to silence requests for more, or as a 'put-off' when asked to contribute a tale. These characteristically begin 'I'll tell you a story of Jack a Manory,' but refuse to do so. Northall has

> I'll tell you a tale, the back of my nail,
> A pinch of snuff and a pint of good ale.

And

> I'll tell you a tale.
> Shall I begin it?
> There's nothing in it.

While *märchen* were often told in heightened language, some of which might be memorized word-for-word, legends and jocular tales are generally told in a more relaxed and spontaneous fashion, in a manner close to ordinary discourse. The BBC Sound Archives (13637–8) contain 'The Story of a Local Butcher', a rambling but amusing comic narrative recorded in the Black Country in 1948 from Joseph Wilkes, of whom it is noted: 'This storyteller is over seventy and more or less earns his living by story-telling in "pubs". He cannot read.' He opens his tale:

> Well now then my dear friends there'll be some more short stories as I'll have to give you I might give you one now and, I heard some time ago about a man there was him and his wife he was a butcher now this butcher he was rather a low ignorant man, but he was making a lot of money in the meat trade . . .

His delivery is fast and unpunctuated, the practised flow of a man determined not to be interrupted. In contrast, the late Sid Boddy, a lifelong resident of the village of Seer Green in Buckinghamshire, adopted a much more relaxed delivery, with plenty of cunning pauses and a good deal of expression in his tone, when telling three local place-name legends at an entertainment in the new village hall on 9 January 1981. He began:

> The stories I am going to tell you were told to me by my mother and father and to them by their parents, grandparents and great-grandparents, and so on back through the families. I may say that both my mother and father's families had been in this area for 400 years and probably much longer, so there's a good foundation for the stories that I'm going to tell.
>
> And my first one, I'm going to take you back a very long time, about 2000 years, to the time when the Romans occupied the greater part of our country. I say the greater part because, of course, they didn't conquer Seer Green.
>
> In fact, this was really due to the fact that the Romans didn't want Seer Green . . .

In chapter 34 of his *Down and Out in Paris and London* (1933), George Orwell describes tramps telling stories, and while he only summarizes most of them, he gives a good flavour of the delivery of one man, Bill, 'a genuine sturdy beggar of the old breed':

> I ain't goin' far in – Kent. Kent's a tight country, Kent is. There's too many bin' moochin' about 'ere. The – bakers get so as they'll throw their bread away sooner'n give it you. Now Oxford, that's the place for moochin', Oxford is. When I was in Oxford I mooched bread, and I mooched bacon, and I mooched beef, and every night I mooched tanners for my kip off of the students. The last night I was twopence short of my kip, so I goes up to a parson and mooches 'im for threepence. He give me threepence, and

the next moment he turns round and gives me in charge for beggin'. 'You bin beggin',' the copper says. 'No I ain't,' I says, 'I was askin' the gentleman the time,' I says. The copper starts feelin' inside my coat, and he pulls out a pound of meat and two loaves of bread. 'Well, what's all this, then?' he says. The beak give me seven days. I don't mooch from no more – parsons. But Christ! what do I care for a lay-up of seven days?

The vibrant expressive qualities of this man's speech, the way he slips from reminiscence into story, the brief, well-paced sentences and crisp delivery reflect the hardiest strain of English storytelling, one which is still very much alive. One finds it, in a gentler rural note, in the observation of an old Wiltshire man to John U. Powell in 1895 (*Folk-Lore*, vol. 12, 1901):

I've heard 'em say that Adam were made and then put up again' a wold hurdle to dry.

The best of the stories in this book – 'Jack the Giant Killer', 'The Small-Tooth Dog', 'Sorrow and Love', 'Tom Tit Tot', 'The Story of Mr Fox', 'The Independent Bishop' and so on – are among the best English short stories. They have a succinct brevity, a verbal dash and daring, and a potency of image that blends economy of statement with richness of implication and flexibility of application.

A great deal of work still needs to be done to investigate the English folk narrative tradition. Even the chief areas of interest – oral storytelling as a narrative art; the personalities, repertoires and techniques of individual storytellers; the varying contexts in which stories are told; the storytelling traditions of particular localities, occupations and families; the folktale as an element in social history; the interplay between folktales and literature; the methods of the folktale collectors – remain largely unexplored.

In the meantime, we can all enjoy what is – despite textual problems and lost evidence – a full and varied corpus of tales, in the uncritical spirit of the listeners to the story within a story that effects the denouement of Wasti Gray's 'De Little Fox' (p. 76):

Deah wuz all de ladies an' gentlemen clappin' an' sayin', 'Speak an, my little fox.' 'Well tole, my little fox!' 'Werry good tale indeed!'

Neil Philip
August 1992

Author's Note

THIS COLLECTION OF ENGLISH folktales from authentic sources has been arranged primarily for the reader's pleasure, as a representative anthology of the English tradition of oral storytelling. But it is also intended to serve as a reference and sourcebook. The notes appended to the stories are particularly concerned with the tales' journey from mouth to page, and what has happened to them on the way. I have tried to place the stories in the context of the wider folktale tradition, in particular by specifying, where it seems useful, applicable 'tale-type' numbers. These numbers refer to two indexes of the international folktale. AT numbers refer to *The Types of the Folktale* by Antti Aarne (translated and enlarged by Stith Thompson, *Folklore Fellows Communications*, no. 184, 1981). ML numbers refer to *The Migratory Legends* by Reidar Th. Christiansen (*Folklore Fellows Communications*, no. 175, 1958). Not all folktales fit happily into these indexes, which enable the researcher to track down other stories with the same basic plot, but many do. For instance, the story 'Clever Jack' (see p. 17), which was told to Henry Mayhew in the casual ward of a London workhouse by a sixteen-year-old boy from Wisbeach, is a good version of the tale type AT1525 'The Master Thief'. Ernest W. Baughman's *Type and Motif Index of the Folk-Tales of England and North America (Indiana University Folklore Series*, no. 20, 1966) will guide the reader to other versions told in English, while D. L. Ashliman's *A Guide to Folktales in the English Language* (*Greenwood Press Bibliographies and Indexes in World Literature*, no. 11, 1987) offers a first selection of versions from other cultures, including the story which gives the type its name, the Grimms' 'The Master Thief'. Stith Thompson also produced a very detailed *Motif-Index of Folk Literature* (1955–8) that enables folklorists to reduce any tale to a skeleton of motif numbers, but I have only referred to these numbers on a few occasions.

Jack and the Beanstalk

Source: Joseph Jacobs, *English Fairy Tales*, 1890, pp. 57–67.

Narrator: Jacobs recalling 'my old nurse', Australia (presumably Sydney), *c.* 1860.

Type: AT328 'The Boy Steals the Giant's Treasure'.

THERE WAS ONCE UPON a time a poor widow who had an only son named Jack, and a cow named Milky-white. And all they had to live on was the milk the cow gave every morning which they carried to the market and sold. But one morning Milky-white gave no milk and they didn't know what to do.

'What shall we do, what shall we do?' said the widow, wringing her hands.

'Cheer up, mother, I'll go and get work somewhere,' said Jack.

'We've tried that before, and nobody would take you,' said his mother; 'we must sell Milky-white and with the money do something, start shop, or something.'

'All right, mother,' says Jack; 'it's market day today, and I'll soon sell Milky-white, and then we'll see what we can do.'

So he took the cow's halter in his hand, and off he starts. He hadn't gone far when he met a funny-looking old man who said to him: 'Good morning, Jack.'

'Good morning to you,' said Jack, and wondered how he knew his name.

'Well, Jack, and where are you off to?' said the man.

'I'm going to market to sell our cow here.'

'Oh, you look the proper sort of chap to sell cows,' said the man; 'I wonder if you know how many beans make five.'

'Two in each hand and one in your mouth,' says Jack, as sharp as a needle.

'Right you are,' said the man, 'and here they are the very beans themselves,' he went on pulling out of his pocket a number of strange-looking beans. 'As you are so sharp,' says he, 'I don't mind doing a swop with you – your cow for these beans.'

'Walker!' says Jack; 'wouldn't you like it?'

'Ah! you don't know what these beans are,' said the man; 'if you plant them overnight, by morning they grow right up to the sky.'

'Really?' says Jack; 'you don't say so.'

'Yes, that is so, and if it doesn't turn out to be true you can have your cow back.'

'Right,' says Jack, and hands him over Milky-white's halter and pockets the beans.

Back goes Jack home, and as he hadn't gone very far it wasn't dusk by the time he got to his door.

'What back, Jack?' said his mother; 'I see you haven't got Milky-white, so you've sold her. How much did you get for her?'

'You'll never guess, mother,' says Jack.

'No, you don't say so. Good boy! Five pounds, ten, fifteen, no, it can't be twenty.'

'I told you you couldn't guess, what do you say to these beans; they're magical, plant them overnight and—'

'What!' says Jack's mother, 'have you been such a fool, such a dolt, such an idiot, as to give away my Milky-white, the best milker in the parish, and prime beef to boot, for a set of paltry beans? Take that! Take that! Take that! And as for your precious beans here they go out of the window. And now off with you to bed. Not a sup shall you drink, and not a bit shall you swallow this very night.'

So Jack went upstairs to his little room in the attic, and sad and sorry he was, to be sure, as much for his mother's sake, as for the loss of his supper.

At last he dropped off to sleep.

When he woke up, the room looked so funny. The sun was shining into part of it, and yet all the rest was quite dark and shady. So Jack jumped up and dressed himself and went to the window. And what do you think he saw? Why, the beans his mother had thrown out of the window into the garden, had sprung up into a big beanstalk which went up and up and up till it reached the sky. So the man spoke truth after all.

The beanstalk grew up quite close past Jack's window, so all he had to do was to open it and give a jump on to the beanstalk which was made like a big plaited ladder. So Jack climbed and he climbed and he climbed and he climbed and he climbed and he climbed and he climbed till at last he reached the sky. And when he got there he found a long broad road going as straight as a dart. So he walked along and he walked along and he walked along till he came to a great big tall house, and on the doorstep there was a great big tall woman.

'Good morning, mum,' says Jack, quite polite like. 'Could you be so kind as to give me some breakfast.' For he hadn't had anything to eat, you know, the night before and was as hungry as a hunter.

'It's breakfast you want, is it?' says the great big tall woman, 'it's breakfast you'll be if you don't move off from here. My man is an ogre and there's nothing he likes better than boys broiled on toast. You'd better be moving on or he'll soon be coming.'

'Oh! please mum, do give me something to eat, mum. I've had nothing to eat since yesterday morning, really and truly, mum,' says Jack. 'I may as well be broiled, as die of hunger.'

Well, the ogre's wife wasn't such a bad sort, after all. So she took Jack into the kitchen, and gave him a junk of bread and cheese and a jug of milk. But Jack hadn't half finished these when thump! thump! thump! the whole house began to tremble with the noise of some one coming.

'Goodness gracious me! It's my old man,' said the ogre's wife, 'what on earth shall I do? Here, come quick and jump in here.' And she bundled Jack into the oven just as the ogre came in.

He was a big one, to be sure. At his belt he had three calves strung up by the heels, and he unhooked them and threw them down on the table and said: 'Here, wife, broil me a couple of these for breakfast. Ah! what's this I smell?

Fee-fi-fo-fum,
I smell the blood of an Englishman,
Be he alive, or be he dead
I'll have his bones to grind my bread.'

'Nonsense, dear,' said his wife, 'you're dreaming. Or perhaps you smell the scraps of that little boy you liked so much for yesterday's dinner. Here, go you and have a wash and tidy up, and by the time you come back your breakfast'll be ready for you.'

So the ogre went off, and Jack was just going to jump out of the oven and run off when the woman told him not. 'Wait till he's asleep,' says she; 'he always has a snooze after breakfast.'

Well, the ogre had his breakfast, and after that he goes to a big chest and takes out of it a couple of bags of gold and sits down counting them till at last his head began to nod and he began to snore till the whole house shook again.

Then Jack crept out on tiptoe from his oven, and as he was passing the ogre he took one of the bags of gold under his arm, and off he pelters till he came to the beanstalk, and then he threw down the bag of gold which of course fell in to his mother's garden, and then he climbed down and climbed down till at last he got home and told his mother and showed her the gold and said: 'Well, mother wasn't I right about the beans. They are really magical, you see.'

So they lived on the bag of gold for some time, but at last they came to the end of that so Jack made up his mind to try his luck once more up at the top of the beanstalk. So one fine morning he got up early, and got on to the beanstalk, and he climbed and he climbed and he climbed and he climbed and he climbed and he climbed till at last he got on the road again and came to the great big tall house he had been to before. There, sure enough, was the great big tall woman a-standing on the doorstep.

'Good morning, mum,' says Jack, as bold as brass, 'could you be so good as to give me something to eat?'

'Go away, my boy,' said the big, tall woman, 'or else my man will eat you up for breakfast. But aren't you the youngster who came here once before? Do you know, that very day, my man missed one of his bags of gold.'

'That's strange, mum,' says Jack, 'I dare say I could tell you something about that but I'm so hungry I can't speak till I've had something to eat.'

Well the big tall woman was that curious that she took him in and gave him something to eat. But he had scarcely begun munching it as slowly as he could when thump! thump! thump! they heard the giant's footstep, and his wife hid Jack away in the oven.

All happened as it did before. In came the ogre as he did before, said: 'Fee-fi-fo-fum,' and had his breakfast off three broiled oxen. Then he said: 'Wife, bring me the hen that lays the golden eggs.' So she brought it, and the ogre said: 'Lay,' and it laid an egg all of gold. And then the ogre began to nod his head, and to snore till the house shook.

Then Jack crept out of the oven on tiptoe and caught hold of the golden hen, and was off before you could say 'Jack Robinson'. But this time the hen gave a cackle which woke the ogre, and just as Jack got out of the house he heard him calling: 'Wife, wife, what have you done with my golden hen?'

And the wife said: 'Why, my dear?'

But that was all Jack heard, for he rushed off to the beanstalk and climbed down like a house on fire. And when he got home he showed his mother the wonderful hen and said 'Lay' to it; and it laid a golden egg every time he said 'Lay'.

Well, Jack was not content, and it wasn't very long before he determined to have another try at his luck up there at the top of the beanstalk. So one fine morning, he got up early, and went on to the beanstalk, and he climbed and he climbed and he climbed and he climbed till he got to the top. But this time he knew better than to go straight to the ogre's house. And when he got near it he waited behind a bush till he saw the ogre's wife come out with a pail to get some water, and then he crept into the house and got into the copper. He hadn't been there long when he heard thump! thump! thump! as before, and in came the ogre and his wife.

'Fee-fi-fo-fum, I smell the blood of an Englishman,' cried out the ogre; 'I smell him, wife, I smell him.'

'Do you, my dearie?' says the ogre's wife. 'Then if it's that little rogue that stole your gold and the hen that laid the golden eggs he's sure to have got into the oven.' And they both rushed to the oven. But Jack wasn't there, luckily, and the ogre's wife said: 'There you are again with your fee-fi-fo-fum. Why of course it's the laddie you caught last night that I've broiled for your breakfast. How forgetful I am, and how careless you are not to tell the difference between a live un and a dead un.'

So the ogre sat down to the breakfast and ate it, but every now and then he would mutter: 'Well, I could have sworn—' and he'd get up and search the larder and the cupboards, and everything, only luckily he didn't think of the copper.

After breakfast was over, the ogre called out: 'Wife, wife, bring me my golden harp.' So she brought it and put it on the table before him. Then he said: 'Sing!' and the golden harp sang most beautifully. And it went on singing till the ogre fell asleep, and commenced to snore like thunder.

Then Jack lifted up the copper-lid very quietly and got down like a mouse and crept on hands and knees till he got to the table when he got up and caught hold of the golden harp and dashed with it towards the door. But the harp called out quite loud: 'Master! Master!' and the ogre woke up just in time to see Jack running off with his harp.

Jack ran as fast as he could, and the ogre came rushing after, and would soon have caught him only Jack had a start and dodged him a bit and knew where he was going. When he got to the beanstalk the ogre was not more than twenty yards away when suddenly he saw Jack disappear like, and when he got up to the end of the road he saw Jack underneath climbing down for dear life. Well, the ogre didn't like trusting himself to such a ladder, and he stood and waited, so Jack got another start. But just then the harp cried out: 'Master! master!' and the ogre swung himself down on to the beanstalk which shook with his weight. Down climbs Jack, and after him climbed the ogre. By this time Jack had climbed down and climbed down and climbed down till he was very nearly home. So he called out: 'Mother! mother! bring me an axe, bring me an axe.' And his mother came rushing out with the axe in her hand, but when she came to the beanstalk she stood stock still with fright for there she saw the ogre just coming down below the clouds.

But Jack jumped down and got hold of the axe and gave a chop at the beanstalk which cut it half in two. The ogre felt the beanstalk shake and quiver so he stopped to see what was the matter. Then Jack gave another chop with the axe, and the beanstalk was cut in two and began to topple over. Then the ogre fell down and broke his crown, and the beanstalk came toppling after.

Then Jack showed his mother his golden harp, and what with showing that and selling the golden eggs, Jack and his mother became very rich, and he married a great princess, and they lived happy ever after.

⚜

'Jack and the Beanstalk' is often regarded as the quintessential English folktale. Although the story's motifs (the foolish bargain gaining a magic treasure, the ascent to the other-world, the theft of the giant's treasures and so on) can be widely found elsewhere, this particular tale is limited to England and its colonies.

I have placed this text first because it illustrates so well the profound problems facing any student of the English tale. For even with this most well-known and distinctive of English stories, we have no really reliable text. Jacobs dismissed the chapbook version (the first we know of is Tabart's of 1807/9) as 'very poor', and relied instead on his own memories of the story as told to him by his childhood nursemaid. His note laconically states, 'I tell this as it was told to me in Australia, somewhere about the year 1860.' In 1860 Jacobs was six years old.

Even if Jacobs is remembering the story word for word, we may question this version's Englishness: Jacobs did not trouble to give any details about his storytelling nurse. In fact, though, this text is clearly a literary construct, in which Jacobs is mixing memories of a childhood telling (quite possibly based on a chapbook) with a recent dissatisfied reading of the chapbook texts. Peter and Iona Opie go so far in their *The Classic Fairy Tales* as to state that 'close examination shows that the version given by Jacobs in *English Fairy Tales*, as collected in Australia about 1860, is no more than a literary retelling of the text that had been in print for more than half a century.' Katharine Briggs, on the other hand, accepts this in her *Dictionary* as 'probably the original form'.

The truth lies, I think, somewhere between these two statements. We cannot know what the 'original' form of the story was; equally, we need not doubt that Jacobs was relying in part on a genuine memory of an oral narration. His lively, funny, supple telling is certainly much closer than the stiff chapbook texts to the oral versions of this story collected in North America (see Leonard Roberts, *Old Greasybeard: Tales From the Cumberland Gap* (1969) and Richard Chase, *The Jack Tales* (1943)).

Jacobs's text is the best we have; though it is interesting to compare it not just with the chapbook and American versions, but also with the version the

Romany *rai* Thomas William Thompson – to whose incomparable collection of English gypsy folktales this book is much indebted – noted from Noah Lock at Rhosneigr Common, Anglesey on 15 August 1914. Thompson's is an idiosyncratic version, and the beanstalk-treasure stealing sequence is only the second half of the tale. The first half begins with the characteristically Scottish motif J.229.3 (*Choice: a big piece of cake with my curse or a small piece with my blessing*) and then relates Jack's attempt to earn his fortune as a ploughman. (There are echoes of another of Noah Lock's tales, 'Strong Jack', a version of AT650 'Strong John'; a feature of which is that the treasure is stolen from an old woman rather than a giant.)

It was published by Thompson in 'English Gypsy Folk-Tales and other Traditional Stories' (*JGLS*, new series, 8, iii, 1914–15, pp. 216–19); there is an alternative text, written out in Thompson's old age, in Notebook E of the Thompson manuscripts at Leeds. It is this tale that the Briggs *Dictionary* mistakenly attributes to Eva Gray. There is also a 'portmanteau' story from Taimi Boswell (Oswaldtwistle, 10 January 1915) in Notebook 9 that contains elements of 'Jack and the Beanstalk'. This conglomerate of motifs was given by Boswell as an example of a muddled story. Thompson notes:

> He had a good 'Jack and the Beanstalk' tale, but I did not record it. It was very like Noah Lock's, except that only *one bean* got planted, and that by *accident* [as in this portmanteau story], and that the gold, jewels, etc. were stolen from an old *giant*, who was killed when Jack chopped down the beanstalk . . . rhyme 'Fee, Fai, Fo, Fum' occurred. Not helpful wife. No note of opening incident, but Jack had job on a farm before sale of cow for a small handful of beans. [This from a very brief note made next day.]

The story was clearly once very widely known. A skit on the tale, 'Enchantment Demonstrated in the Story of Jack Spriggins and the Enchanted Bean', was included in *Round About Our Coal-Fire: Or Christmas Entertainments* (published by J. Roberts *c.* 1730); parody implies popularity. There is no evidence of chapbook publication until the early nineteenth century, which gives us a verse text, *The History of Mother Twaddle, and the Marvellous Atchievements of Her Son Jack*, by B.A.T. (published by John Harris, 1807), and a prose one, *The History of Jack and the Bean-Stalk, Printed from the Original Manuscript, Never Before Published* (published by Benjamin Tabart, 1809). This text is given in *Classic Fairy Tales* by the Opies, who date it 1807. 'Printed from the original manuscript' can be ignored, though it makes an interesting point about what Tabart's customers expected of a story; this text seems to have been 'edited' by Mrs Godwin (Mrs Clairemont, not Mary Wollstonecraft), or possibly William Godwin himself. Both it and the Harris text must derive ultimately, if not directly, from oral tradition, though neither retains much of the feel of an oral narration. The Tabart text, which is, as the Opies say, the basis of almost every subsequent retelling (including, for instance, that of 'Felix Summerly', Sir Henry Cole, in his *Home Treasury* of 1843–7), is marred by laborious prose and an excruciating, moralizing fairy.

In his *Shepherd's Calendar* ('January: A Cottage Evening'), John Clare recalls hearing the tale in his childhood (Clare was born in 1793, in the village of Helpston, Northamptonshire). His version may derive from a chapbook text but, like his other remembered childhood favourites, it exhibits some independence of storyline and incident, arguing for an element of oral tradition or adaptation in the narrations he heard. It is, anyway, a beautifully concise and vivid telling of the tale. Clare remembers:

> The boy that did the jiants slay
> And gave his mothers cows away
> For magic mask that day or night
> When on woud keep him out of sight
> And running beans not such as weaves
> Round poles the height of cottage eves
> But magic ones that travelld high
> Some steeples journeys up the sky
> And reachd a jiants dwelling there
> A cloud built castle in the air
> Where venturing up the fearfull height
> That servd him climbing half the night
> He searchd the jiants coffers oer
> And never wanted wealth no more
> While like a lion scenting food
> The jiant roard in hungry mood
> A storm of threats that might suffice
> To freeze the hottest blood to ice
> And make when heard however bold
> The strongest heart strings cramp wi cold
> But mine sleeps on thro fear and dread
> And terrors that might wake the dead
> When like a tiger in the wood
> He snufts and tracks the scent of blood

And vows if aught falls in his power
He'll grind their very bones to flower
I hear it now nor dream of harm
The storm is settld to a calm
Those fears are dead what will not dye
In fading lifes mortality
Those truths are fled and left behind
A real world and a doubting mind

(John Clare, *The Shepherd's Calendar*,
ed. Eric Robinson and Geoffrey Summerfield, 1964).

Jack the Giant Killer

Source: Ella Mary Leather, *The Folklore of Herefordshire*, 1912, pp. 174–6.
Narrator: W. Colcombe at Weobley, 1909.
Type: AT300 'The Dragon-Slayer', AT328 'The Boy Steals the Giant's Treasure', AT1088 'Eating Contest', AT1930 'Schlaraffenland'.

ONCE UPON A TIME – a very good time it was – when pigs were swine and dogs ate lime, and monkeys chewed tobacco, when houses were thatched with pancakes, streets paved with plum puddings, and roasted pigs ran up and down the streets with knives and forks on their backs crying 'Come and eat me!' That was a good time for travellers.

Then it was I went over hills, dales, and lofty mountains, far farther than I can tell you tonight, tomorrow night, or any other night in this new year. The cocks never crew, the winds never blew, and the devil has never sounded his bugle horn to this day yet.

Then I came to a giant castle; a lady came out of the door with a nose as long as my arm. She said to me, she says, 'What do you want here? If you don't be off my door I'll take you up for a pinch of snuff.' But Jack said 'Will you?' and he drew his sword and cut off her head. He went into the castle and hunted all over the place. He found a bag of money, and two or three ladies hanging by the hair of their heads. He cut them down and divided the money between them, locked the doors, and started off.

Then it was I went over hills and dales, etc.

Then Jack came to another giant's castle, but there was a drop over the door. He slipped in as quickly as he could, but nevertheless the drop struck him on the side of the head and killed him. And the old giant came out and buried him. But in the night three little dogs named Swift, Sure, and Venture, came and dug him up. One scratched him out of the ground, one breathed breath into his nostrils and brought him to life, while the other got him up out of the grave. Then Jack put on his cloak of darkness, shoes of swiftness, and cap of knowledge. He went once more to the giant's door and knocked; when the giant came out, of course he could see nobody, Jack being invisible. He at once drew his sword and struck the giant's head off. He plundered the house, taking all the money he could find, and went into all the rooms. He found four ladies hung up by their hair, and again dividing the money between them, turned them out and locked the door.

Then he went off again over hills and dales and lofty mountains; etc.

Then Jack came to another giant's castle. He knocked at the door, and an old lady came out; he told her he wanted a night's lodging. She said 'My husband is sorely against Englishmen, and if he comes in he will smell the house all over to find one. But never mind, I'll put you in the oven.' When the woman's back was turned, Jack got out of the oven and went upstairs into a bedroom. He put a lump of wood in the bed and hid underneath. By and bye the old giant came in. He said:

> Fee, fi, fum,
> I smell the blood of an Englishman.
> Let him be alive or let him be dead,
> I'll have his flesh to eat for my bread
> And his blood to drink for my drink.

He then went down to supper, and after it he slept. On waking up he said to his wife, 'Now I will find the man that's here.' He went upstairs, club in hand, and hit the log in the bed three times. Every time Jack groaned under the bed the giant said 'I think I've finished ye now.' He went down again, talked to his wife for a bit, and went to bed.

At breakfast next morning he was much astonished to see Jack, and said 'How d'ye feel this morning?' Jack said 'All right, only in the night a mouse gave me a slap with his tail!' Then they had breakfast; it was a hasty pudding. There was poison in Jack's, and instead of eating it he put it in a little leather bag inside his shirt. When they had breakfasted, Jack said: 'I can do something more than you.' The giant said 'Can you?' 'Yes,' said Jack, and pulling a knife out of his pocket he slit the leather bag, and loosed all the pudding out on the ground. The giant, trying to follow Jack's example, pulled out a knife, and wounding himself, fell dead immediately. Then Jack found two or three ladies hanging up, cut them down, took a bag of money that was lying on the table, and then went out and locked the doors.

> Be bow bend it,
> My tales ended.
> If you don't like it,
> You may mend it.

This text shows clearly the interdependence of voice and print in English popular tradition. It is the only oral narration noted in Britain of one of our most famous tales, and was collected in 1909 by Ella Mary Leather from an eighty-year-old man named W. Colcombe at Weobley in Herefordshire. She writes that, 'he learnt it from an old chapbook, when a small boy'. But though this text derives from a chapbook, it has a number of distinctive characteristics that show the hackneyed literary text radically reshaped by oral tradition.

The first known chapbook edition of 'Jack and the Giants' is that printed by J. White of Newcastle in 1711, on which Halliwell based his bowdlerized text in *Popular Rhymes and Nursery Tales of England*. No copy of this edition is now traceable, but textually it seems virtually identical to that of the Eddowes and Cotton edition published in two parts in Shrewsbury in the 1750s or 60s and reprinted verbatim in the Opies' *The Classic Fairy Tales*. This must serve as the base for evaluation of later chapbooks, which though they often simplified and shortened the tale as given here, all accept it – albeit sometimes at several removes – as their authority.

In their succinct and erudite introduction to the chapbook text, the Opies write: 'The story of Jack the Giant Killer, as we know it, appears to consist of a number of classic anecdotes strung together by an astute publisher in the not-so-long-ago.' Thus the first part of the chapbook opens with a couple of time-worn anti-clerical quips attributed to Jack as a youth, then moves into a succession of giant-killing feats, the last of which involves the tricks of pretending to have suffered the blows given to a log and pretended disembowelment: standard folktale ruses of the type which are found, for instance, in the Grimms' 'The Valiant Little Tailor'. Coincidence between these ruses and incidents in Norse mythology (for instance, the story of Thor and Skrymir in the Prose *Edda)* seem, to me, to argue for folktale elements in the Norse stories rather than a Norse ancestry for Jack.

The story of 'Jack and the Giants', then, mutates into a story of the 'Grateful Dead' type, in which Jack, impressed by King Arthur's son's generosity in ransoming the body of a dead man, attaches himself to the Prince and, with the aid of a cap of knowledge, a cloak of invisibility, shoes of swiftness and a sword of sharpness (items that may well have been taken over for this tale from 'The History of Tom Thumbe', for which, see Opie, op. cit.), wins for his patron the hand of an enchanted princess. The earliest recorded Grateful Dead tale is the apocryphal story of Tobias and the angel in the Book of Tobit. The motif of the

Grateful Dead man (E. 341) and the stories with which it is associated have been studied by Gordon H. Gerould (*The Grateful Dead*, 1908). In Peek's *Old Wives' Tale*, the Grateful Dead man is called Jack.

The second part of the chapbook text is much less interesting, being simply a catalogue of further giant-slayings, with a distinctly literary flavour. The best things about it are a certain low comedy (for instance, the picture of one vanquished giant, subdued by a cunning thrust up the rear, capering 'with the sword in his arse, crying out, he should die, he should die with the griping of his guts') and the famous threat:

> Fee, fau, fum,
> I smell the blood of an *English* man,
> Be he alive, or be he dead,
> I'll grind his bones to make my bread.

Otherwise the second part is as weak as most sequels.

The introduction of King Arthur into the chapbook story is presumably based on similar passages in 'The History of Tom Thumbe', and offers the excuse for the rough parody in Jack's later adventures of various giant encounters in Malory. As early as Chaucer's *The Wife of Bath's Tale* the 'olde dayes of the Kyng Arthour' had substituted for 'once upon a time' as the opening of a tale. 'The History of Tom Thumbe' begins, 'In the old time, when King *Arthur* ruled this land'; the chapbook 'Jack and the Giants' begins, 'In the reign of King Arthur'.

The opening of Mr Colcombe's version is very different, and is unrelated to any chapbook text I have seen. It is, rather, one of the best preserved of the opening formulae that once must have been the common currency of English storytellers.

Such formulae are characteristic of *märchen*, though not of legends, setting off the tale from the mundane world. In thriving folk narrative traditions, the formal rigmaroles of opening and closure can be very elaborate, as, for instance, those in J. F. Campbell's *Popular Tales of the West Highlands* (1860–61) and Jones and Kropf's *The Folk-Tales of the Magyars* (1886). English storytellers also had at their disposal mechanisms for entering and leaving the story world and the story timescale. We cannot speak with confidence about the distribution, frequency and variation of these formulae, but they do preserve, often separated from the stories themselves, a number of time-worn phrases and frills.

An opening that incorporates many of these, and relates specifically to Mr Colcombe's formula, is given in *Folk-Lore* (12, 1901, p. 76) by John U. Powell ('Folklore Notes from South-West Wilts'), dated 1895:

An old man would tell a story in the following way: 'There were a time, 'tweren't in my time, neither in your time, nit [nor yet] in anybody else's time; 'twere when magpies built in old men's beards and turkey-cocks chewed bacca; all over hills, dales, mountains, valleys, so far as I shall tell you tonight, or tomorrow night, or ever I shall tell you before I've done, if I can.'

Powell thought there was something missing from this before 'all over hills': the present text allows us to tentatively restore the words, 'then it was I went . . .'

This passage, recurring in Mr Colcombe's narration at each change of scene, is the nearest thing in recorded English tradition to the 'runs' of Gaelic storytelling: gabbled and often garbled set-piece poetic prose passages that mark a repeated action in a tale, performing the function of a scene-change at the theatre. It is extremely interesting to find an English storyteller using such a punctuating device. What is still more interesting is the way the 'run' allows the narrator to make the transition from 'I' to 'he'. One of the things that allows us to feel confidence in this as an oral text is that Ella Leather preserved in it apparent confusions which left her feeling, when Jack appears from nowhere, that part of the story must have been forgotten. It is clear, however, that while Mr Colcombe has been selective in the incidents he had remembered or chosen to retell from the chapbook, he is relating a whole, not a fragmentary, story. The key is that the narrator is enabled by the verbal formulae to identify himself with the hero: '*I* went over hills . . . Then *I* came to a giant castle; a lady came out of the door with a nose as long as *my* arm. She said to *me*, she says, "What do you want here? If you don't be off my door I'll take you up for a pinch of snuff." But *Jack* said "Will you?"' The only thing that impedes this smooth transition from 'I' to 'Jack' is the retention in the first repetition of the run of 'I' rather than the 'he' of the subsequent version.

Mr Colcombe's narration consists of three parts, plus the formulaic opening and closing passages and the thrice-repeated run. In the first of these Jack kills the long-nosed lady, who stands in for the giant who never appears. In the second, in an extraordinary incident that bears no relation to anything in the chapbook (save in so far as Jack takes on a dead man's role), Jack is killed, and revived by three dogs, 'Swift, Sure and Venture'. (In a Scottish story collected by Hamish Henderson from Andrew Stewart, 'The Three Dogs', summarized in Briggs (*Dictionary*, Part A, vol. 2), three dogs called Swift, Able and Noble are disenchanted by decapitation and revealed as Jack's three long-lost brothers.) We then learn that Jack owns a cloak of darkness, shoes of swiftness and a cap of knowledge, with which he overcomes a giant. In the third section, Jack takes lodging with a giant and his wife, his host being – in a memory of the chapbook's mockery of the Welsh – 'sorely against Englishmen', and Jack tricks the giant into killing himself. This passage is quite close to the chapbook, which is worth quoting for its colourful and expressive phrasing:

> Soon after the giant arose, and went to his Breakfast with a Bowl of Hasty-Pudding, containing four Gallons, giving *Jack* the like Quantity, who being loth to let the Giant know he could not eat with him, got a large Leathern Bag, putting it artificially under his loose Coat, into which he secretly conveyed the Pudding, telling the Giant he would shew him a Trick; then taking a large Knife ript open the Bag, which the Giant supposed to be his Belly, and out came the Hasty-Pudding, which the Giant seeing cried out, *Cotsplut, hur can do that Trick hurself:* then taking a sharp Knife he ript open his own Belly from the Bottom to the Top, and out dropt his Tripes and Trolly-Bubs, so that hur fell down dead.

An unexplained element in Mr Colcombe's narration is the discovery in each 'giant castle' of ladies 'hung up by the hair'. These are taken over from the chapbook, in which they offer Jack the following explanation for their plight:

> Their Husbands had been slain by the Giant, and they were kept many Days without Food, in order to feed upon the Flesh of their murdered Husbands, which they could not, if they were to Starve to death.

Between the first chapbook printing sometime around the turn of the eighteenth century and Mr Colcombe's version in 1909, the story of Jack and the Giants had a lively time in countless chapbook editions and retellings, establishing itself as a subject for popular drama (the first recorded play was a comi-tragical farce, *Jack the Gyant-Killer*, performed at the Haymarket in 1730, featuring an aptly named character called Mr Plotless), and engaging the affections and interest of generations of uneducated readers such as Mr Colcombe: readers for whom John Clare speaks in his spirited defence of chapbooks, and in his recognition, in one of his last poems, of 'Jack the jiant killer's high renown' ('To John Clare', in Robinson and Powell (ed.), *The Later Poems of John Clare, 1837–64,* II, pp. 1102–3, 1984). In addition, both Dr Johnson and Boswell confessed to a taste for his adventures; he was famous enough for Fielding to refer to him in the first chapter of *Joseph Andrews* (1742); and for John Newberry to employ him as a letter-writer in *A Little Pretty Pocket-Book* (1744), the publication of which is generally reckoned as the starting-point of modern children's literature.

Such literary references and employments, however, are tangential to Jack's real career as a prime figure in the imaginative fictions of the English unlettered reader, sustained in that position by chapbooks based, no doubt, on oral narrations, and oral narrations based on chapbooks. One thinks of Kit in *The Old Curiosity Shop*, outside the Garlands' cottage:

> sitting on the box thinking about giants' castles, and princesses tied up to pegs by the hair of their heads, and dragons bursting out from behind gates, and other incidents of the like nature, common in story-books to youths of low degree on their first visit to strange houses.

As with 'Jack and the Beanstalk', 'Jack the Giant Killer' has been collected from oral sources several times among communities of English derivation in North America.

Clever Jack

Source: Henry Mayhew, *London Labour and the London Poor*, vol. III, 1861, pp. 389–90.

Narrator: A sixteen-year-old boy from Wisbeach, in the casual ward of a London workhouse, *c.* 1860.

Type: AT1525 'The Master Thief'.

YOU SEE, MATES, THERE was once upon a time, and a very good time it was, a young man, and he runned away, and got along with a gang of thieves, and he went to a gentleman's house, and got in, because one of his mates sweethearted the servant, and got her away, and she left the door open. And the door being left open, the young man got in and robbed the house of a lot of money, 1000*l.*, and he took it to their gang at the cave. Next day there was a reward out to find the robber. Nobody found him. So the gentleman put out two men and a horse in a field, and the men were hidden in the field, and the gentleman put out a notice that anybody that could catch the horse should have him for his cleverness, and a reward as well; for he thought the man that got the 1000*l.* was sure to try to catch that there horse, because he was so bold and clever, and then the two men hid would nab him. This here Jack (that's the young man) was watching, and he saw the two men, and he went and caught two live hares. Then he hid himself behind a hedge, and let one hare go, and one man said to the other, 'There goes a hare,' and they both run after it, not thinking Jack's there. And while they were running he let go the t'other one, and they said, 'There's another hare,' and they ran different ways, and so Jack went and got the horse, and took it to the man that offered the reward, and got the reward; it was 100*l.*; and the gentleman said 'D—n it, Jack's done me this time.' The gentleman then wanted to serve out the parson, and he said to Jack, 'I'll give you another 100*l.* if you'll do something to the parson as bad as you've done to me.' Jack said, 'Well, I will'; and Jack went to the church and lighted up the lamps, and rang the bells, and the parson he got up to see what was up. Jack was standing in one of the pews like an angel, when the parson got to the church. Jack said, 'Go and put your plate in a bag; I'm an angel come to take you up to heaven.' And the parson did so, and it was as much as he could drag to church from his house in a bag; for he was very rich. And when he got to the church Jack put the parson in one bag, and the money stayed in the other; and he tied them both together, and put them across his horse, and took them up hills and through water to the gentleman's, and then he took the parson out of the bag, and the parson was wringing wet. Jack fetched the gentleman, and the gentleman gave the parson a horsewhipping, and the parson cut away, and Jack got all the parson's money and the second 100*l.*, and gave it all to the poor. And the parson brought an action against the gentleman for horsewhipping him, and they both were ruined. That's the end of it.

This story celebrates a more down-to-earth type of thievery than 'Jack and the Beanstalk'. Mayhew gives it as an example of the sort of story admired by the vagrants of his day; his informant told him, 'That's the sort of story that's liked best, sir.' This 'intelligent-looking boy' dressed in 'a series of ragged coats' is one of Mayhew's most heart-breaking informants. He had twice run away from home, not liking his apprenticeship to a brutal tailor and hankering for the sea; now destitute, he told Mayhew he would even go back to the tailor rather than 'hunger about like this'. That use of 'hunger' as a verb is an indication of the robust expressive qualities of his quiet speech, which benefited not only from oral tradition but also from reading, for 'I was what people called a deep boy for a book'.

The boy told Mayhew that in the casual wards

> we told stories sometimes; romantic tales, some; others blackguard kind
> of tales, about bad women; and others about thieving and roguery; not so
> much about what they'd done themselves, as about some big thief that was
> very clever at stealing, and could trick anybody. Not stories such as Dick
> Turpin or Jack Sheppard, or things that's in history, but inventions.

'Clever Jack' was this boy's contribution to the entertainment. He describes it as 'one story that I invented till I learnt it'.

The boy's claim to have 'invented' the story is not a lie, but an indication of his attitude to the story, which has been carefully thought out and memorized. A seventeen-year-old Manchester boy is quoted in the same tantalizing passage as reciting his version of AT1940 'The Extraordinary Names', 'very readily, as if by rote'. It is this boy who makes the point that, 'the best man in the story is always called Jack.' This is certainly true of a great many gypsy and Traveller narratives, and it seems likely that if Mayhew had been a folklorist rather than a social investigator, he could have recovered a large number of 'Jack tales' from his informants. As it is, we must rely on the evidence from the Appalachian Mountains (see Richard Chase, *The Jack Tales*, 1943) to fill out our picture of this once-thriving genre.

The Little Red Hairy Man

Source: S. O. Addy, *Household Tales with Other Traditional Remains: Collected in the Counties of York, Lincoln, Derby and Nottingham*, 1895, pp. 50–53.

Narrator: Unknown, Wensley, Derbyshire; communicated by R. F. Drury, Esq., of Sheffield.

Type: AT301a 'Quest for a Vanished Princess'.

ONCE UPON A TIME there was a lead miner in Derbyshire who had three sons, and he was very poor. One day the eldest son said he would go and seek his fortune, so he packed up his kit, and took something to eat with him and set off. After he had walked a long way he came to a wood, and being very tired he sat down upon a large stone by the wayside, and began to eat the bread and cheese that he had brought with him. Whilst he was eating he thought he heard a voice. So he looked about him and saw a little red man coming out of the wood covered with hair, and about the height of nine penn'orth of copper. He came close up to the eldest son, and asked for something to eat. But instead of giving him food the eldest son told him to be off, and kicked his foot out at the little man and hurt him, so that he went limping back into the wood.

Then the eldest son went on his way, and after a long time came home again as poor as he had left.

After the eldest son had returned, the second son said that he would go out and seek his fortune. When he came to the wood he sat down to rest and eat, and whilst he was eating the little red hairy man came out and begged for some food. But the second son went on eating until he had done, and threw the little man the crumbs and bits that were left. Then the little man told the second son to go and try his luck in a mine that he would find in the middle of the wood.

So the second son went to look for the mine, and when he had found it he said to himself, 'Why, it's only an old worn-out mine, and I'm not going to waste my time over that.' So he set off on his way, and after a long time came home again as poor as he had left.

Now by this time Jack, the youngest son, had grown up, and when the second son came home he said to his father, 'I will go now and seek my fortune.'

So when he was ready he left home in the same way that his brothers had done. And when he came to the wood and saw the stone on the way side, he sat down on it, and pulled out his bread and cheese and began to eat, and in a few minutes he heard somebody say, 'Jack, Jack'. So he looked about him and saw the same little red hairy man that his brothers had seen. The little man said he was hungry, and asked Jack to give him some of his bread and cheese, and Jack said he would and welcome. So he cut him a good lump, and told him he could have more if he wanted. Then the little man came close up to Jack and told him that he only wanted to try him to see what sort he was.

'And now,' said the little man, 'I will help thee to get thy fortune, but thou must do as I tell thee.'

So then he told Jack to go and find the old mine in the middle of the wood.

So Jack went, and when he got to the mine he found the little man had got there before him.

The opening of the mine was inside an old hut, and over the pit, in the middle of the floor, was a windlass. So the little man told Jack to get into the bucket, and began to let him down. So Jack went down, and down, and down, till at last he came to the bottom, when he got out and found himself in a beautiful country.

Whilst he was looking round about him the little man stood by him and gave him a sword and armour, and told him to go and set free a princess who was imprisoned in a copper castle in that country. And then the little man threw a small copper ball on the ground, and it rolled away, and Jack followed it until it came to a castle made of copper, and flew against the door. Then a giant came out of the castle, and Jack fought with him and killed him, and set the princess free, and she went back to her own home.

When Jack came back the little man told him that he must go to a silver castle and set another princess free. So the little man threw down a silver ball, and Jack followed it till it came to a splendid silver castle, and struck against the door so loudly that the giant who lived there came out to see what it was. And then Jack fought with him and killed him, and set the princess free.

Now some time after Jack had set free the princess in the silver castle, the little man said that he must now try to set another princess free who lived in a golden castle. So Jack said he would, and the little man threw down a golden ball, and it began to roll away, and Jack followed it until it came in sight of a magnificent gold castle, and then it went faster and faster until it struck the castle door, and made the giant who lived there come out to see what was the matter. Then Jack and the giant fought, and the giant nearly killed Jack, but at last Jack killed the giant, and then went into the castle and found a beautiful lady there. Jack fell in love with her, and brought her to the little man, and he married them, and helped Jack to get as much gold from the gold castle as he wanted. And then he helped Jack and his wife up the mine, and they went to Jack's home.

Jack built a fine house for himself and another for his father and mother. But his two brothers were envious, and went off to the mine to see if they could not get some gold as well as Jack. And when they got into the hut they quarrelled as to who should go down first, and as they were struggling to get into the bucket the rope broke, and they both fell to the bottom of the pit. As they did not come back Jack and his father went to seek them. And when they got to the mine they saw that the sides of the pit had given way, and blocked it up. And the hut had fallen down, and the place was covered up for ever.

'The Little Red Hairy Man' is paralleled in almost every aspect by a story called 'The Little Red Man' collected by T. W. Thompson at Oxenholme near Kendal on 7 September 1914 from the gypsy Muli Lee (Thompson mss, Brotherton Collection, Notebook C).

Jack the Butter-Milk

Source: S. O. Addy, *Household Tales with Other Traditional Remains*, 1895, pp. 6–9.
Narrator: Unknown, Nottinghamshire.
Type: AT327c 'The Devil Carries the Children Home'.

JACK WAS A BOY who sold butter-milk. One day as he was going his rounds he met a witch who asked him for some of his butter-milk, and told him that if he refused to give it she would put him into a bag that she carried over her shoulders.

But Jack would not give the witch any of his butter-milk, so she put him into her bag, and walked off home with him.

But as she was going on her way she suddenly remembered that she had forgotten a pot of fat that she had bought in the town. Now Jack was too heavy to be carried back to the town, so the witch asked some men who were brushing the hedge by the roadside if they would take care of her bag until she came back.

The men promised to take care of the bag, but when the witch had gone Jack called out to them and said, 'If you will take me out of this bag and fill it full of thorns I will give you some of my butter-milk.'

So the men took Jack out of the bag and filled it with thorns, and then Jack gave them some butter-milk, and ran home.

When the witch came back from the town she picked up her bag, threw it over her shoulder, and walked away. But she had not gone far before the thorns began to prick her back, and she said, 'Jack, I think thou'st got some pins about thee, lad.'

As soon as she had got home she emptied the bag upon a clean white sheet that she had ready. But when she found that there was nothing in the bag but thorns she was very angry and said, 'I'll catch thee tomorrow, Jack, and I'll boil thee.'

The next day she met Jack again, and asked him for some butter-milk, and told him that if he would not give it her she would put him into her bag again.

But Jack said he would give her no butter-milk, so she put him into her bag, and again she bethought her that she had forgotten something for which she would have to go back to the town.

This time she left the bag with some men who were mending the road. Now as soon as the witch had gone Jack called out to them and said, 'If you will take me out and fill this bag full of stones I will give you some of my butter-milk.'

Then the men took Jack out of the bag, and he gave them the butter-milk.

When the witch came back she threw the bag over her shoulder as before, and when she heard the stones grinding and rattling she chuckled and said, 'My word, Jack, thy bones do crack.'

When she got home she emptied the bag on the white sheet again. But when she saw the stones she was very angry, and swore that she would boil Jack when she caught him.

The next day she went out as before, and met Jack again, and asked for some butter-milk. But Jack said 'No' again, so she put him into her bag, and went straight home with him, and threw him out upon the white sheet.

When she had done this she went out of the house and locked Jack in, intending to boil him when she came back. But whilst she was away Jack opened all the cupboards in the house and filled the bag with all the pots that he could find. After he had done this he escaped through the chimney, and got safe home.

When the witch came back she emptied the bag upon the sheet again, and broke all the pots that she had in the house. After this she never caught Jack any more.

<hr />

Sidney Oldall Addy (1848–1933) is one of the most important figures in the study of English folk custom and belief, as well as folk narrative. The fifty-odd folktales in his collection are mostly short and not very well told, but should be cherished precisely because we can be sure that Addy did not polish and refine them. He noted them from dictation or occasionally from written copies, and endeavoured to give them 'in the very words of the narrators'.

Lazy Jack

Source: J. O. Halliwell, *Popular Rhymes and Nursery Tales of England*, 1849, pp. 37–9.

Narrator: Unknown, Yorkshire.

Type: AT1696 'What Should I Have Said (Done)'.

ONCE UPON A TIME there was a boy whose name was Jack, and he lived with his mother on a dreary common. They were very poor, and the old woman got her living by spinning, but Jack was so lazy that he would do nothing but bask in the sun in the hot weather, and sit by the corner of the hearth in the winter time. His mother could not persuade him to do anything for her, and was obliged at last to tell him that if he did not begin to work for his porridge, she would turn him out to get his living as he could.

This threat at length roused Jack, and he went out and hired himself for the day to a neighbouring farmer for a penny; but as he was coming home, never having had any money in his possession before, he lost it in passing over a brook. 'You stupid boy,' said his mother, 'you should have put it in your pocket.' 'I'll do so another time,' replied Jack.

The next day Jack went out again, and hired himself to a cow-keeper, who gave him a jar of milk for his day's work. Jack took the jar and put it into the large pocket of his jacket, spilling it all, long before he got home. 'Dear me!' said the old woman; 'you should have carried it on your head.' 'I'll do so another time,' replied Jack.

The following day Jack hired himself again to a farmer, who agreed to give him a cream cheese for his services. In the evening, Jack took the cheese, and went home with it on his head. By the time he got home the cheese was completely spilt, part of it being lost, and part matted with his hair. 'You stupid lout,' said his mother, 'you should have carried it very carefully in your hands.' 'I'll do so another time,' replied Jack.

The day after this Jack again went out, and hired himself to a baker, who would give him nothing for his work but a large tom-cat. Jack took the cat, and began carrying it very carefully in his hands, but in a short time pussy scratched him so much that he was compelled to let it go. When he got home, his mother said to him, 'You silly fellow, you should have tied it with a string, and dragged it along after you.' 'I'll do so another time,' said Jack.

The next day Jack hired himself to a butcher, who rewarded his labours by the handsome present of a shoulder of mutton. Jack took the mutton, tied it to a string, and trailed it along after him in the dirt, so that by the time he had got home the meat was completely spoilt. His mother was this time quite out of patience with him, for the next day was Sunday, and she was obliged to content herself with cabbage for her dinner. 'You ninnyhammer,' said she to her son, 'you should have carried it on your shoulder.' 'I'll do so another time,' replied Jack.

On the Monday Jack went once more, and hired himself to a cattle-keeper, who gave him a donkey for his trouble. Although Jack was very strong, he found some difficulty in hoisting the donkey on his shoulders, but at last he accomplished it, and began walking slowly home with his prize. Now it happened that in the course of his journey there lived a rich man with his only daughter, a beautiful girl, but unfortunately deaf and dumb; she had never laughed in her life, and the doctors said she would never recover till somebody made her laugh. Many tried without success, and at last the father, in despair, offered her in marriage to the first man who could make her laugh. This young lady happened to be looking out of the window, when Jack was passing with the donkey on his shoulders, the legs sticking up in the air; and the sight was so comical and strange, that she burst out into a great fit of laughter, and immediately recovered her speech and hearing. Her father was overjoyed, and fulfilled his promise by marrying her to Jack, who was thus made a rich gentleman. They lived in a large house, and Jack's mother lived with them in great happiness until she died.

This story, collected by Halliwell from oral tradition, is unusual in ending with the motif of making the princess laugh, familiar from the Grimms' 'Golden Goose' (AT571 'All Stick Together'). A version collected by T. W. Thompson on 6 September 1914 from Terence Lee at Oxenholme, near Kendal, 'Silly Jack's Rewards and What He Did With Them', shares this feature.

The Grey Castle

Source: Dora E. Yates, *A Book of Gypsy Folk-Tales*, 1948, pp. 161–7.
Narrator: Rosie Griffiths.
Type: Variant of AT313 'The Girl as Helper in the Hero's Flight'.

ONCET UPON A TIME, and it wasn't in your time nor my time but it was in jolly good days, Jack left home. In his home he's left his poor old mother ahind on an owld box. And he was retermined to see life, 'cos he's never seen life afore.

He tramps along a dreary muddy road for miles and miles, and at long last he took a seat and reconsidered hisself, and he shook his head. 'Why did I, poor foolish boy, leave my home? What is mine own mother doing now 'ithout me? I wonder.'

He shook his head again, but he plucked up courage, brushed his coat and his cap, and started on tramp once more again. 'Now, Jack, dere's only yourself you got to talk to,' says he, as he sighs his way along the dreary road. He begins to feel tired again so he rests his weary foot. De night is dark and bright stars above him, but he could not speak to de stars.

All at oncet dere stood a bright light in front of him, so he glared at it a-one-side, and with his brain and his heart wondered and plondered what was going to be at de end. 'Well, Jack old boy, cheer up, and now you must take a sleep.'

At long last de morn is comed and de birds begin deir bright singing, what lightened his heart a great deal. And the sun was shining so beautiful he could see de rocks and meadows clearly, and a large grey castle on a hill in front of him. 'Jack, my lad, you do not know what's afore you: dat castle may be your fortune.'

Jack sighed again, tired and dreary, hungry and dirsty, he gazed a-one-side at a grey owld farmhouse. He ventured to open de gate and knocked at de farm door and asked de owld woman for a drink. De owld farmer-woman asked him quite snubbily as she handed him de tea: 'What is a young man like you doing about de country: have you no work?' 'No, dere isn't no work for Poor Jack', says he to dat owld farmer-woman. 'Why?' she asks. 'Well,' says Jack, 'it's like a good few of you farmers, you's a bit juberstitious of a man's stealing summat. But bein' as you's made such a brag and a boast 'bout

it, we'll begin with you, missus. Is dere any work for poor Jack from you?'
'Well, my man, only haarrd work!'

Jack laughed as she stood wid her coarse apron at de door. 'Give me de chancet, missus, to see what I could do.' 'Well!' says she, quite sneery, 'what *can* you do?' 'Excuse me,' says Jack, quite on de laughing side, pulling his cap off so p'litely and brushing back his black hair, 'I'll give you an offer of work now this instant minute. I'll chop dat big tree for you, missus, into logs for your oven, for a little bite to eat.' 'Well,' says the woman, 'here's my chopper.' Jack smiles to hisself and mutters: 'She's a hard piece of brick, is dat farmer-woman.'

He worked away did Jack and, feeling very dreary, hungry and dirsty, brought de wood to de door. 'Jack,' says she (quite de thing now, you sees) 'you've done more work nor any one of my men has done. Seat yourself down at dat table dis instant minute', she says, 'and eat and drink of de best.' 'Now', thinks Jack to hisself, 'it's only de start of a dream for you, my boy, it's only de first lesson. But somehow dese hard-hearted manly women comes soft-hearted at de end.'

A'ter he'd done his food, he sits hisself down by de fireside and has a little smoke and plonders very deeply about his poor owld mother. And he starts to make amend very smartly, and asks de missus could he have a wash. 'Ev course,' says she, quite cheerful, 'it'll afresh you Jack.' And out he goes with de bucket and soap (in a farmhouse you sees), and de farmer-woman hurries a'ter him and relivers him de towel. 'Thank you kindly,' says Jack, 'you bin just like a mother to me, but not ezackly like my poor owld mammie: she used to cling to me and pray for me more nor anybody in de world.'

Well, de owld woman fetches him a suit now, b'longing to one of her sons, and begs him to stay de night. But all he says is: 'How far is de next village from here, mum?' 'You don't mean to say you will walk twenty miles tonight, Jack? I want you to stay wid me and I'll give you good money and good food. Do you know owt about ploughing?' 'No,' he said quite stern to de owld woman, 'de best ploughing as ever I done, mum, is ploughing de hard road. So I'll stay no longer nor tonight, and mind you call me up six o'clock in de mornin'!'

De next morning is comed. He hears de gentle creak up de stairs, and up he jumps on de cheerful side. 'Well, Jack,' he says to hisself, 'you do look a smart, brisk lad now. And you'll soon make away for your dear hard road.' He enjoys his breakfast with de missus and tells her straight he must leave dis same morning. (He still has dat grey castle on his mind – he would do oncet he'd seen it.) 'Poor foolish Jack,' says she with a jeery laugh, 'I s'pose you's thinking of dat castle what you told me of. Dere's nowt dere for you, my boy, nowt whatsumdever! De very idea of you's going dere! poor foolish lad.' 'Well,' says Jack, 'I'm retermined to see life, and life I *will* see.'

So off he goes, carrying a little food wid him. He shuts de gate ahind him merrily, and starts a-laughing. 'Thank God', he says, 'I'm on de hard road again.' He starts a bit of hard walking, as he didn't think nothing of dat twenty miles. So he walked and he walked till he see'd de castle grinning at him. He sits hisself down and has a little smoke and he smiles to hisself. 'I'll soon make dat castle speak for itself too,' says he; 'it's bin on my brain long enough,' he says.

Now he sees de lodge of dat castle, but he sees no light in dat lodge. But when he goes to de front door, he sees a bright light inside. So he smartens hisself and makes a 'tempt to knock at dat hard knocker. Now who comes out to him dere but an owld grey lady. She opens de door and gives him a little smile. 'Whatever do you want here, my boy?' says she. 'What a diff'rent voice she has', thinks Jack, 'towards dat hard brick!' And he laughs. 'I wants to know, mother,' he says, 'who lives up at dat owld grey castle.' 'You come in, my boy, and I'll 'tempt to 'splain to you. But you's very late: it's turned seven!' (It's in the night, you see, in dem country places.)

'Are you looking for work?' asked the old lady. 'Well, I bin here dese thirty years', she says 'and I've seen no men like you walking about de land.' (Poor hopes for Jack!) 'But dere's no harm in you's going up. Dere's only an owld gentleman dere', she says, 'and he's hard o' hearing.' (God help poor Jack!) 'Ah!' says Jack, 'never enter, never will.' (He was cheering hisself up.) 'When dere's a will, dere's a way. And I'm going up, mother,' he says. 'Good night, my boy, take care of you's self: you's got still two mile yet to go up to dat castle.'

Jack goes along through two big iron gates and makes his way up to de castle. (Thank God!) He goes over owld humpy, owld bumpy, owld stones, of course, but he doesn't care nowt for dese humpy, bumpy stones. He comed to de door of dat castle – dirty big lumps of lead on de door but a beautiful big knocker. He knocked on dat door.

Suddenly de door opened but he seen no one dere. He could not understand it. Dat door closened again. He knocked again. Suddently de door opened again. But still he seen no one dere.

So Jack stepped in den, cheekily. And what stood afore him? (Don't frighten!) A little hairy owld man! 'What can I do for you, my strange man?' he says. 'I want work, Sir.' 'Ha! ha! ha!' says he, '*work* you want, is it? Come dis way, I'll show you work. Did anyone send you up here?' 'No', says Jack, quite cheerful. 'I must say you're a brave young man. Dere hasn't been anyone up here for thirty years. Well,' he said, 'I'll see about getting some work for you. When did you have something to eat last, my boy?' 'Oh! I don't feel hungry, thank you', says Jack. 'Well, I do,' says de owld hairy man. 'Come dis way,' he say, 'you have not seen de Master yet.'

Jack begins to shiver. Jack begins to stare. And who should sit down at the great dinner table but a big Giant! Jack stared and stared. 'Well, my brave man,' he says, 'come to look here for work, have you? Ha! ha! I'll give you work, if work it is you want!' Jack begins to miss de little hairy man.

'Sit down here,' he says. (Dat's de Giant.) Jack begins to look around and shivers. He sees a 'normous plate afore him. 'You've to eat all dat!' (Poor Jack! he must have a big belly too.) 'Remember you haven't seen your master *yet*.' 'How many masters must I see?' thinks poor Jack to hisself. 'You'll want a place to sleep in, won't you?' 'Yes,' says Jack.

'Come here, and I'll show you' – and dere stands his dear little hairy man again. Jack steps into the room and sees a 'normous big bed: 'Too big for me', he thinks to hisself. And who drops in dere but a bigger Giant nor what he'd seen afore, what would have been the mainstay of two Giants. 'You're not sleeping with me?' says Jack, and he begins to shiver again. 'No, my man, dat is your bed to you's self.' 'Well, I'll be very glad of a rest,' says Jack. And he pulls his shoes off, does Jack, and he puts his head down on de pillow (thank God he did!) and he snores and snores till morning. (You wouldn't hardly know was it morning dere, it was always so dark – dat's why it's called de grey castle, you see!)

A ten-pound knock comed to de door and shook de bed from under him. 'Come down for your breakfast, my man, come down!' Poor Jack goes down for his breakfast (certainly he would do, wouldn't you too?). And he sees de two Giants and the little s'rimp, de hairy man. 'Jack,' says de Giant, 'I want you to do some very hard work today. You'll have to go into de green room today. Dere stands a table before you, my boy, and you'll have to sleep dere for three nights, my boy, and unpick every single bit of rag dat's in dat great big rug.' 'I'll try my best, Sir,' says poor Jack shivering again. The Giant went away and slammed the door on him.

Dere only stood two candles for his work. (God help him! he must have had good eyes too.) So he picked up de rug and started working. At last he begin to tremble: he partly knew dere was *somebody* about. And de 'normous big Giant with his glistening eyes came in. 'Well, Jack, have you found anything? Have you seen anything?' 'What d'you want me to see or find?' says Jack. 'Is dere anything in dis dark room to find or to see?' he says. 'Seek not for inflammation!' said de big Giant, 'but get on wid your work!' De door goes slam, wid a fast lock. (Poor Jack!)

Jack begins to work again, and suddenly he looks towards a big long chest what stood in de darkest corner. And he hears a whisper: 'Pull it from de middle, Jack, and your three days' job will soon be finished. But do not say dat you heard anything.'

De Giant comes in (dat Giant is a Devil, you know!) shining de room up wid his glittering eyes. 'You're doing your work wonnerful, Jack, but I'm not quite satisfied. You must have seen someone to help you do dat rug.' 'I don't know what you's talking about', says Jack. The Giant goes out de same old way with a slam of de door.

It suddenly struck Jack about de owld chest what stood in de corner. He stepped up to it and was 'tempted to undo de lock. (Go ahead, Jack!) De word was spoken: 'You can't undo dat lock. Look on de shelf, Jack, and look pretty sharp, and you'll find de key of de chest.' Jack looks sharp and finds de key.

He unlocks de chest and suddenly de lid opens, and he staggers back. He sees inside de glitter of a beautiful green dress and a figure wid a pale face: a lovely lady. Den she up and spoke to Jack afore she lays down again. 'Jack,' she says, 'I have been locked in dis chest for de last thirty years.' Jack is staggered. 'Are you a ghost?' he asks. 'No,' says she, 'I'm human like what you are, dere's still a bit of life in me. I'm in my wedding dress,' she says. 'You are my brave man, Jack,' she says, 'and dose two Giants are 'chanted and dat little hairy man is my father. And now, Jack, I've told you my secret. So don't hesitate, Jack; close de chest, fasten de lock and say nothing.' By this time de whole rug is unpicked.

At last bum! bum, bum! de Giant is coming. 'Come in!' cries Jack. 'My word, you have worked dat cloth beautiful, Jack. You must have found something, or seen someone.' 'Dere's only one more thing, Jack,' he says, 'you've got to do for me: to go to dat pond outside de castle and find two diamond rings.' 'Well,' says Jack, very disheartened, 'it's impossible, Sir, to find two diamond rings.' The Giant glared at him quite furiously.

Poor Jack goes out to dis dirty black pond, and he plondered to hisself could he find dese two diamond rings. At long last he sees a beautiful white swan and Jack thinks to have a chat with dis swan. Suddenly it made up to him. And Jack got more frightened of de swan nor what he got of de Giants. 'Poor Jack,' says she, 'just follow me and I'll show you where are dose diamond rings.' Jack followed de swan up to de pond. 'Don't get disheartened, Jack, I've got dose diamond rings for you.' And de swan lifted up her bill and dere were de rings she'd picked up from de bottom of de pond. 'And now, Jack, go back to dat Giant and tell him you've seen no one, and give dose two rings into his own hands.'

Back goes Jack, quite cheerful, steps into de green room, goes up to de chest de first thing and opens de lid, and speaks gently to de lovely green lady. He shows her de diamond rings. 'Jack,' says she, 'my good lad, give dem to dat Brute and do not return here again to me. You will find me somewhere else.'

Jack goes bravely from her, and steps up to de big Giant, quite cheeky. 'Here you are, you Brute!' he says. 'What! what! what!' says de Giant, 'dose same two diamond rings what caused a lot of bloodshed? Well!' he says to Jack (quite de thing now, you sees) 'you've fulfilled your work, you've beat me, Jack. And you've won de grey castle. You'll be "poor" Jack no longer! I must leave you for a minute. Go into de green room, Jack, and you shall have your reward.'

Poor Jack goes into de other room quite happy and proud. And a nice gentleman met him at de door. He was looking for de little hairy owld man, but he couldn't see him – only dis very nice gentleman to keep poor Jack company.

Suddenly he seed de castle all of a light-shine, what he'd never seed afore. De gentleman dances him into another great big room, and he could see de table laid out with chickens and ducks and all sorts of good things, and he was plondering where were de guests. And suddenly two beautiful young gentlemen appear, shining like de rising sun. He was looking for de two Giants, and lo and behold! – dese two young gentlemen.

Jack was quite excited and quite exhausted. Den who comes in a'ter, but a lovely lady in a pale green dress and a green veil. She comes up to Jack and says: 'Jack, my boy, you have brokened our 'chantment.' With dat, she throws back her green veil and stands afore him – the handsomest young lady in all de land.

Den dey all gathered together – de father, de two brothers and Jack and de lady – 'ithout one enemy in de world. And Jack married de lovely lady. And so dey lived happy for ever more after.

This remarkable story slots uneasily into the Aarne–Thompson classification, relating to a number of tale types while conforming to none. Briggs allies it to AT400 'The Man on a Quest for his Lost Wife' and AT326a 'Soul Released from Torment'. It is essentially an individual welding of common motifs, making a unique and powerful story. It most resembles those versions of AT313 in which the hero falls in love with a swan maiden, takes service with her ogre father and, helped surreptitiously by her, achieves impossible tasks. Usually this is followed by the incident of the obstacle flight, and perhaps more complications; here, however, the achievement of the tasks disenchants all the other characters.

On the evidence of this text – despite its sometimes unsuccessful attempt to preserve verbal idiosyncracies – Rosie Griffiths was a marvellous storyteller: the language is full of flavour, the narrative is tightly controlled, the whole text is relaxed, yet full of life. She was a close friend of Dora Yates, who recorded this story from her, and devotes a chapter of her memoir, *My Gypsy Days*, to their friendship.

Lousy Jack and His Eleven Brothers

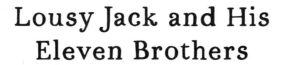

Source: T. W. Thompson mss, Brotherton Collection, Leeds, Notebook H.
Narrator: Taimi Boswell, 9 January 1915, Oswaldtwistle.
Type: AT551 'The Sons on a Quest for a Wonderful Remedy for Their Father' (variant) with elements of AT410 'Sleeping Beauty'.

DERE WAS AN OWLD woman what 'ed twelve sons. Eleven on 'em was fine enough fellas in deir way, but de youngest, Jack, was rale lousy, and good for nothing at all. Lousy Jack he was called, and ivvrybody kicked him and knocked him about.

His eleven brothers decided to go out into de world to seek deir fortunes, and Lousy Jack said as he'd go as well. What was de use of him going, dey said: de only fortune he'd meet wid was kicks and blows, anless somebody took pity on him and cut his head off. He would go nonedeless, and his mother says: 'Yes, let him.'

De brothers cam to twelve road ends, and agreed to part dere, and to meet agen at de same place in a year and a day. Dey left Jack de dirtiest road; and a wery bad road it was. He kept going on and going on, till at last he cam to a big castle. Dere was a Golden Phoenix over de door. 'If you ventures into dis castle,' it says, 'you'll see things as'll mek your blood run cowld.' 'Oh!' says Jack, and teks no more notice on it 'an if it hedn't bin dere. He goes in and looks round. He sees all de sarvants standing dere at deir work but not stirring: nivver a one of 'em moves hand or foot: it was as if dey'd bin turned to stone. He goes upstairs: it's de same dere. Dere is nobody anywheres what's any diffrent: it's as if dey'd all bin turned to stone in de middle o' doing summat. He goes into de stables, and de horses and grooms is just de same. One groom looks at first sight as if he was brushing down a horse, but neether it nor him ivver moves. It's de same wid de dogs, and de beeas [cows] in de shippon. Christians [humans] and animals alike, dey's all silent and still. Dey's all in a trance or under a spell: ivvry living thing's bin 'chanted.

Besides being lousy, Jack was a fool, and he hedn't de sense to be afeared. And as it happened he was wery curious. So he goes nosing and exploring all ower de castle, even down into de cellars. He don't know it, but de king's daughter bin put down in de bottommost cellar, and a great heap o' thorns piled over her. It's pitch dark down dere, and a wery bad place to find. But Lousy Jack comes on it in time, and goes groping among de thorns. Being such a lousy fella he liked de scratching he got, and kept on pushing his way through 'em on dat account, just for de sake 'n de scratching, you un'erstand: he'd nothing else in mind. But by chance – and it was only a chance – he touched de princess; and when dat happened de cellar was lit up, and she came to life agen. Wi'out knowing it he'd broke de spell as 'd bin put on her, in de only way as it could be broke. He soon hed de thorns shifted off 'n her, and set her free. He fun as de 'chantment didn't howld no longer anywheres as he went. De sarvants was tripping about agen and chattering, de dogs barking, de horses pawing, and de groom gitting on wid his brushing-down. Christians and animals, dey was all alive agen.

De princess wanted to know how he'd come to do all dis, and he telt her de same as I've telt you: it was all a lucky accident, he said, due to him being curious, and to his liking a good scratching because he was lousy. She'd 'ev hed him stop at de castle al'ays, and he dided dere till it was time for him to go and meet his brothers. He must do dat, he said, as he'd give his word as he would and couldn't go back on it. So off he went, and in a year and a day de twelve brothers met agen at de place where dey'd parted. For a long time all de talk was about what de tother eleven 'ed met wid, but at de last dey ext Jack how he'd got on. He telt 'em about de Castle of de Golden Phoenix, and how he rescued de princess dere from de deepest, darkest cellar, where he'd fun her spell-bound under a big heap o' thorns; telt 'em ivvrything, he did, but didn't happen to mention his reason for pushing on and on into de thorns.

Soon after, dis princess give out as she wanted to see agen de man as 'ed broke de spell and rescued her. On hearing about dis, Jack's brothers took and throw'd him into a dyke, thinking to drownd him so 'at one o' dem could hev de credit for what he'd done. De owldest brother den goes and tells de princess it was him as ended de 'chantment and set her free. He must prove it, she says, by telling her just how he did it, and exac'ly how it come to pass; and he must answer all her questions correc'ly. Well, he tells her exac'ly all as he'd heeard Jack say, and can answer all her questions but one. He's not de man, she tells him, but doesn't say why. All de tother brothers goes in turn, and tells de story as dey'd heeard it from Jack. But dere's al'ays one thing dey missed out, one question dey can't answer correc'ly; and one after another she turns 'em all down. De reason was as none 'n 'em said or could tell her why he'd kept on pushing about among de thorns in de dark when he didn't know as nobody was dere. But she didn't tell 'em dis: all she said was as none 'n 'em was de man as 'ed liberated her.

At de finish she ext 'em if dey hedn't got another brother. Well, yes, dere *was* one, but it was no use trying to find him, dey said, as he was dead or 'ed disappeared. Besides, it wouldn't be him as 'ed rescued her: he was de fool 'n de family. And if she's sin him once, she'd nivver want to see him agen as he was lousy: Lousy Jack he'd alays bin called. Dat's what dey telt de princess, but she pays no heed, and sends 'em away.

Jack warn't dead; he'd somehow managed to save hissel', and scram'le out 'n de dyke into which his brothers 'ed throw'd him; and after dat he'd turned tramp. He's in de neighbourhood o' de Castle o' de Golden Phoenix once more, and hears what de princess 'es give out. So he goes and says as he'd be de man she's exing for, as it was him 'at broke de spell and set her free. And she know'd it was him when he telt her, as he'd done at de time, 'at it was all due to him liking a good scratching, being as he was lousy. Well, Jack and de princess gits married, and when her father died he become king. But to de end of his days he was a lousy fellow, and like a good scratching.

This tale is either a truncated version, or a parody, of a long story – 'The Castle o' the Golden Phoenix, the Bottle o' Eversee Water and the Three Sleeping Beauties' – known to have been in the repertoire of both Taimi Boswell and another renowned gypsy storyteller, Jimmy Smith, but never recorded from either of them. Thompson notes before the summary text in Notebook 9 (pp. 25–32) that, 'this story was only outlined, and Taimi did not make it very clear.' The present text was expanded in Thompson's old age. Thompson writes that it was told 'in outline only last thing at night', and a note at the end reads, 'in my original record there is needless confusion and vagueness in latter part. My fault. It was righted later, and is here.' There is no way of telling what he meant by 'original record': the two surviving texts are very close to each other, although the late, expanded version printed here attempts to convey something of the sound and cadence of Taimi's delivery.

According to Thompson's informant, Johnny Smith, Jimmy Smith took six hours to tell his complete 'Castle of the Golden Phoenix' tale. It seems unlikely that such a long story would have depended on Lousy Jack's mock-heroic motivation, and it seems likely that 'Lousy Jack' is a skit on the longer story (which sounds as if it was a version of AT551 'The Sons on a Quest for a

Wonderful Remedy for Their Father'). 'Lousy Jack' lacks the motif of the quest for the water of life (the 'Eversee Water'), although the story would make more sense were it present, as then the brothers would make their false claim to their father, who genuinely would not know who was being truthful. The fact that Taimi only told the tale in outline perhaps accounts for this lacuna, and for the absence of any explanation as to why the princess is enchanted, or account of what happened to the eleven false brothers.

Parody has always been a vital element of oral tradition. Thompson recorded a romantic tale, 'The Bride Who Had Never Been Kissed', hinging on the common motif of a ring cast away in the sea subsequently found in a fish, from Eva Gray, and a joke story to cap it from her brother Reuben, in which a young man throws a ring into the sea and tells two girls he will marry the one who gives it back to him. Years later, one of the girls cuts open the fish, and what do you think she finds inside – 'the guts'. Augustus Hare collected a similar tale from Miss Hosmer in Rome in 1892 (*The Story of My Life*, vol. 4, p. 285), in which the answer is slightly politer – 'the fishbone'.

The Magic Knapsack

Source: T. W. Thompson mss, Brotherton Collection, Leeds, Notebook F, pp. 11–13; collected by John Myers.

Narrator: 'Ashton', a traveller from Hull, June 1911, Newport, Monmouthshire.

Type: AT569 'The Knapsack, the Hat and the Horn'.

WUNS UPON A TIME ther wus a poor lad called Jack, and he set off to seek his fortune. He wandered on till he felt hungry, and he cum to a house and asked summat to eat. So the people in this house axed him in, and they laid a spread-cloth and said 'spread vittles', and with that all sorts of vittles cum onto this cloth. So Jack sat down, and had plenty to eat and plenty to drink, and when he'd finished eating he snatched this spread-cloth and run. They all off after him, but he'd got a good start, and he left them.

Now on the road he fell in with an old soldier, and this here old soldier begged from him. So to show off Jack puts down his spread-cloth and says 'spread vittles', and all sorts of food and drink cum onto it. So they sat down and helped themselves. When they'd finished this old soldier takes his knapsack and kicks it, and out comes a regiment of soldiers, and every time he kicked out cum another regiment. This old soldier orders 'em all back, and then offered to swap his knapsack for the spread-cloth. So Jack agrees, and t'fust thing he done was to order his soldiers to take the spread-cloth off the old man, and off he sets home with both.

When he got home he found his poor old father and mother in vury bad trouble, and his poor old mother was weeping 'cos they were going to be turned out. So Jack says, 'Cheer up, mother, ther isn't anybody can turn you out', and he lays the spread-cloth and says 'spread vittles' and ther wus all kinds of food and drink, so when they were eating some soldiers cum to turn 'em out, and Jack kicks his knapsack, and a whole regiment of soldiers cum out, and these soldiers what had cum to turn 'em out was frightened, and they went and tell't t'king. This med t'king so angry that he sent his whole army, but Jack just kicked his knapsack, and fetched regiment after regiment, and t'king was so frightened that he had to ask for mercy. So Jack told t'king if he'd mek him heir to t'throne and give him his daughter he'd call his soldiers off and help t'king against his enemies. Now in them days ther wus kings and queens in every county and sheer, and Jack set to work like Oliver Cromwell, only better, to conquer 'em all. Now them as giv in was alright, them as fowt was eaten up and at t'finish he was king over all t'country.

◦◦◦

Myers recorded three tales from this man (the others are 'The Cleverest Thief in the World' and 'The Three-Legged Hare'), who also knew a fourth, 'How the Smith got to Heaven'. He then sent the texts to Thompson, who spent much energy trying to discover whether or not 'Ashton' (the name was apparently an alias) had got his tales, as he claimed, from one of the Grays. The present text is in Thompson's hand; Myers' texts do not seem to have survived, though correspondence between the two men has. Thompson writes in 'The Gypsy Grays as Tale-Tellers', 'Ashton had none of the fine arts of tale-telling: he simply got through his stories as quickly as possible, and seemed glad when he had finished.' This may have been true in the uncomfortable situation of having his narrations noted down by a stranger, but even so this compact and lively tale does not seem to support Thompson's assertion. Its cheerful amorality needs just such a crisp pace to avoid callousness.

This is one of the few native English tales that actually begins 'Once upon a time'. The formula towards the end that, 'in them days there was kings and queens in every county and shire', was also a standard story opening. My only amendment to this text is to make Jack ask to be made 'heir', rather than 'heiress', which is apparently what Ashton actually said.

The History of the Four Kings

Of Canterbury, Colchester, Cornwall and Cumberland, Their Queens and Daughters; Being the Merry Tales of Tom Hodge and His School-Fellows

Source: Chapbook text reprinted in Robert Hays Cunningham, *Amusing Prose Chapbooks Chiefly of the Last Century*, 1889, pp. 187–200.

Narrator: Unknown.

Type: (III) AT853 'Hero Catches the Princess with Her Own Words', (IV and V) AT480 'The Spinning Women by the Spring', (VII) AT1534 'Series of Clever Unjust Decisions', (VIII) AT921 'The King and the Peasant's Son'.

Preface

Not to detain the reader with many words to little purpose, I shall only here observe that Tom Hodge, with the rest of his old companions, belonging to the school of Cockermouth, were walking on a very pleasant morning in May, and having tired themselves with pranks and intrigues, towards evening they sat themselves down on a green bank, beneath a lovely oak, where they agreed amongst themselves that everyone should tell a tale, or pay a fine; and because Tom was the eldest scholar, it was concluded and agreed upon that he should begin first.

> Says Tom, 'With all my heart,
> So I'll begin my part.'

Tale I

Once upon a time, when the opinion was common in England that those whose age and experience enabled them to determine the consequences of certain actions were wizards and witches, there was a queen in this realm, whose name was Elizabeth; and by reason that the famous town of Lancaster was strangely pestered with witches, the queen sent some judges down to arraign and try them in order to bring them to justice.

Now the news of this court being to be kept in Lancaster, spread through all the country, so that a husbandman living near forty miles from that place, hearing of this news, and believing they were come to tell the folks whether they were witches or not, resolved to go to be satisfied in himself, for he was possessed with a fear that he was a witch, because he had a wart grew on his neck, which he imagined to be a dug.

His wife, who had a friend in a corner, and was therefore glad of his absence, did not only give her consent, but also dressed him in his best leathern suit and broad-brimmed hat. So taking leave of his good wife Joan, he trudged on day and night until he came to the place where the court was kept; so rushing on and pressing through the crowd, the crier of the court believing him to be some evidence, gave orders that they should let him in, which was soon done, and he was required to speak what he had to say. 'Why,' says the countryman, 'd'ye see, I've a dug upon my neck, which makes me afraid I am a witch, and volks tell me that these vine gentlemen (pointing to the judges) can tell a body whether one is a witch or no.' The crier of the court seeing the simplicity of the man, said, 'No, no, my friend, I can assure thee thou art no witch; thou lookest more like a cuckold than a witch or a conjurer.' 'I thank you, zur; and zo zays these vine gentlemen.' Then having given three or four scrapes and half a dozen congees, he came back as wise as Waltham's calf. The next day he was met by his wife, who waited for his return at the town's end, to whom she said, 'Well, husband, what do the gentlemen say? are you a witch or no?' 'A witch, sweet wife, no; they tells a body one looks more like a cuckold than a witch or a conjurer.' 'Why say you so?' replied she; 'I prithee go back and have them taken up for witches; for except they had been so, they would not have known you were a cuckold.'

This merry tale so pleased them that they set up a hearty laugh, which, being ended, the second boy began his tale in the following manner.

Tale II

In the days of yore, when this land was governed by many kings, among the rest the king of Canterbury had an only daughter, and she was wise, fair, and beautiful. Her father sent forth a decree that whoever would watch one night with his daughter, and neither sleep nor slumber, he should have her the next day in marriage; but if he did either, he should lose his head. Many knights and squires attempted it, but lost their heads.

Now it happened a young shepherd, grazing his flock near the road, said to his master, 'Zur, I zee many gentlemen ride to the court at Canterbury, but ne'er see 'em return again.' 'O, shepherd!' said his master, 'I know not how they should; for they attempt to watch with the king's daughter, according to the decree, and not performing it, they are all beheaded.' 'Well,' said the shepherd, 'I'll try my vorton; zo now vor a king's daughter or a headless shepherd.' And taking his bottle and bag, he trudged to court. Now, in his way, he was to cross a river, over which lay a plank; down he sits, and pulls off his shoes and stockings to wash his feet, lest the smell of his toes might be the means of keeping her awake. While he was washing his feet a fish came smelling and biting his toes; he caught it and put it into his bag: after which came a second, a third, and a fourth, which he caught and put in his bag likewise. This done, and dried his feet, he put on his stockings and shoes, and pursued his journey till he came to the palace, where he knocked loudly with his crook. He was no sooner let in, and having told his business, but he was conducted to a hall, prepared for that purpose, where the king's daughter sat ready to receive him; and the better to lull his senses, he was placed in a rich easy chair, having delicious wines for his supper, with many fine dishes of fruit, etc., of which the shepherd ate and drank plentifully, insomuch that he began to slumber before midnight. 'O shepherd,' said the lady, 'I have caught you napping?' 'Not, zweet ally, I was busy.' 'At what?' said she. 'Why a feeshing.' 'Nay, shepherd, there is no fish-pond in the hall.' 'No matter: vor that, I have been feeshing.' Says the lady, 'Where do you fish?' 'O,' quoth he, 'in my bag.' 'O me, have you catched e'er a one?' 'Ay, lady,' said he. 'I'd willingly see it,' replied she. 'Ay, an't please you, you shall with all my heart.' This said, he slyly drew one of the fishes out of his bag, at the sight of which she was greatly pleased, and praised it for a pretty fish: and withal said, 'Dear shepherd, do you think you could catch one in mine too?' 'Ay, ay, doubtless I can.' Then he fell to fishing, and in a short time drew a second fish out of the bag pretending he drew it from her. The king's daughter was so pleased with it that she kissed it, declaring it was the finest she ever saw. And about half an hour after she said, 'Shepherd, do you think you could get me one more?' He answered, 'Mayhap I may, when I have baited my hook.' 'Then make haste, for I am impatient till I have another.' Then the shepherd acted as before, and so presented her with another fish, which she also extolled and praised, saying, 'It was ten times finer than the other'; and then gave him leave to sleep, promising to excuse him to her father.

In the morning the king came into the hall as usual, followed by the headsman with a hatchet; but the lady cried out, 'You may return with your hatchet, here is no work for you.' 'How so,' said the king, 'has he neither slumbered nor slept?' 'No, royal father, he has not.' 'How has he employed himself?' 'In fishing.' 'Why, there is never a fish-pond; where did he catch them?' 'One in his own bag, and two in this one of mine.' 'Say you so? Well, friend, dost thou think thou can'st catch one in mine?' 'An't please you, my liege, I believe I can.' Then directing the king to lie down, he poked him with a packing needle, which made him cry out exceedingly; at which time he drew the other fish out of the bag, and showed it to the king. His majesty said, 'I never knew such sort of fishing before; however, take my daughter, according to my royal decree.' And so they were married, and the wedding kept in great triumph, and the shepherd became a king's son.

'O that was mighty well,' said the third boy, 'he had wonderful good fortune. This puts me in mind of a story, which I will now tell in my turn.'

Tale III

If I may believe my old grandmother, there lived in the county of Cumberland a nobleman, who had three sons. Two of them were comely and tall youths, wise and learned; the third a merry fool, and went often in a party-coloured coat and steeple crowned hat, at the top of which was a tassel. In this dress he made a comical figure. At this time the king of Canterbury had a fine daughter, adorned with all the gifts of nature, joined to an ingenious education, she being very ripe-witted, as appeared by her ready answers and the comical questions she put forth. The king, her father, published a decree, that whoever should come to the court, and answer his daughter three questions, without study or stumbling, should have her in marriage, and also be heir to the crown at his decease. On publishing this decree, the said gentleman's two sons agreed between themselves to go and try how favourable fortune might be to them in this undertaking; but all their care was what they should do with their silly brother Jack; for, as they said, if he follows us, he will out with some foolish bolt, and so spoil our business. At length it was agreed on going to the court, to go out of the back door, which led to the road over several fields, about a mile from the house. They did so, but were no sooner got into the highway, but looking behind, they saw their brother Jack coming capering and dancing after them, saying, with a loud laughter, 'So you are going to get a king's daughter, but I will pursue you.' They saw there was no way to get rid of him, but by walking fast and leaving him behind, hoping thereby to get entrance before Jack, and then have the gates shut against him. They had not gone half a mile before Jack set up a great fit of laughter, at which one of his brothers said, 'What's the fool found out now?' 'Why, I've found an egg.' 'Put it in thy pocket,' said his brothers. 'Adad, and so I will,' says Jack. Presently after he was taken with another fit of laughter. 'What's the fool found now?' 'What have I found!' says Jack, 'why a crooked stick.' They bid him put that in his pocket also. 'Ay, marry, will I.' They had not walked much farther before Jack burst into a greater fit of laughter than before. His brothers said, 'What's the fool found now?' 'Found! why an orange.' 'Put that in your pocket likewise.' 'I intend it,' says Jack. Now, by this time they were come near the palace gate, at which they no sooner knocked but they were admitted. But Jack never stood for ceremonies, but ran through the midst of the court, and as the wise brothers were making their addresses, Jack was laughing at the ladies, unto whom he said, 'What a troop of fair ladies are got here!' 'O yes, yes,' said the king's daughter, who was among them, 'we are fair ladies, for we carry fire in our bosom.' 'Do you?' said Jack; 'then roast me an egg.' 'How will you get it out again?' 'By a crooked stick which I have.' 'Ay, you will?' said she. 'I have it in my pocket,' says Jack. In this Jack answered the three questions proposed. Then he was preferred to that honour which was mentioned in the decree. His two wise brothers then went home like two fools, and left foolish Jack to be reverenced at court with the king's fair daughter.

Said the fourth boy, 'This verifies the old proverb, "Fools have fortune"; besides, it has put me in mind of a story that was told me by my aunt.'

Tale IV

Long before Arthur and the Knights of the Round Table, here reigned, in the easterly part of this land, a king who kept his court at Colchester. He was witty, strong and valiant, by which means he subdued his enemies abroad and planted peace among his subjects at home.

Nevertheless, in the midst of all his earthly glory, his queen died, leaving behind her an only daughter, about fifteen years of age, under the care of her royal husband. This lady, from her courtly carriage, beauty, and affability, was the wonder of all that knew her; but, as covetousness is the root of all evil, so it happened here.

The king hearing of a lady who had likewise an only daughter, for the sake of her riches had a mind to marry her, though she was old, ugly, hook-nosed, and hump-backed, yet all could not deter him from marrying her. The daughter of the said piece of deformity was a yellow dowdy, full of envy and ill-nature; and, in short, was much of the same mould as her mother. This signified nothing, for in a few weeks the king, attended by the nobility and gentry, brought the said piece of deformity to his palace, where the marriage rites were performed. Long they had not been in the court before they set the king against his own beautiful daughter, which was done by false reports and accusations. The young princess, having lost her father's love, grew weary of the court, and on a certain day meeting with her father in the garden, she desired him, with tears in her eyes, to give her a small subsistence and she would go and seek her fortune, to which the king consented, and ordered her mother-in-law to make up a small sum according to her discretion. To her she went, who gave her a canvas bag of brown bread, a hard cheese, with a bottle of beer. Though this was but a very pitiful dowry for a king's daughter, she took it, returned thanks, and so proceeded, passing through groves, woods, and valleys, till at length she saw an old man sitting on a stone at the mouth of a cave, who said, 'Good morning, fair maiden, whither away so fast?' 'Aged father,' says she, 'I am going to seek my fortune.' 'What hast thou in thy bag and bottle?' 'In my bag I have got bread and cheese, and in my bottle good small beer; will you please to partake of either?' 'Yes,' said he, 'with all my heart.' With that the lady pulled out her provision, and bid him eat and welcome. He did, and gave her many thanks, telling her there was a thick thorny hedge before her, which will appear to you impassable, but take this wand in your hand, strike three times, and say, 'Pray hedge, let me come through'; and it will open immediately. Then a little further you will find a well, sit down on the brink of it, and there will come up three golden heads which will speak; and what they require, that do. Then promising she would, she took her leave of him. Coming to the hedge, and following the old man's direction, the hedge divided and gave her a passage. Then coming to the well, she had no sooner sitten down, but a golden head came up with a singing note, 'Wash me, comb me, lay me down softly.' 'Yes,' said the young lady; then putting forth her hand, with a silver comb performed the office, placing it upon a primrose bank. Then came up a second, and a third, saying as the former, which she complied with; and then pulling out her provision, ate her dinner. Then said the heads one to another, 'What shall we do for this lady, who hath used us so very kindly?' The first said, 'I will cause such addition to her beauty as shall charm the most powerful prince in the world.' The second said, 'I will endow her with such perfume, both in body and breath, as shall far exceed the sweetest flowers.' The third said, 'My gift shall be none of the least, for as she is a king's daughter. I'll make her so fortunate that she shall become queen to the greatest prince that reigns.' This done, at their request she let them down into the well again, and so proceeded on her journey. She had not travelled long before she saw a king hunting in the park with his nobles. She would have shunned him, but the king having a sight of her, made towards her, and between her beauty and perfumed breath, was so powerfully smitten that he was not able to subdue his passion, but proceeded on his courtship, where, after some compliments and kind embraces, he gained her love. And bringing her to his palace, he caused her to be clothed in the most magnificent manner.

This being ended, and the king finding that she was the king of Colchester's daughter, ordered some chariots to be got ready that he might pay him a visit. The chariot in which the king and queen rode was beautified with rich ornamental gems of gold. The king, her father, was at first astonished that his daughter had been so fortunate as she was till the young king made him sensible of all that happened. Great was the joy at court among the nobility, except the queen and her club-footed daughter, who were ready to burst with malice, and envied her happiness; and the greater was their madness because she was now above them all. Great rejoicings, with feasting and dancing, continued many days. Then at length, with the dowry that her father gave her, they returned home.

'Well,' said the fifth boy, 'had she not been kind and beautiful, such good fortune had never come to her lot. And pray what became of her hump-backed sister-in-law!' 'Indeed I know not.' 'Why, then,' said the fifth boy, 'I can tell you something of her.'

Tale V

She, perceiving that her sister was so happy in seeking her fortune, would needs do the same; so disclosing her mind to her mother, all preparations were made; not only rich apparel, but sweetmeats, sugar, almonds, etc., in great quantities, and a large bottle of Malaga sack. Thus furnished she went the same road as her sister, and coming near the cave, there sat the old man, who said, 'Young woman, whither so fast?' 'What is that to you?' said she. Then said he, 'What have you in your bag and bottle?' She answered, 'Good things, what you shall not be troubled with.' 'Won't you give me some?' said he. 'No, not a bit nor a drop, unless it would choke you.' The old man frowned, saying, 'Evil fortune attend thee.' Going on, she came to the hedge, through which she espied a gap, where she thought to pass, but going in the hedge closed, and the thorns run into her flesh, so that with great difficulty she got out. Being now in a bloody condition, she looks for water to wash herself, and looking round she saw a well, and sitting down, one of the heads came up to her, saying, 'Wash me, comb me, lay me down softly.' But she banged it with her bottle, saying, 'Hang you, take this for your washing.' So the second and third heads came up, and met with no better welcome than the first. Whereupon the heads consulted among themselves what evils to plague her with for such usage. The first said, 'Let her be struck with leprosy in her face.' The second said, 'Let an additional stink be added to her breath.' The third bestowed on her a husband, though but a poor country cobbler. This done, she goes on till she came to a market town, and it being market day, the people smelt a stink, and seeing such a mangy face, all fled but a poor cobbler, who not long before had mended the shoes of an old hermit, who having no money, gave him a box of ointment for the cure of the leprosy, and a bottle of spirits for a stinking breath. Now the cobbler having a mind to do an act of charity, was minded to try an experiment; so going up to her, asked her who she was? 'I am', she said, 'the king of Colchester's daughter-in-law.' 'Well,' said the cobbler, 'if I restore you to your natural complexion, and make a sound cure both in face and breath, will you in reward take me for a husband?' 'Yes, friend,' replied she, 'with all my heart.' With this the cobbler applied the remedies, and they worked the effect in a few weeks, which being done, they were married. After some few days spent in town, they set forward for the court at Colchester. At length coming there, and the queen understanding she had married nothing but a poor cobbler, fell into distraction, and in wrath hanged herself. The death of the queen pleased the king much, who was glad he had got rid of her so soon. Having buried her, he gave the cobbler one hundred pounds, on condition that he and his lady would quit the court. The cobbler received it, and promised he would. Then setting up his trade in a remote part of the kingdom, they lived many years, he mending shoes, and she spinning thread.

Quoth the sixth boy, 'I think for a king's daughter she hath spun a very fine thread, but now for my story.'

Tale VI

A tinker in our town had but one daughter, whose name was Tib, and because her father would not let her marry a miller's man named Jobson, nothing would serve her but she must go and seek her fortune, so over hills and mountains, through groves and lonesome woods she passed, till at length she met with an old woman, who said unto Tib, 'Where are you going?' 'To seek service,' says Tib. 'Will you live with me?' replied the old woman; 'my family is small, myself, my cat, and my dog.' Tib answered, 'With all my heart.' So home they went to her cottage, which stood by the side of a grove on the bank of a pleasant river. She no sooner entered in at the door than she beheld the shelves furnished with abundance of earthenware and glasses. She had not lived long with her before Tib had committed a fault, for which the old woman was resolved to break every bone in her skin. For that end she put her into a sack, and having tied the mouth of the same, she went to the grove to cut a stick; but while she was gone, Tib with a penknife opened the sack and got out; and put the dog and cat into it, filling it up with pans, pipkins, etc., then dragged it to the door, that the old woman might not come in to miss them, who, on her return, thinking that Tib had rolled thither, began to lay on like fury, when the dog howled, the cat mewed, and the pipkins cracked; while the old woman cries out, 'Ah! howl if you will and be poxed, for before you come out of this sack I'll thrash your bones to chaff.' Now Tib stood at a distance laughing to see how busy she was in destroying her own furniture, then fled for it, and never after returned.

'It was well she did,' replied the seventh boy, 'or else the old woman would certainly have been revenged on Tib at last. But now for my story, which shall be the last at this meeting.'

Tale VII

A young man having found a purse in which was five pounds, he made a proclamation that if anyone would lay any just claim to it to come to such a tavern, and they would have it again. To the tavern he went, where, in meat and drink, he spent a crown. At last when the young man was ready to go the owner came and demanded the purse, which he was ready to surrender; but the owner, on knowing a crown was spent, would not receive it, unless he made up the whole sum. The young man told him he could not; so an officer was sent for, but before he came the youth took to his heels, and ran for it with that swiftness, that, an ass standing in his way, he took hold of his tail to swing himself by, and twitched it off. A little farther he overthrew a woman with a child and caused her to fall. At length he was taken and brought before a justice by the three sufferers. Having heard their complaints he turned to the young man, and said, 'Young man, several complaints are here laid against you, which I shall clear up. First, keep the money you have found, and trade with it till you have improved it so far as to make him satisfaction, and then let him have it. You take the ass, and work him till a new tail grows, then give him to his owner. And you take the woman home, till she is as quite recovered as she was before, and then send her home to her husband.' So with these determinations, he dismissed them.

Tale VIII

In the reign of King Arthur, near the Land's End of England, namely the county of Cornwall, there lived a wealthy farmer, who had one only son, commonly known by the name Jack Hornby. He was brisk and of a ready wit, so that whatever he could not perform by strength, he completed by ingenious wit and policy.

For instance, when he was no more than seven years of age, his father sent him into the field to look after his oxen. The laird, by chance coming across the field, asked Jack many questions, particularly, 'How many commands there were?' Jack told him there were nine. The laird replied there were ten. 'Nay,' quoth Jack, 'sir, you are out of that; it is true there were ten, but you broke one of them when you coveted my father's bull.' The landlord replied, 'Thou art an arch wag, Jack.'

'But, sir,' says Jack, 'can you tell me how many sticks goes to build a crow's nest?' 'Why,' says the landlord, 'there are as many goes as are sufficient for the size of the nest.' 'Oho, you are out again, sir,' quoth Jack, 'there is none goes, they are all carried.'

The landlord finding himself so fooled, trudged away, leaving Jack in a fit of laughter.

'The History of the Four Kings' exemplifies the chapbook practice of combining various tales, and types of tales, in one text. There are seven stories here: six jocular tales and one *märchen* spread over two 'chapters'.

Tale I is a very simple joke about a cuckold, of a type which might still be told, suitably updated, in a public bar.

Tales II and III, stories of a princess won by wit and cunning, have similar structures and, indeed, Joseph Jacobs, retelling them as 'The Princess of Canterbury', combined the two. Motifs such as the princess offered to the suitor who can defeat her in repartee, or who can make her laugh, or who can watch over her for a night are commonplace. Tale III is a distinct type, AT853; but it has been somewhat bowdlerized in the printed version. T. W. Thompson collected an oral version, 'The Foolish Brother', from Shani Gray on 31 October 1914, in which the three objects collected are, as usual, an egg, a crooked stick and a turd (Notebook 3, Brotherton Collection). If the reader substitutes this third object for the text's incongruous orange, and remembers that the princess's fire is located not in her bosom but 'in my tail', then the obscurities of the dialogue will become clear.

Tales IV and V are versions of the international wonder-tale known as 'The Spinning-Women by the Spring', whose various forms have been analysed by W. E. Roberts in *The Tale of the Kind and Unkind Girls* (1958). The British versions have two characteristic forms, that of the present tale and that of 'The Old Witch' (p. 55); these may seem quite separate stories, but their close relationship can be seen in 'The Green Lady' (p. 51).

The story of 'The Three Gold Heads in the Well', as it is often called, is one of the folktales interwoven in George Peek's play *The Old Wives' Tale* of 1595. Two girls are sent to a well to fetch the water of life. The handsome girl breaks her pitcher on the head which speaks to her from the well, the ill-favoured one combs corn from it, and then gold from a second head. The speech of the head is often reprinted as an independent poem, for the sensuous beauty of its language:

> Gently dip: but not too deepe;
> For feare you make the goulden beard to weep.
> Faire maiden white and red,
> Combe me smoothe, and stroke my head:
> And thou shalt have some cockell bread.
> Gently dip, but not too deepe,
> For feare thou make the goulden beard to weep.
> Faire maide, white, and redde,
> Combe me smoothe, and stroke my head;
> And every haire, a sheave shall be,
> And every sheave a goulden tree.

There is an erotic connotation to the phrase 'cockell bread', explained by John Aubrey (*Three Prose Works*, p. 254):

> Young Wenches have a wanton sport, which they call *moulding of Cocklebread:* viz. they gett upon a Table-board, and then gather-up their knees and their Coates with their hands as high as they can, and then they wabble to and fro with their Buttocks as if they were kneading of Dowgh with their Arses, and say these words, viz. –

> > My dame is sick and gonne to bed
> > And I'le go mowld my Cockle-bread.

The Opies plausibly suggest (*The Classic Fairy Tales*, p. 157) that the motif of the heads in the well connects with Celtic traditions which associate wells with severed heads. The British 'oikotype' of AT480 may have assimilated, in this way, a very old element of Celtic belief and practice.

In most instances the heads speak in verse. *Songs for the Nursery* (1805) contains an isolated rhyme clearly associated with the tale, and incorporated by Halliwell in his text:

> Wash me, and comb me,
> And lay me down softly,
> And lay me on a bank to dry,
> That I may look pretty,
> When somebody comes by.

The single incident in Tale VI relates to British versions of AT372 'The Children and the Ogre' and also to the other British strand of AT480 represented by 'The Old Witch' (p. 55). John Clare, who recalled 'The Three Heads in the Well' in his *Shepherd's Calendar* (see introduction, p. xviii), also knew this tale, in chapbook form, as he tells in his poem 'St Martin's Eve' (*The Oxford Authors: John Clare*, pp. 174–80):

> And Tib a Tinkers daughter is the tale
> That doth by wonder their rude hearts engage
> Oer young and old its witchcraft scenes prevail
> In the rude legend of her pilgrimage.
> How she in servitude did erst engage
> To live with an old hag of dreadful fame
> Who often fell in freaks of wonderous rage
> And played with Tib full many a bitter game
> Till een the childern round cried out for very shame
>
> They read how once to thrash her into chaff
> The fearful witch tied Tibby in a sack
> And hied her to the wood to seek a staff
> That might be strong enough her bones to whack
> But lucky Tib escaped ere she came back
> And tied up dog and cat her doom to share
> And pots and pans – and loud the howl and crack
> That rose when the old witch with inky hair
> Began the sack to thrash with no intent to spare.

Tale VII is one of many folktales about clever or witty judgements; this one, by making conscientiously unjust decisions in each case, guys more serious stories in which the judge's wisdom is likened to that of Solomon. The story has no doubt been euphemized: in oral telling the woman would have lost her baby, giving point to the judgement that the young man should take her home and only give her back to her husband when she was in the same condition as before.

Tale VIII is a version of a widespread story also represented in this volume by a locally collected tale, 'The Landlord and the Farmer's Boy' (p. 211). The chapbook of 'Jack the Giant Killer' opens with a variant of this tale.

The Green Lady

Source: Contributed by Alice Gomme to *Folk-Lore*, 7, 1896, pp. 411–14.
Narrator: Mary Ann Smith.
Type: AT480 'The Spinning-women by the Spring'.

ONCE UPON A TIME there was an old man who had two daughters. Now one of these girls was a steady decent girl, and the other was a stuck-up, proud, conceited piece; but the father liked her best, and she had the most to eat and the best clothes to wear.

One day the nice girl said to her father: 'Father, give me a cake and a bottle of beer, and let me go and seek my fortune.' So the father gave her a cake and a bottle of beer, and she went out to seek her fortune. After she had walked a weary while through the wood she sat down by a tree to rest herself, and eat her cake and drink her beer. While she was eating, a little old man came by, and he said: 'Little girl, little girl, what are you doing under my tree?' She said: 'I am going to seek my fortune, sir; I am very tired and hungry, and I am eating my dinner.' The old man said: 'Little girl, little girl, give me some dinner too.' She said: 'I have only some cake and a bottle of beer; if you like to have some of that, you may.' The old man said he would; so he sat down, and they ate the cake and drank the beer all up. Then the little girl was going on further, and the old man said: 'I will tell you where to seek your fortune. Go on further and further into the wood, until you come to a little old cottage where the green lady lives. Knock at the door, and when she opens it tell her you've come to seek service. She will take you in; mind you be a good girl and do all she tells you to do, and you'll come to no harm.' So the little girl thanked him kindly and went on her way. Presently she came to the little cottage in the wood, and she knocked at the door. Then the door was opened by a pretty green lady, who said: 'Little girl, little girl, what do you want?' 'I've come to seek service, ma'am,' said the little girl. 'What can you do?' said the green lady. 'I can bake, and I can brew, and about the house can all things do,' said the little girl. 'Then come in,' said the green lady; and she took her into the kitchen. 'Now,' said she, 'you must be a very good girl; sweep the house well, make the dust fly; and mind you don't look through the keyhole, or harm will befall you.' The little girl swept the house well and made the dust fly. Then the green lady said: 'Now go to the well and bring in a pail of nice clean water to cook the supper in. If the water isn't clear, change it and change it till it is.' Then the little girl took a pail and went to the well. The first pail she drew, the water was so muddy and dirty she threw it away. The next pailful she drew, the water was a little clearer, but there was a silver fish in it. The fish said: 'Little girl, little girl, wash me and comb me and lay me down softly.' So she washed it and combed it and laid it down softly. Then she drew another pailful. The water was a little clearer, but there was a gold fish in it. The fish said: 'Little girl, little girl, wash me and comb me and lay me down softly.' So she washed it and combed it and laid it down softly. Then she drew another pailful. This was clean water, but there was still another fish who said the same thing as the others had done; so she washed this one too, combed it and laid it down softly. Then she drew another pailful, and this was quite clear and fresh. Then the three fish raised their heads and said:

> They who eat the fairies' food
> In the churchyard soon shall dwell.
> Drink the water of this well,
> And all things for thee shall be good.
> Be but honest, bold, and true,
> So shall good fortune come to you.

Then the little girl hasted to the house, swept up the kitchen, and made the dust fly quickly; for she thought she would surely be scolded for being away so long, and she was hungry too. The green lady then showed her how to cook the supper and take it into the parlour, and told her she could take some bread and milk for herself afterwards. But the little girl said she would rather have a drink of water and some of her own cake; she had found some crumbs in her pocket, you must know. Then the green lady went into the parlour, and the little girl sat down by the fire. Then she was thinking about her place and what the fish had said, and she wondered why the green lady had told her not to look through the keyhole. She thought there could not be any harm in doing this, and she looked through the keyhole, when what should she see but the green lady dancing with a bogey! She was so surprised that she called out: 'Oh! what can I see, a green lady dancing with a bogey!' The green lady rushed out of the room and said: 'What can you see?' The little girl replied: 'Nothing can I see, nothing can I spy, nothing can I see till the days high die!' Then the green lady went into the parlour again to have her supper, and the little girl again looked through the keyhole. Again she sang: 'Oh! what can I see, a green lady dancing with a bogey!' The green lady rushed out: 'Little girl, little girl, what can you see?' The girl said: 'Nothing can I see, nothing can I spy, nothing can I see till the days high die!' This happened a third time, and then the green lady said: 'Now you shall see no more'; and she blinded the little girl's eyes. 'But,' said the green lady, 'because you have been a good girl and made the dust fly, I will give you your wages and you shall go home.' So she gave her a bag of money and a bundle of clothes, and sent her away. So the little girl stumbled along the path in the dark, and presently she stumbled against the well. Now there was a fine young man sitting on the brink of the well; and he told her he had been sent by the fish of the well to see her home, and would carry her bag of money and her bundle for her. He told her, too, before starting on their journey to bathe her eyes in the well. This she did; and she found her eyes come back to her, and she could see as well as ever. So the young man and the little girl went along together until they arrived at her father's cottage; and when the bag was opened there was all sorts of money in it, and when the bundle was opened there was all sorts of fine clothes in it. And the little girl married the young man, and they lived happy ever after.

Now, when the other girl saw all the fine things her sister had got, she came to her father and said: 'Father, give me a cake and a bottle of beer, and let me go and seek my fortune.' Her father gave her a cake and a bottle of beer, and the same things happened to her as to her sister. But when the old man asked her for some dinner she said: 'I haven't enough for myself, so I can't give you any'; and when she was at the green lady's house she didn't make the dust fly, and the green lady was cross with her; and when she went to the well and the fish got into her pails of water, she said the fishes were wet, sloppy things, and she wasn't going to mess her hands and clean frock with them, and she threw them back roughly into the well; and she said she wasn't going to drink nasty cold water for her supper when she could have nice bread and milk; and when the green lady took out her eyes for looking through the keyhole she didn't get a bag of money and a bundle of clothes for her wages, because she hadn't made the dust fly, and she had no one to help her and take her home. So she wandered about all night and all day, and she died; and no one knows where she was buried or what became of her.

Lady Gomme suggests plausibly that 'the days high die' is 'the day I die'. This is another story remembered from the narration of a nursemaid in childhood. Mary Ann Smith was from Hertfordshire. Lady Gomme notes:

> There should be another rhyme said when the girl is to bathe her eyes at the well, but I have no remembrance of it. The previous one said by the fish at the well is not complete; there were, I think, two or three more lines. Neither do I think the story is quite correct or in its original form; but this is as I learnt it as nearly as I can remember.

The substitution of fish for heads seems like an attempted rationalization, though it makes the rhyme they chant, 'wash me and comb me and lay me down softly', mysterious in the extreme.

This text was followed immediately by a 'variant from Norfolk' contributed by W. B. Gerish, also called 'The Green Lady'. It was 'told by an old Norfolk woman, ninety-five years of age, who had heard the tale told "score o' times" in her youth, but had never seen it in print.' This informant was born in 1799. Her story starts as above, except there are three daughters. The first two take service with two witches and have their heads cut off; the third daughter follows them, discovers the corpses, and escapes with them, relying on gooseberry bushes to hide her and misdirect the witches into the river, where they drown. The dead sisters are not revivified, but presumably once were. This text lacks the motif of the heads or fish in the well, and is much closer to the next tale, 'The Old Witch', and its variants, all still versions of AT480.

The Old Witch

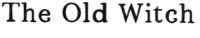

Source: Contributed by Alice Gomme to Joseph Jacobs, *More English Fairy Tales*, 1894, pp. 94–8.

Narrator: Nora, aged nine; recorded by Ellen Chase in Deptford, 1892.

Type: AT480 'The Spinning-women by the Spring'.

ONCE UPON A TIME there were two girls who lived with their mother and father. Their father had no work, and the girls wanted to go away and seek their fortunes. Now one girl wanted to go to service, and her mother said she might if she could find a place. So she started for the town. Well, she went all about the town, but no one wanted a girl like her. So she went on farther into the country, and she came to a place where there was an oven where there was lots of bread baking. And the bread said, 'Little girl, little girl, take us out, take us out. We have been baking seven years, and no one has come to take us out.' So the girl took out the bread, laid it on the ground, and went on her way. Then she met a cow, and the cow said, 'Little girl, little girl, milk me, milk me! Seven years have I been waiting, and no one has come to milk me.' The girl milked the cow into the pails that stood by. As she was thirsty she drank some, and left the rest in the pails by the cow. Then she went on a little bit farther, and came to an apple-tree, so loaded with fruit that its branches were breaking down, and the tree said, 'Little girl, little girl, help me shake my fruit. My branches are breaking, it is so heavy.' And the girl said, 'Of course I will, you poor tree.' So she shook the fruit all off, propped up the branches, and left the fruit on the ground under the tree. Then she went on again till she came to a house. Now in this house there lived a witch, and this witch took girls into her house as servants. And when she heard that this girl had left her home to seek service, she said that she would try her, and give her good wages. The witch told the girl what work she was to do. 'You must keep the house clean and tidy, sweep the floor and the fireplace; but there is one thing you must never do. You must never look up the chimney, or something bad will befall you.'

So the girl promised to do as she was told, but one morning as she was cleaning, and the witch was out, she forgot what the witch said, and looked up the chimney. When she did this a great bag of money fell down in her lap. This happened again and again. So the girl started to go off home.

When she had gone some way she heard the witch coming after her. So she ran to the apple-tree and cried:

> Apple-tree, apple-tree hide me,
> So the old witch can't find me;
> If she does she'll pick my bones,
> And bury me under the marble stones.

So the apple-tree hid her. When the witch came up she said:

> Tree of mine, tree of mine,
> Have you seen a girl
> With a willy-willy wag, and a long-tailed bag,
> Who's stole my money, all I had?

And the apple-tree said, 'No, mother; not for seven year.'

When the witch had gone down another way, the girl went on again, and just as she got to the cow she heard the witch coming after her again, so she ran to the cow and cried:

> Cow, cow, hide me,
> So the old witch can't find me;
> If she does she'll pick my bones,
> And bury me under the marble stones.

So the cow hid her.

When the old witch came up, she looked about and said to the cow:

> Cow of mine, cow of mine,
> Have you seen a girl
> With a willy-willy wag, and a long-tailed bag,
> Who's stole my money, all I had?

And the cow said, 'No, mother; not for seven year.'

When the witch had gone off another way, the little girl went on again, and when she was near the oven she heard the witch coming after her again, so she ran to the oven and cried:

Oven, oven, hide me,
So the old witch can't find me;
If she does she'll break my bones,
And bury me under the marble stones.

And the oven said, 'I've no room, ask the baker.' And the baker hid her behind the oven.

When the witch came up she looked here and there and everywhere, and then said to the baker:

Man of mine, man of mine,
Have you seen a girl,
With a willy-willy wag, and a long-tailed bag,
Who's stole my money, all I had?

So the baker said, 'Look in the oven.' The old witch went to look, and the oven said, 'Get in and look in the furthest corner.' The witch did so, and when she was inside the oven shut her door, and the witch was kept there for a very long time.

The girl then went off again, and reached her home with her money bags, married a rich man, and lived happy ever afterwards.

The other sister then thought she would go and do the same. And she went the same way. But when she reached the oven, and the bread said, 'Little girl, little girl, take us out. Seven years have we been baking, and no one has come to take us out.' The girl said, 'No, I don't want to burn my fingers.' So she went on till she met the cow, and the cow said, 'Little girl, little girl, milk me, milk me, do. Seven years have I been waiting, and no one has come to milk me.' But the girl said, 'No, I can't milk you, I'm in a hurry,' and went on faster. Then she came to the apple-tree, and the apple-tree asked her to help shake the fruit. But the girl said, 'No, I can't; another day p'raps I may,' and went on till she came to the witch's house. Well, it happened to her just the same as to the other girl – she forgot what she was told, and one day when the witch was out, looked up the chimney, and down fell a bag of money. Well, she thought she would be off at once. When she reached the apple-tree, she heard the witch coming after her, and she cried:

Apple-tree, apple-tree, hide me,
So the old witch can't find me;
If she does she'll break my bones,
And bury me under the marble stones.

But the tree didn't answer, and she ran on further.
Presently the witch came up and said:

> Tree of mine, tree of mine,
> Have you seen a girl,
> With a willy-willy wag, and a long-tailed bag,
> Who's stole my money, all I had?

The tree said, 'Yes, mother; she's gone down that way.'
So the old witch went after her and caught her, she took all the money away
from her, beat her, and sent her off home just as she was.

For 100 years this retelling by Joseph Jacobs has been the only available
text of this lively story; Jacobs misleadingly claimed that it was 'collected
by Mrs Gomme at Deptford'. The original text collected by Ellen Chase
has now turned up in the Gomme papers in the Folklore Society archives,
and it is at once clear that the Gomme/Jacobs text is a radical revision of
the original, rather than a slight brushing-up for publication. In particular,
the original ending, with the marriage to the publican, has been rigorously
censored. The original text, collected from a nine-year-old girl called Nora,
who 'could not remember what happens next, but believes there is more',
was first printed, with one gap, in *FLS News* (No. 10, 1990), as 'The Witch
and Her Servant'.

Once there was a witch and she wanted a servant and so this little girl
come. So she said 'I'm going out and I'll leave you in, and you must take
care of the place.'
So an old witch come in and she was making puddins. So the witch said
'Give me a bit,' so the little girl said no, I wont. So she said 'all right then
I'll come at night when you're in bed and I'll kill you!'
So the little gal went to bed. So the witch came up and the other witch
who lived there killed her. So the strange witch's husband come and the old
witch kills him, and then the son comes and she kills him.
Then she said to the girl 'Take the chopper down,' and the little girl stole
all her money away.
And she went to a apple tree and said—

> Apple tree, apple tree hide me
> In case the old witch will find me
> If she do she'll break my bones
> And bury me under the marble stones.

The apple tree says, 'I haven't any room – you better go to the pear tree.'
Then she went to the pear tree and said—

> Pear tree, pear tree hide me
> In case the old witch will find me
> If she do she'll break my bones
> And bury me under the marble stones.

The pear tree says, 'I haven't any room – you better go to the orange tree.'
Then she went to the orange tree and said—

> Orange tree, orange tree hide me
> In case the old witch will find me

[A page of the manuscript appears to be missing here]
and the pear tree said—

'No, I never see the girl.' Then she went to the orange tree – then she went to the baker. They said they hadn't seen her. Then she went to the public house and they said, 'We haven't seen her'; and she was laughing inside!

So she married the publican and lived happy ever after.

'The Old Witch' is the fullest of a number of English versions of this tale. Others include one contributed by the artist Joseph Crawhall as an appendix to the second (1879) edition of Henderson's *Notes on the Folklore of the Northern Counties of England and the Borders* (pp. 349–50), in which the unkind girl preceded the kind, and a defective Nottinghamshire version in Addy's *Household Tales* (pp. 11–12), 'The Little Watercress Girl', in which there is only one girl. Addy also collected two other versions, 'The Glass Ball' (*Household Tales*, pp. 18–22; from Norton in Derbyshire) and 'The Glass House' (*Derbyshire Folk-Lore*, pp. 358–9; Briggs, *Dictionary*, Part A, vol. 1, pp. 270–71). This latter tale was related by a fourteen-year-old girl, Sarah Ellen Potter, at Castleton in 1901, and, like 'The Witch and Her Servant', is an interesting example of a folktale told by a child and clearly adapted for her own purposes. The girl goes into service with a lady who lives in a glass house, breaks a window pane, and flees, asking first a gooseberry tree, then a butcher, then a baker to

> hide me
> For fear my mistress should find me,
> For if she does, she'll break my bones,
> And bury me under the marble stones.

The baker hides her in a bread box, and nails it down. The lady searches for her, and 'when she came to the box that was nailed she shivered, and she made him undo the nails, and out came the girl.' However, on the way home, the girl simply pushes the lady into a river, and she is drowned, 'And the little girl went singing merrily till she got to the glass house, and kept it as her own.'

The rhyme in Crawhall's version is worth noting:

> Gate o' mine, gate o' mine,
> Have you seen a maid o' mine,
> With a ji-jaller bag,
> And a long leather bag,
> With all the money in it
> That I ever had?

See also 'The Green Lady' (p. 51) and 'The History of the Four Kings' (p. 39).

The Small-Tooth Dog

Source: S. O. Addy, *Household Tales with Other Traditional Remains*, 1895, pp. 1–4.
Narrator: Unknown, Norton, Derbyshire.
Type: AT425c 'Beauty and the Beast'.

ONCE UPON A TIME there was a merchant who travelled about the world a great deal. On one of his journeys thieves attacked him, and they would have taken both his life and his money if a large dog had not come to his rescue and driven the thieves away.

When the dog had driven the thieves away he took the merchant to his house, which was a very handsome one, and he dressed his wounds and nursed him until he was well.

As soon as he was able to travel the merchant began his journey home, but before starting he told the dog how grateful he was for his kindness, and asked him what reward he could offer in return, and he said he would not refuse to give him the most precious thing that he had.

And so the merchant said to the dog, 'Will you accept a fish that I have that can speak twelve languages?'

'No,' said the dog, 'I will not.'

'Or a goose that lays golden eggs?'

'No,' said the dog, 'I will not.'

'Or a mirror in which you can see what anybody is thinking about?'

'No,' said the dog, 'I will not.'

'Then what will you have?' said the merchant.

'I will have none of such presents,' said the dog, 'but let me fetch your daughter and take her to my house.'

When the merchant heard this he was grieved, but what he had promised had to be done, so he said to the dog, 'You can come and fetch my daughter after I have been at home for a week.'

So at the end of the week the dog came to the merchant's house to fetch his daughter, but when he got there he stayed outside the door, and would not go in.

But the merchant's daughter did as her father told her, and came out of the house dressed for a journey and ready to go with the dog.

When the dog saw her he looked pleased, and said: 'Jump on my back, and I will take you away to my house.'

So she mounted on the dog's back, and away they went at a great pace until they reached the dog's house, which was many miles off.

But after she had been a month at the dog's house she began to mope and cry.

'What are you crying for?' said the dog.

'Because I want to go back to my father,' she said.

The dog said, 'If you will promise me that you will not stay at home more than three days I will take you there. But, first of all,' said he, 'what do you call me?'

'A great, foul, small-tooth dog,' said she.

'Then,' said he, 'I will not let you go.'

But she cried so pitifully that he promised again to take her home. 'But before we start,' said he, 'tell me what you call me.'

'Oh,' she said, 'your name is Sweet-as-a-honeycomb.'

'Jump on my back,' said he, 'and I'll take you home.'

So he trotted away with her on his back for forty miles when they came to a stile.

'And what do you call me?' said he, before they got over the stile.

Thinking that she was safe on her way, the girl said, 'A great, foul, small-tooth dog.'

But when she said this he did not jump over the stile, but turned right round about at once, and galloped back to his own house with the girl on his back.

Another week went by, and again the girl wept so bitterly that the dog promised her again to take her to her father's house.

So the girl got on his dog's back again, and they reached the first stile as before, and then the dog stopped and said, 'And what do you call me?'

'Sweet-as-a-honeycomb,' she replied.

So the dog leaped over the stile, and they went on for twenty miles until they came to another stile.

'And what do you call me?' said the dog, with a wag of his tail.

She was thinking more of her father and her own home than of the dog, so she answered, 'A great, foul, small-tooth dog.'

Then the dog was in a great rage, and he turned right round about and galloped back to his own house as before.

After she had cried for another week the dog promised again to take her back to her father's house. So she mounted upon his back once more, and when they got to the first stile the dog said, 'And what do you call me?'

'Sweet-as-a-honeycomb,' she said.

So the dog jumped over the stile, and away they went – for now the girl made up her mind to say the most loving things she could think of – until they reached her father's house.

When they got to the door of the merchant's house the dog said, 'And what do you call me?'

Just at that moment the girl forgot the loving things that she meant to say, and began, 'A great—' but the dog began to turn, and she got fast hold of the door latch, and was going to say 'foul', when she saw how grieved the dog looked and remembered how good and patient he had been with her, so she said, 'Sweeter-than-a-honeycomb'.

When she had said this she thought the dog would have been content and have galloped away, but instead of that he suddenly stood up on his hind legs, and with his fore legs he pulled off his dog's head and tossed it high in the air. His hairy coat dropped off, and there stood the handsomest young man in the world, with the finest and smallest teeth you ever saw.

Of course they were married, and lived together happily.

The only real 'Beauty and the Beast' story recorded in England, this succinct narration seems to me a much more potent text than Madame Leprince de Beaumont's wordy and literary 'La Belle et la Bête' (1756), which has been the basis of almost every retelling ever since.

The Glass Mountain

Source: Mabel Peacock, 'The Glass Mountain: A Note on Folk-Lore Gleanings from County Antrim', *Folk-Lore*, 4, 1893, pp. 322–5.
Narrator: Female farmhouse servant, north Lincolnshire.
Type: AT425 'The Search for the Lost Husband'.

A VERY LONG TIME back, I don't know how long, there was a woman who lived in a lone cottage with her three daughters. Well, one evening when it was getting on to dusk, a man knocked at the door and asked if he could not spend the night there, as he had come a long way, and no other shelter was near at hand. The woman did not much like taking a stranger in, but hers was the only house for miles round, so she could not very well turn him away; and the end of it was she let him lie down by the fire. Then, when morning came, nothing would do for him but he must have the youngest of the three daughters for his wife; and the lass, she liked his looks well enough, so it was settled that way. They were married, and he took her off home with him. A fine, big place she found his house was, with everything in it anybody could want so she thought she should do well enough there. But there was just one thing that was out of the way queer. When the grey of night-time began to come on, the man said to her: 'Now, you have got to choose which way it is to be: I must take the shape of a bull either by day or by night, one or the other; how will you have it?'

'You shall be a bull by day, and a man by night,' the girl answered; and so it always was. At sunrise he turned into a bull, then at sundown he was a man again.

Well, use is everything, so after a while his wife got to think as much of him as if he had been like other folks. However, when a year had gone by, and she was likely to have a bairn, she began to think long of seeing her mother and sisters again, and asked her husband to let her go home to them for her confinement. He did not like that: he was quite against it, for fear she should let out what he was. 'If you ever opened your mouth to anyone about what you know, ill-luck would come of it,' he said.

But still she hankered after her mother, and begged so hard that, being as she was, he could not deny her, and she got her own way.

Well, that time everything went as right as could be. The child was a boy, and fine and proud she was when her husband came to see it. The only trouble she had was that her mother and sisters were as curious as curious to find out why he never came to see her by daylight; and they had no end to their questions. So at last, when she was strong again, she was glad to go away home with him.

Still, the year after, the same thing happened again. She took such a longing to be nursed by her mother when the next bairn was to be born, that, willing or not, her husband had to let her have her liking. 'But mind,' he said, 'we shall have the blackest of trouble if you ever tell what you know of me.' Then she promised by all that was good to keep a quiet tongue about him; and she held to her word. Whenever her mother and sisters began to wonder and to ask, she put them off with one thing or another, so that when she took her second boy home with her she left them no wiser than they were before.

Well, the next year another child was coming, and then she had just the same tale to her husband: she must go back to her mother, she could not bide away from her.

'If you will, why you will,' said the man, 'but remember what will come of it if you speak'; and then, though it went sorely against him, he let her and the children go.

This time, do as she would, her mother and sisters gave her no peace; they were fairly bursting with curiousness to know the far-end of her husband's comings and goings; and at last, on the day her third boy was born, they plagued her so much with their inquisitiveness that she could not hold out, and just told them the truth of it. Well, when evening drew on, she thought her husband would be coming to see the child, but the sunset went by, and the dusk went by, and the night went by, without a sight or sign of him. Then, after that, days and days slipped past, but still he stayed away.

When she was up and about again she grew that sick of waiting and waiting, that she took her bairns with her and set off to seek him . . .

[Here the story is defective. I believe the wife returned to her husband's house, and, finding it desolate, wandered out into the world in search of him, meeting with adventures analogous to those which befell the heroine of the Leitrim legend. My memory takes up the tale at the point where she is endeavouring to release her husband from the spell which prevents him recognizing her.]

So she sat down outside his door, combing her hair, and sang:

> Bare bull of Orange, return to me,
> For three fine babes I have borne to thee,
> And climbed a glass hill for thee,
> Bare bull of Orange, return to me.

But his stepmother had given him a sleeping-drink, so he never heard her . . . Then on the second night she came to his door again, and sat combing her hair, and sang:

> Bare bull of Orange, return to me,
> For three fine babes I have borne to thee,
> And climbed a glass hill for thee,
> Bare bull of Orange, return to me.

And this time he turned in his bed and groaned, but his stepmother's sleeping-drink hindered him knowing that he heard his wife's voice . . . Then on the third night it was her last chance, and she sat outside the threshold of his door, and combed her hair, and sang:

> Bare bull of Orange, return to me,
> For three fine babes I have borne to thee,
> And climbed a glass hill for thee,
> Bare bull of Orange, return to me.

And he started up and opened his chamber door; and so the stepmother's spells were all broken. He had his shape again by day and by night like other men, and they lived with their three children in peace and quietness ever after.

This story was contributed to *Folk-Lore* by Mabel Peacock in response to the Irish story 'The Glass Mountains' (*Folk-Lore*, 4, 1893, pp. 190–4); hence the reference to Leitrim at the point where this tale breaks down. In the Irish tale, the husband is 'my bonny bull of oranges'. There are also Scottish versions, of which the best is 'The Black Bull of Norroway' in Robert Chambers' *Popular Rhymes of Scotland*, in which the heroine serves seven years in a smith's house to earn shoes to climb a glass hill, at the top of which she washes out her lover's bloody shirt. The knight is convinced that another girl has washed the shirt, and is set to marry her. The heroine buys three nights with him, with jewels she finds when she breaks open a magic apple, pear and plum she has been given, and sings each night her famous haunting plea:

> Seven lang years I served for thee,
> The glassy hill I clamb for thee,
> The bluidy shirt I wrang for thee;
> And wilt thou no wauken and turn to me?

Mabel Peacock writes:

The following imperfect variant of 'The Glass Mountain' was related to me when I was a child by a rough, illiterate, farmhouse servant, a native of Brigg in north Lincolnshire, or of one of the adjacent villages. The story has no point of resemblance with any of our local folk-beliefs, so, I imagine, the girl heard it from a member of the colony of Irish labouring people at Brigg, an opinion which is confirmed by the fact that she told the tale with an air of great reserve and mystery, as something particularly extraordinary and uncanny, cautioning me never to 'let on' that I was acquainted with it, which she would scarcely have thought of doing had one of our own commonplace traditions of boggard, ghost, or wizard been in question.

Wherever the girl heard the tale, it evidently meant something special to her. Two English variants of the same tale type, 'The Three Feathers' and 'Sorrow and Love', follow; in them, the magical atmosphere can be seen slowly being accommodated into a surface realism, though 'The Three Feathers' retains the husband's animal transformation and gives the wife magical powers through him, while the brooding 'Sorrow and Love' still features a magic pear.

For a survey of this tale type, see Jan-Öjvind Swahn, *The Tale of Cupid and Psyche* (1955).

Three Feathers

Source: Joseph Jacobs, *More English Fairy Tales*, 1894, pp. 34–8; supplied by Alice Gomme, probably collected by Ellen Chase.
Narrator: 'Some hop-pickers', near Deptford.
Type: AT425 'The Search for the Lost Husband'.

ONCE UPON A TIME there was a girl who was married to a husband that she never saw. And the way this was that he was only at home at night, and would never have any light in the house. So the girl thought that was funny, and all her friends told her there must be something wrong with her husband, some great deformity that made him want not to be seen.

Well, one night when he came home she suddenly lit a candle and saw him. He was handsome enough to make all the women of the world fall in love with him. But scarcely had she seen him when he began to change into a bird, and then he said: 'Now you have seen me, you shall see me no more, unless you are willing to serve seven years and a day for me, so that I may become a man once more.' Then he told her to take three feathers from under his side, and whatever she wished through them would come to pass. Then he left her at a great house to be laundry-maid for seven years and a day.

And the girl used to take the feathers and say: 'By virtue of my three feathers may the copper be lit, and the clothes washed, and mangled, and folded, and put away to the missus's satisfaction.'

And then she had no more care about it. The feathers did the rest, and the lady set great store by her for a better laundress she had never had. Well, one day the butler, who had a notion to have the pretty laundry-maid for his wife, said to her, he should have spoken before but he did not want to vex her. 'Why should it when I am but a fellow-servant?' the girl said. And then he felt free to go on, and explain he had £70 laid by with the master, and how would she like him for a husband.

And the girl told him to fetch her the money, and he asked his master for it, and brought it to her. But as they were going up stairs, she cried, 'O John, I must go back, sure I've left my shutters undone, and they'll be slashing and banging all night.'

The butler said, 'Never you trouble, I'll put them right,' and he ran back, while she took her feathers, and said: 'By virtue of my three feathers may the shutters slash and bang till morning, and John not be able to fasten them nor yet to get his fingers free from them!'

And so it was. Try as he might the butler could not leave hold, nor yet keep the shutters from blowing open as he closed them. And he *was* angry, but could not help himself, and he did not care to tell of it and get the laugh on him, so no one knew.

Then after a bit the coachman began to notice her, and she found he had some £40 with the master, and he said she might have it if she would take him with it.

So after the laundry-maid had his money in her apron as they went merrily along, she stopt, exclaiming: 'My clothes are left outside, I must run back and bring them in.' 'Stop for me while I go; it is a cold frost night,' said William, 'you'd be catching your death.' So the girl waited long enough to take her feathers out and say, 'By virtue of my three feathers may the clothes slash and blow about till morning, and may William not be able to take his hand from them nor yet to gather them up.' And then she was away to bed and to sleep.

The coachman did not want to be every one's jest, and he said nothing. So after a bit, the footman comes to her and said he: 'I have been with my master for years and have saved up a good bit, and you have been three years here, and must have saved up as well. Let us put it together, and make us a home or else stay on at service as pleases you.' Well, she got him to bring the savings to her as the others had, and then she pretended she was faint, and said to him: 'James, I feel so queer, run down cellar for me, that's a dear, and fetch me up a drop of brandy.' Now no sooner had he started than she said: 'By virtue of my three feathers, may there be slashing and spilling, and James not be able to pour the brandy straight nor yet to take his hand from it until morning!'

And so it was. Try as he might James could not get his glass filled, and there was slashing and spilling, and right on it all, down came the master to know what it meant!

So James told him he could not make it out, but he could not get the drop of brandy the laundry-maid had asked for, and his hand would shake and spill everything, and yet come away he could not.

This got him in for a regular scrape, and the master when he got back to his wife said, 'What has come over the men, they were all right until that laundry-maid of yours came. Something is up now though. They have all drawn out their pay, and yet they don't leave, and what can it be anyway?'

But his wife said she could not hear of the laundry-maid being blamed, for she was the best servant she had and worth all the rest put together.

So it went on until one day as the girl stood in the hall door, the coachman happened to say to the footman: 'Do you know how that girl served me, James?' And then William told about the clothes. The butler put in, 'That was nothing to what she served me,' and he told of the shutters clapping all night.

So then the master came through the hall, and the girl said: 'By virtue of my three feathers may there be slashing and striving between master and men, and may all get splashed in the pond.'

And so it was, the men fell to disputing which had suffered the most by her, and when the master came up all would be heard at once and none listened to him, and it came to blows all round, and the first they knew they had shoved one another into the pond.

So when the girl thought they had had enough she took the spell off, and the master asked her what had begun the row, for he had not heard in the confusion.

And the girl said, 'They were ready to fall on any one; they'd have beat me if you had not come by.'

So it blew over for that time, and through her feathers she made the best laundress ever known. But to make a long story short, when the seven years and a day were up, the bird-husband, who had known her doings all along, came after her, restored to his own shape again. And he told her mistress he had come to take her from being a servant, and that she should have servants under her. But he did not tell of the feathers.

And then he bade her give the men back their savings.

'That was a rare game you had with them,' said he, 'but now you are going where there is plenty, so leave them each their own.' So she did; and they drove off to their castle, where they lived happy ever after.

An interesting feature of this 'Cupid and Psyche' variant is that the girl does not need to search for the husband – as in 'The Glass Mountain', p. 64 – but is instead placed as a servant by him, to await his return. Therefore her cavalier treatment of her suitors, common in AT313c 'The Forgotten Fiancée', is not to gain money to buy three nights in which to win her husband's recognition, but is rather a sort of chastity test, as in the medieval fabliau 'The Wright's Chaste Wife' (from Adam de Cobham; see Briggs, *Dictionary*, Part A, vol. 2, pp. 503–4). The girl's life in service links 'Three Feathers' with the gypsy 'Sorrow and Love' (see p. 71); it is likely that Lady Gomme's hop-pickers either were gypsies or had heard this story from them.

Sorrow and Love

Source: T. W. Thompson mss, Brotherton Collection, Leeds, Notebook 2, pp. 2–16.
Narrator: Gus Gray, Cleethorpes, 26 September 1914.
Type: AT 425 'The Search for the Lost Husband'.

OLD FARMER HAD EITHER two or three daughters – we'll say three. All very beautiful, but the youngest was most beautiful of all. Once a year he took them to market with him as a great treat. Eldest didn't want to go, second didn't, youngest did. Father said she couldn't as others weren't – she shouldn't want to as they didn't. She sobbed and fretted. He said she should go next year. Long time to wait – it was, wasn't it? He said she was young yet.

Farmer said he'd bring them all back whatever they fancied. Eldest – blue silk with stars on it to make a dress for Xmas parties. Second – something else. Youngest wouldn't have anything. Pressed. She said she'd have 1d. of sorrow and love.

Old man went to market. Had some difficulty in getting what two eldest wanted. Didn't know where to get what youngest had asked for. Should he try chemist, ironmonger, mason or builder. Tried each in turn. Didn't stock it didn't even know what it was. Tried everywhere. Got tired of asking for 1d. worth, so asked for 10/- worth, £1 worth. Even tried doctor. No success.

Going home sad because he hadn't got the sorrow and love; his old milk-cob, doing its eight miles an hour, champ, champ, champing along. Young gentleman overtook him riding a blood horse, a chestnut mare with four white legs. He reined this in and spoke to the old farmer. Farmer looked at him. 'Well my daughter is handsome, but for a man I haven't seen anybody as handsome as this young gentleman is. What a fine figure and what a noble face, and when he speaks his voice is like a band playing.' The gentleman was pulling up with all his strength to keep in his horse – bit hard against the back of its mouth – double bridle – veins in its arched neck stood out like cords, foam dropped from its mouth, sweat dropped off it like a hail of bullets, it was picking up its front legs to its shoulders, coat black with sweat and so glossy that you could see yourself in it. Asked old man if he was in difficulty about reckoning up his money. Was he short? No. Explained why. Couldn't get some sorrow and love for youngest daughter. No one had even heard of it. Young gentleman said he knew what it was. Old farmer pleased at this. Young gentleman asked how much sorrow and love he wanted. Farmer said daughter had only ordered 1d. worth, but he'd buy any amount if only he could get some. Young gentleman said he could get it for him, but he must see his daughter. It was out of his way, but he would go along with him then.

They came up the drive together. Mother and daughters wondered who fine gentleman could be. All agog with excitement. All peeping behind curtains. Young gentleman left outside. Old farmer gave eldest hers, second hers, told youngest he had not been able to get hers, what difficulties he'd had, and how the young gentleman outside was going to get it for her. But first she must go out and speak with him. She was a bit bashful, but went. First and second wished now they'd had 1d. of sorrow and love. Young gentleman only stayed a few seconds. Said she was to be there at eight o'clock next morning and he would bring her some sorrow and love. Touched horse and it jumped down the drive in one stride. That evening all the talk was of the young gentleman. Youngest said to father what a lot of trouble to put him to for the sake of 1d. She was madly in love with him, thought of him all night, couldn't sleep, wishing for eight o'clock to come. Came to minute; said he was sorry he hadn't brought it – it was very difficult to get. Said she was to meet him at eight o'clock next morning at crossroads to save him coming so far out of his way: he would give her it then. Stayed only a few seconds. She was more madly in love with him than ever.

Next morning she went to the crossroads trembling with excitement. She was just one second late. 'You're too late' he said 'it's past eight o'clock.' He got off his horse, took hold of her hand, removed her glove, and then bit off the end of her little finger. With it he made three bloodstains on the front of his white shirt. Then he jumped on his horse. 'My name is Squire King Kaley: if you ever find me again then I'll make you my wife.' He set off. She hung on by the stirrup for a bit. It was no use however as his horse was like a swallow flying. Didn't put spur to it until she was forced to leave go. Then he did and disappeared like the wind.

She followed. Had only thin slippers on, and soon began to look more and more like a tramp. Gave away all her jewellery in exchange for food, except pearl necklace – an heirloom. Did not know how to beg, as she had been brought up a lady. Asked everywhere for Squire King Kaley, but no one knew the name. Nearly starved.

At last came to a big moat on the other side of which was a mansion. An old man was there. Asked him about Squire King Kaley and he said he lived over other side. Moat frozen over. He said no one could get across without they wore a pair of pattens. She gave him her pearl necklace for a pair.

She went across, and went to the house. Woman there who thought she was going to marry the young squire and she was over all the servants and household arrangements. Young lady asked for work and woman told her she would be taken on to clean knives and peel potatoes and clean grates and such like.

One of other servants befriended her, and gave her a print dress. She washed her face and hair and put this on, leaving hair down back – it reached to the ground nearly – a beautiful head of hair. Lady of house came and saw her. Dreadfully jealous. 'The idea. Put hair up at once, black face with black lead brush. Look as if she'd been working or she'd get the sack.' Lady so jealous of her beauty that she dismissed her – turned her out of doors. Young girl entreated, 'let me stay', but no use.

She did not go very far. Sat down and cried. An old woman came up to her. Asked what was matter. Was told about dismissal. Said if she could cry her a bowl full of tears she would give her something that would see her through the world. Young girl says she can, as she is full of tears. Does very quickly. Old woman gives her a pear, told her to cut it in halves with a penknife and then she would hear the most beautiful music in the world. The charm of it would get her anything she wanted.

Young girl now went in front of house, on lawn. Cut pear in two, and music began. Lady came out, and wanted to know all about it. Tried to buy pear. 'No,' said the young girl 'money didn't buy it, and money won't buy it.' Offered to give it to lady if she would take her back for three weeks. Lady didn't want to, but eventually did so.

So she went back. Lady said she was never to let her hair down and never wash her face. 'Can't I when I go to bed to refresh myself a bit?' 'Yes, but must only use a very little cold water and no soap.'

Young girl saw shirt with three bloodstains in dirty linen basket. Squire had said whoever washed them out should be his wife. Lady tried and better tried, then let other servants try – no result. Young girl saw them all scrubbing away at it first one and then another. Young girl asked to be allowed to try. 'The idea: a slut and tramp like you knowing how to wash, etc.' The friendly servant asked lady to let her try it, and so eventually she did. Young girl dipped shirt in water, squeezed it where bloodstains were, and lifted it out – spotless. Lady drove her away and abused her – 'A slut like you couldn't have washed the spots out when all my best laundry maids have failed' – and bribed other servants with £10 a piece to say as it was she who had washed shirt clean. Young girl driven away.

But the boots had been peeping. He was going to get married to friendly servant, who had told him about new girl, how she was different from others, how beautiful she was, what nice hands she had, nails manicured, etc. So the boots was interested in the new maid, and peeped.

Young girl crept away from house, dejected and sad. She was near kennels. Saw her master coming on horseback. Slipped into one of kennels. Master saw her. Spoke kindly to her, told her he would set her over other servants to see that they did their work, and took her back to the house. When Lady saw her: 'Oh, there's this poor tramp again. I do hope the master won't give her in charge, poor thing. It looks as if he was going to.' Master brings her into house, and tells Lady that he wants to set her over the servants to see that they do their work. Lady is horrified. 'The idea, a tramp like that, etc. Turn her out.' Master, 'No give her a trial: it is my wish.' Lady has to give way.

Lady now takes shirt to master, and tells him that she has washed bloodstains out, and servants come in one after another and say that they saw her do it. Lady thinks she will now get married to young gentleman. He says, 'The one that has washed out the bloodstains, she I will make my wife.'

This comes to boots' ears. Lady is in drawing room with *rai*, and they were carrying on. Boots says he wants to speak to young gentleman. Tells him what he saw. Young gentleman says, 'Yes, there was only one could wash out those stains.'

Lady presses on preparation for marriage – hers she thinks. Young gentleman says the one whom he is going to marry must have tip of little finger missing and must be able to wear a certain glove he has in his possession. Lady goes and cuts off end of little finger. Young gentleman not deceived: says that has only just been cut off. He said there was someone in house who had tip of finger missing. All came. Young lady only one who has tip of little finger missing. Lady protests. They try on glove. Lady has big coarse hands and can't get it on. Young lady puts it on as easily as possible: it exactly fits her. She the squire proclaims as his bride.

Lady prepares to leave. Asks servants for money back. One had given to her mother, another had sent it home and so on. She leaves.

Squire took bride in his arms and kissed her. 'You've had your sorrow; now you are going to have love.'

T. W. Thompson noted nine stories from Gus Gray on this occasion. This is the only text of 'Sorrow and Love', and except for altering Thompson's paragraphing on one occasion and slightly tidying up the punctuation, it is printed as found.

Gus was the youngest of the family (born in 1870 at Hogsthorpe in Lincolnshire), and learned most of his stories from his sister Eva. Eva knew 'Sorrow and Love', but Thompson did not record it from her. She had two other tales about Squire King Kaley: 'Doctor Forster' (p. 145) and another which Thompson did not record.

'Sorrow and Love' is a curious tale, in which the magical atmosphere of the 'Cupid and Psyche'/'Beauty and the Beast' cycle is deliberately tamped down. The Grays valued believability and down-to-earth detail in a tale, and although this sometimes leads to incongruity (e.g. the farmer's daughter's possession of jewellery), it does lend the story a distinctive homely air: a frozen moat instead of a glass mountain; a deliberate and rather cruel test of affection rather than a mysterious enchantment.

T. W. Thompson disliked some of the modern details and rationalizations in Gus Gray's storytelling (the mention of manicure in this story provokes him to note, 'this is a damnably modern touch'), but nevertheless regarded him highly as a narrator. In his essay 'The Gypsy Grays as Tale-Tellers', he writes:

Gus's style of tale-telling is closely similar to Eva's. His artistry is a little more conscious, a trifle more deliberate, and though he does not, perhaps, maintain the same average level of excellence, he is capable nevertheless of rising to higher flights in purely descriptive passages. I remember particularly (who could forget it?) his description of Squire King Kaley's mare in 'Sorrow and Love' as the rider reined her in to keep pace with the old farmer's cob. 'The bit was hard back in her mouth, and the foam flying like big flakes o' snow; the veins on her neck was standing out like rope; the sweat dripping off her like a hail o' bullets; her chestnut coat black wi' sweat, and shiny like jet. She was all of a dither; at a touch she'd ha' jumped out'n her skin.' Even in ordinary conversation Gus is, as one of our members wrote to me recently after seeing him for the first time, 'a man of beautiful speech'.

De Little Fox

Source: John Sampson, 'Tales in a Tent', *JGLS*, 3, 1892, pp. 204–7
Narrator: Wasti Gray, Liverpool.
Type: AT708 'The Wonder-Child'.

IN OLE FORMEL TIMES, when dey used to be kings an' queens, deah wuz a king an' queen hed on'y one darter. And dey stored this darter like de eyes in dere head, an' dey hardly would let de wind blow an her. Dey lived in a 'menjus big park, an' one way of de park deah wuz a lodge-house, an' de oder en' deah wuz a great moat of water. Now dis queen died an' lef' dis darter, an' she wur a werry han'some gal – you're sure she mus' be, bein' a queen's darter!

In dis heah lodge-house deah wuz an ole woman lived and in dem days deah wur witchcraft, an' de ole king used to sont fur her to go up to de palast to work, an' she consated herself an' him a bit. So one day dis heah ole gentleman wuz a-talking to dis ole woman, an' de darter gat a bit jealous, an' dis ole woman fun' out dat de darter wuz angry, an' she didn't come anigh de house fur a long time.

Now de ole witch wuz larnin' de young lady to sew. So she sont fur her to come down to de lodge-house afore she hed her breakfast. An' de fust day she wents, she picked up a kernel of wheat as she wuz coming along, an' eat it. An' de witch said to her, 'Have you hed your breakfast?' an' she says 'No!' 'Have you hed nothin'?' she says. 'No!' she says, 'on'y a kernel of wheat.' She wents two marnin's like dat, an' picked up a kernel of wheat every marnin', so dat de witch would have no powah over her – God's grain you know, *rai*! But de third marnin', she on'y picked up a bit av orange peel, an' den dis ole '*guzberi gorji*' witchered her, an' after dat she never sont fur her to come no more.

Now dis young lady gat to be big. An' de witch wuz glad. So she goned to de king an' she says, 'Your darter is dat way. Now, you know, she'll hev to be 'stry'd.' 'What! my beautiful han'some darter to be in de fambly way! Oh! no! no! no! et couldn't be!' 'But it can be so, an' et es so!' said de ole witch.

Well, it wuz so, an' de ole king fun' it out and was well-nigh crazy. An' when he fun' it out, for shuah dem days when any young woman had a misforchant, she used to be burnt, an' he ordered a man to go an' get an iron chair, an' a cartload of faggots, an' she hed to be put in dis iron chair, an' dese faggots set of a light rount her, an' she burnt to death.

As dey had her in dis chair, and a-goin' to set it of a-light, deah wur an ole gentleman come up – Dat was my ole dubel to be shuah! – an' he says, 'My noble leech, don't burn her, nor don't hurt her, nor don't 'stry her, for dere's an' ole wessel into de bottom of dat park; put her in dere an' let her go where God d'rect her to.' So dey did do so, an' nevah think'd no more about her.

Durin' time dis young lady wuz confined of a little fox, and d'rectly as he was bornt he says: 'My mammy, you mus' be werry weak an' low bein' confined of me, an' nothin' to eat or drink, but I must go somewheres, an' get you somethin'.' 'Oh! my deah little fox, don't leave me. Whatever shall I do witout you? I shall die broken-hearted.' 'I'm a-goin' to my gran'fader, as I suppose,' says de little fox. 'My deah, you mustn't go, you'll be worried by de dogs.' 'Oh! no dogs won't hurt me, my mammy.' Away he gone'd, trittin' an' trottin' tell he got to his gran'fader's hall. When he got up to de gret boarden gates, dey wuz closed, an' deah wuz two or tree dogs tied down, an' when he goned in de dogs never looked at him.

One of de women comed outer de hall, an' who should it be but dis ole witch. He says, 'Call youah dogs in, missis, an' don't let 'em bite me. I wants to see de noble leech belonging to dis hall.' 'What do you want to see him fur?' 'I wants to see him for somethin' to eat an' drink fur my mammy, she's werry poorly.' 'An' who are youah mammy?' 'Let him come out, he'll know.' So de noble leech comed out an' he says: 'What do you want, my little fox?' He put his hen' up to his head, such manners he had! 'I wants somethin' to eat an' drink fur my mammy, she's werry poorly.' So de noble leech tole de cook to fill a basket wid wine an' wittles. So de cook done so, and bring'd it to him. De noble leech says: 'My little fox you can never carry it, I will sen' some one to carry it.' But he says, 'No! thank you, my noble leech,' an' he chucked it on his little back, an' wents tritting an' trotting to his mammy.

When he got to his mammy, she says, 'Oh! my deah little fox, I've bin crazy about you. I thought de dogs had eaten you.' 'No, my mammy, dey turn't deir heads de oder way.' An' she took'd him an' kissed him an' rejoiced over him. 'Now, my mammy, have somethin' to eat an' drink,' says de little fox, 'I got dem from my gran'father as I suppose it is.'

So he wents tree times. An' de secon' time he wents, de ole witch began smellin' a rat, an' she says to de servants, 'Don't let dat little fox come heah no more; he'll get worried.' But he says, 'I wants to see de noble leech,' says de little fox. 'Youah werry plaguesome to de noble leech, my little fox.' 'Oh no! I'm not,' he says.

De las' time he comes, his moder dressed him in a beautiful robe of fine needlework. Now de noble leech comes up again to de little fox, an' he says, 'Who is youah mammy, my little fox?' 'You wouldn't know p'raps, ef I wuz to tell you.' An' he says, 'Who med you dat robe, my little fox?' 'My mammy, to be shuah! who else should make it?' An' de ole king wept an' cried bitterly when he seed dis robe he had an, fur he think'd his deah child wur dead.

'Could I have a word wi' you, my noble leech?' says de little fox. 'Could you call a party dis afternoon up at your hall?' He says, 'What fur, my little fox?' 'Well, ef you call a party, I'll tell you whose robe dat is, but you mus' let my mammy come as well.' 'No! no! my little fox, I couldn't have youah mammy to come.' 'Well, I shan't come ef my mammy arn't to come.' Well, de ole king agreed, an' de little fox tell'd him: 'Now deah mus' be tales to be telled, an' after we have dinner, let's go an' walk about in de garden; but you mus' 'quaint as many ladies an' genlemen as you can to dis party, an' be shuah to bring de ole lady what live at de lodge.'

Well, dis dinner was called, an' dey all had 'nuff to eat, an after dat wur ovah, de noble leech stood up in de middlt an' called for a song or tale. Deah wuz all songs sing't and tales tell't, tell it camed to dis young lady's tun. An' she says, 'I can't sing a song er tell a tale, but my little fox can.' 'Pooydorda!' says de ole witch, 'tun out de little fox, he stinks!' But dey all called an de little fox, an' he stoods up an' says: 'Once ont a time,' he says, 'deah wuz an' ole-fashn't king an' queen lived togeder, an' dey only had one darter, an' dey stored dis darter like de eyes into deir head, an' dey 'ardly would let de wint blow an her.' 'Pooydorda!' says de ole witch, 'tun out de little fox, it stinks.' But deah wuz all de ladies an' gentlemen clappin' an' sayin', 'Speak an! my little fox.' 'Well tole! my little fox.' 'Werry good tale, indeed!'

So de little fox speak'd an, and tell't dem all about de ole witch, an' how she wanted to 'stry de king's darter, an' he says: 'Dis heah ole lady she fried my mammy a egg an' a sliced of bacon, an' ef she wur to eat it all, she'd be in de fambaley way wid some bad animal, but she only eat half on it, an' den she wor so wid me. An' dat's de ole witch deah!' he says, showin' de party wid his little paw.

An' den, after dis wuz done, an' dey all walked togeder in de garden, de little fox says: 'Now, my mammy, I've done all de good I can for you, an' now I'm a-goin' to leave you,' an' he strip't aff his little skin, an' he flewed away in de beautifulest white angel you ever seed in your life. An' de ole witch was burnt in de same chair dat wuz meant fur de young lady.

John Sampson's 'Tales in a Tent' marked a new height in the notation and presentation of English folktales. Sampson – an expert on William Blake and Librarian of University College, Liverpool – managed, by some exceptional sympathy of ear and emotion, to capture the swing of the storytelling in his prose. Never had atmosphere and context been so powerfully communicated, allied to authentic and carefully transcribed texts. Another 'Romany Rai', Francis Hindes Groome, said of Sampson (*Gypsy Folk Tales*, pp. lv–lvi):

> He possesses the rare gift of being able to take down a story in the very words, the very accents even, of its teller. Hundreds of times have I listened to Gypsies' talk, and in these stories of his I seem to hear it again: a phonograph could not reproduce it more faithfully.

Possessed of this rare gift, Sampson, in his devotion to the Welsh dialect of Romani, then chose to ignore it. The painstaking Welsh Romani texts of folktales gathered from Matthew Wood, which Sampson published in the *Journal of the Gypsy Lore Society*, are a pious fraud. Wood habitually told his marvellous tales in English, but instead of the word-for-word transcriptions he could have given, Sampson's English texts (some of which are to be found in his book *XXI Welsh Gypsy Folk Tales*, 1933) are stiff, archaic translations from the Romani.

'De Little Fox' is a lively version of the international wonder-tale known as 'The Wonder-Child'. A particularly interesting Breton version of this tale type interwoven with themes from the Cinderella cycle, 'The Black Cat', can be found in Philip, *The Cinderella Story*: pp. 122–136. The animal form of the wonder-child is variable: here it is a fox, in the Breton tale it is a cat, and in the only other English versions, both collected from gypsies by T. W. Thompson, it is a squirrel. Thompson's stories were collected from Shani Gray and Taimi Boswell and can be found in Notebooks 3 and 8 of the Thompson manuscripts in the Brotherton Collection. In a draft version of his article 'The Gypsy Grays as Tale-Tellers' (Eng. misc., c 765, Bodleian Library), Thompson writes:

> I have a tale from Shanny, known also to Eva and Josh, called 'The Little Squir'l', which is identical in plot with 'De Little Fox', collected by Dr Sampson from Johnny Gray's wife, Wasti. The main difference is in the particular animal to which the king's daughter gives birth, the animal being a principal actor in the tale. Further, Josh maintains that the kindly white-bearded old gentleman who intercedes on the Princess's behalf with her father is the *duvel*, and that the little squirrel was really an angel, but

Shanny does not accept this, nor does Eva I believe; yet in Wasti's version they are as Josh says . . . My Grays know that the tale is sometimes told with a little fox in place of the little squirrel, and the two versions they say have existed side by side ever since they can remember. They do not regard one as right and the other as wrong, nor, I might well add, does Taimi Boswell who tells the story as 'De Little Squir'l' (with no mention of God or an angel), which he regards as the older version.

It is interesting that in Sampson's text the line 'Dat was my ole dubel [God] to be shuah!', while not differentiated from the main narrative, is an interjection from the audience (presumably Johnny Gray), and this is certainly true of Josh Gray's cries of 'That was the Lord' and 'It was really an angel' during Shani's narration.

A *guzberi gorji* is a witch (literally, wise woman). Sampson glosses 'my noble leech' as 'liege'.

De Little Bull-Calf

Source: John Sampson, 'Tales in a Tent', *JGLS*, 3, 1892, pp. 208–10.
Narrator: Johnny Gray, Liverpool, *c.* 1890.
Type: AT511a 'The Little Red Ox', AT300 'The Dragon-slayer'.

CENTERS OF YEAHS AGO, when all de most part of de country wur a wilderness place, deah wuz a little boy lived in a pooah bit of a poverty *ker*, an' dis boy's father guv him a deah little bull-calf. De boy used to tink de wurl' of dis bull-calf, an' his father gived him everyting he wanted fur it.

Afterward dat his father died, an' his mother got married agin, an' dis wuz a werry wicious stepfather an' he couldn't abide dis little boy, an' at last he said, if de boy bring'd de bull-calf home agin, he wur a-goin' to kill it. Dis father should be a willint to dis deah little boy, shouldn't he, my Sampson?

He used to gon out tentin' his bull-calf every day wid barley bread, an' arter dat, deah wus an ole man comed to him, an' we have a deal of thought who dat wuz, *hoi*? An' he d'rected de little boy: 'You an' youah bull-calf had better go away an' seek youah forchants.'

So he wents an, an' wents an, as fur as I can tell you tomorrow night, an' he wents up to a farmhouse an' begged a crust of bread, an when he comed back he broked it in two, and guv half an it to his little bull-calf.

An' he wents an to another house, an begs a bit of cheese crud, an' when he comed back, he wants to gin half an it to his bull-calf. 'No!' de little bull-calf says, 'I'm a-goin' acrost dis field into de wild wood wilderness country, where dere'll be tigers, lepers, wolfs, monkeys, an' a fiery dragin, an' I shall kill dem every one excep' de fiery dragin, an' he'll kill me.' (De Lord could make any animal speak dose days. You know trees could speak onst. Our blessed Lord he hid in de eldon bush, an' it tell't an him, an' he says, 'You shall always stink,' and so it always do; but de ivy let him hide into it, and he says, 'It should be green both winter an' summer.')

An' dis little boy did cry, you'ah shuah, and he says, 'Oh! my little bull-calf, I hope he won't kill you.' 'Yes, he will,' de little bull-calf says, 'an you climb up dat tree, an' den no one can come anigh you but de monkeys, an' ef dey come de cheese crud will sef you. An' when I'm kilt de dragin will go away fur a bit, an' you come down dis tree, an skin me, an get my biggest gut out, an' blow it up, an' my gut will kill everyting as you hit wid it, an' when dat fiery dragin come, you hit it wid my gut, an' den cut its tongue out.' We know deah were fiery dragins dose days, like George an' his dragin in de Bible, but deah! it arn't de same wurl' now. De wurl' is tun'd ovah sense, like you tun'd it ovah wid a spade!

In course he done as dis bull-calf tell't him, an' he climb't up de tree, and de monkeys climb't up de tree to him, an' he helt de cheese crud in his hend, an' he says, 'I'll squeese youah heart like dis flint stone.' An' de monkey cocked his eye, much to say, 'Ef you can squeeze a flint stone an mek de juice come outer it, you can squeeze me.' An' he never spoked, for a monkey's cunning, but down he went. An' de little bull-calf wuz fightin' all dese wild things on de groun', an' de little boy wuz clappin' his hands up de tree an sayin': 'Go an, my little bull-calf! Well fit, my little bull-calf!' An' he mastered everyting barrin' de fiery dragin, an' de fiery dragin kilt de little bull-calf.

An' he wents an, an' saw a young lady, a king's darter staked down by de hair of her head. Dey wuz werry savage dat time of day, kings to deir darters, ef dey misbehavioured demselfs, an' she wuz put deah fur de fiery dragin to 'stry her.

An' he sat down wid her several hours, an she says, 'Now, my deah little boy, my time is come when I'm a-goin' to be worried, an' you'll better go.' An' he says: 'No!' he says, 'I can master it, an' I won't go.' She begged an prayed an him as ever she could to get him away, but he wouldn't go.

An' he could heah it comin' far enough, roarin' an' doin', an' dis dragin come spitting fire, wid a tongue like a gret speart, an' you could heah it roarin' fur milts, an' dis place wheah de king's darter wur staked down, was his beat wheah he used to come.

An when it comed, de little boy bit dis gut about his face tell he wuz dead, but de fiery dragin bited his front finger affer him.

Den de little boy cut de fiery dragin's tongue out, an' he says to de young lady: 'I've done all dat I can, I mus' leave you.' An' youah shuah she wuz sorry when he hed to leave her, an' she tied a dimant ring into his hair, an' said goodbye to him.

Now den, bime bye, de ole king comed up to de werry place where his darter was staked by de hair of her head, 'mentin' an' doin', an' espectin' to see not a bit of his darter, but de prents of de place where she wuz. An' he wuz disprised, an' he says to his darter 'How come you seft?' 'Why, deah wuz a little boy comed heah an' sef me, daddy.' Den he untied her, an' took'd her home to de palast, for youah shuah he wor glad, when his temper comed to him agin.

Well, he put it into all de papers to want to know who seft dis gal, an' ef de right man comed he wur to marry her, an' have his kingdom an' all his destate. Well, deah wuz gentlemen comed fun all an' all parts of England, wid' deah front fingers cut aff, an' all an' all kinds of tongues, foreign tongues an' beastes tongues, an' wile animals' tongues. Dey cut all sorts of tongues out, an' dey went about shootin' tings a purpose, but dey never could find a dragin to shoot. Deah wuz gentlemen comin' every other day wid tongues an' dimant rings, but when dey showed deir tongues, it warn't de right one, an' dey got turn't aff.

An' dis little ragged boy comed up a time or two werry desolated like, an' she had an eye on him, an' she looked at dis boy, tell her father got werry angry an' turn't dis boy out. 'Daddy,' she says, 'I've got a knowledge to dat boy.'

You may say, deah wuz all kinds of kings' sons comin' up showin' deah parcels, an' arter a time or two dis boy comed up agin dressed a bit better. An' de ole king says, 'I see you've got an eye on dis boy, an' ef it is to be him, it has to be him.' All de other *ryas* wuz fit to kill him, and dey says, 'Pooh! pooh! tun dat boy out; it can't be him.' But de ole king says, 'Now, my boy, let's see what you got.' Well, he showed de dimant ring, with her name into it an' de fiery dragin's tongue. *Dordi!* how dese gentlemen were mesmerized when he showed his 'thority, and de king tole him, 'You shall have my destate, an' marry my darter.'

An he got married to dis heah gal, an' got all de ole king's destate, an' den de stepfather came an' wanted to own him, but de young king didn't know such a man.

———

'De Little Bull-Calf' must be one of the most vividly narrated and skilfully notated folktales in the whole English corpus. Johnny Gray, who is also the narrator of 'Bobby Rag' (p. 142), is completely in charge of the pace and mood of his complicated story: so confident that he can slip in a little religious legend about the elder and the ivy without losing any momentum. The intimacy of this telling, with its lovely asides to 'my Sampson', who was writing it down, has survived all the obstacles in its way to lift off the page and into the air with the practised cadences and inflections of a master storyteller miraculously intact.

The tale itself is the male version of the 'One-Eye, Two-Eyes and Three-Eyes' stories in the Cinderella cycle, mutating, as is quite common with this type, into a 'Dragon-slayer' ending.

The Frog Lover

Source: W. H. Jones and L. L. Kropf, *The Folktales of the Magyars*, 1889, pp. 404–5.

Narrator: Unknown, Holderness.

Type: AT440 'The Frog King'; with elements of AT480 'The Spinning-women by the Spring'.

THERE WAS A STEPMOTHER who was very unkind to her step-daughter and very kind to her own daughter; and used to send her stepdaughter to do all the dirty work. One day she sent her to the pump for some water when a little frog came up through the sink and asked her not to pour dirty water down, as his drawing room was there. So she did not, and as a reward he said pearls and diamonds should drop from her mouth when she spoke. When she returned home it happened as he said; and the stepmother, learning how it had come about, sent her own daughter to the pump. When she got there the little frog spoke to her and asked her not to throw dirty water down, and she replied 'Oh! you nasty, dirty little thing, I won't do as you ask me.' Then the frog said 'Whenever you speak, frogs and toads and snakes shall drop from your mouth.' She went home and it happened as the frog had said. At night when they were sitting at the table a little voice was heard singing outside –

> Come bring me my supper,
> My own sweet, sweet one.

When the stepdaughter went to the door there was the little frog. She brought him in in spite of her stepmother; took him on her knee and fed him with bits from her plate. After a while he sang –

> Come, let us go to bed,
> My own sweet, sweet one.

So, unknown to her stepmother, she laid him at the foot of her bed, as she said he was a poor, harmless thing. Then she fell asleep and forgot all about him. Next morning there stood a beautiful prince, who said he had been enchanted by a wicked fairy and was to be a frog till a girl would let him sleep with her. They were married, and lived happily in his beautiful castle ever after.

───·❦·───

The title is provided by me. This is one of a number of English folktales included by W. H. Jones in his notes to his outstanding volume of Hungarian stories. He writes, 'I have often had this tale told to me by my nurse when a child, and heard the following version a short time ago in Holderness, and was informed it had been told thus for ages.' He noted that the lines of verse were sung to a traditional air, and commented, 'this is one of the few folk-stories I have been able to collect from the lips of a living storyteller in England.'

Although the story of the Frog King is best known to us now in the Grimms' version, there is evidence that it was once widely known in native forms throughout England. Thomas Keightley writes (*Tales and Popular Fictions*, p. 13), 'this story was also related to me by a woman from Somersetshire . . . My Somerset friend concluded it by saying, "and I came away".' Halliwell claimed to have collected a set of rhymes, but not the story to go with them, in the north of England, and published them with his own prose text in *Popular Rhymes and Nursery Tales*; these rhymes may simply be anglicized from the Scottish ones in R. Chambers' *Popular Rhymes of Scotland*. The frog asks the girl to 'Open the door', then 'Go wi' me to bed', and then:

> Chop off my head, my hinny, my heart,
> Chop off my head, my own darling;
> Remember the words you spoke to me,
> In the meadow by the well-spring.

A good and full version from Oxfordshire was printed in *Notes and Queries* (V, 15 May 1852, p. 460). In this, as usual in such stories, the girl is unwilling to accede to the frog's requests to 'cuddle my back', etc. A nice touch is that the frog is attired in 'boots and spurs'. In the morning he has turned into 'the handsomest gentleman that ever was seen'.

In the present text the usual Frog King story has been confused slightly by the addition of the motif of the kind and unkind girls.

The Frog Sweetheart

Source: T. W. Thompson mss, Brotherton Collection, Leeds, loose sheets, 7pp.
Narrator: John Lock, August 1923, Clun Forest, Salop.
Type: AT440 'The Frog King'.

ONCE ON A TIME when things was a bit diff'rent to now there was a king wid three daughters. This king was took bad, and had one doctor after another to see him, but none 'n 'em did him the leastest good, and he didn't mend of hisself. So after a bit he sends for a wise man, and axes him what he should do now to get better. 'The cure's at hand,' says the wise man. 'All you need is a draught o' pure water from your own well. But mind,' he says, 'it must be drawed by one 'n your own daughters.'

When the king hears this he sends for his three daughters and tells 'em. Then he says to the owldest: 'For pity's sake, my love, go and get me what I must have to save my life.' Of course she goes as fast as her legs 'ld carry her; but when she draws the water she finds as it's muddy, and anfit for annybody to drink. She's real puzzled: the water'd never been like that afore, not as she knowed on. She looks down into the well – it warn't all that deep – and sees as there's a frog into it. It comes to the surface now, the frog does, and looks up at her; then it jumps onto the rim o' the well, and lands right aside of her. 'Fair lady,' it says, 'promise as you'll be my sweetheart,' it says, 'then you can draw all the clear water as you wish for.' 'What!' she says, 'me have a nasty, clammy creature like you for a sweetheart; me, a king's daughter!' 'Will you promise me?' it axes agen. 'No,' she says. 'Well then,' it says, 'you shan't have no clear water from this well.' And it jumped down into it agen, and took care as she didn't.

The king then says to his second daughter, 'Go *you*, my love, and see if *you* can't get me the only thing as 'll save my life.' But it's just the same wid her, exac'ly the same, so I'll pass straight on to the youngest. She was diff'rent, she was. When the frog axes her to promise as she'll be its sweetheart she bursts out laughing; and when it axes a second time she says, thinking as she might as well please it, 'Yes, I will; truly I will.' She didn't mean it serious; it was just a bit o' joking as she looked at it. Annyways, she was able to draw the clear water her

– 86 –

father was badly in want of, and believe it or not, he was certain sure as it saved his life. That was one up for her, and one up for the wise man. You may be sure the king rewarded him. She had her reward an well, but that's another story.

She never thought no more for three or four days about the frog, and the promise she'd made to it. Then one night as soon as she'd got into bed she heeard it calling outside 'n her door; axing to come in it was. 'You promised as you'd be my sweetheart,' it says, 'promised faithful, you did.' There's no denying that, she thinks, so up she gets, and opens the door a teeny bit, just enough for it to get through. Then she nips back into bed, and waits quite quiet to see what it'll do. After a bit it jumps up onto the bottom o' the bed, and lies still there as if it was sattled for the night. But in the morning it's gone, and isn't nowheres to be seen, neether in the room nor outside.

It come agen the next night, and the carry-on was 'dentic'ly the same, or as near as makes no matter. The third night she tells it she'll let it in once more, but for the last time. What it does on this visit is to wait till she's fast asleep, when it jumps up onto the top end o' the bed nigh agen her face, and there it lies half in and half out 'n the bed. She didn't waken up during the night, but when in the morning she fun' out where it was she shrieked and hollered, and threw it on to the floor.

It disappeared, and in its place what did she see but a very handsome young gentleman dressed in the grandest o' clothes; walking-out clothes, they was. The young princess, she was proper dumbfoundled. But she never took her eyes off of him, and when at last she fun' her tongue agen she axes him, 'And who in the world are you, and what in Heaven's name are you doing here in my bedroom?' 'Well,' he says, 'you promised as you'd be my sweetheart, and it was you 'at let me in: don't that signify?' 'On my honour,' she says, 'I never let no young gentleman into my bedroom, only a frog, and that come about through a bit o' foolishness o' mine a few days back.' 'Maybe it did,' he says, 'but annyways it was uncommon kind of you, and I'll tell you for why. I was the frog. Strange thing for a king's son to be, but I'd been witched, and was under a spell. Now, what you promised and done 's broke the spell, and lifted the curse off of me. It's a miracle you've worked, like what the dear Lord did in the owlden times it tell of in the Book; mainly what the same as casting out devils from people, but happen a bit diff'rent from what you can make out.' Wid that he walks off, but at the door he stops and turns. 'You'll be mine,' he says, 'mine for good, or it won't be for the axing. I'm going to have a word wid you father soon as he's up and about.'

And for sure he did. He towld the king his story, and said as he was son and heir of another king as lived not above twenty mile away. Then he axed the king

– the first king that is – for his youngest daughter in marriage. 'She saved me from a life as was worser 'an death,' he says, 'and I'd cherish her, sir, to the end o' my days.' 'Well,' says the king, 'I'll talk it over wid your father; but first,' he says, 'you must show up at home, and make sure as you're still heir to the throne.'

So d'rec'ly after breakfast the young prince starts off for his father's palace, on a horse as the king lends him, and wid one 'n his grooms in attendance. He'd orders, the groom had, to keep his eyes and ears open what time he was there, and to be back wid the both horses afore night. Which he was, and wid plenty o' daylight to spare. Had he stopped long at the tother end, the king axes him. 'Just long enough, your majesty, to bait and rest the horses,' he says, 'and at the same time to get a bite and sup misel.' 'Yes,' says the king, 'we can take that for granted. But didn't you see or hear annything about the prince?' 'Well, you majesty, the butler towld me as the king and royal fam'ly, and ev'rybody at the palace, was beside thersels wid joy and rejoicement when the prince landed up, and they seen as he was a christian [human] agen; ev'ry inch a christian, no manner o' doubt about it, and nobody could tell as he's ever been annything diff'rent. And there was another thing, your majesty. Just afore I come away the prince hissel give me this message for you, sir. I was to tell you most pertic'lar, he said, as him and his father, God willing, 'ld be wid you the day after tomorrow.

Nothing happended to hinder 'em from coming, and soon as they civilly could the two kings got down to business; bargaining some 'ld call it, and that's near about what it was, if you ax me. It come to an end in time wid the fixing of the dower as was to be handed over wid the princess, and once that was agreed on, the two kings decided as arrangements for the wedding was to go for'et right away, and as all the titled and quality folk in both the kingdoms was to be bid to it. A real grand affair it was by all accounts. The wedding feast, wid the speeches, toasts, and cetera, lasted ev'ry bit o' three hours. And after the bride and bridegroom 'd been bedded, there was music, and songs, and dancing till the break of another day. It don't say who pervided the music, but like as not it 'ld be some of our people.

———— ✦ ————

This story only exists in this late, expanded text. I have slightly modified Thompson's punctuation and paragraphing, and have amended 'the' to 'there' and 'cartian' to 'certain' in the interests of clarity.

Thompson writes about John Lock in *JGLS* (3rd series, vol. 4, pp. 63–6). Ella Mary Leather had collected folkdance tunes from him from 1908 on, but did not record his tales, though she alerted Thompson to the existence of this one in 1922. John Lock turned out to be a first cousin of one of Thompson's earliest informants, Noah Lock. Thompson met him only once and noted just this one story from him, though he knew others: 'The Green Leaves of the Forest', and one about a tree on which golden apples grew. Thompson urged Mrs Leather to publish this story and collect the others, but she was unable to do so.

This lengthy 'Frog King' story is notable for the down-to-earth, unromantic conclusion, in which the expected marriage is delayed to allow the young man's prospects to be investigated, and the two fathers to haggle over the dowry. Thompson asked Lock whether there was any more about the wise man: 'No, *rai*, not to speak of, only as he couldn't be come by when the princess's father sent for him the day the prince axed for her in marriage, nor yet the day after; and as the prince met wid him later on near his father's palace, and give him a 'stantial reward out 'n the dower the princess had brought him.' It is noteworthy that this text contains no rhymes.

This story should not be confused with another 'Frog Sweetheart' in the Thompson manuscripts, collected from Gus Gray on 26 September 1914: that story, also known as 'Mister Frog', is a 'Beauty and the Beast' variant.

Snow-White

Source: T. W. Thompson mss, Brotherton Collection, Leeds, loose sheets, 16pp.

Narrator: Traienti Lovell, 13 September 1914, Blackburn.

Type: AT709 'Snow White'.

THER WAS ONCE A king and queen as hadn't bin married more 'an a few months. It was into the wintertime, and as the queen was sitting by the window sewing it begun to snow, and afore so long ev'rything was white over. Now and agen she'd stop working, and watch the snowflakes falling: pure white, they was, and uncommon big. Then accidental – or careless – like she went and pricked her finger; so she opened the window for a moment, and let the drops o' blood fall into the snow as covered the sill. Three red marks they made, and looking at 'em through the window she thought what a pretty sight they made on the white snow. Ther was a baby on the way, and she got wishing and dreaming about it – day-dreaming that is – seeing it as a little girl grown to be seven or eight, wid skin as white as snow except for two rosy-cheeks, and lips as red as blood. And what she dreamt come true, as true as ever she could ha' wished. But she, poor thing, was never to see it happen, for she died when Snow-white was born.

A year or two later the king got married agen. His second wife was a very handsome woman, and by gum didn't she know it. She'd a big looking-glass in her room 'at she used to ax who was the most beautiful woman in the land, and awlus it replied as she was, till one day it followed this up by saying as while she was the most beautiful lady, little Snow-white, then seven years owld, was even more beautiful.

It had awlus towld the truth, this mirror had, so now the Queen's proper put out, and beside hersel wid jealousy of her stepdaughter. The mirror kept telling her the same thing ev'ry time she axed it, and more and more her jealousy grew till she couldn't bear the sight o' Snow-white; and in the end what does she do but give orders to her groom to take the poor child into the king's forest and kill her. He was to cut her heart out, and bring it back wid him to prove as he'd carried out his orders.

The groom took Snow-white into the forest alright, but kill her he couldn't. When he drew his long knife she begun to cry, and begged and prayed of him to spare her life; and she being so young and so lovely he felt 'at he'd sooner risk his, and, mind you, it was a risk he was taking. All the same he warn't sorry to hear her say as she'd go on and on, and never return to the palace: he thought as the wild beasts 'ld be sure to get her, poor little thing, but that warn't as bad he reckoned as him murdering her in cowld blood. He watched her out o' sight, and then turned for home. He hadn't gone far when he comes on a young pig, or boar it might ha' bin, rooting in the forest. He kills it, and cuts its heart out; and this he takes to show the queen. She has it cooked, and eats it, thinking all the time as it's Snow-white's.

The little girl, when she's left to hersel all alone in the forest, is frightened to death, but goes on and on as she's said she would. She sometimes has to make her way as best she can through thorns and briars and thick undergrowth, and sometimes over rough stones, or boggy places. And once some wolves was quite near to her; but they didn't seem to see or scent her; anyways they let her a-be. At last, after what must ha' bin hours and hours, she struck a bit of a path. By then she was near done in, and sat down under a tree to rest. She hadn't bin ther not above five minutes when she heeard voices, men's voices, not far away, and getting nearer ev'ry minute. She'd a mind to run and hide, but afore she could get onto her feet agen the men was atop of her. Big rough men they was, but they spoke to her ever so kindly. 'What might you be doing here, little lady?' one 'n 'em axes. Another tells her that if it's help she's wanting she can count on it from them. And a third says as they'd heeard about her, and the danger she was in, and was coming to look for her. 'And now as we've 'lighted on you,' he says, 'you must come home wid us: you'll be safe then, and can get rested.' Though Snow-white didn't know it, they was robbers, these three men was, as lived in a cave in the rocks about a couple o' miles further on. Seeing the state she was in, they helped her up, and took it in turns to carry her in their arms all the way to their place; and then put her straight to bed and give her a glass o' wine, and a sip o' brandy and water.

Next morning they axed her what was her name, and she towld 'em it was Snow-white. That was when they brought her some breakfast, and said as she was to stop in bed a bit longer, or the best part o' the day if she liked. They'd be going out presently, they towld her, but she'd be quite safe. Ther was a door to the cave, and they'd shut it behind 'em; which meant as nobody could get in as didn't know the passwords, and nobody did excepting thersels. On no account was she to go out, they warned her, as it wasn't safe for her to show hersel at present. She heeded all they said, but when they'd bin gone a while she got up, and had a real good look round. She liked this little house they'd brought her to, but thought how untidy and un-cared for it was, and set to work to rid it up.* She was only a girl, and not used to that kind o' work, but she made a real good job of it. When they landed home agen the robbers was proper surprised, and could hardly credit it as their good fairy was little Snow-white. What's more, they was very pleased wid her for cleaning and tidying up the place, and said they'd be glad for her to stop wid 'em as long as ever she liked. But for her own sake she wasn't to open the door to anybody as called, still less to go out unless they was at home. Very strong on this they was.

She stopped wid the robbers a long time, Snow-white did, and after a bit begun to get their meals ready as well as clean the house. They was very good to her, and kept bringing her presents; but they never let on what they did, and she never really fun' out. In the evenings one or another of 'em 'ld sometimes go out wid her in the forest for a bit, but never far or for long. Still they was a nice change for her, these little outings was, and give her a chance to get a few flowers, and berries, and nuts. Ther was a tidy few blackberries and bilberries nearby to the cave, but what she liked best was the flowers and blossoms. She'd use 'em to decorate their little house as she called it, and these seeming rough men, they 'preciated it. But they wouldn't hear of her going out by hersel to pick flowers and that. It was her stepmother they was set on guarding her agen, they towld her in the end. And it was the truth, that was.

After the queen had eated what she truly believed was Snow-white's heart her jealousy died down, and for a long time she didn't even think of axing her magic mirror who was the most beautiful woman in the land. When she did, she got the shock of her life, for it towld her as in the palace and in the capital she was the most beautiful lady, but the most beautiful little lady of all was Snow-white. She lived in the forest near as far as you could travel in it. That's what the mirror said. 'Anpossible,' the queen cries out. 'She's dead and gone: why I eated her heart mysel!' And she axes the mirror agen, but only to get the same answer. It had awlus towld the truth afore, and she was forced into believing 'at the groom had deceived her, and 'at Snow-white was still alive. She couldn't do nothing to the groom: he'd left soon after, and gone right away. But Snow-white: she vowed as she'd make an end o' her as quick as ever she could.

What she did first was to send for the huntsman and ax him how far it 'ld be to the opposite end o' the forest, and if anybody lived getting on for that end. He towld her it 'ld be happen ten to a dozen miles, and 'at he'd never sin any

* clean it.

sign o' human life hissel, but had heeard tell of a robber-gang living in a cave there when they was at home. That was enough to set her thinking as Snow-white could ha' fallen into their hands, and be wid 'em still. She mentioned this to him, and offered him good money for anything he could find out about them or her. He begins to spend more time at that end o' the forest, and in time he finds out where the cave is, and after he's marked out a fairly easy way to it, he takes and shows the queen. For that he gets a good reward, and the offer of three times as much if he catch sight o' Snow-white. In the end he succeeds: he sees her picking flowers in a green hollow near the cave, and a man standing by and watching her.

She then promises him ten times as much as she first give him if he brings Snow-white to her: 'Alive or dead,' she says, 'it's matterless which.' He sees her out o' doors two or three times more, but awlus ther's a man wid her, and he doesn't fancy his chance o' getting her off of him. So instead he calls at the cave when he thinks Snow-white is there by herself. He's right, she is; but she won't open the door to him, and he can't open it. He calls out to her as he's come to rescue her, and take her back to the palace, but that doesn't serve as a bait; she might never ha' heeard him for all the difference it makes. He tries agen another day and a third wid the same result; and then tells the queen as he can't get howld o' Snow-white for her, no-how he can't, and 's not for trying any more.

But the queen means to be rid of her one way or another. And first she dresses hersel up as a woman hawker, and calls at the cave wid her basket. Among the things in it was a very pretty neck-band, and her plan was to sell it cheap to Snow-white, and then insist on putting it on for her, and so get the chance to throttle her. Things didn't pan out like that though. The door was opened to her alright, but by one o' the robbers as happened to ha' stopped at home. He took her basket off of her, and any money or jewellery she'd got wid her, and then he sent her packing. But she didn't leave it at that for more 'an two or three weeks. She then tries to poison Snow-white. This time she gets hersel up as a poor country woman trying to earn a few pennies by selling apples and posies o' garden flowers. The apples is rosy cheeked, and contains a deadly poison; and into her basket is more poison, just as deadly, to put on the flowers just afore she gets to the cave. She knocks on the door, and tries to wheedle her way in, but Snow-white won't open it to her. So she calls out as she's leaving one o' the posies just outside for her, and slips into a hiding place. But no, Snow-white doesn't open the door to get it. The queen then looks about for the green hollow where the huntsman'd sin the girl picking flowers. In no time she finds it, and where the prettiest flowers is she puts down in the grass three or four o' the poisoned apples.

When the robbers got home they fun' the posy by the door. It had bin put down a-purpose, they thought, and when Snowwhite towld 'em how it come to be there one 'n 'em made a fire and burnt it. They was suspicious of it, and rightly so. But they didn't know nothing about the apples and no more did Snow-white; ther'd never bin any mention of 'em, you see. Well, she didn't have the chance to go out that evening, Snow-white didn't; but on the next the chief o' the robbers takes her out for a short while. She makes straight for the green hollow to pick some flowers, and very soon finds one o' the rosy apples. 'Look what I fun',' she calls out, and takes a bite of it. As soon as he sees what it is he tells her not to eat it; but it's too late; the deadly poison's done its work, and she drops down dead.

The robber chief kneels down, and bends over her. Her breath's stopped, her heart's still. Ther's no sign o' life at all. He calls the tothers, and all three men weep over her; no wailing, but they can't keep the tears back. Then after a bit they stir thersels, and see if they can rouse her. They can't; so they carry her into the cave, and lie her on the bed where she'd bin used to sleeping. And that night, let me tell you, the queen put the usual question to her magic mirror, and got the answer she wanted wid no mention o' Snow-white.

Next day, when the robbers carried her out into the daylight, they noticed 'at her cheeks was rosy and her lips red. More, they was just the same the day after, aye, and on the day after that. Looking at her you couldn't tell she was dead, only 'at she'd stopped breathing. Being as that was so, they couldn't bring thersels to bury her. So they had a coffin made wid a glass lid to it, and laid her in it, dressed in her best clothes, and wid all her jewellery on. The lid wasn't fastened down, so she could get out if ever she come alive agen, and they could put things in whenever they wanted to. To begin wid they tried things to eat, but they was never touched, so after a while they give this up. They'd made a bier to stand the coffin on, and when it was fine enough they took the two outside into the green hollow, or some other flowery spot, and left 'em there for a time. Weeks and months passed, and still they kept and treasured Snow-white, her body that is; and still it stayed the very same as it had bin that evening she dropped down dead after eating a bite o' one 'n the poisoned apples. Indeed, seven years passed and even then no change could be seen in her.

The robbers didn't tell nobody about her, but one day when the seven years was up a young prince – the son of a nearby king he was – come on the coffin by chance. He'd bin out hunting, and didn't rightly know just where he was; he'd never bin that way afore. But having noticed the coffin, he thinks he'll take a closer look at it. One 'n the robbers bars his way. 'Begging yer pardon, sir, but what might you be wanting?' he axes. 'I saw the coffin,' says the prince, 'and was curious about it, that's all.' The tother two robbers then come on the scene, and the prince was relowed to see the girl laid in the coffin.

He gazed and gazed at her thinking o' nothing else but how beautiful she was, by far the most beautiful he'd ever set eyes on. Who was she? he axed 'em, and they towld him about her, and how her stepmother'd treated her; as good as murdered her twice, they said. 'If only she were mine,' says the prince, and offers 'em any price they like to name for her body. 'No,' they tells him, 'it's above price to us.' But as he begs and prays of 'em to let him have it, and swears as he can't live without it, they decided in the end to give it to him. And, believe me, that was the best thing they ever did for her.

The prince called on two of his servants to shoulder the coffin, and carry it to his father's palace. They'd gone part o' the way when the one at the head-end tripped up over a tree root or summat, and couldn't save hissel from falling. As a result the coffin come tum'ling after him, and the lid was partly what throwed off of it. The prince was on the spot in no time – he'd bin following a bit behind – and was just going to curse 'em for their carelessness when he sin as Snow-white'd opened her eyes, and raised hersel up. He watches, thinking to hissel can she ha' come alive agen. She half sits up, and pushes the coffin lid out of her way. Then she looks about her bewildered like. 'Where am I?' she calls out. The prince is sure now 'at she's come alive agen. 'Wid me,' he tells her, 'the son o' king So and So, and your true love as long as ever I live.'

She's just as puzzled. 'But I've never sin you afore,' she says. 'No,' he says, 'but I've sin you, and soon as I did I knowed as I couldn't live widout you.' 'Well where are we going now?' she axes. 'To my father's palace,' he says, and begs of her to 'comp'ny him. To this she regrees, and is carried the rest o' the way there. Her appetite come back right away, and soon she was able to walk about agen, and go for rides wid the prince.

Then he made love to her in earnest, and said as he wanted to marry her. She consented, and a wedding was arranged. It was at the prince's father's palace, and a very grand affair it was.

This tale only survives in a late, expanded text made in the 1960s, which I have printed as found save for minor amendment of punctuation and paragraphing. It is the only English version of this story, and is fairly clearly based on Grimm, though not on Grimm alone as the substitution of robbers for dwarfs is frequently found in oral versions of 'Snow White'.

The hurried ending of this otherwise full and vivacious narrative was caused by Thompson's need to leave and catch a train. However, 'a grown-up daughter of Traienti's, who had listened to the tale, and who came part of the way to the railway station with me, said that on the morning after the wedding Snow-white's wicked stepmother was "roasted alive in the king's brick-kil", and that was the end of her, and the finish of the story.'

Traienti was married to Ephraim Heron, alias Young; she was a sister of Taimi Boswell's second wife Kashi Lovell. She spent her youth in the Manchester area, and after her marriage travelled around the West Riding wool towns.

Thompson writes:

To bring folk-tales into the conversation I told Traienti and Ephraim of my visit earlier in the day to Morjiána Lee at Preston, and outlined her tale of the young princess whose hands were cut off. Ephraim listened politely, but showed no interest in it. Traienti was all eagerness. 'Wait till I've got these tea things put away,' she said, 'then *I'll* tell you a tale, *rai*, about another young princess and *her* jealous stepmother.' In a few minutes she was ready to begin, and Ephraim excused himself. She told it very fluently, and with obvious relish; and what an interesting variant it is of the Grimms' 'Little Snow-White'. It was the only time I ever saw her, worse luck.

Morjiána Lee's tale, which does not survive in any form among Thompson's manuscripts, sounds like a version of AT706 'The Maiden Without Hands', which is otherwise unreported in England. It seems possible that the outline summaries of these two tales, and others such as the 'Golden Bird' story evidently collected from Harry Lock in 1914, were contained in Notebook 1 of Thompson's numbered notebooks, which is missing from the Leeds collection.

The story, with its disturbing notion of childhood innocence preserved unsullied by a coma into sexual maturity – matching the Victorian ideal of a 'child-wife' – might be seen as a repressive male fantasy; it is interesting to note that this text and the Grimms' were collected from women, and that it is female jealousy, not male desire, that provides the story's dynamic.

Tom Tit Tot

Source: Lady Eveline Camilla Gurdon, *Suffolk (County Folklore: Printed Extracts No. 2)*, 1893, pp. 43–8.

Narrator: The unnamed childhood nurse of the writer, Anna Walter Thomas, West Suffolk; written in 1878 from memory of the 1850s.

Type: AT500 'The Name of the Helper'.

WELL, ONCE UPON A time there were a woman, and she baked five pies. And when they come out of the oven they was that overbaked, the crust were too hard to eat. So she says to her darter:

'Maw'r,' says she, 'put you them there pies on the shelf an' leave 'em there a little, an' they'll come again.' – She meant you know, the crust 'ud get soft.

But the gal, she says to herself, 'Well, if they'll come again, I'll ate 'em now.' And she set to work an' ate 'em all, first and last.

Well, come supper time the woman she said: 'Goo you and git one o' them there pies. I dare say they've come agin now.'

The gal she went an' she looked, and there warn't nothin' but the dishes. So back she come, and says she, 'Noo, they ain't come agin.'

'Not none on 'em?' says the mother.

'Not none on 'em,' says she.

'Well, come agin, or not come agin,' says the woman, 'I'll ha' one for supper.'

'But you can't, if they ain't come,' says the gal.

'But I can,' says she. 'Goo you an' bring the best of 'em.'

'Best or worst,' says the gal, 'I've ate 'em all, an' you can't ha' one till that's come agin.'

Well, the woman she were wholly bate, an' she took her spinnin' to the door to spin, and as she spun she sang:

> My darter ha' ate five, five pies today.
> My darter ha' ate five, five pies today.

The King, he were a' comin' down the street an' he hard her sing, but what she sang he couldn't hare, so he stopped and said:

'What were that you was a singin' of, maw'r?' The woman, she were ashamed to let him hare what her darter had been a doin', so she sang, 'stids o' that:

My darter ha' spun five, five skeins today.
My darter ha' spun five, five skeins today.

'S'ars o' mine!' said the King, 'I never heerd tell of anyone as could do that.'

Then he said: 'Look you here, I want a wife and I'll marry your darter. But look you here,' says he, ''leven months out o' the year she shall have all the vittles she likes to eat, and all the gownds she likes to git, and all the cump'ny she likes to hev; but the last month o' the year she'll ha' to spin five skeins ev'ry day, an' if she doon't, I shall kill her.'

'All right,' says the woman, for she thowt what a grand marriage that was. And as for them five skeins, when te come tew, there'd be plenty o' ways o' gettin' out of it, an' likeliest, he'd ha' forgot about it.

Well, so they was married. An' for 'leven months the gal had all the vittles she liked to ate, and all the gownds she liked to git, an' all the cump'ny she liked to hev.

But when the time was gettin' oover, she began to think about them there skeins an' to wonder if he had 'em in mind. But not one word did he say about 'em, an' she whoolly thowt he'd forgot 'em.

Howsivir, the last day o' the last month, he takes her to a room she'd nivir set eyes on afore. There worn't nothin' in it but a spinnin' wheel and a stool. An' says he, 'Now me dear, hare yow'll be shut in tomorrow with some vittles and some flax, and if you hain't spun five skeins by the night, yar hid'll goo off.'

An' awa' he went about his business. Well, she were that frightened. She'd alius been such a gatless mawther, that she didn't so much as know how to spin, an' what were she to dew tomorrer, with no one to come nigh her to help her.

She sat down on a stool in the kitchen, an' lork! how she did cry!

Howsiver, all on a sudden she hard a sort of a knockin' low down on the door. She upped and oped it, an' what should she see but a small little black thing with a long tail. That looked up at her right kewrious, an' that said:

'What are yew a cryin' for?'

'What's that to yew?' says she.

'Nivir yew mind' that said. 'But tell me what you're a cryin' for?'

'That oon't dew me noo good if I dew,' says she. 'You doon't know that,' that said, an' twirled that's tail round.

'Well,' says she, 'that oon't dew no harm, if that doon't dew no good,' and she upped and told about the pies an' the skeins an' everything.

'This is what I'll do,' says the little black thing. 'I'll come to yar winder iv'ry mornin' an' take the flax an' bring it spun at night.'

'What's your pay?' says she.

That looked out o' the corners o' that's eyes an' that said: 'I'll give you three guesses every night to guess my name, an' if you hain't guessed it afore the month's up, yew shall be mine.'

Well, she thowt she'd be sure to guess that's name afore the month was up. 'All right,' says she, 'I agree.'

'All right,' that says, an' lork! how that twirled that's tail.

Well, the next day, har husband he took her inter the room, an' there was the flax an' the day's vittles.

'Now there's the flax,' says he, 'an if that ain't spun up this night off goo yar head.' An' then he went out an' locked the door.

He'd hardly goon, when there was a knockin' agin the winder.

She upped and she oped it, and there sure enough was the little oo'd thing a settin' on the ledge. 'Where's the flax?' says he.

'Here te be,' says she. And she gonned it to him.

Well, come the evenin', a knockin' come agin to the winder.

She upped an' she oped it and there were the little oo'd thing, with five skeins of flax on his arm.

'Here te be,' says he, an' he gonned it to her.

'Now what's my name?' says he.

'What, is that Bill?' says she.

'Noo, that ain't,' says he. An' he twirled his tail.

'Well, is that Ned?' says she.

'Noo that ain't,' says he. An' he twirled his tail.

'Well, is that Mark?' says she.

'Noo that ain't,' says he. An' he twirled harder, an' awa' he flew.

Well, when har husband he come him, there was the five skeins riddy for him. 'I see I shorn't hev for to kill you tonight, me dare,' says he. 'Yew'll hev yar vittles and yar flax in the mornin',' says he, an' awa' he goes.

Well, ivery day the flax an' the vittles, they was brought, an' ivery day that there little black impet used for to come mornin's and evenin's. An' all the day the mawther she set a tryin' fur to think of names to say to it when te come at night. But she niver hot on the right one. An' as that got to-warts the ind o' the month, the impet that began for to look soo maliceful, an' that twirled that's tail faster and faster each time she gave a guess.

At last te come to the last day but one.

The impet that come at night along o' the five skeins, an' that said:

'What, hain't yew got my name yet?'

'Is that Nicodemus?' says she.

'Noo t'ain't,' that says.

'Is that Sammle?' says she.

'Noo t'ain't,' that says.

'A-well, is that Methusalem?' says she.

'Noo t'ain't that norther,' he says.

Then that looks at her with that's eyes like a cool o' fire, an' that says, 'Woman, there's only tomorrer night, an' then yar'll be mine!' An' awa' te flew.

Well, she felt that horrud. Howsomediver, she hard the King a comin' along the passage. In he came, an' when he see the five skeins, he says, says he:

'Well my dare,' says he. 'I don't see but what you'll ha' your skeins ready tomorrer night as well, an' as I reckon I shorn't ha' to kill you, I'll ha' supper in here tonight.' So they brought supper, an' another stool for him, and down the tew they sat.

Well, he hadn't eat but a mouthful or so, when he stops an' begins to laugh.

'What is it?' says she.

'A-why,' says he, 'I was out a huntin' today, an' I got awa' to a place in the wood I'd never seen afore. An' there was an old chalk pit. An' I heerd a sort of a hummin', kind o'. So I got off my hobby, an' I went right quiet to the pit, an' I looked down. Well, what should there be but the funniest little black thing yew iver set eyes on. An' what was that dewin' on, but that had a little spinnin' wheel, an' that were spinnin' wonnerful fast, an' a twirlin' that's tail. An' as that span that sang.

> Nimmy nimmy not,
> My name's Tom Tit Tot.

Well, when the mawther heerd this, she fared as if she could ha' jumped outer her skin for joy, but she di'n't say a word.

Next day, that there little thing looked soo maliceful when he come for the flax. An' when night came, she heerd that a knockin' agin the winder panes. She oped the winder, an' that come right in on the ledge. That were grinnin' from are to are, an' Oo! tha's tail were twirlin' round so fast.

'What's my name?' that says, as that gonned her the skeins.

'Is that Solomon?' she says, pretendin' to be afeard.

'Noo t'ain't,' that says, an' that come fudder inter the room.

'Well, is that Zebedee?' says she agin.

'Noo t'ain't,' says the impet. An' then that laughed an' twirled that's tail till yew cou'n't hardly see it.

'Take time, woman,' that says; 'next guess an' you're mine.' An' that stretched out that's black hands at her.

Well, she backed a step or two, an' she looked at it, an' then she laughed out, an' says she, a pointin' of her finger at it,

> Nimmy nimmy not,
> Yar name's Tom Tit Tot.

Well, when that hard her, that shruck awful, an' awa' that flew into the dark, an' she niver saw it noo more.

_ⲁ๙๒ⲗ_

After the Jack tales, 'Tom Tit Tot' is surely the best-known of all English folktales, the Suffolk equivalent of the Grimms' 'Rumpelstiltskin'. Edward Clodd based a whole book, *Tom Tit Tot: An Essay on Savage Philosophy in Folk-Tale* (1898), on it.

The story was sent to Francis Hindes Groome for inclusion in his 'Suffolk Notes and Queries' column in the *Ipswich Journal*, where it first appeared on 15 January 1878. The writer was Anna Walter Thomas (née Fison), who remembered the story from the telling of her childhood nurse, who was also the narrator of the story's sequel, 'The Gypsy Woman' (p. 103), and of the Cinderella variant 'Cap o' Rushes' (p. 106). From this humble start, the tale was quickly taken up by folklorists and storytellers, somewhat to its writer's chagrin. Pasted into Clodd's own copy of *Tom Tit Tot* in the Brotherton Library is a letter to the editor of *The Times* of 31 October 1898 complaining about Joseph Jacobs's use of the tale in his *English Fairy Tales* without payment or acknowledgement to her. She writes:

> 'Tom Tit Tot' was told to me very far back in the fifties by a servant; the
> dialect was hers, and was then the common speech in west Suffolk. I wrote
> it down, years after, for Archdeacon Groome (or his son), who told me
> he had sent it and 'Cap o' Rushes', which I also gave him, to the *Ipswich
> Journal*. Many years after, when I had almost forgotten the circumstance,
> I found the stories to my astonishment in Mr Jacobs's book of fairy tales.

In fact the tale had also been reprinted by Clodd, E. S. Hartland and others. While Mrs Thomas's indignation is understandable, the note of authorial pride may warn us not to regard her text as the simple, faithful transcript it appears.

There are several other English and Scottish variants of 'The Name of the Helper', including 'Habetrot', 'Peerifool', 'Titty Tod' and 'Whuppity Stoorie'. The most interesting in the context of 'Tom Tit Tot' is the Cornish variant, 'Duffy and the Devil', which can be found in Robert Hunt's *Popular Romances of the West of England* and William Bottrell's *Traditions and Hearthside Stories of West Cornwall: Second Series*. Both authors recall seeing this performed in the early nineteenth century as a Christmas play or Guise-dance. Bottrell writes:

> Great part of the dialogue appears to have been improvised, as the actor's fancy dictated. Yet there were some portions of rude verse, which would seem to have been handed down with little variation. Mimical gesticulation expressed much of the story; and when there was unwonted delay in change of scene, or any hitch in acting, in came the hobby-horse and its licenced ride, to keep the mirth from flagging.

The 'mirth' was, as Bottrell notes, of a 'rude and simple' kind; both Bottrell and Hunt were obliged to bowdlerize. In Hunt's text the demon's name is Terrytop, but Bottrell follows the words of one of the last of the semi-professional Cornish droll-tellers, Billy Foss of Sancreed, who asserted that 'some, who know no better, call Duffy's devil Terrytop; but his ancient and proper name is Tarraway'.

Tales of this type were undoubtedly widespread throughout Britain. In her *Small Books and Pleasant Histories* (1981), Margaret Spufford instances a young boy of Willingham in Cambridgeshire who in the early years of this century was told tales in bad weather by older farmworkers, including 'the story of the princess who had three chances to guess "the imp's name correctly"'.

The Gypsy Woman

Source: Lois A. Fison and Anna Walter Thomas, *Merry Suffolk*, 1899,
pp. 18–22.
Narrator: Anna Walter Thomas's old nurse, West Suffolk, 1850s.
Type: AT501 'The Three Old Women Helpers'.

WELL, THE HOOL O' that yare the mawther she'd the best o' livin' an' the best o' cump'ny, till the 'leventh month was nare over.

An' then har husban' says to her, says he,

'Well, me dare, today that's the end o' the month, an' tomorrer you'll ha' to begin an' spin yar five skeins ivvery day.'

She hadn't nivver given a thowt but what he'd clane forgotten about it, an' now what te dew she did not know. She knew she couldn't reckon noo moor on Tom Tit Tot, an' she couldn't spin a mite herself; an' now har hid 'ud hav to come off!

Well, pore toad, she set herself down agin on a stule in the back-house, an' she cried as if har heart 'ud break. All at onst, she hared someone a-knockin' at the door. Soo she upped an' onsnecked it, an' there stood a gipsy woman, as brown's a berry.

'Why, wha's this te-dew hare?' sez she. 'What air yew a-cryin' for like that?'

'Git awa', yew golderin' mawther,' says she. 'Doon't yew come where yew ain't noo good.'

'Tell me yar trouble, an' may be I shall be some good,' says the woman.

Well she looked soo onderstandin' that the queen she upped an' toold her.

'Wha's that all?' sez she. 'I ha' hoped folks out o' wuss than this, an' I'll help yew out o' this.'

'Ah, but what de yew arst for dewin' of it?' sez the queen, for she thowt how she'd nare gonned herself awa' to that snaisly little black impet.

'I doon't ask nothun' but the best suit o' clothes yew ha' got,' the gipsy said.

'Yow shall hev 'em an' welcome,' says the queen, an' she runned an' ooped the hutch where har best gownd an' things was, an' giv 'em to the woman, an' a brooch o' gay goold. For she thowt to herself, 'If she's a chate, an' can't help me, an' my hid is cut off, that woon't make no matters, if I hev giv awa' my best gownd.'

The woman she looked rarely plazed when she see the gown, an' sez she,

'Now, then, yow'll ha' to ask all the fooks yew know to a stammin' grand partery. An' I'll come tew it.'

Well, the mawther she went to her husband, an' says she,

'My dare, being that 'tis the larst night afoor I spin, I should like to hev a partery.'

'All right, me dare,' sez he. Soo the fooks wuz all arst, an' they come in their best clothes: silks an' sattuns, an' all mander o' fine things. Well, they all had a grand supper o' the best o' vittles, an' they liked theirselves rarely well. But the gipsy woman she nivvir come nigh, an' the queen, har heart was in har mouth. One of the lords as was right tired o' dancin' said that worn't far from bull's noon, an' te wuz time te goo.

'Noo, noo, dew yew sta' a little longer,' says the queen. 'Le's hev a game o' blind man's buff fust.'

So thev began to play. Just then the door that flew open, an' in come the gipsy woman. She'd woished herself an' coomed har hair, an' whelmed a gay an' gah handkercher round har hid, an' put on the gran' gownd till she looked like the queen come in.

'S'ars o' mine, whu's that?' says the king.

'Oo, tha's a frind o' mine,' says the queen. An' she looked to see what the gipsy 'ud dew.

'What! are yew a-playin' blind man's buff?' sez she. 'I'll jine in along o' ye.'

An' soo she did. But in har pocket what wuz there but a little gotch of cold cart grease, an' as she run, she dipped har hand in this hare grease, an' smudged it on the fooks as she run by.

That worn't long afore somebody hollered out, 'Oo, lork! there's some rare nasty stuff on my gownd!'

'Why, soo there is on mine,' sez another. 'That must ha' come off of yow.'

'Noo, that that din't. Yew ha' put it on to me.'

An' then nigh ivverybody began to holler an' quarrel with ache other, ache one a-thinkin' that the tother had gone an' smirched 'em.

Well, the king he come forrerd an' he heerd what was the matter. The ladies was a-cryin' an' the gentlemen was a-shouten', an' all their fine things was daubed over.

'Wha's this?' he sah, for there was a great mark on his coat-sleeve, an' says he, 'Why, that's cart grease!'

'Noo, that ain't,' sez the gipsy woman. 'That's off my hand. Tha's spindle grease.'

'Why, wha's spindle grease?' sez he.

'Well,' says she, 'I ha' been a great spinner i' my time, an' I span an' span an' span five skeins a day. An' becos I span se much the spindle grease, that, worked inter my hands, and now woish 'em as often as I may, I naster everything I touch. An' if yar wife spins like I, she'll ha' spindle grease like I.'

Well, the king he looked at his coat-sleeve, an' he rubbed it, an' then he said,

'Look yew hare, me dare, an' listen what I sa' to yew. If ivver I see yew with a spindle agin in yar hands, yar hid'll goo off.'

An' tha's all.

Reviewing *Merry Suffolk in Folk-Lore* (XI, 1900, pp. 204–5), E. S. Hartland remarks on

the softening down of the catastrophe of the sequel to 'Tom Tit Tot' . . . The true catastrophe as told in Suffolk is less fit perhaps for the parlour than Mrs Thomas's version; but then it did not originate in the parlour . . . The story is the same up to the introduction of the gipsy-confederate into the party. She has put a dozen rotten eggs in her pocket. She sits down and 'jiffeys and jiffeys' until they are broken. The lords and ladies all freely accuse each other 'o' stinkin' like a fummard; till there was sech a te-dew that the King he said: "I'll ha' te know hew 'tis a-stinkin' like that." So he made 'em set down all round. Then the gipsy-woman she got up an' said: "'Tis me as stinks." "A-well, yew naster pug, git hoom and woish yerself, and doon't yew come hare ne moore," says he. "Woishin' oon't dew it," says she. "When I were a gal, I were a great spinner, an' I span an' span, till my twatlin' thrids was broke; an' what's moore, if yar wife spins like I, she'll stink like I." An' soo the King he says: "Look yew hare, me dare, an' listen what I sa' te yew. If ivver I see yew with a spindle agin in yar hands, yar hid'll goo off." An' tha's all.'

Presumably Anna Walter Thomas herself provided Hartland with this more indelicate but more authentic ending to her story. It matches the ending of Bottrell's 'Duffy and the Devil', in which Old Betty warns Squire Lovell that 'as sure as I sit here with a broken twadling-string it will soon be the same with my lady there, if it's true, what I do hear, that you keep her to spin from morn till night most every day of the year.'

Cap o' Rushes

Source: Lady Eveline Camilla Gurdon, *Suffolk (County Folklore: Printed Extracts No. 2)*, 1893, pp. 40–43.

Narrator: Anna Walter Thomas's old nurse, West Suffolk, 1850s.

Type: AT510b 'The Dress of Gold, of Silver and of Stars'.

WELL, THERE WAS ONCE a very rich gentleman, and he'd three darters. And he thought to see how fond they was of him. So he says to the first, 'How much do you love me, my dear?' 'Why,' says she, 'as I love my life.' 'That's good,' says he.

So he says to the second, 'How much do you love me, my dear?' 'Why,' says she, 'better nor all the world.' 'That's good,' says he.

So he says to the third, 'How much do *you* love me, my dear?' 'Why,' she says, 'I love you as fresh meat loves salt,' says she. Well, he were that angry. 'You don't love me at all,' says he, 'and in my house you stay no more.' So he drove her out there and then, and shut the door in her face.

Well, she went away, on and on, till she came to a fen. And there she gathered a lot of rushes, and made them into a cloak, kind o', with a hood, to cover her from head to foot, and to hide her fine clothes. And then she went on and on till she came to a great house.

'Do you want a maid?' says she.

'No, we don't,' says they.

'I hain't nowhere to go,' says she, 'and I'd ask no wages, and do any sort o' work,' says she.

'Well,' says they, 'if you like to wash the pots and scrape the saucepans, you may stay,' says they.

So she stayed there, and washed the pots and scraped the saucepans, and did all the dirty work. And because she gave no name, they called her Cap o' Rushes.

Well, one day there was to be a great dance a little way off, and the servants was let go and look at the grand people. Cap o' Rushes said she was too tired to go, so she stayed at home.

But when they was gone, she offed with her cap o' rushes and cleaned herself, and went to the dance. And no one there was so finely dressed as her.

Well, who should be there but her master's son, and what should he do but fall in love with her the minute he set eyes on her. He wouldn't dance with anyone else.

But before the dance were done, Cap o' Rushes she stepped off and away she went home. And when the other maids was back she was framin' to be asleep with her cap o' rushes on.

Well, next morning, they says to her:

'You did miss a sight, Cap o' Rushes!'

'What was that?' says she.

'Why the beautifullest lady you ever see, dressed right gay and ga'. The young master, he never took his eyes off of her.'

'Well I should ha' liked to have seen her,' says Cap o' Rushes.

'Well, there's to be another dance this evening, and perhaps she'll be there.'

But, come the evening, Cap o' Rushes said she was too tired to go with them. Howsumdever, when they was gone, she offed with her cap o' rushes, and cleaned herself, and away she went to the dance.

The Master's son had been reckoning on seeing her, and he danced with no one else, and never took his eyes off of her.

But before the dance was over, she slipped off and home she went, and when the maids came back, she framed to be asleep with her cap o' rushes on.

Next day they says to her again:

'Well, Cap o' Rushes, you should ha' been there to see the lady. There she was again, gay an ga', and the young master he never took his eyes off of her.'

'Well, there,' says she, 'I should ha' liked to ha' seen her.'

'Well,' says they, 'there's a dance again this evening, and you must go with us, for she's sure to be there.'

Well, come the evening, Cap o' Rushes said she was too tired to go, and do what they would she stayed at home. But when they was gone, she offed with her cap o' rushes, and cleaned herself, and away she went to the dance.

The master's son was rarely glad when he saw her. He danced with none but her, and never took his eyes off her. When she wouldn't tell him her name, nor where she came from, he gave her a ring, and told her if he didn't see her again he should die.

Well, afore the dance was over, off she slipped, and home she went, and when the maids came home she was framing to be asleep with her cap o' rushes on.

Well, next day they says to her: 'There, Cap o' Rushes, you didn't come last night, and now you won't see the lady, for there's no more dances.'

'Well, I should ha' rarely liked to ha' seen her,' says she.

The master's son he tried every way to find out where the lady was gone, but go where he might, and ask whom he might, he never heard nothing about her. And he got worse and worse for the love of her till he had to keep his bed.

'Make some gruel for the young master,' they says to the cook, 'He's dying for love of the lady.' The cook she set about making it, when Cap o' Rushes came in.

'What are you a' doin' on?' says she.

'I'm going to make some gruel for the young master,' says the cook, 'for he's dying for love of the lady.' 'Let me make it,' says Cap o' Rushes.

Well, the cook wouldn't at first, but at last she said yes; and Cap o' Rushes made the gruel. And when she had made it, she slipped the ring into it on the sly, before the cook took it upstairs.

The young man, he drank it, and saw the ring at the bottom.

'Send for the cook,' says he. So up she comes.

'Who made this here gruel?' says he.

'I did,' says the cook, for she were frightened, and he looked at her.

'No you didn't,' says he. 'Say who did it, and you shan't be harmed.'

'Well, then, 'twas Cap o' Rushes,' says she.

'Send Cap o' Rushes here,' says he.

So Cap o' Rushes came.

'Did you make the gruel?' says he.

'Yes, I did,' says she.

'Where did you get this ring?' says he. 'From him as gave it me,' says she. 'Who are you then?' says the young man.

'I'll show you,' says she. And she offed with her cap o' rushes, and there she was in her beautiful clothes.

Well, the master's son he got well very soon, and they was to be married in a little time. It was to be a very grand wedding, and every one was asked, far and near. And Cap o' Rushes' father was asked. But she never told nobody who she was.

But afore the wedding she went to the cook, and says she, 'I want you to dress every dish without a mite o' salt.'

'That will be rarely nasty,' says the cook.

'That don't signify,' says she. 'Very well,' says the cook.

Well, the wedding day came, and they was married. And after they was married, all the company sat down to their vittles.

When they began to eat the meat, that was so tasteless they couldn't eat it. But Cap o' Rushes' father, he tried first one dish and then another, and then he burst out crying.

'What's the matter?' said the master's son to him.

'Oh!' says he, 'I had a daughter. And I asked her how much she loved me. And she said, "As much as fresh meat loves salt." And I turned her from my door for I thought she didn't love me. And now I see she loved me best of all. And she may be dead for aught I know.'

'No, father, here she is,' says Cap o' Rushes.

And she goes up to him and puts her arms round him. And so they was happy ever after.

This tale type is one of the chief elements of the Cinderella cycle. This particular version has the 'King Lear' opening with its characteristic 'love like salt' motif. In many versions the underlying tensions of the tale are made even clearer by making the father have incestuous designs on the daughter, thus causing her to flee. Thus in the fragmentary Cornish story, 'The Princess and the Golden Cow' (*Folk-Lore*, 1, 1890, p. 149), we are told unequivocally, 'Once there was a King who had a daughter, being very beautiful, and he loved her so much he wanted to marry her.' For a full discussion of the relation of these stories to *Cinderella*, see Neil Philip, *The Cinderella Story* (1989).

The text of this tale was first published, with 'Tom Tit Tot', in the *Ipswich Journal* in 1878.

The Ass, the Table
and the Stick

Source: Contributed by Sabine Baring-Gould to William Henderson, *Notes on the Folklore of the Northern Counties of England and the Borders*, 1866, pp. 327–9.

Narrator: Unknown, West Riding of Yorkshire; Unknown, East Riding of Yorkshire.

Type: AT563 'The Ass, the Table and the Stick'.

West Riding version

A lad was once so unhappy at home through his father's ill-treatment, that he made up his mind to run away and seek his fortune in the wide world.

He ran, and he ran, till he could run no longer, and then he ran right up against a little old woman who was gathering sticks. He was too much out of breath to beg pardon, but the woman was good-natured, and she said he seemed to be a likely lad, so she would take him to be her servant, and would pay him well. He agreed, for he was very hungry, and she brought him to her house in the wood, where he served her for a year and a day. When the twelvemonth had passed, she called him to her, and said she had good wages for him. So she presented him with an ass out of the stable, and he had but to pull Neddy's ears to make him begin at once to ee–aw! And when he brayed there dropped from his mouth silver sixpences, halfcrowns and golden guineas.

The lad was well pleased with the wage he had received, and away he rode till he reached an inn. There he ordered the best of everything, and when the innkeeper refused to provide them without some assurance of being paid, the boy hied him to the stable, pulled the ass's ears, and obtained his pocket full of money. The host had watched the proceedings through a crack in the door, and when night came on he substituted an ass of his own for the precious Neddy of the poor youth, who, unconscious of any change having been made, rode away next morning to his father's house.

Now I must tell you that near the paternal cottage dwelt a poor widow with an only daughter. The lad and the maiden were fast friends and trueloves; but when Jack asked his father's leave to marry the girl, 'Never, till you have the money to keep her,' was the reply. 'I have that, father,' said the lad, and going to the ass he pulled its long ears. Well, he pulled and he pulled, till one of them came off in his hands; but Neddy, though he brayed lustily, let fall no halfcrowns or guineas. The father picked up a hayfork and beat his son out of the house. I promise you he ran. Ah! he ran and ran till he came bang against the door; and burst it open, and there he was in a joiner's shop. 'You're a likely lad,' said the joiner: 'serve me for a twelvemonth, and I will pay you well.' So he agreed and served the carpenter for a year and a day. 'Now,' said the master, 'I will give you your wage': and he presented him with a table, telling him he had but to say, 'Table, be covered,' and at once it would be spread with an abundant feast.

Jack hitched the table on his back, and away he went with it till he came to the inn. 'Well, host,' shouted he, 'my dinner today, and that of the best.'

'Very sorry, but there is nothing in the house but ham and eggs.'

'Ham and eggs for me!' exclaimed Jack. 'I can do better than that – Come, my table, be covered!'

At once the table was spread with turkey and sausages, roast mutton, potatoes and greens. The publican opened his eyes, but said nothing.

That night he fetched down from his attic a table very similar to that of Jack, and exchanged the two. Jack, none the wiser, next morning hitched the worthless table on his back and carried it home. 'Now, father, may I marry my lass?' he asked.

'Not unless you can keep her,' replied the father.

'Look here!' exclaimed Jack. 'Father, I have a table which does all my bidding.'

'Let me see it,' said the old man.

The lad set it in the middle of the room, and bade it be covered; but all in vain, the table remained bare. In a rage, the father caught the warming-pan down from the wall and warmed his son's back pretty effectually with it, so that the boy fled howling from the house, and ran and ran till he came to a river and tumbled in. A man picked him out and bade him assist him in making a bridge over the river; and how do you think he was effecting this? Why, by casting a tree across; so Jack climbed up to the top of the tree and threw his weight on it, so that when the man had rooted the tree up, Jack and the tree-head dropped on the farther bank.

'Thank you,' said the man, 'and now for what you have done I will pay you:' so saying, he tore a branch from the tree, and fettled it up into a club with his knife. 'There,' exclaimed he: 'take this stick, and when you say to it, "Up stick and fell him", it will knock anyone down who angers you.'

The lad was overjoyed to get this stick – so away he went with it to the inn, and as soon as the publican appeared, 'Up stick and fell him!' was his cry. At the word the cudgel flew from his hand and battered the old publican on the back, rapped his head, bruised his arms, tickled his ribs, till he fell groaning on the floor: still the stick belaboured the prostrate man, nor would Jack call it off till he had recovered the stolen ass and table. Then he galloped home on the ass, with the table on his shoulders, and the stick in his hand. When he arrived there his father was dead, so he brought his ass into the stable, and pulled its ears till he had filled the manger with money.

It was soon known through the town that Jack had returned rolling in wealth, and accordingly all the girls in the place set their caps at him. 'Now,' said Jack. 'I shall marry the richest lass in the place; so tomorrow do you all come in front of my house with your money in your aprons.'

Next morning the street was full of girls with aprons held out, and gold and silver in them; but Jack's own sweetheart was among them, and she had neither gold nor silver, naught but two copper pennies, that was all she had.

'Stand aside, lass,' said Jack to her, speaking roughly. 'Thou hast no silver nor gold – stand off from the rest.' She obeyed, and the tears ran down her cheeks, and filled her apron with diamonds.

'Up stick and fell them,' exclaimed Jack; whereupon the cudgel leaped up, and running along the line of expectant damsels, knocked them all on the heads and left them senseless on the pavement. Jack took all their money and poured it into his truelove's lap. 'Now, lass,' he exclaimed, 'thou art the richest, and I shall marry thee.'

East Riding version

There was once a poor woodcutter who had three sons. They lived in a great forest and worked hard all day making faggots. The eldest of the three one day declared he was tired of his work, and should go and seek his fortune. He flung down his axe and started at once; he walked on and on till he was tired, and then sat down on a hillside to rest. Just as he was falling asleep, a little man, not so high as his knee, stood before him, and asked where he was going. 'To seek my fortune,' said the lad. 'Well,' said the little man, 'go on over yon hills, and you will come to a white house. Say Harry-cap has sent you, and you will be admitted.' The boy got up and travelled on till he came to the white house. He said what the little man had bade him, and was at once told to enter. He slept well, and on the morrow, when about to come away, the people of the house brought him as a present a purse, which had, and always would have, one piece of money in it – no matter what piece was required, it was always there – never more than needed, never less. Delighted with his acquisition, the boy instantly set off homewards. He saw no more of Harry-cap, but thanks to the purse he lacked nothing on the road.

One evening when drawing homewards he stayed at an inn. The landlord's daughter, who brought him refreshments, noticed his purse, and being a witch knew its powers and value. She instructed her mother to make one exactly like it, and in the dead of night, while the lad was fast asleep, she stole into his room, and exchanged the purses.

The counterfeit purse had one piece in it, just what she took care to charge him for breakfast, so that the defrauded lad did not discover his loss. On his arrival at home, he told the household the good news, and they called in the neighbours to hear it too. The neighbours did not know how to praise him enough, and at last, in a fit of generosity, he said he would give a piece of money to each. This, of course, he was unable to do. Finding out the miserable cheat, the neighbours loaded him with abuse, and, had not his own folk stood up for him, would have maltreated him in other ways. For what is so despicable as an empty purse?

The poor lad had to take to the woods again, but his example stirred up the second son to seek his fortune also. He set out, met Harry-cap in the same place, was directed to the same white house, and received as a parting gift from its inhabitants a round table, which at his bidding would immediately be covered with all manner of dainty food. Overjoyed with his treasure, he set off homewards, but staying at the same inn where his brother had tarried, he was in a similar way cheated by the witch-daughter.

The neighbours were called in as before, and when disappointed of a promised feast, they cudgelled the poor lad unmercifully.

Now the third son was a silent, thinking lad. He mused over the stories of his two brothers, and resolved to profit by their experience; he set off, met Harry-cap, went to the white house, and when coming away received a stick which, when bidden by its owner, would thrash his enemies, and which was also a great help to him when journeying. Bearing in mind how his brothers had stopped at the same inn on the way home, and had missed their treasures soon afterwards, he resolved to be on the lookout.

In the dead of the night he spied the witch-daughter creep into the room, and lay her hand on the stick. 'Stick, bang her!' he cried, and the cudgel (as if possessed by the whole Irish nation) began immediately to thrash the witch all round the room. In vain she begged for mercy till she offered him a purse always containing one piece of money, and a table that would always supply a dinner on demand. He took the treasures and set off homewards cheerily enough, stick in hand, purse in pocket, table over shoulder; and so he entered the house. Summoning the neighbours as before, they were sumptuously regaled, and after dinner he presented each with the piece of money promised them before. Then he said to them: 'When my brothers returned and could not entertain you as they anticipated, you took no heed of their goodwill in offering you a share of their good fortune, but abused them instead of sharing their sorrow', and, turning to the stick, he exclaimed 'Bang 'em!' So out of the house it drove them, through the streets, and over the bridge, till the bridge bended, and my tale's ended.

Richard Blakeborough printed a further text of this tale from the North Riding in his *Wit, Character, Folklore and Customs of the North Riding of Yorkshire* (1898), remarking that it was often 'told to the little ones'. Why this international tale should be so popular in Yorkshire and unreported elsewhere in England is unclear.

Blakeborough's North Riding text features a boy who runs away from a cruel stepmother, wins and loses a gold-dropping ass and a self-replenishing hamper, and then regains them and visits his revenge on the stepmother with the magic stick, which answers to the command, 'Come out, stick, and bend yourself.'

Another version of AT563, 'The Seven Mysteries of Luck', was told by the gypsy Jonathan Ayres to Alfred James near Cardiff in 1915, and printed by T. W. Thompson in 'English Gypsy Folk-Tales and Other Traditional Stories' (*JGLS*, 3rd series, 1, 1922, pp. 224–7). Again, each adventure is given to a separate character. The title of 'Seven Mysteries' is unclear, as there are, as usual, only three magic objects: a horse that drops sovereigns, a table that spreads itself with food and drink, and magic clogs which on the command 'Clogs kick' win back the stolen treasures. Jonathan Ayres added a sardonic postscript in which two of the characters go to the docks to look for work: one falls in and cries, 'Send us a line'. He is told: 'It will be a mystery if you wants a line where you are going', and drowns. Apparently this gruesome joke was what Ayres most valued in the tale. On an earlier occasion Ayres ended the tale with the formula:

> Old Buzzie Lock trod on a piece of tin,
> It bended,
> An' my story's ended.

The Story of Mr Vinegar

Source: J. O. Halliwell, *Popular Rhymes and Nursery Tales of England*, 1849, pp. 26–9.
Narrator: Unknown, the west of England.
Type: AT1415 'Lucky Hans'.

MR AND MRS VINEGAR lived in a vinegar bottle. Now one day, when Mr Vinegar was from home, Mrs Vinegar, who was a very good housewife, was busily sweeping her house, when an unlucky thump of the broom brought the whole house clitter-clatter, clitter-clatter, about her ears. In a paroxysm of grief she rushed forth to meet her husband. On seeing him she exclaimed, 'Oh, Mr Vinegar, Mr Vinegar, we are ruined, we are ruined: I have knocked the house down, and it is all to pieces!' Mr Vinegar then said, 'My dear, let us see what can be done. Here is the door; I will take it on my back, and we will go forth to seek our fortune.' They walked all that day, and at nightfall entered a thick forest. They were both excessively tired, and Mr Vinegar said, 'My love, I will climb up into a tree, drag up the door, and you shall follow.' He accordingly did so, and they both stretched their weary limbs on the door, and fell fast asleep. In the middle of the night Mr Vinegar was disturbed by the sound of voices beneath, and to his inexpressible dismay perceived that a party of thieves were met to divide their booty. 'Here, Jack,' said one, 'here's five pounds for you; here, Bill, here's ten pounds for you; here, Bob, here's three pounds for you.' Mr Vinegar could listen no longer; his terror was so intense that he trembled most violently, and shook down the door on their heads. Away scampered the thieves, but Mr Vinegar dared not quit his retreat till broad daylight. He then scrambled out of the tree, and went to lift up the door. What did he behold but a number of golden guineas! 'Come down, Mrs Vinegar,' he cried, 'come down, I say; our fortune's made, our fortune's made! come down, I say.' Mrs Vinegar got down as fast as she could, and saw the money with equal delight. 'Now, my dear,' said she, 'I'll tell you what you shall do. There is a fair at the neighbouring town; you shall take these forty guineas and buy a cow. I can make butter and cheese, which you shall sell at market, and we shall then be able to live very comfortably.' Mr Vinegar joyfully assents, takes the money, and goes off to the fair. When he arrived, he walked up and down, and at length saw a beautiful red cow. It was an excellent milker, and perfect in every respect. Oh! thought Mr Vinegar, if I had but that cow I should be the happiest man alive; so he offers the forty guineas for the cow, and the owner declaring that, as he was a friend, he'd oblige him, the bargain was made. Proud of his purchase, he drove the cow backwards and forwards to show it. By and by he saw a man playing the bagpipes, Tweedle dum, tweedle de; the children followed him about, and he appeared to be pocketing money on all sides. Well, thought Mr Vinegar, if I had but that beautiful instrument I should be the happiest man alive – my fortune would be made. So he went up to the man: 'Friend,' says he, 'what a beautiful instrument that is, and what a deal of money you must make.' 'Why, yes,' said the man, 'I make a great deal of money, to be sure, and it is a wonderful instrument.' 'Oh!' cried Mr Vinegar, 'how I should like to possess it!' 'Well,' said the man, 'as you are a friend, I don't much mind parting with it; you shall have it for that red cow.' 'Done,' said the delighted Mr Vinegar; so the beautiful red cow was given for the bagpipes. He walked up and down with his purchase, but in vain he attempted to play a tune, and instead of pocketing pence, the boys followed him hooting, laughing, and pelting. Poor Mr Vinegar, his fingers grew very cold, and, heartily ashamed and mortified, he was leaving the town, when he met a man with a fine thick pair of gloves. 'Oh, my fingers are so very cold,' said Mr Vinegar to himself; 'if I had but those beautiful gloves I should be the happiest man alive.' He went up to the man, and said to him, 'Friend, you seem to have a capital pair of gloves there.' 'Yes, truly,' cried the man; 'and my hands are as warm as possible this cold November day.' 'Well,' said Mr Vinegar, 'I should like to have them.' 'What will you give?' said the man; 'as you are a friend of mine, I don't much mind letting you have them for those bagpipes.' 'Done,' cried Mr Vinegar. He put on the gloves, and felt perfectly happy as he trudged homewards. At last he grew very tired, when he saw a man coming towards him with a good stout stick in his hand. 'Oh,' said Mr Vinegar, 'that I had but that stick! I should then be the happiest man alive.' He accosted the man – 'Friend! what a rare good stick you have got.' 'Yes,' said the man, 'I have used it for many a long mile, and a good friend it has been, but if you have a fancy for it, as you are a friend, I don't mind giving it to you for that pair of gloves.' Mr Vinegar's hands were so warm, and his legs so tired, that he gladly exchanged. As he drew near to the wood where he had left his wife, he heard a parrot on a tree calling out his name – 'Mr Vinegar, you foolish man, you blockhead, you simpleton; you went to the fair, and laid out all your money in buying a cow; not content with that, you changed it for bagpipes, on which you could not play, and which were not worth one-tenth of the money. You fool, you – you had no sooner got the bagpipes than you changed them for the gloves, which were not worth one quarter of the money; and when you had got the gloves, you changed them for a poor miserable stick; and now for your forty guineas, cow, bagpipes, and gloves, you have nothing to show but that poor miserable stick, which you might have cut in any hedge.' On this the bird laughed immoderately, and Mr Vinegar falling into a violent rage, threw the stick at its head. The stick lodged in the tree, and he returned to his wife without money, cow, bagpipes, gloves, or stick, and she instantly gave him such a sound cudgelling that she almost broke every bone in his skin.

Halliwell says this text was obtained from oral tradition. There is a gypsy variant, 'Jack's Wonderful Bargains', in Notebook C of the T. W. Thompson manuscripts, collected from Mulli Lee on 6 September 1914 at Oxenholme, near Kendal.

The Golden Ball

Source: Contributed by Sabine Baring-Gould to William Henderson, *Notes on the Folklore of the Northern Counties of England and the Borders*, 1866, pp. 333–5.

Narrator: Two unnamed informants (the passages in square brackets being from the second), Yorkshire.

Type: AT326a 'Soul Released from Torment'.

THERE WERE TWO LASSES, daughters of one mother, and as they came home from t' fair, they saw a right bonny young man stand i' t' house-door before them. They niver seed such a bonny man afore. He had gold on t' cap, gold on t' finger, gold on t' neck, a red gold watch-chain – eh! but he had brass. He had a golden ball in each hand. He gave a ball to each lass, and she was to keep it, and if she lost it, she was to be hanged. One o' the lasses, 't was t' youngest, lost her ball. [I'll tell thee how. She was by a park-paling, and she was tossing her ball, and it went up, and up, and up, till it went fair over t' paling; and when she climbed up to look, t' ball ran along green grass, and it went raite forward to t' door of t' house, and t' ball went in and she saw't no more.]

So she was taken away to be hanged by t' neck till she were dead, a cause she'd lost her ball.

[But she had a sweetheart, and he said he would get ball. So he went tut park-gate, but 't was shut: so he climbed hedge, and when he got tut top of hedge, an old woman rose up out of t' dyke afore him, and said, if he would get ball, he must sleep three nights in t' house. He said he would.

Then he went into t' house, and looked for ball, but could na find it. Night came on and he heard spirits move i' t' courtyard: so he looked out o' t' window, and t' yard was full of them, like maggots in rotten meat.

Presently he heard steps coming upstairs. He hid behind door, and was as still as a mouse. Then in came a big giant five times as tall as he were, and giant looked round but did not see t' lad, so he went tut window and bowed to look out: and as he bowed on his elbows to see spirits i' t' yard, t' lad stepped behind him, and wi' one blow of his sword he cut him in twain, so that the top part of him fell in the yard, and t' bottom part stood looking out of t' window.

There was a great cry from t' spirits when they saw half the giant come tumbling down to them, and they called out, 'There comes half our master, give us t' other half.'

So the lad said, 'It's no use of thee, thou pair of legs, standing aloan at window, as thou hast no een to see with, so go join thy brother'; and he cast the bottom part of t' giant after top part. Now when the spirits had gotten all t' giant they were quiet.

Next night t' lad was at the house again, and now a second giant came in at door, and as he came in t' lad cut him in twain, but the legs walked on tut chimney and went up them. 'Go get thee after thy legs,' said t' lad tut head, and he cast t' head up chimney too.

The third night t' lad got into bed, and he heard spirits striving under the bed, and they had t' ball there, and they was casting it to and fro.

Now one of them has his leg thrussen out from under bed, so t' lad brings his sword down and cuts it off. Then another thrusts his arm out at other side of the bed, and t' lad cuts that off. So at last he had maimed them all, and they all went crying and wailing off, and forgot t' ball, but he took it from under t' bed, and went to seek his truelove.]

Now t' lass was taken to York to be hanged; she was brought out on t' scaffold, and t' hangman said, 'Now, lass, tha' must hang by t' neck till tha be'st dead.' But she cried out:

> Stop, stop, I think I see my mother coming!
> Oh mother, hast brought my golden ball
>   And come to set me free?

> I've neither brought thy golden ball
>   Nor come to set thee free,
> But I have come to see thee hung
>   Upon this gallows-tree.

Then the hangman said, 'Now, lass, say thy prayers, for tha must dee.' But she said:

> Stop, stop, I think I see my father coming!
> O father, hast brought my golden ball
>   And come to set me free?

> I've neither brought thy golden ball
> Nor come to set thee free,
> But I have come to see thee hung
> Upon this gallows-tree.

Then the hangman said, 'Hast thee done thy prayers? Now, lass, put thy head intut noo-is.'

But she answered, 'Stop, stop, I think I see my brother coming!' &c. After which, she excused herself because she thought she saw her sister coming, then her uncle, then her aunt, then her cousin, each of which was related in full: after which the hangman said, 'I wee-nt stop no longer, tha's making gam of me. Tha must be hung at once.'

But now she saw her sweetheart coming through the crowd, and he had over head i' t' air her own golden ball; so she said:

> Stop, stop, I see my sweetheart coming!
> Sweetheart, hast brought my golden ball
>   And come to set me free?

> Aye, I have brought thy golden ball
>   And come to set thee free;
> I have not come to see thee hung
> Upon this gallows-tree.

'The Golden Ball' is a version of a tale widespread in England and America. In it, as Tristram Coffin has shown in 'The Golden Ball and the Hangman's Tree' (*Folklore International*, 1967, pp. 23–8), the folktale of the man braving the horrors of a night in a haunted house has been intertwined with the ballad-story of 'A Maid Freed from the Gallows', four versions of which can be found in Albert B. Freedman's *The Penguin Book of Folk Ballads of the English-Speaking World* (pp. 131–7). Freedman suggests that the precious 'golden ball', which the condemned girl has lost, is a symbol of virginity. In England, the ballad became the basis of a children's game known as 'Mary Brown' (see Alice B. Gomme's *The Traditional Games of England, Scotland and Ireland*, vol. 1, pp. 364–8). M. Damant contributed a version, called 'The Three Golden Balls', collected from a young woman from Romsey, to *Folk-Lore* in 1895, which is close to the ballad: the three sisters are called Pepper, Salt and Mustard. Morley Roberts heard it in Barnstaple and put it into the mouth of a Devonshire nursemaid in his novel *Red Earth* (1894, pp. 289–90), and his notes on it in the *Athenaeum* the following year brought reports of the tale from the Midlands, Oxford, Buckinghamshire, Durham, Shrewsbury and Derbyshire.

Mr Miacca

Source: Joseph Jacobs, *English Fairy Tales*, 1890, pp. 164–6.
Narrator: Mrs B. Abrahams.
Type: AT327c 'The Devil Carries the Children Home in a Sack'.

TOMMY GRIMES WAS SOMETIMES a good boy, and sometimes a bad boy; and when he was a bad boy, he was a very bad boy. Now his mother used to say to him: 'Tommy, Tommy, be a good boy, and don't go out of the street, or else Mr Miacca will take you.' But still when he was a bad boy he would go out of the street; and one day, sure enough, he had scarcely got round the corner, when Mr Miacca did catch him and popped him into a bag upside down, and took him off to his house.

When Mr Miacca got Tommy inside, he pulled him out of the bag and set him down, and felt his arms and legs. 'You're rather tough,' says he; 'but you're all I've got for supper, and you'll not taste bad boiled. But body o' me, I've forgot the herbs, and it's bitter you'll taste without herbs. Sally! Here, I say, Sally!' and he called Mrs Miacca.

So Mrs Miacca came out of another room and said: 'What d'ye want, my dear?'

'Oh, here's a little boy for supper,' said Mr Miacca, 'and I've forgot the herbs. Mind him, will ye, while I go for them.' 'All right, my love,' says Mrs Miacca, and off he goes. Then Tommy Grimes said to Mrs Miacca: 'Does Mr Miacca always have little boys for supper?'

'Mostly, my dear,' said Mrs Miacca, 'if little boys are bad enough, and get in his way.'

'And don't you have anything else but boy-meat? No pudding?' asked Tommy.

'Ah, I loves pudding,' says Mrs Miacca. 'But it's not often the likes of me gets pudding.'

'Why, my mother is making a pudding this very day,' said Tommy Grimes, 'and I am sure she'd give you some, if I ask her. Shall I run and get some?'

'Now, that's a thoughtful boy,' said Mrs Miacca, 'only don't be long and be sure to be back for supper.'

So off Tommy pelters, and right glad he was to get off so cheap; and for many a long day he was as good as good could be, and never went round the corner of the street. But he couldn't always be good; and one day he went round the corner, and as luck would have it, he hadn't scarcely got round it when Mr Miacca grabbed him up, popped him in his bag, and took him home.

When he got him there, Mr Miacca dropped him out; and when he saw him, he said: 'Ah, you're the youngster what served me and my missus that shabby trick, leaving us without any supper. Well, you shan't do it again. I'll watch over you myself. Here, get under the sofa, and I'll set on it and watch the pot boil for you.'

So poor Tommy Grimes had to creep under the sofa, and Mr Miacca sat on it and waited for the pot to boil. And they waited, and they waited, but still the pot didn't boil, till at last Mr Miacca got tired of waiting, and he said: 'Here, you under there, I'm not going to wait any longer; put out your leg, and I'll stop your giving us the slip.'

So Tommy put out a leg, and Mr Miacca got a chopper, and chopped it off, and pops it in the pot.

Suddenly he calls out: 'Sally, my dear, Sally!' and nobody answered. So he went into the next room to look out for Mrs Miacca, and while he was there, Tommy crept out from under the sofa and ran out of the door. For it was a leg of the sofa that he had put out.

So Tommy Grimes ran home, and he never went round the corner again till he was old enough to go alone.

This cautionary tale seems to have been a family story, like 'The Pear-Drum' (p. 128), rather than a common property; it is constructed along the lines of a tale such as 'Jack the Butter-Milk' (p. 23). I have retained Jacobs's text as printed, as he never published the original and the whereabouts of his manuscripts are unknown. He admits that, 'I have transposed the two incidents, as in her version Tommy Grimes was a clever carver and carried about with him a carven leg.' Mrs Abrahams remembered the story from her mother's telling c. 1840; Mr Miacca was not just a bogey figure, but also a rewarder of good children. The name Tommy Grimes perhaps shows the influence of moralizing children's literature.

The Rose-Tree

Source: Contributed by Sabine Baring-Gould to William Henderson, *Notes on the Folklore of the Northern Counties of England and the Borders*, 1866, pp. 314–17.

Narrator: Unknown, Devonshire.

Type: AT720 'My Mother Slew Me, My Father Ate Me'.

THERE WAS ONCE UPON a time a good man who had two children: a girl by a first wife, and a boy by the second. The girl was as white as milk, and her lips were like cherries. Her hair was like golden silk, and it hung to the ground. Her brother loved her dearly, but her wicked stepmother hated her. 'Child,' said the stepmother one day, 'go to the grocer's shop and buy me a pound of candles.' She gave her the money; and the little girl went, bought the candles, and started on her return. There was a stile to cross. She put down the candles whilst she got over the stile. Up came a dog and ran off with the candles.

She went back to the grocer's, and she got a second bunch. She came to the stile, set down the candles, and proceeded to climb over. Up came the dog and ran off with the candles.

She went again to the grocer's, and she got a third bunch; and just the same event happened. Then she came to her stepmother crying, for she had spent all the money and had lost three bunches of candles.

The stepmother was angry, but she pretended not to mind the loss. She said to the child: 'Come, lay thy head on my lap that I may comb thy hair.' So the little one laid her head in the woman's lap, who proceeded to comb the yellow silken hair. And when she combed, the hair fell over her knees, and rolled right down to the ground.

Then the stepmother hated her more for the beauty of her hair; so she said to her, 'I cannot part thy hair on my knee, fetch a billet of wood.' So she fetched it. Then said the stepmother, 'I cannot part thy hair with a comb, fetch me an axe.' So she fetched it.

'Now,' said the wicked woman, 'lay thy head down on the billet whilst I part thy hair.'

Well! she laid down her little golden head without fear: and whist! down came the axe, and it was off. So the mother wiped the axe and laughed.

Then she took the heart and liver of the little girl, and she stewed them and brought them into the house for supper. The husband tasted them and shook his head. He said they tasted very strangely. She gave some to the little boy, but he would not eat. She tried to force him, but he refused, and ran out into the garden, and took up his little sister, and put her in a box, and buried the box under a rose-tree; and every day he went to the tree and wept, till his tears ran down on the box.

One day the rose-tree flowered. It was spring, and there among the flowers was a white bird; and it sang, and sang, and sang like an angel out of heaven. Away it flew, and it went to a cobbler's shop, and perched itself on a tree hard by; and thus it sang:

> My wicked mother slew me,
> My dear father ate me,
> My little brother whom I love
> Sits below, and I sing above
> Stick, stock, stone dead?

'Sing again that beautiful song,' asked the shoemaker. 'If you will first give me those little red shoes you are making.' The cobbler gave the shoes, and the bird sang the song; then flew to a tree in front of a watchmaker's, and sang:

> My wicked mother slew me,
> My dear father ate me,
> My little brother whom I love
> Sits below, and I sing above
> Stick, stock, stone dead.

'Oh, the beautiful song! sing it again, sweet bird,' asked the watchmaker. 'If you will give me first that gold watch and chain in your hand.' The jeweller gave the watch and chain. The bird took it in one foot, the shoes in the other, and flew away, after having repeated the song, to where three millers were picking a millstone. The bird perched on a tree and sang:

> My wicked mother slew me,
> My dear father ate me,

My little brother whom I love
Sits below, and I sing above
Stick!

Then one of the men put down his tool and looked up from his work,

Stock!

Then the second miller's man laid aside his tool and looked up,

Stone!

Then the third miller's man laid down his tool and looked up,

Dead!

Then all three cried out with one voice: 'Oh, what a beautiful song! Sing it, sweet bird again.' 'If you will put the millstone round my neck,' said the bird. The men complied with the bird's request, and away to the tree it flew with the millstone round its neck, the red shoes in the grasp of one foot, and the gold watch and chain in the grasp of the other. It sang the song and then flew home. It rattled the millstone against the eaves of the house, and the stepmother said, 'It thunders.' Then the little boy ran out to see the thunder, and down dropped the red shoes at his feet. It rattled the millstone against the eaves of the house once more, and the stepmother said again, 'It thunders.' Then the father ran out and down fell the chain about his neck.

In ran father and son, laughing and saying. 'See, the thunder has brought us these fine things!' Then the bird rattled the millstone against the eaves of the house a third time; and the stepmother said, 'It thunders again, perhaps the thunder has brought something for me,' and she ran out; but the moment she stepped outside the door, down fell the millstone on her head; and so she died.

This tale is best-known as the Grimms' 'Juniper Tree'; it is very widespread, and a number of English versions have been recorded. Joseph Jacobs used Baring-Gould's text for his *English Fairy Tales*, and notes that 'I heard this in Australia', and that Israel Gollancz told him he remembered a version called 'Pepper, Salt, and Mustard' with the refrain,

My mother killed me,
My father picked up my bones,
My little sister buried me
Under the marble stones.

This is almost the same as the rhyme in several other versions (e.g. that given in Gutch and Peacock's *Examples of Printed Folk-Lore Concerning Lincolnshire* (*County Folk-Lore*, vol. V, 1908), p. 325, 'Orange and Lemon').

Richard Blakeborough prints a Yorkshire text, 'The Cruel Stepmother and her Little Daughter', in his *Wit, Character, Folk-Lore and Humour of the North Riding of Yorkshire* (pp. 273–6), which is very similar to Baring-Gould's (and possibly based on it). There is a highly dramatic text with plenty of lively dialogue in Jones and Kropf's *The Folk-Tales of the Magyars* (pp. 418–20), collected by Jones from 'old nurses in Holderness', also under the title 'Orange and Lemon'. Orange and Lemon are sisters, the favourites respectively of the mother and father. S. O. Addy collected a version from C. R. Hirst in Sheffield in June 1896 and printed it as 'The Satin Frock' in 'Four Yorkshire Folktales' (*Folk-Lore*, 8, 1897, pp. 394–5); Hirst got it from a girl aged about thirteen, and it is spectacularly gruesome but lacks the motif of reincarnation as a bird. The father merely remarks, 'This broth is nice, but it does taste like my Mary', discovers the crime and kills his wife. Another story collected by Addy in Sheffield, 'The Broken Pitcher' (*Household Tales*, pp. 29–30), also features sisters called Orange and Lemon, and is essentially a happy version of this story, presumably invented to counteract the terrors induced by the real tale. It was probably based on the story 'Patty and her Pitcher' in *Mother Goose's Nursery Rhymes and Fairy Tales* (*c.* 1880).

Katharine Briggs recorded a version, 'Little Rosy', from Ruth Tongue in 1963, and printed it in Briggs and Tongue's *Folktales of England*, together with a tune for the rhyme. J. Roby's *Traditions of Lancashire* (1829, p. 134) contains an historical legend, 'Fair Ellen of Radcliffe', which as Briggs points out (*Dictionary*, Part A, vol. 2, pp. 47–8) is essentially a naturalized version of AT720. Like all Roby texts it is very long-winded.

The Pear-Drum

Source: Contributed by J. Y. Bell to *Folk-Lore*, 66, 1955, p. 303.
Narrator: Family story.
Type: AT779b 'Disrespectful Children Punished'.

ONCE UPON A TIME there were two little girls. Their names were Blue-Eyes and Turkey. Blue-Eyes was named after the colour of her eyes and Turkey after the red dress she wore. They lived in a little house on a moor with their mother and the baby. Their father was a sailor voyaging to far away lands.

One day Blue-Eyes and Turkey went for a walk upon the moor, and they met a Gipsy Girl playing on a pear-drum. When she played, a little man and woman came out of the drum and danced. Blue-Eyes and Turkey were enchanted, and begged her to give them the pear-drum. 'I will give it you,' she said, 'but only if you are very naughty! Come back tomorrow.'

So Blue-Eyes and Turkey were very naughty. They shouted, and spilled their food, and refused to go to bed, and scribbled on their books. Their mother was grieved, but next day they both got up very early and went out on the moor. There they met the Gipsy Girl, and again she played the pear-drum. 'We were very naughty,' they cried. 'Can we have it?' 'Tell me what you did,' she replied. So they told her. 'Oh, no,' said the Gipsy Girl, 'you were only a little naughty. You must be far worse than that.'

So that day they were as naughty as they could be. They threw their cups on the floor, and tore their clothes, and walked in the mud up to their knees; and pulled up all the flowers in the garden, and let the pig out so that it ran away. Their mother was still more grieved than before, but next day they got up very early and went out to meet the Gipsy Girl. Again she told them they had not been naughty enough. 'You must be really bad,' she said.

So they went home. This time they broke the chairs and smashed the china, and tore their clothes to pieces, and whipped the dog and struck the baby and beat their mother with their fists. Their mother said sadly, 'Blue-Eyes and Turkey, you must not be so naughty. If you do not stop, I shall have to go away, and instead there will come a new mother with glass eyes and a wooden tail to live with you.' But still they thought of the wonderful pear-drum and said to each other, 'Tomorrow we will be good. Once we have got the pear-drum we will be good again.'

Next morning they got up very early and went out on the moor. There was the Gipsy Girl, but she had no pear-drum. 'Where is the pear-drum?' they cried. The Gipsy Girl laughed. 'It is gone. We Gipsies are all going away today. I am the last to leave.' 'But we did as you told us' – and they told her all the things they had done. The Gipsy Girl laughed again. 'Yes,' she said, 'you have been really naughty, and now your mother has gone away, far, far away to find your father, and instead you have a mother with glass eyes and a wooden tail.'

Blue-Eyes and Turkey wandered about on the moor all day, but when evening came, they went back to their house. There were no lamps lit, but in the glow of the firelight they could see through the window the glitter of their new mother's glass eyes, and hear the thump of her wooden tail.

In her note on this tale, Katharine Briggs remarks that it is 'a family story, and was probably a cautionary tale invented by the first teller in the family. The mother with glass eyes and a wooden tail is an unusual invention, but there is an authentic thrill about her.' In fact, this remarkable and chilling tale is an adaptation of a short story called 'The New Mother' by Mrs Lucy Clifford, first published in *Anyhow Stories* in 1899. This story is forty-four pages long; J. Y. Bell's text retains every key element. This is rare testimony to the refining and condensing processes of oral narration at work on a story with a known history. The story does contain a more detailed description of the mysterious pear-drum, which is

> a good deal like a guitar in shape; it had three strings, but only two pegs by which to tune them. The third string was never tuned at all, and thus added to the singular effect produced by the pear-drum's music. Yet, oddly enough, the music was not made by touching the strings, but by turning a little handle cunningly hidden on one side.

The potent images of Lucy Clifford's story are of the kind to lodge in the mind; the historian of children's literature, F. J. Harvey Darton, was haunted by the figure of the new mother, recording in his *Children's Books in England* (3rd edn, 1982, p. 196) that, 'Getting on for fifty years after I met her first, I still cannot rid my mind of that fearful creation.' Oddly enough, the story fits perfectly into the tale type AT779b, though this is one of the rare types for which only a single (Russian) text is listed.

The Flyin' Childer

Source: M. C. Balfour, 'Legends of the Lincolnshire Cars: Part 3', *Folk-Lore*, 2, 4 December 1891, pp, 403–9.

Narrator: Unnamed man, Lindsey, Lincolnshire.

Type: ML4020 'The Unforgiven Dead'.

A'M SKERS SURE EF a can tell 'ee 't ahl right, but a guess a mind it as 't wor tell't me'a. Le'ssee, na'ow! Theer wor wanst a chap 's wor gra'at fur tha wimmen-fo'ak, an' cud'n't kep out o' tha wa'ay ef a tried ever so; th' varry soight o' a pittyco't ha'f a mile off'n th' road 'd ca'all un fur to foller 'n. 'N' wan da'ay, as 't mout be, a come ker-bang ra'ound a co'ner, 'n' theer wor a rampin' maid, settin' her lo'an an' washin' asel', an' th' fond chap wor ahl outer's wit's to wanst. An' th' upshot o' 't wor, 's a sweer a'd wed her, ef her'd come ho'am wi' 'm; 'n' says she:

'A'll come, 'n' welcome!' says she, 'but thou'll mun sweer as thou'll wed ma.'

'A will,' says he, 'a sweer 't!' – an' a thowt to 'msel', 'ower th' lef' showther, that!'

'Thou'll mun wed ma i' cho'ch,' says she.

'A will!' says he – 'Ef a iver put foot in,' he thowt to 'msel'.

'An' ef thou do'ant, what'll a forspell 'ee?' says she.

'Lawks,' says he, fur a wor feared o' bein' forspellt, which be main mischancy, seest tha; 'do'ant 'ee overlook ma, do'ant 'ee! Ef a do'ant wed tha, mout th' wo'ms e'at ma' – ('Ther ba'oun' fur to do 't annywa'ays!' thinks he to 'msel') – 'an' th' childer hey wings 'n' fly awa'ay.' ('An' none gra'at matter ef tha do!' says he to 'msel'.)

But th' maid didn't know as a wor thinkin', an' a want wi' 'm. An' by-'n'-by tha coom to 'n' cho'ch.

'Thou'll can wed ma here-by,' says she, tweakin's arm.

'No'a!' says he, 'th' pa'asson's a-huntin'.' So tha went on a bit furder, an' coom to 'nother cho'ch.

'Wal', here-by?' says she.

'No'a!' says he; 'pa'asson 's none sober 'nuff, 'n' clerk's drunk.'

'Wal'!' says she, 'mebbe tha'll can wed 's, fur ahl thar i' liquor.'

'Houts!' says he, an' gi's her a kick.

So on tha want ag'ean, an' by-'n'-by, a meets wi' a t'ylorman, an' a says, says a, 'Wheer's th' me'aster?'

'Ooh, da'own-by!' says th' au'd feller.

So a went on a bit furder, while tha coom to a wise woman, plaitin' straws, an' a says to a, 'Wheer's th' au'd mun?'

'Da'own-by!' says she.

So on tha want, while a coom to 'n bit cottage by th' la'ane side, an' a knockit an' kicked at th' door tell't shuk, but niver a wo'd coom f'um inn'ard. So a wa'alked ra'at in, an' theer wor 'n au'd mun lyin' slepin' 'n' snorin' on's bed.

Wal', th' young chap keck't aba'out 'un fur summat handy, 'n' seen 'n axe, so a oop wi' 't 'n' brained th' au'd feller, 'n' chopped's feet 'n' han's off'n 'um. An' than a set to 'n' cle'aned oop th' pla'ace, 'n' thrung th' corp out o' winder, 'n' lat fire i' th' hearth, while ahl wor smart 'n' natty.

An' by-'n'-by, keckin' ower 's showther, a seed th' wise woman stealin' th' corp awa'ay wi' a.

'Hi!' says th' chap; 'th' corp's mine, seest tha. What thou do' n' wi' 'm?'

'A'll barry'm fur tha,' says she.

'No'a thou wunt,' says he, 'a'll do 't masel'.'

'Wall, then,' says she, 'a'll stan' by.'

'No'a, thou wunt!' says he, 'a'll can do 't better ma lo'an.'

'Ta'ake thy wa'ay, fool,' says she, 'but gi' ma th' axe, then, 'stead o' th' corp.'

'No'a, a wunt!' says he; 'a mout want her age'an.'

'Hi!' says th' wise woman, 'none give, none have; red han' an' lyin' lips!'

An' a want awa'ay, mutterin' an' twistin' 's fingers.

So th' chap buried th' corp, but less a furgot wheer't wor, a lef' wan arm stickin' oot o' th' gra'oun', an' th' feet 'n' han's a chuck to th' pigs, an' says he to th' gal:

'A'll ga 'n snare a cony; see thou kep to th' ha'ouse'; 'n' off a want.

Th' gal diddle-daddled aba'out, 'n' presently th' pigs 'gun squealin' 's if a wor kill't.

'An' oh!' says th' gal, 'what 'n 's amiss wi' 'm, fur so to squeal?'

An' th' dead feet up an' said, 'We be amiss, us'll trample th' pigs tell thou bury us!'

So a took th' feet, an' put 'em i' yarth.

An' by-'n'-by th' pigs la'ay da'own 'n' died.

'Oh! oh!' says th' gal, 'what be th' matter wi' 'm fur so to die?'

An' th' dead han's up an' cried, 'We be th' matter, we's chocked um!'

So a want 'n' barried 'em too.

An' by-'n'-by a heerd summat a-callin', 'n' a-callin' on her, an' a want fur to see what a wanted.

'Who be a-ca'allin'?' says she.

'Thou 's put us wrong!' said th' feet an' han's; 'we be feelin', an' we be creepin', an' we ca'ant fin' th' rest o' 's annywheers. Put us by th' au'd mun, wheer 's arm sticks oot o' groun', or we'll tickle tha wi' fingers an' tread tha wi' toes, till thou loss tha wits.'

So a dug 'em up, 'n' put 'em by th' au'd mun.

An' by-'n'-by th' young chap coom back, an' ca'alled fur 's dinner.

'Wheer's th' childer?' says he.

'Ooh, gath'rin' berries!' says she.

'Berries i' *spring*?" says he; an' kep on wi' 's eatin'.

But when noight coom an' tha wornt ho'am:

'Wheer's th' *childer*? says he.

'Gone a fishin',' says she.

'Ay,' says he, "'n' th' babby, too?'

An' coom th' mornin', a shuk th' gal oop sudden, an' bawled in's earn:

'Wheer's th' CHILDER?'

'Ooh!' says she 'n a hurry, 'flown awa'ay, th' childer hev!'

'Tha hev?' says he. 'Then thou'll can goo arter'm!'

An' a oop wi' th' axe 'n' chopped her i' pieces 'n' shuv th' bits unner th' bed.

Wal, by-'n'-by, th' childer coom flyin' back, an' keck't aba'out fur th' mother, but tha seed nowt.

'Wheer's mother?' tha said to th' chap.

'Gone to buy bacon,' says he, feelin' oneasy.

'Bacon?' says tha; 'an' wi' flitches hangin' ready?'

'N' presently tha comes age'an, 'n' says:

'Wheer's mother na'ow?

'Gone to seek *thou*,' says a, shakin' unner th' cloes.

'Ay?' says tha, 'an' we here!'

An' fore a cud get oot o' bed tha coom ahl ra' ound un, an' pointed at un wi' 's fingers:

'Wheer's mother TO-NA'OW?'

'Ooh!' a squealed, 'unner th' bed!' An' a put's head unner th' blunket.

Tha childer pulled oot th' bits, an' fell to weepin' an' wailin' as tha pieced un togither. An' th' chap, a want fur to crep to th' door 'n' get awa'ay, but tha cot un, an' took th' axe 'n' chopped un oop loike th' gal, an' lef un lyin' whiles tha want awa'ay grattin'.

Soon's a wor sure a wor de'ad, up a got 'n' shook 's 'sel, an' theer wor th' gal, stannin' waitin' fur 'n wi' 's long claws a'out, an' 's teeth gibberin' an' 's eyne blazin' loike a green cat, gan' to spring. An' nat'rally th' chap wor feared, an' a runned, an' runned, an' runned, so's to git awa'ay; but she runned efter, wi' 's long claws strot out, till a cu'd feel un ticklin' th' back o' 's neck, an' strainin' wi' th' longin' to chock un. An' a ca'lled a'out to the thunner:

'Strike ma de'ad!'

But th' thunner wud'n't, for a wor de'ad a'ready.

An' a runned to th' fire an' begged:

'Burn ma oop!'

But tha fire wud'n't, fur th' chill o' de'ath put 'n a'out.

An' a thrung's sel' in th' watter, an' said:

'Draown me blue!'

But th' watter wudn't, fur th' death-colour wor comin' in 's fa'ace a'ready.

An' a tuk th' axe 'n' tried to cut 's thro'at, but th' axe wud'n't.

An' to last, a thrung 's sel' into th' gra'ound, an' ca'alled fur th' wo'ms to eat un, so's a cu'd rest in's grave an' be quit o' th' woman.

But by-'n-by oop crep a gra'at wo'm, an' a stra'ange an' gra'at thing 't wor, wi' th' gal's head o' th' en' o' its long slimy body, an' 't crep oop aside un an' ra'oun' about, 'n' over un, while a druv awa'ay all th' other wo'ms, an' than a set to, to eat un's sel'.

'Ooh, eat ma quick, eat ma quick!' a squeels.

'Stiddy, na'ow!' says th' wo'm, 'good food's wuth th' meal-toime. Thou ho'd still, 'n' let ma 'njoy masel'.'

'Eat ma quick, eat ma quick!' said he.

'Do'ant thou haste ma, a tell 'ee,' says th' wo'm, 'a 's gettin' on fine. Thou'st nigh gone na'ow.' An' a smacked's lips wi' th' goodness o' 't.

'Quick!' a whispit age'an.

'Whist, thou'st 'n onpatient chap,' says th' wo'm.

An' a' swallowed th' last bit, an' th' lad wor all go'an, an' a' got awa'ay fum th' gal to last.

An' that's ahl.

<hr />

This is one of the most terrible of all English folktales; few will ever forget its climax, when the murderous husband pleads with the huge slimy worm with his dead wife's head to 'eat me quick, eat me quick', and is answered with the unspeakably sinister homily, 'Good food's worth the meal-time.'

It was narrated to Marie Clothilde Balfour by a man from the Wolds, in a small inn, on the only occasion she met him. She took the tale down in the rough notes given below, and later expanded them for publication as one of her 'Legends of the Lincolnshire Cars', published in *Folk-Lore* (2, 1891, pp. 145–70, 257–83, 401–18):

Not quite sure if remember – think can tell as told me. Once was a lad – fond of girls – couldn't keep away from petticoats. Came round corner 'kerbang' on girl washing herself – swore he'd wed her, if she'd follow him. She makes him swear – he does it 'ower th' lef shouther'. In church, she says. Says he will, 'if ever he goes in' (aside). Threatens to 'forespell' him if he doesn't. He says, 'Mout th' wo'ms eat ma ef a don't' – 'Bound do it anyway' – and children fly away – 'no great matter' (aside). So they went on – came to church – girl wants to go in. He says no, parson hunting. Go on to next church – says, 'No; parson's tipsy, and clerk's drunk.' She says might wed them for all that. He kicks her. Meet a tailor – ask him for the master. 'Down-by'. Meet wise woman plaiting straws. 'Wheer's au'd mun?' 'Down-by.' Come to cottage, knock – no answer, go in – old man asleep on bed. Lad takes axe, brains him, chops feet and hands – throws out of window. Cleaned place – lit fire. Wise woman tries to steal corpse. 'Hi, that's mine.' 'I'll bury it.' 'No, do 't masel'.' 'I'll stand by.' 'No, do better alone.' 'Give axe instead.' 'No might need it.' 'None give, none have; red hand, lying lips.' He buries corpse – leaves arm sticking up – feet and hands to the pigs. Says to gal, 'Get cony; you keep house.' Girl diddle-daddles – pigs squeal. 'What's amiss?' Dead feet say, 'We trample pigs – bury us.' She does. Pigs die. 'What's matter?' Dead hands say, 'Choking pigs – bury us.' She does. They call – she goes. Say, 'Can't feel body -must be buried by it, or haunt her.' She does. Lad comes home. 'Where's childer?' 'Gathering berries.' 'In spring?' Night comes. 'Where's childer?' 'Fishing.' 'Baby too?' Morning – wakes her suddenly. 'Where's *childer*?' 'Flown away.' 'You go too.' Chops her – puts under bed. Children come back. 'Where's mother?' 'Buying bacon.' 'With flitches here?' 'Wheer's mother?' 'Seeking you.' 'We here?' Crowd round bed. '*Where's mother?*' 'Under bed!' They pull her out – weep – chop him up too. He gets up – shakes. Girl up too – 'wi' long claws out' – gibbering – eyes green. He runs – she runs after – claws out – tickle his neck – longs to choke him. He calls thunder – strike him dead. 'No, dead already.' To fire, 'Burn ma oop.' 'No, 'chill o' death' put out fire.' Water, 'Drown ma blue.' 'No, dead blue already.' Axe, 'Cut throat.' Wouldn't. Went to ground, calls worms – great worm comes – drives off others. Girl's head. 'Eat ma quick.' 'Good food's worth meal-time.' 'Eat ma quick.' 'No haste – nigh gone.' 'Quick.' 'You're impatient.' Last bit – all gone – got rid of girl. That's all.

Suppose all rubbish – but murderers may be chased by people they kill – think likely.

She denigrates this narrator – 'He was a poor storyteller and did not seem to realize the incoherency of the tale' – and certainly despite the power of the images their progression is not always clear. Another of her Lincolnshire stories, 'Sam'l's Ghost', also personifies death as a worm. In the repeated queries as to the whereabouts of the children, and in the macabre atmosphere, there is also some affinity with the children's game 'The Witch' (see Alice Gomme, *The Traditional Games of England, Scotland and Ireland*, vol. 2, 1898, pp. 391–6).

However this, like Mrs Balfour's other stories, is sufficiently strange and unlike anything else collected even in Lincolnshire by folklorists such as Ethel Rudkin and Mabel Peacock, as to raise a real doubt as to the authenticity of the material, despite the circumstantial information provided about the narrators, and the printing in three cases of field notes. Joseph Jacobs, who was a shrewd judge, accepted the stories as genuine, as have scholars such as Katharine Briggs and Richard Dorson since. But the F. J. Norton manuscripts contain a note expressing his doubts, and these I share.

Lindsey was never a discrete social or economic area to sustain such a distinctive and atavistic culture; Mrs Balfour's claim to have discovered – even in the by then drained and fertile fenland – inhabitants speaking 'almost pure Saxon', and possessed of such grim and violent imaginations, is not really supported by any other evidence.

The dialect of the Balfour texts presents a number of problems. It varies considerably from that in Mabel Peacock's *Tales and Rhymes in the Lindsey Folk-Speech* (1886); Ethel Rudkin writes ('Folklore of Lincolnshire', *Folk-Lore*, 66, 4, 1955, pp. 396) that 'the dialect is shocking'. Certainly in the above text the exclamation 'Houts!', however spelt, has a Scottish rather than a Lincolnshire ring.

Clothilde Balfour was married to Dr James Craig Balfour, and was hence an aunt by marriage to Robert Louis Stevenson. She contributed stories and articles to periodicals such as *Macmillan's Magazine*, sent further folktales to Jacobs for *More English Fairy Tales*, and gathered together material from printed sources for the Northumberland volume of the Folklore Society's *County Folklore Series* (*County Folklore*, 4, 1903).

She claims to have recorded (or at least heard) Lincolnshire versions of such familiar tales as 'Jack the Giant Killer' and 'Beauty and the Beast', but these she does not print; nor have I been able to turn up any manuscript material. Her 'Tattercoats' in Jacobs's *More English Fairy Tales* is a rather literary Cinderella variant supposedly recorded from 'a little girl named Sally Brown' whose mother worked for Mrs Balfour in the Cars. None of the other eleven stories from the Cars bears much resemblance to anything else in the recorded English tradition. The stories are: 'The Flyin' Childer' and 'Fred the Fool', from the same narrator; 'The Green Mist' (p. 359); 'The Tiddy Mun', from an old woman; 'The Dead Moon' and 'Sam'l's Ghost' from a crippled girl of nine; 'The Dead Hand'; 'The Strangers' Share'; 'Yallery Brown'; and 'A Pottle o' Brains' and 'Coat o' Clay' from the same narrator (this last tale being printed first by Andrew Lang in *Longman's Magazine*, and then in *Folk-Lore*, 1, Sept. 1890).

Whatever their provenance – and they may of course be, as Mrs Balfour claimed, accurate records of oral narrations, set down as near as possible 'exactly as told to me' – the 'Legends of the Cars' are remarkable for their ability to give shape to the most intimate horrors of the mind: they represent a high achievement of the Gothic imagination. A central theme of the stories, that we create or provoke our own demons, is given clear expression in 'The Dead Moon', narrated by the crippled child Fanny, in the description of a man in the grip of the 'Horrors':

An a' tha evil thoughts an' deeds o's life cam' an' whispet in 's ears, an'
da'anced aboot an' shooted oot tha secret things o's ain heart, till a shrieked
an' sobbed wi' pain an' shame.

The Story of Mr Fox

Source: J. O. Halliwell, *Popular Rhymes and Nursery Tales of England*, 1849, pp. 47–8.

Narrator: Contributed by Blakeway to Malone's *Variorum Shakespeare*, 1821.

Type: AT955c 'Mr Fox'.

ONCE UPON A TIME there was a young lady called Lady Mary, who had two brothers. One summer they all three went out to a country seat of theirs which they had not before visited. Among the other gentry in the neighbourhood who came to see them was a Mr Fox, a bachelor, with whom they, particularly the young lady, were much pleased. He used often to dine with them, and frequently invited Lady Mary to come and see his house. One day, when her brothers were absent elsewhere, and she had nothing better to do, she determined to go thither, and accordingly set out unattended. When she arrived at the house and knocked at the door, no one answered. At length she opened it and went in, and over the portal of the door was written:

> Be bold, be bold, but not too bold.

She advanced, and found the same inscription over the staircase; again at the entrance of the gallery; and lastly, at the door of a chamber, with the addition of a line:

> Be bold, be bold, but not too bold,
> Lest that your heart's blood should run cold!

She opened it, and what was her terror and astonishment to find the floor covered with bones and blood. She retreated in haste, and coming down stairs, she saw from a window Mr Fox advancing towards the house with a drawn sword in one hand, while with the other he dragged along a young lady by the hair of her head. Lady Mary had just time to slip down, and hide herself under the stairs, before Mr Fox and his victim arrived at the foot of them. As he pulled the young lady up stairs, she caught hold of one of the bannisters with her hand, on which was a rich bracelet. Mr Fox cut it off with his sword: the hand and bracelet fell into Lady Mary's lap, who then contrived to escape unobserved, and got safe home to her brother's house.

A few days afterwards Mr Fox came to dine with them as usual. After dinner the guests began to amuse each other with extraordinary anecdotes, and Lady Mary said she would relate to them a remarkable dream she had lately had. I dreamt, said she, that as you, Mr Fox, had often invited me to your house, I would go there one morning. When I came to the house, I knocked at the door, but no one answered. When I opened the door, over the hall I saw written, 'Be bold, be bold, but not too bold'. But, said she, turning to Mr Fox, and smiling, 'It is not so, nor it was not so.' Then she pursued the rest of the story, concluding at every turn with, 'It is not so, nor it was not so,' till she came to the discovery of the room full of bones, when Mr Fox took up the burden of the tale, and said:

> It is not so, nor it was not so,
> And God forbid it should be so!

which he continued to repeat at every subsequent turn of the dreadful story, till she came to the circumstance of his cutting off the young lady's hand, when, upon his saying, as usual,

> It is not so, nor it was not so,
> And God forbid it should be so!

Lady Mary retorts by saying,

> But it is so, and it was so,
> And here the hand I have to show!

at the same moment producing the hand and bracelet from her lap. Whereupon the guests drew their swords, and instantly cut Mr Fox into a thousand pieces.

The related types of 'The Robber Bridegroom' (AT955) and 'Bluebeard' (AT311 and 312) are among the most popular of all stories in England. Although their ostensible subject matter is murder and attempted murder, the theme of these tales is sexual violence. A man who preys on women receives his comeuppance through the wiliness of his intended victim. The imagery of severed hands, cellars of blood and open graves queasily encodes an apprehension of rape and sexual shock that serves in its atmosphere of terror as a warning to young girls and in its denouement as a warning to male predators. See also 'Bobby Rag' (p. 142), 'Doctor Forster' (p. 145), 'Captain Murderer' (p. 162), 'The Wooden Leg' (p. 167), 'Wanted, a Husband' (p. 171) and 'The Hand of Glory' (p. 173).

Interestingly Perrault's story of 'Bluebeard', although available in chapbook form from *c.* 1750, seems not to have made much impression on the native tradition, which Baughman assigns its own subtype AT955c 'Mr Fox'. 'The Story of Mr Fox' was contributed by Blakeway to the Malone–Boswell *Variorum Shakespeare*, as a gloss on Benedick's words in *Much Ado About Nothing*: 'Like the old tale, my Lord, "It is not so, nor t'was not so, but indeed, God forbid it should be so."'

Stories written down in the nineteenth century to explain references in Shakespeare, for instance the cante-fable of Childe Rowland in Jamie-son's *Illustrations of Northern Antiquities* (1814), should be treated with caution, but this story has a large number of close variants in English tradition, albeit none with this particular Shakespearian refrain. Blakeway learnt it from his great aunt, who was born in 1715.

In the commonest form of the tale, a girl is seduced by a man and then lured by him to a rendezvous at a lonely spot. She arrives early, and climbs a tree for safety. Her lover arrives, sometimes with an accomplice, and she observes him digging a grave. Later, she exposes the plot, and the man is brought to summary justice. In one version, 'The Oxford Student' (Halliwell, *Popular Rhymes and Nursery Tales of England*, 1849), which Halliwell 'obtained in Oxfordshire from tradition', the girl confronts her suitor alone, and is herself killed. This ending of the story, peculiar to Oxford, seems to relate to the Town–Gown riots of 1214, during which townspeople hanged two students who allegedly helped a fellow student murder a local girl he had seduced (see *The Early Oxford Schools*, ed. J. I. Catto, 1934, p. 26; and *The Melrose Chronicles*, ed. A. and M. Andersen, 1936, p. 53). Until 1984 a sum was still paid yearly to the university in compensation for the locals' revenge (see the *Guardian*, 29 June 1984).

The girl in 'The Oxford Student' reveals her knowledge by means of a rhymed riddle of which Halliwell gives two versions:

> One moonshiny night, as I sat high,
> Waiting for one to come by,
> The boughs did bend; my heart did ache
> To see what hole the fox did make.

In the second version, the student – named as Fox – had been accompanied:

> As I went out in a moonlight night,
> I set my back against the moon,
> I looked for one, and saw two come;
> The boughs did bend, the leaves did shake,
> I saw the hole the fox did make.

Variants of this rhyme have been recorded over and over again. M. A. Courtney prints in *Cornish Feasts and Folk-Lore* (from the Reverend S. Rundle in the *Transactions of the Penzance Natural History and Antiquarian Society*, 1885–6):

> Riddle me! Riddle me right!
> Guess where I was to last Saturday night.
> Up in the old ivy tree,
> Two old foxes under me,
> Digging a grave to bury me.
> First I heard the wind blow,
> Then I heard the cock crow,
> Then I saw the chin-champ chawing up his bridle,
> Then I saw the workman working hisself idle.

The chin-champ is the horse on which the gravedigger rode; 'working hisself idle' is working in vain. This is close to the version in the story of 'The Lass 'at Seed Her Awn Graave Dug' in Mabel Peacock's *Tales and Rhymes in the Lindsey Folk-Speech* (1886, pp. 72–5). In Gutch and Peacock's *County Folk-Lore V: Lincolnshire* (1908), this tale is singled out as a 'widely known story'.

Other versions of this form of the tale are 'The Girl Who Got up the Tree' (S. O. Addy, *Household Tales*, pp. 10–11) and 'Mr Fox's Courtship' (Briggs and Tongue's *Folktales of England*, pp. 90–4; recorded from Ruth Tongue, with music for the rhyme and two extended sets of words for it). As late as January 1938, E. M. Wilson could take down from J. E. Bland, a labourer of Endmoor, Westmorland, the following version (loose leaf XXXIX of loose sheets attached to vol. 6 of the Norton Collection):

A young man had got a young woman into trouble. So he told her to meet him in Paddy Lane and they'd make arrangements to be married and one thing and another. And (when she got there) something told her to get up into the branches of a tree – a Scotch fir, which she did. And after a bit the young man came with a pick and a spade and he dug a grave under the tree. And this is the verse:

> The boughs did bend,
> The leaves did shake,
> I saw the hole
> The fox did make.

Paddy Lane is a road two miles east of Kendal. Such specific localization of the tale is not uncommon. In two other local versions, 'The Lonton Lass' (Gutch, *County Folk-Lore II: North Riding of Yorkshire*, 1901, p. 207) and a Devonshire tale related to Augustus Hare by George Russell at luncheon at Lady Florentia Hughes's on 17 May 1879 (*The Story of My Life*, vol. 5, pp. 193–5), the girl is saved not because she hides up a tree, but because a farmer (in the Hare version, her employer) has a warning dream.

Bobby Rag

Source: John Sampson, 'Tales in a Tent', *JGLS*, 3, April 1892, pp. 201–3.
Narrator: Johnny Gray.
Type: AT955 'The Robber Bridegroom'.

YEAHS AN' YEAHS AN' double yeahs ago, deah wuz a nice young Gypsy gal playin' round an ole oak tree. An' up comed a squire as she wur a-playin', an' he failed in love wid her, and asked her ef she'd go to his hall, an' marry him. An' she says: 'No, sir! you wouldn't have a pooah Gypsy gal like me.' But he meaned so, an' stoled her away an' married her.

Now, when he bring'd her home, his mother warn't 'greeable to let hisself down so low as to marry a Gypsy gal. So she says: 'You'll hev to go and 'stry her in de hundert mile wood, an' strip her star'-mother-naked, an' bring back her clothes and her heart and pluck wid you.'

And he took'd his hoss, and she jumped up behint him, and rid behint him into de wood. You'll be shuah it wor a wood! an ole-fashioned wood we know it should be, wid bears, an' eagles, an' sneks, an' wolfs into it. And when he took'd her in de wood he says: 'Now, I'll ha' to kill you here, an' strip you star'-mother-naked and tek back your clothes an' your heart an' pluck wid me, and show dem to my mammy.'

But she begged hard fur herself, an' she says: 'Deah's an eagle into dut wood, an' he's gat de same heart an pluck as a Christ'n; take dat home an' show it to your mammy, an' I'll giv you my clothes as well.'

So he stript her clothes affer her, an' he kilt de eagle, and took'd his heart an' pluck home, an' showed it to his mammy, an' said as he'd kilt her.

And she hear'd him rode aff, an' she wents an, an' she wents an, an' she wents an, an' she crep' an' crep' an her poor dear hen's an' knees, tell she fun' a way troo de long wood. Youah shoah she'd have hard work to fin' a way troo it! an' long an' by last she got to de hedge anear de road, so as she'd hear any one go by.

Now, in de marnin' deah wuz a young gentleman comed by an hoss-back, an' he couldn't get his hoss by for love nor money; an' she hed herself in under de hedge, fur she wur afrightened 'twor de same man come back to kill her agin, an' besides youah shuah she wor ashamed of bein' naked.

An' he calls out: 'Ef you're a ghost go 'way! but ef you 're a livin' Christ'n, speak to me!' An' she med answer direc'ly: 'I'm as good a Christ'n as you are, but not in parable.' An' when he sin her, he pull't his deah, beautiful topcoat affer him, an' put it an her, an' he says: 'Jump behint me.' An' she jumped behint him, an' he rid wi' her to his own gret hall. An' deah wuz no speakin' tell dey gat home. He knowed she wuz deah to be kilt, an' he galloped as hard as he could an his blood-hoss, tell he got to his own hall.

An' when he bring'd her in, dey wur all struck stunt to see a woman naked, wid her beautiful black hair hangin' down her back in long rinklets. Dey asked her what she wuz deah fur, an' she tell'd dem, an' she tell'd dem, an' youah shuah dey soon put clothes an her, an' when she wuz dressed up, deah warn't a lady in de land more han'some nor her, an' his folks wor in delight av her.

Now, dey says: 'We'll have a supper for goers an' comers an' all gentry to come at.' Youah shuah it should be a 'spensible supper an' no savation of no money. And deah wuz to be tales tell'd an' songs sing'd, an' everywan dat didn't sing't a song had to tell't a tale; an' every door wuz bolted for fear any wan would mek a skip out.

An' it kem to pass to dis Gypsy gal to sing a song; an de gentleman dat fun' her says: 'Now, my pretty Gypsy gal, tell a tale'; an' de gentleman dat wuz her husband knowed her, an didn't want her to tell a tale, and he says: 'Sing a song, my pretty Gypsy gal.'

An' she says: 'I won't sing a song, but I'll tell a tale.' An' she say -

> Bobby rag! Bobby rag!
> Roun' de oak tree—

'Pooh! pooh!' says her husband, 'dat tale won't do.' (Now, de ole mother an' de son, dey knowed what wuz comin' out.) 'Go an! my pretty Gypsy gal!' says de oder young gentleman. 'A werry nice tale indeed!'

So she goes an —

> Bobby rag! Bobby rag!
>   Roun' de oak tree.
> A Gypsy I wuz born'd;
>   A lady I wuz bred;
> Dey made me a coffin
>   Afore I wuz dead.

'An' dats de rogue deah!' An' she tell't all de tale into de party, how he wur agoin' to kill her, an' tek her heart and pluck home.

An' all de gentry took'd an' gibbeted him alive, both him an' his mother; an' dis young squire married her, an' med her a lady for life. 'Ah!' concludes Johnny musingly, 'ef we could know her name, an' what breed she wur, what a beautiful ting dat would be, but de tale doan' say.'

This story of Johnny Gray's is described as 'one of the old *Märchen* current among the Gypsies when he was a lad, but now less frequently heard, and looked down on as "poor simple things" by the younger generation.' It is an idiosyncratic variant of this tale type. Sampson glosses 'parable' as 'apparel'.

Doctor Forster

Source: T. W. Thompson mss, Bodleian Library, Eng. misc., c765, pp. 55–70.
Narrator: Eva Gray at Grimsby, 18 November 1914.
Type: AT955 'The Robber Bridegroom'.

THER'S A CERTAIN PLACE down in the South of England – I shall call its name to mind just now – where one 'n these white chalky roads runs for twenty miles betwixt gret large woods. On both sides 'n the road the trees hangs right over all the whol way; in fact in some parts they join in the middle, and you med think as you was going through a tunnel. People going on the road would stop and peer into the woods, but you couldn't see in not above a yard or two, they was that thick. They was that thick even as game and varmint couldn't live there, and all the wild creatures as anybody ever sin was a few birds and a squir'l or two, and ther was precious few of them. It was the handsomest bit o' road in all England, they say: for the whol twenty miles ther wa'n't not a single house nor a dwelling of any kind, excepting one very large hotel, which stood by the roadside at a place where ther was a bit of clearing in the woods.

It was a very notified place this hotel was. All the coaches used to stop there to change horses, and gentlemen and ladies used to come and visit it from miles around. It was fitted upon parpose for their intertainment. Ther was a croquet ground at the back for gentlemen, all properly fitted up. Ther was a gret range of stables for their horses, with twenty or thirty ostlers just to look after 'em; and ther was kennels for the hounds as well. Inside it was just the same: ther was everything as anybody could think of for intertaining ladies and gentlemen. Downstairs was a big billiard room where they used to howld towrnaments and that, and upstairs was what they called the 'long ballroom' – a very fine room that was – where they used to have dances twice a week, on Wednesdays and Saturdays. Then of course ther was the lounge, and the smoking room, and the dinner room, and a very large supper room: in fact ther was everything.

The landlord of this hotel, and his family, they was wonderful interprising people – al'ays getting summat up. They had a meet of hounds there twice a month, and the tother weeks very likely they'd have a coursing match instead; and they had dances, and supper parties, and concerts, and games and towrnaments of all soarts. No matter what day you went there ther'd be sure to be summat going on, summer and winter alike. Ther' was just the one son, a very sporty young gentleman of about twenty-fower or twenty-three years of age; and they'd only but one daughter too. She was just turned twenty-two, and such a handsome girl you never sin in your life. Everybody as come to the hotel used to pass remarks on her good looks, and even the ladies was bound to admit as she was handsome, so she must ha' bin. And such a nice young lady she was too: such a nice feeling way she had with her. She used to help in the bar – a very select bar this one was where nobody served excepting the family. It was where all the squires and lords and that used to go, and of course they was very fond of having a bit of chat with her; that goes without saying.

Now among the young gentlemen as used to come reg'lar to this hotel ther was one as was called Squire King Kaley. Both a squire and a king he was, and Mr Kaley was his plain name. No matter what time o' day you called you'd be sure to find him there. He was a tall, dark, very handsome young gentleman, well set up, and al'ays dressed in the height of fashion, though very quiet mind, and he had very good manners and very taking ways with him. He al'ays come on horseback – gen'rally what he used to ride a little chestnut blood-mare with a star on its forehead and four white feet – and as soon as ever he got in at the gate you should ha' sin the way the ostlers run to wait on him. They al'ays used to give his horse a spicially good brush down, and they'd wash its legs and that, and put it in the best stall. They knew what they was a-doing on: ther wa'n't anybody as come to the hotel as tipped them as large as what Squire King Kaley did. (Not 'at they ever asked for anything. Oh! dear no. Such a thing wa'n't allowed on there.) Inside the house he was just as free with his money. He'd order champagne and wine by the bottle, and whisky and spirits as well, and often he'd pay for a dinner all round, or a supper or summat. And he was al'ays foremost in everything, no matter what was going on.

This Squire King Kaley he was on partic'lar friendly terms with the landlord's son. He'd often ask him to come for rides with him, or have a game of billiards, or anything else he was doing: in fact they was nearly al'ays together. And after a time he begun to pay attentions to the daughter. It got more and more noticeable every day this did. He never let a chance slip past him of having a bit of chat with her across the counter, and if ther was nobody else in the bar you'd be sure to find him there. Very noticeable that was. She had a liking for him too: in fact she was very fond of him: in a way you med even say they was two sweethearts, though she'd never bin for a walk with him nor nothing like that. Her father and mother wouldn't never have allowed on such a thing: they kept her very strict.

Well, one day when they was talking together over the counter same as two sweethearts do (How do they? I'm sure I don't know), he asked her would she come and have dinner with him at his home tomorrow night at eight o'clock. 'You know, my dear,' he says, 'never a day passes but what I come to see you, and yet you've never as much as once bin to see me. I should like for you,' he says, 'to meet my mother and sisters. Why only last night,' he says, 'they was saying how anxious they was to see you.' 'Well I don't think as I can,' she says. 'Father and mother is that strict with me they're sure to say no.' 'If you don't,' he says, 'you can't care much about me, and I sha'n't never come to see you again,' 'Oh! it isn't as I don't want to,' she says, 'for ther's nothing in all the world as I should like better, and of course I shall ask my father and mother.' She'd really med up her mind to go whatever they said. 'Very well then,' he says, 'I shall expect you.' 'Oh! no,' she says. 'I don't think as they'll consent, not for one minute. But in case they should,' she says, 'how shall I find my way, and how shall I know your house when I get there, for you must remember,' she says, 'as I've never bin afore? In fact,' she says, 'I don't even know whereabouts you live.' It was the truth: she didn't. He'd bin scoares and scoares o' times to the hotel but he'd never once said where he lived; he'd never towld none 'n 'em. 'Oh! I'll soon arrange for that, my dear,' he says. 'I'll kill a pig from your doar to mine, and you must follow the bloodstains.' 'Very well,' she says, 'I'll do my best to get off, but don't expect me,' she says, 'whatever you do.' 'I shall,' he says, 'and if you disappoint me I'll never come a-nigh you again.' Wi' that he went off.

She sat herself down and thought it all over. She'd go, yes she'd go whatever come or went. And she'd go on Bessy, she decided. Bessy was a little black mare she had: it was a blood-mare, and a wonderful fast trotter: it could do a mile in three minutes any time o'day. Of course she was a good rider; that goes without saying: she'd rode to hounds ever since she was no height, and ther wa'n't a fence or a ditch anywheres about as she couldn't jump. She'd soon be ther on Bessy, she thought, even if it was a long way, and after when it was all over Bessy would soon bring her home again. She wouldn't be afeard of anything if she was on Bessy, not even if she had to come back by herself in the night, but Squire King Kaley would never let her do that; she was sure he wouldn't, quite sure he wouldn't. It was a bit funny though, she thought, as nobody knew where he lived; and killing a pig from her doar to his, well that was a bit funny too. Such a ancivilized thing to do! Still it might be the custom where he come from, she thought, and very likely he didn't think nothing of it. Anyway she'd go: she'd med up her mind to that, of course she'd ask her father and mother first and see what they said, but in any case she'd go. She did wonder what his mother and sisters would be like, and how they'd receive her.

Her brother comes into the bar. 'Oh! George,' she says, 'Squire King Kaley has asked me to go to dinner with him tomorrow night.' 'Hm!' he says, 'I thought ther must be summat atween you and him, else he'd never ha' took so much notice o' me. But I'm glad to hear of it, Lily,' he says, ''cause he is a real squire for you now: he's not only squire by name but he's got squire's ways to him.' 'Would you go George if you was me?' she asks him. 'Yes,' he says; 'why ever not, Lily?' 'Oh!' she says, 'I wa'n't quite sure whether it'd be alright or not, but of course if you say so, George . . .' 'Now look here, Lily,' he says, 'don't you go saying as I said you should go. I know your ways. You go and ask your father and mother.'

She'd better try her mother first, she thought, so she goes and tells her all about the invitation. 'Well,' says her mother, 'I should strongly advise you not to go, Lily. Ther's no knowing what young gentlemen is.' 'But Mr Kaley, mother! Surely he is alright; him a squire both in his position and his ways. Why I've heard you say so yourself many a time.' 'Yes,' says her mother, 'he's everything as you say when he's here, but we don't know what he is at home.' 'Oh! how can you say that mother when we all know him so well? Why he's George's greatest friend.' 'For sure he is,' says her mother, 'and I'd be the very last to say anything again him, but bear in mind ther's other things to tek into account.' 'What, mother, what?' 'Well,' says her mother, 'whereabouts does he live? We don't none 'n us know that though he comes here so reg'lar, and meks such friends of us all. It med be a long way off, and in any case how are you going to find his house if you don't know where it is?' 'Oh!' says Lily, 'he's arranged for all that: he's going to kill a pig from my doar to his, and I'm to follow the bloodstains.'

'Well!' says her mother, 'whoever heeard 'n such a thing! Outlandish, I call it, right down heathenish.' 'Oh! it's nothing, mother,' says Lily, 'very likely it's the custom where he lives and when a thing is the custom nobody thinks nothing of it.' 'But supposing you do go how shall you get back home again, Lily?' her mother asks. 'You know as well as I do child as it's not fit for a young girl to be out by herself at night-times in such lonesome country.' 'Don't you fret yourself about that, mother,' she says, 'for Squire King Kaley is sure to see me home, and even if he don't I shall be alright on Bessy.' 'Well,' says her mother, 'you'd better go and see your father about it. It isn't for me to say.'

So she went to ask her father now. What nonsense, he said. He'd never heeard of a young girl wanting to do such a thing. Squire King Kaley med be alright as a customer – he'd nothing to say again him on that scoare – and he med be alright as George's friend – he'd never objected to that – but for her to ever think of going to his house by herself, and late at night – she must be out of her senses. And lots more like that he said. Of course she must begin to cry when she sin how he was carrying on: she was an artful little miss. 'It's my only chance, father,' she sobbed, 'for if I don't go he's never coming a-nigh the place again. Oh! it's cruel, cruel!' She took on so about it that her father begun to come round a bit. 'Well, if you must go,' he says, 'mind and you go on the fastest horse we've got, and then if ther is any mischief . . .' 'Oh! Yes, father,' she says, 'I'm going on Bessy. There!' she says, 'I knew you would never stand in my way.'

Next day she got herself up in a nice black riding habit with one of them owld-fashioned long skirts – they was more becoming she thought 'an the newfangled soart – and she put on a hard hat – black it was too – and a nice black veil. She had her whip in her hand and everything just ready to start when she bethought herself as she might as well to tek some of the little fancy cakes and tarts and custards and mince pies as she'd bin abaking of the day afore. It would show his mother and sisters, she thought, what she could do – and she was a very good cook mind, ther was no mistake about that. So she went and got about thirty of 'em altogether, one kind or another, and tied 'em up in a nice white silk handkerchief all ready to tek with her. Then she rung the bell for the ostler to bring Bessy round to the front doar, which he did. He'd give it an extra good brush down – you could see yourself in its coat – and he'd put on the very best bridle and side-saddle they had in the stables. He hands her up and away she goes, waving 'em 'goodbye' all the way down the drive.

As soon as she gets out'n the gate she looks for the bloodstains, and there they was plain enough to see: they stood out well on the white chalky road. She goes straight on for miles and miles on this road betwixt the gret large woods, and every now and again she looks down for the bloodstains, and there they are right enough. It was in the summertime, and she *was* enjoying her ride under the cool of the trees, thinking how nice it would be at the end of it to sit down to dinner with Squire King Kaley and his mother and sisters. Presently she comes to a dead stop. The bloodstains has turned off down a side lane, and she follows this now, on and on and on, till they turn off again into a little bye path just wide enough for her to get down. They're much fainter now – the pig must ha' bin nearly dead by the time it got here, she thinks – but she can mek 'em out easy enough, and on she goes, and on and on and on. At last she begins to feel a bit tired – she must ha' come thirty miles, she thinks – at the very least – and Bessy is getting a bit tired as well. She thinks more about Bessy nor what she does about herself. 'Come Bessy,' she says, and she leans over and whispers in its ears, telling it what a lot of corn it will have when it gets there, and what a nice stable ther'll be for it to lie in and rest till it is time for her to come home. She gives it its wind for a few minutes and then on they go again, and afore very long they come to the end of the path. They pass through a gate into open fields. The bloodstains is very faint here, and she can only just mek 'em out. Ther's a gret tall hedge in front, and on it she spies a little bit of handkerchief dipped in blood, so over she goes. Then she comes to a gret broad ditch, and on the tother side is a cleft stick with a bit of bloodstained handkerchief on it. Over that she goes: it was a beautiful jump. She crosses one more field, and comes out into a road; then the bloodstains stops altogether. 'There now, Bessy, we're at the end of our journey,' she says, and so they was.

She looks round, and there in front of her is a fine, big mansion – newish it is and built of brick. This must be his house, she thinks, and she's all of a flutter with excitement. She rides up to the gate, where ther's a big brass plate affixed. Oh! that'll be his name plate, she thinks, and she reads it. 'Whatever is this?' she says. 'Doctor Forster.' Yes, that's what it says plain enough: 'Doctor Forster. Well: Fancy him going in a wrong name: Oh! I don't like the look of things,' she says, 'The best I can do is to go back home again at once.' She turns Bessy round. 'No,' she says, 'I'll go on now as I've come so far. Besides, poor Bessy wants her supper very bad.' She turns it over in her mind, and over and over again; then she wheels round and opens the gate and canters up the drive into the stable yard.

'Ostler!' she calls, 'ostler!' but nobody come. She calls again, and she calls a third time, but still she can't mek nobody hear. Well! she thinks, this is strange! When Squire King Kaley comes to my house ther's al'ays two or three ostlers runs out to meet him, but here ther isn't one to be found anywheres. I suppose I must stable Bessy myself, but I must say I didn't expect this. She tucks up her riding habit round her middle, and leads Bessy to the stables. The door is stood wide open, so she goes right in and looks round. What stables! she thinks. Nothing only but bare boards to lie on, not a bit of bedding of any kind anywheres to be sin, and the floar all wet and dirty with what the tother horses had done. Doesn't nobody never clean them out? She was sorry for Bessy. 'Poor Bessy!' she says, 'this is all the place ther is for you to lie in, and you used to things so different!' She looks in the crib, but ther's nothing there only but a little teeny bit of dirty, wet, trampled hay. She can't find nothing else anywheres, so she sheks this out so as to mek it seem a bit nicer nor what it was. 'Come Bessy,' she says, 'this is all ther is for you.' Bessy wouldn't have touched it at home, but she is so hungry she revours it up.

The young lady goes over to the house now, and as she crosses the yard she passes a tremendous big dog in a kennel. It was every bit as big as this tent the kennel was, and yet the dog could only just to say get into it: ther med be six inches or a foot to spare at the two sides, but ther certainly wa'n't more; nor yet in the height. It was bigger 'an the largest size of donkey, this dog was; in fact it was the largest dog in the world. But it didn't bark nor nothing as she goes past it; it didn't tek no notice on her at all.

Ther wa'n't a soul about anywheres as far as she could see. She knocked at two or three doars, but nobody answered her, and when she tried 'em she fun as they was locked. It was the same with every one till at last she got to a little side doar quite hid away where nobody would see it, and when she tried that it was open. She walked straight in, and fun herself in a little teeny room which was very very dirty; filthy dirty it was. Ther was nobody there excepting a very owld woman, all wizened up from age and lost in dirt; about ten tons of dirt she had on her. She was sitting down on the floar blowing up the fire; leastways she was blowing at two smowldering sticks laid one across the tother; dirty, wet, green sticks they was, and the smoke was summat awful. Every now and then she'd stop, and give a gret long hollow cough, then she'd at it again, blow, blow, blowing away. Well I didn't expect to find this in a palace, the young lady thinks, and she was nearly on the point of running away. But she plucks up her courage, and she asks the owld woman could she tell her if Squire King Kaley lived there, and whether he was at home or not. The owld woman doesn't answer her not a word; she doesn't even look up, but goes on blowing harder 'an ever afore. So she asks her again, and tells her how she's bin invited to dinner, and what a long journey she's had. The owld woman doesn't tek not the slightest notice; just goes on blowing away at her two sticks. She asks a third time, but again ther's no reply, only this time the owld woman's took with a coughing fit. Queerer and queerer, she thinks, but now as I am into the house I might as well to look round. Besides anything is better than this dirty owld woman a-coughing her insides out.

Ther was only but one doar leading out 'n this little room, so my young lady opens it and goes through. She finds herself now in a gret large room, a very grand room it was, quite becoming a palace. She looks 'round, but she can't see nobody nor nothing there, excepting a very fine poll-parrot hung up in a gret cage all over gilt. 'Ah! Pretty polly!' she says. 'Pretty polly!' But it didn't speak; only cocked its head this way and that way, and looked hard at her with its little bright beady eyes. 'Pretty polly!' she says. 'Oh! You *are* a pretty polly.' But still it didn't speak; only cocked its head on one side, and looked hard at her. 'Pretty polly! Sugar, polly! Polly have some sugar.' Still it wouldn't speak. 'Pretty polly! Pretty polly! Polly speak. Polly speak to me.' This time it did speak, and this is what it said. 'If Doctor Forster catch you here he'll mek your blood run cowld.' 'Oh! Polly! Pretty polly! Polly speak again.' 'If Doctor Forster catch you here he'll mek your blood run cowld. Pretty fair lady! Pretty fair lady! Pretty fair lady! G-o-o-u-t.' 'No, polly, no. I've come to see master.' 'Pretty fair lady! Pretty fair lady! Pretty fair lady! G-o-o-u-t.' 'But polly, pretty polly, where's master, polly?' 'Pretty fair lady! G-o-o-u-t.' 'But polly I must see master.' 'If Doctor Forster catch you here he'll mek your blood run cowld. Pretty fair lady! G-o.' 'I-f D-o-c-t-o-r F-o-r-s-t-e-r c-a-t-c-h m-e h-e-r-e h-e-'l-l m-e-k m-y b-l-o-o-d r-u-n c-o-w-l-d.' 'He will, pretty lady, he will, and if you don't believe me open that trap doar by your feet, and see what it can show. But, pretty fair lady, go afore it is too late.' She pulled up the trap doar and looked down, and what should she see but a gret cellar of blood. She screamed help and blue murders, and rushed out'n the room, past the owld woman blowing at her two crossed sticks, out'n the doar, and straight for Bessy's stable.

At that very minute who should come riding in at the gate but Squire King Kaley; that's Doctor Forster. She'd never ha' sin him very like she was in such an upset, if it hadn't bin for the gate banging, and as it is she has only just time to slip into the dog kennel as he comes riding past. She never stopped to think about the dog, but it didn't tek no notice on her at all; it never med a sound. Just as he is passing the kennel he throws a lady's hand to the dog, which it catches in its mouth. It's beginning to gnaw at it when she outs with her tarts and her custards and mince pies, and she shoves them down its throat instead. It drops the hand, which she picks up, and she puts it in her boosom. Then she slips quietly out, and meks straight to Bessy. 'Come Bessy,' she says as she jumps on its back; 'you must go for your life,' and Bessy understands. She's out'n the gate in the twinkling of an eye, but no sooner does she hear it bang behind her but what it bangs a second time. Squire King Kaley is coming after her.

He'd gone into the house expecting to find her there, and when he didn't he asked the owld woman – she was his mother the owld woman was, and she was a witch – he'd asked her if a young lady hadn't called to see him. Yes, she towld him, she'd bin, and she'd only just now gone, the very minute as he come in. Hadn't he met her on the doarstep? No, he hadn't, he said, and he swore and carried on summat awful, and scowlded her and that. Why hadn't she killed her herself, he asked, if she couldn't keep her till he come? 'Oh! I couldn't,' she says. 'Bad as I am I couldn't bring myself to it, she was such a pretty fair lady, and so young, and so innocent looking.' 'You soft-hearted owld fool,' he says, 'you've lost me the daintiest one as I ever had. But I'll catch her yet.' And wi' that he jumps on his horse, and gallops after her.

He could see her in front of him, and he calls out for her to stop, but she never as much as turns her head, only just leans for'ard and whispers to Bessy. 'Life or death, Bessy,' she says, 'which is it to be?' and Bessy goes like the wind. He could see he wa'n't gaining, so he calls out again. This time she does just turn her head, but she never slackened speed, not an inch. 'It'll be a hard race, Bessy,' she says, 'but we can do it.' And it *was* a hard race. She lay down on Bessy's back and rode like a wild thing, but all the time she could hear Squire King Kaley coming thud, thud, thud, clatter, clatter, clatter behind her. She thought she was gaining, but she couldn't be sure, ther was so little in it. Miles and miles she goes on like this, till at last she is certain as she's leaving him behind; the sounds was getting fainter and fainter. 'We're doing it Bessy, we're doing,' she says. 'Only another mile or two and then.' Squire King Kaley sin he was beaten now, but still he kept coming on, and it wa'n't until she was within sight of the hotel as he give up the chase. 'We've done it, Bessy,' she says, 'we've done it. You've saved my life.'

As soon as she got in she fainted right away – she hadn't had time to afore – but one dashed cowld water over her face, and another run into the bar for some brandy for her, and wi' one thing or another they soon had her round again. Whatever had happened to her, her mother wanted to know. Had somebody bin molesting of her? So she towld them the whol story right from the time when she left home, just the same as I've towld you. 'Yes,' she says, 'and when I got there I sin a brass name plate on the gate, and on it was "Doctor Forster".' 'Oh!' says her mother, 'so he isn't what he pretends to be. Didn't that mek you think of coming straight home, Lily?' 'Well, yes, it did, mother, but I thought I might as well to go on now when I had come all that way. And in the yard,' she says, 'was a tremendous big dog, bigger 'an the largest size of donkey it was.' 'Oh! dear,' says her mother, 'that would ha' bin enough for me.' 'But it was as quiet as a lamb, mother, and didn't tek not the leastest notice 'n me. And when I got inside,' she says, 'ther was a dirty wizened up owld woman wi' ten tons o' dirt on her blowing away at two smowldering, owld, green, wet sticks laid one across the tother.' 'Worse and worse,' says her mother. 'Whyever didn't you rush straight out to Bessy, and come home again as hard as ever you could? Wa'n't you frightened?' 'Well, I was a bit, mother, but I wanted to see what else ther was, so I went on and I got into a gret large room such a grand place, quite becoming a palace, and there I sin a poll-parrot hanging up in a gilt cage. I asked it where master was, but all it would say was "If Doctor Forster catch you here he'll mek your blood run cowld."' 'Well, now,' says her mother, 'didn't that frighten you? I should have screamed the place down.' 'No, mother,' she says, 'it didn't, not to say properly. Then when I asked it again the parrot says, "Pretty

fair lady! Pretty fair lady! Pretty fair lady! G-o-o-u-t", and it kept on a-saying it.'
'It wouldn't ha' had to tell me twice,' says her mother. 'I can't understand you,
Lily; you're timid enough at home. You must ha' bin very anxious to see this
Squire King Kaley.' 'Listen, mother,' she says. 'When I didn't go it towld me
to open the trap doar by my feet, which I did, and I sin a gret cellar of blood.'
'O-h!' says her mother, and she turned as white as a table cloth, and nearly
went off into a swownd. 'And just as I was rushing out'n the doar,' she says –
that's the young lady, 'who should come in at the gate but Squire King Kaley.
I slipped into the dog kennel, and as he come riding past he thro wed a lady's
hand to the dog.' Her mother was feeling a bit better again by now. 'So he's a
murderer then, is he?' she says. 'Yes,' says Lily, 'he's that at the very least. But
do listen mother. I got the tarts and that what I took with me and I shoved
'em down the dog's throat. He let go the hand, and I picked it and put it in
my boosom. Here it is,' she says, and she draws it out and puts it on the table.
'Then,' she says, 'I jumped on Bessy, and galloped home for my life, and Squire
King Kaley after me all the way, but we beat him, Bessy and me did.' 'It's a good
thing you was on Bessy,' says her mother. 'God bless her! She saved your life.'

Now her father had heeard all this, but so far he'd said nowt, not a word.
He was thinking. 'Well, Lily,' he says, after when she is come to the end of her
story, 'you bin very foolish, but you bin plucky as you bin foolish, and I'm very
glad of that. Anyway what's done can't be undone, and all we need bother about
now is to bring this Squire King Kaley to his end. We must be wily,' he says,
'and not show our hands till we've got him fast pinned and nailed. Now as his
plot has failed,' he says, 'his is sure to be here again tomorrow just as if nothing
had happened, and when he comes, Lily, you must be friendly to him and all
that like what you've al'ays bin, and you must mek up some story about how
you was prevented from going to his house last night, and say how sorry you
are, and how disappointed you bin. Tell him the tale proper – you can do it I
know if you set your mind to it – and as for everything else leave it to me. And
mind,' he says, 'let ther be no talking about what has happened when ther's any
customers in the house.'

Well, next day Squire King Kaley was there just as usual. Lily was in the bar
by herself when he come in – of course that was all arranged for – and when
she sin him her first thought was as she'd shoot him there and then. She had
a very handy little pistol which she'd loaded ready in case. How could she as
much as speak to him, she thought, let alone be pleasant and chatty; and as
for love meking, that was out of the question altogether. Still she managed it
all somehow. Oh! how pleased she was, she said, to see him again after what
he'd said about not coming again: she did lay it on. She'd bin all over anxiety,

she said, for fear as he'd tek offence at her not coming to dinner after when he'd bin as good as to ask her. She was very very sorry, she said, but really she couldn't help it a bit. She was just all ready to start, she said, when her mother was suddenly took ill, and her being the only daughter well of course she couldn't leave her. She was sure, she said, as he wouldn't want her to do such a thing, but if only he'd say he forgive her and be just the same to her as he used to be it would tek a terrible strain off her mind. Oh! yes, he said, he'd forgive her under the circumstances, though he had felt a bit hurt about her not coming. 'My mother and sisters,' he said, 'come about ten miles to meet you in the pony carriage, and they was nearly as disappointed as what I was when you didn't come.' 'Well, dear,' she says, 'I've towld you how very sorry I am, and as for being disappointed well nobody could be worse nor what I was. I bin crying pretty near all night,' she says. 'Well never mind,' he says, 'perhaps you'll come another time.' She'd be relighted to, she said, only she couldn't come this week, not now.

They was chatting away like two sweethearts when in comes her father, rubbing his hands – you know the way they has – and beaming all over his face. 'Ah! Squire King Kaley! Just the very gentleman as I want to see! Two brandies and sodas, Lily, and two of the best sixpenny cigars. Your good health, sir.' 'And yours, host.' 'And now, squire, I just want to have a word with you. It's about time,' he says, 'as we was getting up another intertainment – a supper I thought this time, and then afterwards how would it be if each one present was to tell a dream? It would be a bit of novelty that.' 'Capital,' says Squire King Kaley. 'Capital. It would be quite a novel idea in these parts.' 'Well I'm very glad as you think so,' says the landlord, ''cause I al'ays look to you, squire, to keep things going brisk. How would the night after next do: it's Thursday today; that'd be Saturday night? We could get everything ready by then, and ther'd be plenty o' time to let people know.' 'Very good,' says Squire King Kaley. 'I shall be there.' 'And you'll let all your gentleman friends know, won't you, squire? Ther's lots as'll come if they know as you're to be present, just for the sake o' being in your comp'ny.' 'Yes,' he says, Squire King Kaley does, 'I'll do everything as I can to mek it a success.' 'Thankyou, squire, thankyou,' says the landlord. 'I knowed as I could rely on you.' And wi' that he goes bustling out.

He goes straight to the telephone, and he telephones to Scotland Yard, and he tells 'em all what has happened to his daughter, and the arrangements what he's med for the supper on Saturday night. 'I want you,' he says, 'to send me down some retectives to tek the case in hand.' Very good, they said; they'd be sure not to fail him. It was very clever of him, they said, to have thought of such a plan.

Friday ther was a rare bustle going on at Scotland Yard if you could only ha'
sin it. They'd got everything worked out ready the night afore as to how they
should go on so as not to rouse no suspicions. Five or six of 'em was to go down
dressed up as farmers; gentlemen farmers some was to be, and some was to be
more like big dealing. This was just the class of people they thought as might
go to this hotel, and yet not be knowed to Squire King Kaley. Friday morning
they goes out and gets ther clothes, and then of course they must try 'em on
and that, which took 'em the better part of the afternoon. They left London by
the five o'clock train that same day and travelled as far as the nearest big town to
the hotel, which was p'rhaps fifteen or twenty miles distance away from it. They
wanted to be there in good time next day so as to look into things on the quiet
a bit first, and arrange exactly how they should go on at the supper.

It wouldn't be not long after dinner time on Saturday, when the first one
of 'em got to the hotel, and the tothers kept on dropping in by ones and twos
for another hour or so, some on horseback and some in gigs. Of course it
wouldn't never have done for 'em all to come in a bunch: people'd soon ha'
begun asking questions if they had. When they was all there the headmost
man among 'em asked if they could see the young lady in private, and they
got her to tell her story from beginning to end. When she'd finished the one
as was acting as spokesman asked if he could see the hand, so they brought it
him. 'Now, my dear,' he says, 'you must go and mek yourself up as a young
gentleman, and when your turn comes to give your dream you must tell the
story of your visit to Squire King Kaley just the same as you've towld it to us.
And when you come to the end,' he says, 'you must draw out the hand from
your pocket, and throw it on the table for proof.' Well, she'd do her best, she
said, but she didn't know however she was going to act the young gentleman
all through the evening. Would she have to smoke and that? Certainly, they
said, she must have a pipe, only she needn't smoke much, not unless she'd a
mind. And she needn't drink much neither, though a glass or two of port wine
would do her good; she'd be less timid-like after it. And now, they said, she
must go and dress herself up, as there wa'n't over much time to spare. So she
did, and presently she comes back in one 'n her brother's riding suits – a new
one it was which he'd never had on yet. She looked very fine in it too I can tell
you: she was a well built figure of a girl, and men's clothes just suited her. But
ther was her hair. What was she to do with that? A wonderful head of hair she
had too: it reached nearly down to her knees when she anloosed it. Well, one
'n the retectives teks it, and screws it up into next to nothing, and then he slips
a wig over it which he'd brought on purpose, a very nice dark brown wig, just
the colour to suit her eyes and her complexion. That was the finishing touch,

and you couldn't ha' towld now but what she was a young squire or summat; nobody could unless they'd looked very close.

The supper was a very grand affair in no mistake. Ther'd be close on a hundred people there I dar'say: all the squires and hunting gentlemen, and the better class of farmers and dealing men for miles round, ther was hardly one 'n 'em but was present. And of course my young lady was there in her disguise, and the retectives in theirs; one here, one somewhere else they was, all scattered up and down the room. As soon as ever supper is over and the tables has bin cleared the chairman gets up and calls for order. 'Gentlemen,' he says, 'we're to have a very novel intertainment tonight. Instead of a song or a tale,' he says, 'each one has to tell a dream.' They all clapped ther hands at this. 'Very Good.' 'Very Good.' 'And now, gentlemen,' he says, 'the first as I shall call upon is Squire King Kaley.' Squire King Kaley jumps up at once, and as soon as they sin him stood up all the people clapped him and cheered him and that, for he was very pop'lar among 'em. 'Gentlemen,' he says, 'a night or two since I dreamed as I med an appointment with a handsome young lady to come to my house to dinner at eight o'clock. ('Oh! Kaley!' 'I can well believe it Mr Kaley!') And,' he says, 'I was looking for'ard to her coming with a gret deal of pleasure ('No doubt you was, Kaley!' 'Very true, Kaley!'), so you can judge how disappointed I was,' he says, 'when she didn't turn up. ('Better luck next time, Kaley!' 'Go on, Mr Kaley!') In fact,' he says, 'I was that disappointed I wakened up.' He sat down, and they all clapped and cheered him again. 'Very Good, Kaley.' 'Well towld, Mr Kaley.' Then the chairman calls on somebody else, and he give his dream, and so it went on till ther was nobody left only just the young lady.

She'd bin sitting through it all with her legs crossed and her pipe in her mouth just like any other young gentleman, though if you'd took special notice on her you'd ha' sin as she didn't smoke not above two or three draws at a time – she couldn't stomach it at all. Still, she'd played her part wonderful well, and ther wa'n't anybody in the room, excepting of those in the know, as suspected she was anything but what she 'peared. Well, the chairman gets up again. 'Gentlemen,' he says, 'everybody has now towld his dream, all but this young gentleman here,' and he turns to the young lady. 'I don't know your name,' he says, 'in fact you're quite a stranger to me; but I'm very glad I'm sure to see you at our party tonight, and I hope as it won't be the last time as you'll do us the honour of your comp'ny. And now,' he says, 'as everybody present must tell ther dreams I must call on you to give us yours.'

My young lady stood up, and everybody give her a right good clap. 'Gentlemen,' she says, 'I dreamed the tother night as I was a young lady.' They pricked up their ears at this; you know how they would. It's going to be int'resting this is, they thought. 'And,' she says, 'a gentleman med an appointment with me to go to his house to dinner at eight o'clock.' 'Must ha' bin Kaley,' one of 'em calls out, but of course it was meant only in fun, and Squire King Kaley laughed as much as any of 'em, more in fact. 'And,' she says, 'as I didn't know the way he said as he'd kill a pig from my doar to his.' Kaley looked up at this: he was a bit startled. 'And when I got there,' she says, 'I sin a name plate on the gate, and on it was "Doctor Forster". He'd gi'n me a false name it 'pears.' Kaley was getting quite uneasy by now. 'Cut it short,' he says. 'It's too long, and everybody is getting tired of it.' 'Go on, sir; it's very int'resting,' somebody else calls out. 'Hear! Hear! Go on, sir.' They was all for him going on. 'Well,' she says, 'as I crossed the yard I sin a gret large dog, bigger 'an the largest size of donkey.' Squire King Kaley is getting more and more uneasy. 'He must have had a good look round,' he thinks, 'I wonder what can he ha' bin after!' He didn't suspect what was coming though. 'And when I got inside,' she says, 'ther was a dirty wizened up owld woman wi' ten tons o' dirt on her blowing up the fire, which was nothing only but two green, wet, smowldering sticks one laid across the tother.' Kaley begun to smell summat now. 'What a long dream!' he says. 'Let's turn it off into a song.' 'Shut up, Kaley.' 'Tek no notice on him, sir.' 'Go on, sir. Go on.' Some was shouting one thing and some another, and they all wanted to hear the end 'n it, all excepting Squire King Kaley. The chairman call 'em to order, and then the young lady goes on again. 'And then,' she says, 'I got into a gret large room quite becoming a castle where ther was a poll-parrot hung up in a gilt cage. I asked it where master was, but all it would say was: "If Doctor Forster catch you here he'll mek your blood run cowld." And it towld me to go. "Pretty fair lady!" it says, "Pretty fair lady! Pretty fair lady! G-o o-u-t." It kept on saying this, and then as I didn't go it towld me to open up the trap door by my feet, which I did, and I sin a gret cellar of blood.' At this Squire King Kaley got up to go. 'You must excuse me,' he says, 'but I shall ha' to go. You know what a long ride I got and how late it is already.' 'No, no, Kaley.' 'Sit down.' 'Sit down.' They all called for him to sit down again. 'I'm very sorry,' he says, 'but I really must go. I'd hoped,' he says, 'as this'd be a short dream so as I could stop to hear it out, 'cause as you know, gentlemen, I've al'ays bin again anybody going afore the end of a party.' 'Sit down, Kaley.' 'Sit down.' 'Sit down,' and they all made him sit down. Then the chairman gets up, and says how sorry he is as anything like this should ha' happened, and how surprised he is at Squire King Kaley. Ther must be no more interrupting, he says, and no one is to go till the end, no matter how long the dream is. They all clapped this except Squire King Kaley, and he sat still, as white as death, and the sweat powring off him. The young lady goes on with the story now. 'And as I rushed out'n the house,' she says, 'who should come riding in at the gate but Squire King Kaley. It was him,' she says, 'as med the appointment with me, and this was his house.' Kaley sprung up out'n his seat but the retectives collared howld'n him. 'Go on,' they says to the young lady. 'Go on.' 'I hid in the dog kennel,' she says, 'and as he come riding past he throwed in a lady's hand to the dog, but I shoved the tarts and that down its throat, and it let go the hand, which I picked up and put in my boosom. Then I slipped out to Bessy, and jumped on her back, and rode for dear life, him following hard after me all the way. But we beat him,' she says, 'we beat him. It was Bessy,' she says, 'as saved my life.' 'It's a lie,' says Kaley. 'It's a lie.' 'It's the truth,' she says. 'It's the truth. And here is the hand to show,' and she drawed it from her pocket, and throwed it down on the table.

In a minute they was all of an uproar: they'd have pulled Kaley limb from limb only the headmost retective calls for order. 'Silence,' he says, and he teks a paper from his pocket. 'Squire King Kaley,' he says, 'I arrest you in the name of the law on the charge of murdering young ladies. Culprit,' he says, 'have you anything to say?' Kaley didn't open his mouth; he was dumbfounded. So they put the handcuffs on him and led him away, but just as they was doing so one young gentleman what had bin examining of the hand calls out for them to stop. 'I can 'dentify this hand,' he says, 'by the ring what is on it: it belongs to my sweetheart.' He drawed off the ring. 'Now look,' he says, 'whose name is that inside it?' They looked, and it was his right enough.

At the trial Squire King Kaley pleaded guilty, and the judge condemned him to be hanged. Just afore the sentence was carried out they asked him had he any favour he would like to ask as his last on earth. Yes, he had, he said; he'd just one thing he would like to beg of them: could he go home and wring that poll-parrot's neck first? But they wouldn't allow 'n it, and they took him and hanged him at the crossroads on the gallows tree, and if you was to go past tomorrow you'd find his bones still there.

———

Eva Gray was born in Lowestoft in 1858. She was highly regarded as a storyteller, and T. W. Thompson notes that 'Doctor Forster' was 'Eva's favourite tale'. Thompson's original notes of the narration are in Notebooks 4 and 5 in the Brotherton Collection, under the title 'The Cellar of Blood'. There is also another full version in Notebook D, under the present title. All three texts relate to the same telling, though the change of title has misled Katharine

Briggs into listing it as two separate stories. Eva apparently did know two other stories about 'Squire King Kaley': 'Sorrow and Love' (p. 71) and another which was never recorded.

The great clutter of supporting detail in this story is what the Grays particularly prized in Eva's storytelling. Thompson writes:

'What I like about Eva,' said Shanny on one occasion, 'is the way she can fill in as she goes along: I've never heard her equal for that. However she comes to think of it all I can't make out; and it's all so natural, so intimate like, you think she must ha' bin there and sin it all for herself from the way she pictures it. And the little sly touches she puts in; she'll make you laugh with 'em many a time they're so true on the nail.'

'Doctor Forster' has none of the concentrated power of 'The Story of Mr Fox' (p. 137) or 'Bobby Rag' (p. 142). Instead there is a short-story writer's slow build up, with named characters and realistic, psychologically acute dialogue. But the realism only goes so far: the dream-telling party and disguise are not required by the modern short story elements – the detectives could just make an arrest – but are necessary for the emotionally satisfactory unmasking of the villain. The detail is marshalled brilliantly. Everything has its purpose: the white road to show up blood, the dog kennel to hide in. Important moments are marked by repetition, which is also a feature of the tale's structure. But the three-fold repetition is not dull: notice, for instance, how in the final showdown Eva keep's Kaley's reaction in the forefront, to savour his comeuppance.

The reconstruction of this long tale was problematic. T. W. Thompson seems to me to have been particularly sensitive in his paragraphing of the text, in long scenes which give the story a filmic quality. He has kept the interesting and meaningful fluctuations of tense, and manages to convey something of the special qualities of Eva Gray's narrative gift. This was not easy, as she has little of the linguistic vivacity of a showman storyteller such as Taimi Boswell. Instead, wrote Thompson,

Eva's greatest asset . . . in producing the illusion of reality is her impassioned recital of the tale, which unfortunately cannot be conveyed in the printed text. She sweeps you along without pause from beginning to end, words pouring from her lips in a torrent, her hands, her eyes, her face, her whole body reinforcing their meaning and significance. The modulations of her voice, the mimicry, the aptness of the phrasing, you hardly notice these separately they are so perfectly in accord with the theme.

The story of 'Sir Richard Baker, surnamed "Bloody Baker"' (Briggs, *Dictionary*, Part B, vol. 2, pp. 353–4) has many similarities to 'Doctor Forster', including the parrot with its warning rhyme:

> Peepoh, pretty lady, be not too bold,
> Or your red blood will soon run cold.

T. W. Thompson stresses that the sing-song refrain, 'If Doctor Forster catch you here he'll mek your blood run cowld', was invariable, and uses it several times as an example of 'parroted' phrases in folktales. Interestingly, in the earliest notebook version of 'Doctor Forster' the phrase does not occur. It reads, 'If I did speak I could tell you summat as would make your blood run cowld.'

Captain Murderer

Source: Charles Dickens, 'Nurse's Stories', *The Uncommercial Traveller*, 1860
(first published in *All the Year Round*).
Narrator: Dickens remembering the narration of Mary Weller.
Type: AT311 'Three Sisters Rescued from the Mountain'.

THE FIRST DIABOLICAL CHARACTER who intruded himself on my peaceful youth (as I called to mind that day at Dullborough), was a certain Captain Murderer. This wretch must have been an offshoot of the Blue Beard family, but I had no suspicion of the consanguinity in those times. His warning name would seem to have awakened no general prejudice against him, for he was admitted into the best society and possessed immense wealth. Captain Murderer's mission was matrimony, and the gratification of a cannibal appetite with tender brides. On his marriage morning, he always caused both sides of the way to church to be planted with curious flowers; and when his bride said, 'Dear Captain Murderer, I never saw flowers like these before: what are they called?' he answered, 'They are called Garnish for house-lamb,' and laughed at his ferocious practical joke in a horrid manner, disquieting the minds of the noble bridal company, with a very sharp show of teeth, then displayed for the first time. He made love in a coach and six, and married in a coach and twelve, and all his horses were milk-white horses with one red spot on the back which he caused to be hidden by the harness. For, the spot *would* come there, though every horse was milk-white when Captain Murderer bought him. And the spot was young bride's blood. (To this terrific point I am indebted for my first personal experience of a shudder and cold beads on the forehead.) When Captain Murderer had made an end of feasting and revelry, and had dismissed the noble guests, and was alone with his wife on the day month after their marriage, it was his whimsical custom to produce a golden rolling-pin and a silver pie-board. Now, there was this special feature in the Captain's courtships, that he always asked if the young lady could make pie-crust; and if she couldn't by nature or education, she was taught. Well. When the bride saw Captain Murderer produce the golden rolling-pin and silver pie-board, she remembered this, and turned up her laced-silk sleeves to make a pie. The Captain brought out a silver pie-dish of immense capacity, and the Captain brought out flour and butter and eggs and all things needful, except the inside of the pie; of materials for the staple of the pie itself, the Captain brought out none. Then said the lovely bride, 'Dear Captain Murderer, what pie is this to be?' He replied, 'A meat pie.' Then said the lovely bride, 'Dear Captain Murderer, I see no meat.' The Captain humorously retorted, 'Look in the glass.' She looked in the glass, but still she saw no meat, and then the Captain roared with laughter, and suddenly frowning and drawing his sword, bade her roll out the crust. So she rolled out the crust, dropping large tears upon it all the time because he was so cross, and when she had lined the dish with crust and had cut the crust all ready to fit the top, the Captain called out, 'I see the meat in the glass!' And the bride looked up at the glass, just in time to see the Captain cutting her head off; and he chopped her in pieces, and peppered her, and salted her, and put her in the pie, and sent it to the baker's, and ate it all, and picked the bones.

Captain Murderer went on in this way, prospering exceedingly, until he came to choose a bride from two twin sisters, and at first didn't know which to choose. For, though one was fair and the other dark, they were both equally beautiful. But the fair twin loved him, and the dark twin hated him, so he chose the fair one. The dark twin would have prevented the marriage if she could, but she couldn't; however, on the night before it, much suspecting Captain Murderer, she stole out and climbed his garden wall, and looked in at his window through a chink in the shutter, and saw him having his teeth filed sharp. Next day she listened all day, and heard him make his joke about the house-lamb. And that day month, he had the paste rolled out, and cut the fair twin's head off, and chopped her in pieces, and peppered her, and salted her, and put her in the pie, and sent it to the baker's, and ate it all, and picked the bones.

Now, the dark twin had had her suspicions much increased by the filing of the Captain's teeth, and again by the house-lamb joke. Putting all things together when he gave out that her sister was dead, she divined the truth and determined to be revenged. So, she went up to Captain Murderer's house, and knocked at the knocker and pulled at the bell, and when the Captain came to the door said: 'Dear Captain Murderer, marry me next, for I always loved you and was jealous of my sister.' The Captain took it as a compliment, and made a polite answer, and the marriage was quickly arranged. On the night before it, the bride again climbed to his window, and again saw him having his teeth filed sharp. At this sight she laughed such a terrible laugh at the chink in the shutter, that the Captain's blood curdled, and he said: 'I hope nothing has disagreed with me!' At that, she laughed again, a still more terrible laugh, and the shutter was opened and search made, but she was nimbly gone, and there was no one. Next day they went to church in a coach and twelve, and were married. And that day month, she rolled the pie-crust out, and Captain Murderer cut her head off, and chopped her in pieces, and peppered her, and salted her, and put her in the pie, and sent it to the baker's, and ate it all, and picked the bones.

But before she began to roll out the paste she had taken a deadly poison of a most awful character, distilled from toads' eyes and spiders' knees; and Captain Murderer had hardly picked her last bone, when he began to swell, and to turn blue, and to be all over spots, and to scream. And he went on swelling and turning bluer, and being more all over spots and screaming, until he reached from floor to ceiling and from wall to wall; and then, at one o'clock in the morning, he blew up with a loud explosion. At the sound of it, all the milk-white horses in the stables broke their halters and went mad, and then they galloped over everybody in Captain Murderer's house (beginning with the family blacksmith who had filed his teeth) until the whole were dead, and then they galloped away.

Mary Weller, Dickens's childhood nurse, seems to have specialized in tales of the Mr Fox/Robber Bridegroom/Bluebeard type. In his Christmas story 'The Holly Tree', he writes, concerning his memories of inns:

My first impressions of an Inn dated from the Nursery; consequently I went back to the Nursery for a starting-point, and found myself at the knee of a sallow woman with a fishy eye, an aquiline nose, and a green gown, whose specialty was a dismal narrative of a landlord by the roadside, whose visitors unaccountably disappeared for many years, until it was discovered that the pursuit of his life had been to convert them into pies. For the better devotion of himself to this branch of industry, he had constructed a secret door behind the head of the bed; and when the visitor (oppressed with pie) had fallen asleep, this wicked landlord would look softly in with a lamp in one hand and a knife in the other, would cut his throat, and would make him into pies; for which purpose he had coppers, underneath a trap-door, always boiling; and rolled out his pastry in the dead of the night. Yet even he was not insensible to the stings of conscience, for he never went to sleep without being heard to mutter, 'Too much pepper!' which was eventually the cause of his being brought to justice. I had no sooner disposed of this criminal than there started up another of the same period, whose profession was originally house-breaking; in the pursuit of which art he had had his right ear chopped off one night, as he was burglariously getting in at a window, by a brave and lovely servant-maid (whom the aquiline-nosed woman, though not at all answering the description, always mysteriously implied to be herself). After several years, this brave and lovely servant-maid was married to the landlord of a country Inn; which landlord had this remarkable characteristic, that he always wore a silk nightcap, and never would on any consideration take it off. At last, one night, when he was fast asleep, the brave and lovely woman lifted up his silk nightcap on the right side, and found that he had no ear there; upon which she sagaciously perceived that he was the clipped housebreaker, who had married her with the intention of putting her to death. She immediately heated the poker and terminated his career, for which she was taken to King George upon his throne, and received the compliments of royalty on her great discretion and valour. This same narrator, who had a Ghoulish pleasure, I have long been persuaded, in terrifying me to the utmost confines of my reason, had another authentic anecdote within her own experience, founded, I now believe, upon *Raymond and Agnes, or the Bleeding Nun.* She said it happened to her brother-in-law, who was immensely rich – which my father was not; and immensely tall – which my father was not. It was always a point with this Ghoul to present my dearest relations and friends to my youthful mind under circumstances of disparaging contrast. The brother-in-law was riding once through a forest on a magnificent horse (we had no magnificent horse at our house), attended by a favourite and valuable Newfoundland dog (we had no dog), when he found himself benighted, and came to an Inn. A dark woman opened the door, and he asked her if he could have a bed there. She answered yes, and put his horse in the stable, and took him into a room where there were two dark men. While he was at supper, a parrot in the room began to talk, saying, 'Blood, blood! Wipe up the blood!' Upon which one of the dark men wrung the parrot's neck, and said he was fond of roasted parrots, and he meant to have this one for breakfast in the morning. After eating and drinking heartily, the immensely rich, tall brother-in-law went up to bed; but he was rather vexed, because they had shut his dog in the stable, saying that they never allowed dogs in the house. He sat very quiet for more than an hour, thinking and thinking, when, just as his candle was burning out, he heard a scratch at the door. He opened the door, and there was the Newfoundland dog! The dog came softly in, smelt about him, went straight to some straw in the corner which the dark men had said covered apples, tore the straw away, and disclosed

two sheets steeped in blood. Just at that moment the candle went out, and
the brother-in-law, looking through a chink in the door, saw the two dark
men stealing upstairs; one armed with a dagger that long (about five feet);
the other carrying a chopper, a sack, and a spade. Having no remembrance
of the close of this adventure, I suppose my faculties to have been always so
frozen with terror at this stage of it, that the power of listening stagnated
within me for some quarter of an hour.

What we can say for sure is that her stories sank deeply into Dickens's
consciousness, and images from them influence much of his work. Who can
doubt that the figure of Carker in *Dombey and Son*, with his 'gleaming teeth' and
his 'fox's hide', draws his strength from these folktale models? Mr Murdstone
in *David Copperfield* and Rigaud in *Little Dorrit* both echo aspects of Captain
Murderer. Dickens writes:

Hundreds of times did I hear this legend of Captain Murderer, in my early
youth, and added hundreds of times was there a mental compulsion upon
me in bed, to peep in at his window as the dark twin peeped, and to revisit
his horrible house, and look at him in his blue and spotty and screaming
stage, as he reached from floor to ceiling and from wall to wall. The young
woman who brought me acquainted with Captain Murderer had a fiendish
enjoyment of my terrors, and used to begin, I remember – as a sort of
introductory overture – by clawing the air with both hands, and uttering
a long low hollow groan. So acutely did I suffer from this ceremony in
combination with this infernal Captain, that I sometimes used to plead I
thought I was hardly strong enough and old enough to hear the story again
just yet. But, she never spared me one word of it.

Its influence is felt yet again in the story of the 'Bride's Chamber' inserted in
The Lazy Tour of Two Idle Apprentices.

The Wooden Leg

Source: Augustus Hare, *The Story of My Life*, 1900, vol. 5, pp. 33–8.
Narrator: Mrs Henry de Bunsen, 5 October 1877, at Gatton.

THERE WAS, AND THERE is still, living in Cadogan Place, a lady of middle age, who is clever, charming, amiable, even handsome, but who has the misfortune of having – a wooden leg. Daily, for many years, she was accustomed to amble every morning on her wooden leg down Cadogan Place, and to take the air in the Park. It was her principal enjoyment.

One day she discovered that in these walks she was constantly followed by a gentleman. When she turned, he turned: where she went, he went: it was most disagreeable. She determined to put an end to it by staying at home, and for some days she did not go out at all. But she missed her walks in the Park very much, and after a time she thought her follower must have forgotten all about her, and she went out as before. The same gentleman was waiting, he followed her, and at length suddenly came up to her in the Park and presented her with a letter. He said that, as a stranger, he must apologise for speaking to her, but that he must implore her to take the letter, and read it when she got home: it was of great importance. She took the letter, and when she got home she read it, and found that it contained a violent declaration of love and a proposal of marriage. She was perfectly furious. She desired her lawyer to enclose the letter to the writer, and say that she could not find words to describe her sense of his ungentlemanly conduct, especially cruel to one afflicted as she was with a wooden leg.

Several years elapsed, and the lady was paying a visit to some friends in the country, when the conversation frequently turned upon a friend of the house who was described as one of the most charming, generous, and beneficent of mankind. So delightful was the description, that the lady was quite anxious to see the original, and was enchanted when she heard that he was likely to come to the house. But when he arrived, she recognized with consternation her admirer of the Park. He did not, however, recur to their former meeting, and after a time, when she knew him well, she grew to esteem him exceedingly, and at last, when he renewed his proposal after an intimate acquaintance, she accepted him and married him.

He took her to his country house, and for six weeks they were entirely, uncloudedly happy. Then there came a day upon which he announced that he was obliged to go up to London on business. His wife could not go with him because the house in Cadogan Place was dismantled for the summer. 'I should regret this more,' he said, 'but that where two lives are so completely, so entirely united as ours are, there ought to be the most absolute confidence on either side. Therefore, while I am away, I shall leave you my keys. Open my desk, read all my letters and journals, make yourself mistress of my whole life. Above all,' he said, 'there is one cupboard in my dressing-room which contains certain memorials of my past peculiarly sacred to me, which I should like you to make yourself acquainted with.' The wife heard with concern of her husband's intended absence, but she was considerably buoyed up under the idea of the three days in which they were to be separated by the thought of the very interesting time she would have. She saw her husband off from the door, and as soon as she heard the wheels of his carriage die away in the distance, she clattered away as fast as she could upon her wooden leg to the dressing-room, and in a minute she was down on all fours before the cupboard he had described.

She unlocked the cupboard. It contained two shelves. On each shelf was a long narrow parcel sewn up in canvas. She felt a tremor of horror as she looked at them, she did not know why. She lifted down the first parcel, and it had a label on the outside. She trembled so she could scarcely read it. It was inscribed – 'In memory of my dear wife Elizabeth Anne, who died on 24 August 1864.' With quivering fingers she sought for a pair of scissors and ripped open the canvas, and it contained – a wooden leg!

With indescribable horror she lifted down the other parcel, of the same form and size. It also bore a label – 'In memory of my dearest wife Wilhelmine, who died on 6 March 1869', and she opened it, and it contained – another wooden leg!

Instantly she rose from her knees. 'It is evident,' she said, 'that I am married to a Blue Beard – a monster who *collects* wooden legs. This is not the time for sentiment, this is the time for action', and she swept her jewels and some miniatures that she had into a handbag and she clattered away on her own wooden leg by the back shrubberies to the highroad – and there she saw the butcher's cart passing, and she hailed it, and was driven by the butcher to the nearest station, where she just caught the next train to London, intending to make good her escape that night to France and to leave no trace behind her.

But she had not consulted Bradshaw, and she found she had some hours to wait in London before the tidal train started. Then she could not resist employing them in going to reproach the people at whose house she had met her husband, and she told them what she had found. To her amazement they were not the least surprised. 'Yes,' they said, 'yes, we thought he ought to have told you: we do not wonder you were astonished. Yes, indeed, we knew dear Elizabeth Anne very well; she was indeed a most delightful person, the most perfect of women and of wives, and when she was taken away, the whole light seemed blotted out of Arthur's life, the change was so very terrible. We thought he would never rally his spirits again; but then, after two years, he met dearest Wilhelmine, to whom he was first attracted by her having the same affliction which was characteristic of her predecessor. And Wilhelmine was perhaps even a more charming person than Elizabeth Anne, and made her husband's life uncloudedly happy. But she too was, alas! early snatched away, and then it was as if the whole world was cut from under Arthur's feet, until at last he met you, with the same peculiarity which was endeared to him by two lost and loved ones, and we believe that with you he has been even more entirely, more uncloudedly happy than he was either with Wilhelmine or Elizabeth Anne.

And the wife was so charmed by what she heard, that it gave quite a new aspect to affairs. She went home by the next train. She was there when her husband returned; and ever since they have lived perfectly happily between his house in the country and hers in Cadogan Place.

This is, as Katharine Briggs puts it, 'a kind of Bluebeard in reverse'. It is interesting to note that authenticating such stories by attributing them to 'a friend of a friend' is no modern phenomenon. The clinching moment of Mrs de Bunsen's narrative came when she claimed that

> a cousin of hers was repeating this story when dining at the Balfours'.
> Suddenly he saw that his host and hostess were both telegraphing frantic
> signals to him, and by a great effort he turned it off. The lady of the
> wooden leg and her husband were both amongst the guests.

In fact the story of 'The Wooden Leg' can be traced to a short story contributed to the March 1859 number of Dickens's *Household Words* by 'Hesba Stretton' (Sarah Smith), entitled 'The Lucky Leg'. It is possible that she was drawing on an oral source, but just as likely that this negative print of Bluebeard was purely her invention, which then made its way into the oral tradition.

Augustus Hare, who recorded it, had an ineradicable thirst for stories and storytelling (see pp. 367–76 for some of the ghost stories recorded in his massive autobiography), and his own powers as a narrator were much admired in the upper social circles of Victorian England. His next diary entry after this records a visit to Tennyson – 'he has an abrupt, bearish manner, and seems thoroughly hard and unpoetical' – during which 'Tennyson insisted that I should tell him some stories.' There is a biography of Hare by Malcolm Barnes.

Wanted, a Husband

Source: T. W. Thompson, 'Twelve Clod's Tales', *JGLS*, 3rd series, vol. 21, 1942.
pp. 7–8.
Narrator: Reuben Gray at Old Radford, Nottinghamshire on 22 December 1914.
Type: AT955 'The Robber Bridegroom' (variant).

ONCE ON A TIME, when I was a handsome young fellow, an' that ain't bin so very long ago as you can see, I was teking a walk down the street into this very town o' Nottingham when I sin big notices up everywheres, an' heeard the bellman crying, as how some grand lady was in want of a husband. Very good looking she was s'posed to be, an' had no end o' money: in fact I believe she was a princess. Sa I ta'en pertie'lar note'n what sort of a man it was she wanted. Dark he had to be, an' very handsome; not too tall, nor yet too short. That's just me, I thought to myself; an' so it was, mind you – exac'ly my describance. Thinks I to myself then, I'll go tomorrow an' reply for this job, 'specially as she's got plenty o' money, for that's a thing I can do wi'.

Howsoever, I got talking wi' some men in the street, an' towld 'em my intention. 'Don't you go,' they says, 'for she's had seven husbands already, this lady has, an' there's nobody knows what's become on 'em. Ne'er a trace'n any a one of 'em is to be found,' they says. Well, I thought, that don't sound nice; but all the same I'll venture. She won't find me as easy to get rid on as these tothers.

So next day I went an' replied. A maid-servant answered the door, an' axed me had I come to marry the missis. 'Yes,' I says, 'if she's willing.' She went an' towld the lady I was waiting; an' presently she come back to say as I was to go in an' let her – that's the missis – have a look at me. In I went as bowld as brass. Yes, I'd do fine, she said: in fact I was just the very man she was wanting. An' a day or two after – to cut my story short – we was married. A grand wedding an' all we had, I can tell you.

The first night we was together I woke up very early: about the middle'n the night it must ha' bin. My missis wa'n't there. This is very queer, I thought. Howsoever, I turned over an' went to sleep agen; an' next time I wakened up there she was right enough. It was nearly getting up time by then. 'Well, my dear,' I says, 'an' have you had a good night?' 'Yes, thank you,' she says. 'An' you?' 'Very good, thank you, my dear,' I says. The second night it was just the same. By then I was a bit suspicious: I would be, wouldn't I? So the third night I foxed; I didn't go to sleep at all. It would be about the middle'n the night when she slips out o'bed, dresses herself very quietly, puts on some soft slippers, an' goes creeping, creeping downstairs. I followed wi'out letting her see me. She goes pid-padding out'n the house, an' down a little path till she comes to some graves. There is one wi' the soil all loose. She scoops this away wi' her hands, an' gets right down into the grave. I crept close up. There she is, sitting eating little bits o' flesh an' bone. 'Hello! my dear,' I says; 'an' what might you be eating of?' 'CORPSE, YOU BUGGER, CORPSE.'

One word in the final sentence is supplied from the manuscript version in Notebook 6 in the Brotherton Collection. Katharine Briggs classifies this as a variant of AT363 'The Vampire'.

The Hand of Glory

Source: William Henderson, *Notes on the Folklore of the Northern Counties of England and the Borders*, 1866, pp. 201–2.
Narrator: Bella Parkin, High Spital, Co. Durham.
Type: AT956b 'The Clever Maiden Alone at Home Kills the Robbers'.

ONE EVENING, BETWEEN THE years 1790 and 1800, a traveller, dressed in woman's clothes, arrived at the Old Spital Inn, the place where the mailcoach changed horses, in High Spital, on Bowes Moor. The traveller begged to stay all night, but had to go away so early in the morning, that if a mouthful of food were set ready for breakfast, there was no need the family should be disturbed by her departure. The people of the house, however, arranged that a servant-maid should sit up till the stranger was out of the premises, and then went to bed themselves. The girl lay down for a nap on the long settle by the fire, but before she shut her eyes she took a good look at the traveller, who was sitting on the opposite side of the hearth, and espied a pair of man's trousers peeping out from under the gown. All inclination for sleep was now gone; however, with great self-command, she feigned it, closed her eyes, and even began to snore. On this the traveller got up, pulled out of his pocket a dead man's hand, fitted a candle to it, lighted the candle, and passed hand and candle several times before the servant-girl's face, saying as he did so, 'Let those who are asleep be asleep, and let those who are awake be awake.' This done, he placed the light on the table, opened the outer door, went down two or three of the steps which led from the house to the road, and began to whistle for his companions. The girl (who had hitherto had presence of mind enough to remain perfectly quiet) now jumped up, rushed behind the ruffian, and pushed him down the steps. She then shut the door, locked it, and ran upstairs to try and wake the family, but without success: calling, shouting, and shaking were alike in vain. The poor girl was in despair, for she heard the traveller and his comrades outside the house. So she ran down again, seized a bowl of blue [skimmed milk], and threw it over the hand and candle; after which she went upstairs again, and awoke the sleepers without any difficulty. The landlord's son went to the window, asked the men outside what they wanted. They answered that if the dead man's hand were but given them, they would go away quietly, and do no harm to anyone. This he refused, and fired among them, and the shot must have taken effect, for in the morning stains of blood were traced to a considerable distance.

Bella Parkin told this story to Charles Wastell, claiming to be the daughter of the courageous servant-girl. Stories of burglars using a 'hand of glory' to put a household to sleep, but being routed by a resourceful girl, were popular in Yorkshire. Sabine Baring-Gould contributed two further versions to Henderson, and there are several in Richard Blakeborough's books and in his manuscript, known as the Naitby Diary, at Sheffield University. The Calvert Folklore Manuscript at the University of Leeds, which dates from the 1820s, contains a North Riding 'true Recipt for the Pickleing and Claiming of a Hand of Glory'. Versions of this tale without the 'hand of glory' have been recorded in West Norfolk, Kent and elsewhere; John Clare mentions the chapbook of '"Idle Lawrence" who carried that power-spell about him that laid every body to sleep' (*Autobiographical Prose*, p. 56). The best is Noah Lock's 'The Robber and the Housekeeper' (in T. W. Thompson, 'English Gypsy Folk-Tales, and Other Traditional Stories', *JGLS*, new series, vol. 8). Dickens's nurse Mary Weller's tale of the 'brave and lovely servant-maid' (see p. 164) is also of this type.

The Old Man at the White House

Source: S. O. Addy, 'Four Yorkshire Folktales', *Folk-Lore*, 7, 1897, pp. 393–4.
Narrator: C. R. Hirst, aged eighteen, Sheffield/Wakefield.
Type: AT366 'The Man from the Gallows'.

THERE WAS ONCE A man who lived in a white house in a certain village, and he knew everything about everybody that lived in the place.

In the same village there lived a woman who had a daughter called Sally, and one day she gave Sally a pair of yellow kid gloves and threatened to kill her if she lost them.

Now Sally was very proud of her gloves, but she was careless enough to lose one of them. After she had lost it she went to a row of houses in the village and inquired at every door if they had seen her glove. But everybody said 'No'; and she was told to go and ask the old man that lived in the white house.

So Sally went to the white house and asked the old man if he had seen her glove. The old man said: 'I have thy glove, and I will give it thee if thou wilt promise me to tell nobody where thou hast found it. And remember if thou tells anybody I shall fetch thee out of bed when the clock strikes twelve at night.' So he gave the glove back to Sally.

But Sally's mother got to know about her losing the glove, and said: 'Where did thou find it?'

Sally said: 'I daren't tell, for if I do an old man will fetch me out of bed at twelve o'clock at night.'

Her mother said: 'I will bar all the doors and fasten all the windows, and then he can't get in and fetch thee'; and then she made Sally tell her where she had found her glove.

So Sally's mother barred all the doors and fastened all the windows, and Sally went to bed at ten o'clock that night and began to cry. At eleven she began to cry louder, and at twelve o'clock she heard a voice saying in a whisper, but gradually getting louder and louder:

'Sally, I'm up one step.'
'Sally, I'm up two steps.'
'Sally, I'm up three steps.'
'Sally, I'm up four steps.'
'Sally, I'm up five steps.'
'Sally, I'm up six steps.'
'Sally, I'm up seven steps.'
'Sally, I'm up eight steps.'
'Sally, I'm up nine steps.'
'Sally, I'm up ten steps.'
'Sally, I'm up eleven steps.'
'Sally, I'm up twelve steps!'
'Sally, I'm at thy bedroom door!!'
'Sally, I have hold of thee!!!'

This tale is related to AT366 only by the shock climax. Addy was concerned about its unnerving quality, and wrote, 'It is hoped that this tale will not be reprinted in any book intended for children.'

The Golden Arm

Source: Contributed by Sabine Baring-Gould to William Henderson, *Notes on the Folklore of the Northern Counties of England and the Borders*, 1866, pp. 338–9.

Narrator: Unknown.

Type: AT366 'The Man from the Gallows'.

THERE WAS ONCE A man who travelled the land all over in search of a wife. He saw young and old, rich and poor, pretty and plain, and could not meet with one to his mind. At last he found a woman young, fair and rich, who possessed the supreme, the crowning glory, of having a right arm of solid gold. He married her at once, and thought no man so fortunate as he was. They lived happily together, but, though he wished people to think otherwise, he was fonder of the golden arm than of all his wife's gifts besides.

At last she died. The husband appeared inconsolable. He put on the blackest black, and pulled the longest face at the funeral; but for all that he got up in the middle of the night, dug up the body, and cut off the golden arm. He hurried home to secrete his recovered treasure, and thought no one would know.

The following night he put the golden arm under his pillow, and was just falling asleep, when the ghost of his dead wife glided into the room. Stalking up to the bedside it drew the curtain, and looked at him reproachfully. Pretending not to be afraid, he spoke to the ghost, and said, 'What hast thou done with thy cheeks so red?' 'All withered and wasted away,' replied the ghost, in a hollow tone.

'What hast thou done with thy red rosy lips?' – 'All withered and wasted away.'

'What hast thou done with thy golden hair?' – 'All withered and wasted away.' 'What hast thou done with thy *Golden Arm*?' – 'Thou hast it!'

Baring-Gould notes, 'The dialogue progresses in horror, till at the close, the ghost's exclamation is shrieked out at the top of the narrator's voice, the candle extinguished, and the young auditors duly panic-stricken. No one desires to know what became of the avaricious husband.'

This is one of the most frequently recorded stories in English tradition: partly, perhaps, because it is so short and memorable. Many English nursery stories are of a horrific or macabre nature: nannies, as Jonathon Gathorne-Hardy notes in his section on 'Terror by Story-Telling: The Nanny as Bard' in *The Rise and Fall of the British Nanny* (1972), seem to have specialized in frighteners.

The Briggs *Dictionary* gives ten British variants of AT366. In its most basic form, the tale type concerns a poor man driven through hunger to steal flesh from a corpse on the gallows, which the corpse then seeks to regain. Many versions, however, substitute greed for hunger, as here, with motif E.235.4.1 *Return from dead to punish theft of golden arm from grave.*

Joseph Jacobs bases his retelling in *English Fairy Tales* on this text; in his note he observes, 'Sir E. Burne-Jones remembered hearing it in his youth in Warwickshire, where I have also traces of it as "The Golden Leg".' George Sturt's childhood memory of the tale, from his underrated memoir *A Small Boy in the Sixties* (1927, pp. 141–2), is particularly valuable because it is concerned to record the atmosphere, content and manner of the telling, and its meaning to the listener, as well as the words:

My father and mother, glad of the day's rest, spent those Sunday afternoons upstairs in the Front Room, dozing a good deal; and that they might be the quieter, we children were packed off downstairs, in charge of Eliza, the maid-of-all-work – hardly more than a child herself, but expected (as is the fate of working-class girls) to show a little steadier common-sense than other children.

Eliza (the hired girl usually had that name bestowed on her, if it was not already her own) was willing enough, so far as I know, to romp with us, or to chatter. It seems to me I owe to one of the Elizas on one of these Sunday afternoons a certain 'startler', too good to be forgotten. It began in a sepulchral undertone, telling how a girl, having a mistress with a golden arm, stole the arm when her mistress died. And at night, going to bed, the girl saw that a certain cupboard door was open. (I knew that door very well. It was in the corner of a bedroom I sometimes slept in, at my grandmother's at Farnborough – a black door in a shadowy corner.) So, the door being open, the girl shut it. It opened again, and she shut it and locked it. It opened again and out walked her mistress's skeleton. 'Where's your beautiful bright blue eyes?' the girl asked. 'All mouldered away and gone,' said the skeleton, in a low and measured graveyard voice.

'Where's your beautiful flaxen hair?'
'All mouldered away and gone.'
'Where's your beautiful golden arm?'

'YOU got it! YOU got it!'

        This in sudden scream to make you jump.

The Story of the Three Little Pigs

Source: J. O. Halliwell, *The Nursery Rhymes of England* (1842), 1970 reprint, pp. 29–31.

Narrator: Unknown.

Type: AT124 'Blowing the House In'.

ONCE UPON A TIME there was an old sow with three little pigs, and as she had not enough to keep them, she sent them out to seek their fortune. The first that went off met a man with a bundle of straw, and said to him, 'Please, man, give me that straw to build me a house'; which the man did, and the little pig built a house with it. Presently came along a wolf, and knocked at the door, and said –

'Little pig, little pig, let me come in.'

To which the pig answered –

'No, no, by the hair of my chiny chin chin.'

The wolf then answered to that –

'Then I'll huff, and I'll puff, and I'll blow your house in.'

So he huffed, and he puffed, and he blew his house in, and ate up the little pig.

The second little pig met a man with a bundle of furze, and said, 'Please, man, give me that furze to build a house'; which the man did, and the pig built his house. Then along came the wolf, and said –

'Little pig, little pig, let me come in.'

'No, no, by the hair of my chiny chin chin.'

'Then I'll puff, and I'll huff, and I'll blow your house in.'

So he huffed, and he puffed, and he puffed, and he huffed, and at last he blew the house down, and he ate up the little pig.

The third little pig met a man with a load of bricks, and said, 'Please, man, give me those bricks to build a house with'; so the man gave him the bricks, and he built his house with them. So the wolf came, as he did to the other little pigs, and said –

'Little pig, little pig, let me come in.'

'No, no, by the hair of my chiny chin chin.'

'Then I'll huff, and I'll puff, and I'll blow your house in.'

Well, he huffed, and he puffed, and he huffed, and he puffed, and he puffed, and he huffed; but he could *not* get the house down. When he found that he could not, with all his huffing and puffing, blow the house down, he said, 'Little pig, I know where there is a nice field of turnips.' 'Where?' said the little pig. 'Oh, in Mr Smith's Home-field, and if you will be ready tomorrow morning I will call for you and we will go together, and get some for dinner.' 'Very well,' said the little pig, 'I will be ready. What time do you mean to go?' 'Oh, at six o'clock.' Well, the little pig got up at five, and got the turnips before the wolf came – which he did about six – and who said, 'Little pig, are you ready?' The little pig said, 'Ready! I have been, and come back again, and got a nice potful for dinner.' The wolf felt very angry at this, but thought that he would be *up to* the little pig somehow or other, so he said, 'Little pig, I know where there is a nice apple-tree.' 'Where?' said the pig. 'Down at Merry-garden,' replied the wolf, 'and if you will not deceive me I will come for you, at five o'clock tomorrow, and we will go together and get some apples.' Well, the little pig bustled up the next morning at four o'clock, and went off for the apples, hoping to get back before the wolf came; but he had further to go, and had to climb the tree, so that just as he was coming down from it, he saw the wolf coming, which, as you may suppose, frightened him very much. When the wolf came up he said, 'Little pig, what! are you here before me? Are they nice apples?' 'Yes, very,' said the little pig. 'I will throw you down one'; and he threw it so far, that, while the wolf was gone to pick it up, the little pig jumped down and ran home. The next day the wolf came again, and said to the little pig, 'Little pig, there is a fair at Shanklin this afternoon, will you go?' 'Oh yes,' said the pig, 'I will go; what time shall you be ready?' 'At three,' said the wolf. So the little pig went off before the time as usual, and got to the fair, and bought a butter-churn, which he was going home with, when he saw the wolf coming. Then he could not tell what to do. So he got into the churn to hide, and by so doing turned it round, and it rolled down the hill with the pig in it, which frightened the wolf so much, that he ran home without going to the fair. He went to the little pig's house, and told him how frightened he had been by a great round thing which came down the hill past him. Then the little pig said, 'Hah, I frightened you then. I had been to the fair and bought a butter-churn, and when I saw you, I got into it, and rolled down the hill.' Then the wolf was very angry indeed, and declared he *would* eat up the little pig and that he would get down the chimney after him. When the little pig saw what he was about, he hung on the pot full of water, and made up a blazing fire, and, just as the wolf was coming down, took off the cover, and in fell the wolf; so the little pig put on the cover again in an instant, boiled him up, and ate him for supper, and lived happy ever afterwards.

ᴂᏅᎣᴗ

Andrew Lang's version of this story in his *Green Fairy Book* (1892) has no provenance and is probably just a retelling of Halliwell's text. Joseph Jacobs surmises in his note to the story in *English Fairy Tales* that, 'As little pigs do not have hair on their chinny chin-chins, I suspect that they were originally kids, who have.' Other versions, however, generally seem to feature geese rather than pigs or kids, as in 'The History of the Celebrated Nanny Goose' (1813) and 'The History of the Prince Renardo and the Lady Goosiana' (1833), children's stories reprinted in one volume by Judith St John (1973), and the verse telling, 'The Fox and the Geese' in Cundall's *A Treasury of Pleasure Books for Young People* (1856; given in Briggs, *Dictionary*, Part A, vol. 2, pp. 524–8). Perhaps the nearest to Halliwell's text is the story of 'The Fox and the Pixies' printed in the *Athenaeum* in 1846. K. M. Briggs suggests (*Dictionary*, Part A, vol. 2, p. 530) that the 'pixies' in this may be a confusion of 'pigs' with the Devon 'pigsies'.

The Old Woman and Her Pig

Source: J. O. Halliwell, *The Nursery Rhymes of England*, 1842, pp. 159–60.
Narrator: Unknown, contributed by Mr Black.
Type: AT2030 'The Old Woman and Her Pig'.

'AN OLD WOMAN WAS sweeping her house, and she found a little crooked sixpence. "What," said she, "shall I do with this little sixpence? I will go to market, and buy a little pig." As she was coming home, she came to a stile: but piggy would not go over the stile.

'She went a little further, and she met a dog. So she said to the dog, "Dog! bite pig; piggy won't go over the stile; and I shan't get home tonight." But the dog would not.

'She went a little further, and she met a stick. So she said, "Stick! stick! beat dog; dog won't bite pig; piggy won't get over the stile; and I shan't get home tonight." But the stick would not.

'She went a little further, and she met a fire. So she said, "Fire! fire! burn stick; stick won't beat dog; dog won't bite pig," (*and so forth, always repeating the foregoing words*). But the fire would not.

'She went a little further, and she met some water. So she said, "Water! water! quench fire; fire won't burn stick," &c. But the water would not.

'She went a little further, and she met an ox. So she said, "Ox! ox! drink water; water won't quench fire," &c. But the ox would not.

'She went a little further, and she met a butcher. So she said, "Butcher! butcher! kill ox; ox won't drink water," &c. But the butcher would not.

'She went a little further, and she met a rope. So she said, "Rope! rope! hang butcher; butcher won't kill ox," &c. But the rope would not.

'She went a little further, and she met a rat. So she said, "Rat! rat! gnaw rope: rope won't hang butcher," &c. But the rat would not.

'She went a little further, and she met a cat. So she said, "Cat! cat! kill rat; rat won't gnaw rope," &c. But the cat said to her, "If you will go to yonder cow, and fetch me a saucer of milk, I will kill the rat." So away went the old woman to the cow.

'But the cow said to her, "If you will go to the haymakers and fetch me a wisp of hay, I'll give you the milk." So away the old woman went, but the haymakers said to her – "If you will go to yonder stream, and fetch us a bucket of water, we'll give you the hay." So away the old woman went, but when she got to the stream, she found the bucket was full of holes. So she covered the bottom with pebbles, and then she filled the bucket with water, and away she went back with it to the haymakers; and they gave her a wisp of hay; and she brought the hay to the cow.

'As soon as the cow had eaten the hay, she gave the old woman the milk; and away she went with it in a saucer to the cat.

'As soon as the cat had lapped up the milk, the cat began to kill the rat; the rat began to gnaw the rope; the rope began to hang the butcher; the butcher began to kill the ox; the ox began to drink the water; the water began to quench the fire; the fire began to burn the stick; the stick began to beat the dog; the dog began to bite the pig; the little pig in a fright jumped over the stile; and so the old woman got home that night.'

I have substituted Halliwell's alternative version of the 'wisp of hay' paragraph. The original runs:

> But the cow said to her, 'If you will go to yonder haystack, and fetch me a handful of hay, I'll give you the milk.' So away went the old woman to the haystack; and she brought the hay to the cow.

This comical narrative was once very widely known, and a number of versions exist, all fairly similar to each other, including a second in Halliwell's pioneering collection. Seamus Ennis collected a text from Ben Baxter of Southrepps for the BBC in November 1955 (BBC Sound Archive, Record 22157). Thomas Radcliffe's memories of the tale as told to him in Derbyshire in the mid nineteenth century (*Notes and Queries*, 10, iii, 1905, pp. 74–5) include some lively dialect that brings us closer to a genuine oral telling than Halliwell's gentrified 'yonder': 'Dog, dog, bite pig; pig wunner goo o'er th'brig, an' Ah shonner get home to-night!' The old woman is finally helped by a man, and 'The most interesting bit in the story . . . was that the man was Christ himself.' Radcliffe recalls that 'the children used to make a ring, and as they rattled off, "The cat began to kill the rat," etc., danced around merrily.' This connects the tale with children's singing games.

Richard Blakeborough also testifies that 'the children tell the story'. His version (*Wit, Character, Folklore and Customs of the West Riding of Yorkshire*, pp. 263–5) opens with a rhyme evidently influenced by the nursery rhyme, 'There was a crooked man'. Blakeborough offers a fanciful interpretation of the story in terms of Norse mythology, and his text may reflect his conviction that it contained such a meaning. The old woman prays to the wind, and 'a voice among the trembling leaves' orders the brook to sleek the fire, etc. The Briggs *Dictionary* (Part A, vol. 2, p. 538) prints a verse text, 'I went to market and bought me a cat', from *Word-Lore* (1, pp. 274–5), 'Learned in childhood by the late George Sweetman of Wincanton, and subsequently recorded by him'. Opie and Opie's *The Oxford Nursery Rhyme Book* prints a verse chapbook text (pp. 207–9).

The cumulative sequence in 'The Old Woman and her Pig', especially in the Derbyshire version in which Christ appears, stands in an interesting and problematic relation to a hymn in the *Sepher Haggadah*, traditionally sung at Passover, of which the final verse runs:

> Then came *the Holy One*, blessed be He!
> And killed the angel of death,
> That killed the butcher,
> That slew the ox,
> That drank the water,
> That quenched the fire,
> That burned the staff,
> That beat the dog,
> That bit the cat,
> That ate the kid,
> That my father bought
> For two pieces of money: A kid, a kid.

Titty Mouse and Tatty Mouse

Source: J. O. Halliwell, *The Nursery Rhymes of England* (1842), 1970 reprint, pp. 227–8.
Narrator: Unknown.
Type: AT2022 'The Death of the Little Hen'.

Titty Mouse and Tatty Mouse both lived in a house,
Titty Mouse went a leasing, and Tatty Mouse went a leasing,
    So they both went a leasing.

Titty Mouse leased an ear of corn, and Tatty Mouse leased an ear of corn,
    So they both leased an ear of corn.

Titty Mouse made a pudding, and Tatty Mouse made a pudding,
    So they both made a pudding.

And Tatty Mouse put her pudding into the pot to boil,
    But when Titty went to put hers in, the pot tumbled over, and scalded her to death.

Then Tatty sat down and wept; then a three-legged stool said, Tatty, why do you weep? Titty's dead, said Tatty, and so I weep; then said the stool, I'll hop, so the stool hopped; then a besom in the corner of the room said, Stool, why do you hop? Oh! said the stool, Titty's dead, and Tatty weeps, and so I hop; then said the besom, I'll sweep, so the besom began to sweep; then said the door, Besom, why do you sweep? Oh! said the besom, Titty's dead, and Tatty weeps, and the stool hops, and so I sweep; then said the door, I'll jar, so the door jarred; then said the window, Door, why do you jar? Oh! said the door, Titty's dead, and Tatty weeps, and the stool hops, and the besom sweeps, and so I jar; then said the window, I'll creak, so the window creaked. Now there was an old form outside the house, and when the window creaked, the form said, Window, why do you creak? Oh! said the window, Titty's dead, and Tatty weeps, and the stool hops, and the besom sweeps, the door jars, and so I creak; then said the old form, I'll run round the house; then the old form ran round the house. Now there was a fine large walnut-tree growing by the cottage, and the tree said to the form, Form, why do you run round the house? Oh! said the form, Titty's dead, and Tatty weeps, and the stool hops, and the besom sweeps, the door jars, and the window creaks, and so I run round the house; then said the walnut-tree, I'll shed my leaves, so the walnut tree shed all its beautiful green leaves. Now there was a little bird perched on one of the boughs of the tree, and when all the leaves fell, it said, Walnut-tree, why do you shed your leaves? Oh! said the tree, Titty's dead, and Tatty weeps, the stool hops, and the besom sweeps, the door jars, and the window creaks, the old form runs round the house, and so I shed my leaves; then said the little bird, I'll moult all my feathers, so he moulted all his pretty feathers. Now there was a little girl walking below, carrying a jug of milk for her brothers' and sisters' supper, and when she saw the poor little bird moult all its feathers, she said, Little bird, why do you moult all your feathers? Oh! said the little bird, Titty's dead, and Tatty weeps, the stool hops, and the besom sweeps, the door jars, and the window creaks, the old form runs round the house, the walnut-tree sheds its leaves, and so I moult all my feathers; then said the little girl, I'll spill the milk, so she dropt the pitcher and spilt the milk. Now there was an old man just by on the top of a ladder thatching a rick, and when he saw the little girl spill the milk, he said, Little girl, what do you mean by spilling the milk, your little brothers and sisters must go without their supper; then said the little girl, Titty's dead, and Tatty weeps, the stool hops, and the besom sweeps, the door jars, and the window creaks, the old form runs round the house, the walnut-tree sheds all its leaves, the little bird moults all its feathers, and so I spill the milk; Oh! said the old man, then I'll tumble off the ladder and break my neck; and when the old man broke his neck, the great walnut-tree fell down with a crash, and upset the old form and house, and the house falling knocked the window out, and the window knocked the door down, and the door upset the besom, the besom upset the stool, and poor little Tatty Mouse was buried beneath the ruins.

———

This very widely distributed rhyme about a pointless calamity is perhaps best known as the Grimms' 'The Louse and the Flea'. There are Scottish texts, but this is the only English one.

The Story of Chicken-Licken

Source: J. O. Halliwell, *Popular Rhymes and Nursery Tales of England*, 1849, pp. 29–51.

Narrator: Unknown.

Type: AT2033 'A Nut Hits the Cock's Head'.

As Chicken-licken went one day to the wood, an acorn fell upon her poor bald pate, and she thought the sky had fallen. So she said she would go and tell the king that the sky had fallen. So chicken-licken turned back, and met Hen-len. 'Well, hen-len, where are you going?' And hen-len said, 'I'm going to the wood for some meat.' And chicken-licken said, 'Oh! hen-len, don't go, for I was going, and the sky fell upon my poor bald pate, and I am going to tell the king.' So hen-len turned back with chicken-licken, and met Cock-lock. 'Oh! cock-lock, where are you going?' And cock-lock said, 'I'm going to the wood for some meat.' Then hen-len said, 'Oh! cock-lock, don't go, for I was going, and I met chicken-licken, and chicken-licken had been at the wood, and the sky had fallen on her poor bald pate, and we are going to tell the king.'

So cock-lock turned back, and met Duck-luck. 'Well, duck-luck, where are you going?' And duck-luck said, 'I'm going to the wood for some meat.' Then cock-lock said, 'Oh! duck-luck, don't go, for I was going, and I met hen-len, and hen-len met chicken-licken, and chicken-licken had been at the wood, and the sky had fallen on her bald pate, and we are going to tell the king.'

So duck-luck turned back, and met Drake-lake. 'Well, drake-lake, where are you going?' And drake-lake said, 'I'm going to the wood for some meat.' Then duck-luck said, 'Oh! drake-lake, don't go, for I was going, and I met cock-lock, and cock-lock met hen-len, and hen-len met chicken-licken, and chicken-licken had been at the wood, and the sky had fallen on her poor bald pate, and we are going to tell the king.'

So drake-lake turned back, and met Goose-loose. 'Well, goose-loose, where are you going?' And goose-loose said, 'I'm going to the wood for some meat.' Then drake-lake said, 'Oh! goose-loose, don't go, for I was going, and I met duck-luck, and duck-luck met cock-lock, and cock-lock met hen-len, and hen-len met chicken-licken, and chicken-licken had been at the wood, and the sky had fallen on her poor bald pate, and we are going to tell the king.'

So goose-loose turned back, and met Gander-lander. 'Well, gander-lander, where are you going?' And gander-lander said, 'I'm going to the wood for some meat.' Then goose-loose said, 'Oh! gander-lander, don't go, for I was going, and I met drake-lake, and drake-lake met duck-luck, and duck-luck met cock-lock, and cock-lock met hen-len, and hen-len met chicken-licken, and chicken-licken had been at the wood, and the sky had fallen on her poor bald pate, and we are going to tell the king.'

So gander-lander turned back, and met Turkey-lurkey. 'Well, turkey-lurkey, where are you going?' And turkey-lurkey said, 'I'm going to the wood for some meat.' Then gander-lander said, 'Oh! turkey-lurkey, don't go, for I was going, and I met goose-loose, and goose-loose met drake-lake, and drake-lake met duck-luck, and duck-luck met cock-lock, and cock-lock met hen-len, and hen-len met chicken-licken, and chicken-licken had been at the wood, and the sky had fallen on her poor bald pate, and we are going to tell the king.'

So turkey-lurkey turned back, and walked with gander-lander, goose-loose, drake-lake, duck-luck, cock-lock, hen-len, and chicken-licken. And as they were going along, they met Fox-lox. And fox-lox said, 'Where are you going, my pretty maids?' And they said, 'Chicken-licken went to the wood, and the sky fell upon her poor bald pate, and we are going to tell the king.' And fox-lox said, 'Come along with me, and I will show you the way.' But fox-lox took them into the fox's hole, and he and his young ones soon ate up poor chicken-licken, hen-len, cock-lock, duck-luck, drake-lake, goose-loose, gander-lander, and turkey-lurkey, and they never saw the king to tell him that the sky had fallen!

The better-known version of this cumulative tale, 'Henny-Penny' in Joseph Jacobs's *English Fairy Tales*, is a suspect text remembered, like his 'Jack and the Beanstalk', 'as told to me in Australia in 1860'. He points out that 'the fun consists in the avoidance of all pronouns, which results in jaw-breaking sentences'. Halliwell gives no provenance for his text.

Nursery Tale

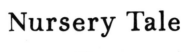

Source: J. O. Halliwell, *Popular Rhymes and Nursery Tales of England* (1849), 1970 reprint, p. 26.

Narrator: Unknown.

Type: AT1930 'Schlaraffenland'.

I SADDLED MY SOW with a sieve full of butter-milk, put my foot into the stirrup, and leaped nine miles beyond the moon into the land of Temperance, where there was nothing but hammers and hatchets and candlesticks, and there lay bleeding Old Noles. I let him lie, and sent for Old Hippernoles, and asked him if he could grind green steel nine times finer than wheat flour. He said he could not. Gregory's wife was up in the pear-tree gathering nine corns of buttered peas to pay St James's rent. St James was in the meadow mowing oat cakes; he heard a noise, hung up his scythe at his heels, stumbled at the battledore, tumbled over the barn-door ridge, and broke his shins against a bag of moonshine that stood behind the stairsfoot door, and if that isn't true you know as well as I.

The Tin Can at the Cow's Tail

Source: T. W. Thompson, 'Twelve Clod's Tales', *Journal of the Gypsy Lore Society*, 3rd series, vol. 21, 1942, pp. 8–10.
Narrator: Pat Lee, Oswaldtwistle, Maundy Thursday, 1916.
Type: AT1875 'The Boy on the Wolf's Tail'.

I WAS COMING OWER Shap Fell once, going to'ards your town, Kendal. I'd a couple o' horses wi' me, an' was riding one an' leading tother. It was night-time; a pretty dark night it was an' all. Well, I'd got to where that owld road joins in – you know, not far from the top – when a robber sprung out at me, an' demanded my watch an' chain. I was carrying a loaded whip, but I didn't let him see it. Instead I took out my watch an' chain, an' med as if I was going to hand 'em ower to him. Then, as he come for'ard to tek 'em, I let fly wi' my whip, crack on his head. He dropped down senseless on the road, an' I galloped ower him.

I went on now till I saw a house wi' a lighted window: a bit away from the road it was. I med for it, an' when I got there I knocked at the dooar, an' axed would they tek me in being as I was nightfast. There was a woman an' her daughter, an' they invited me in. They showed me into a room as had a coffin into it, an' left me there. I sat me down an' lit my pipe, but I couldn't keep my eyes off this coffin. The lid was off, an' I could see as there was a corpse into it. After a bit it moved a hand, this corpse did; then it stretched out an arm; then slowly it raised itsel' an' sat up. I was scared out o' my wits; terrified I was. Then the man spoke; for a man it was into the coffin. He towld me not to be frightened. He wasn't dead, he said, but only shamming. He'd reason to believe, he said, as his missis an' daughter was carrying on wi' a young farmer from thereabouts; an' he was doing this, he towld me, to find 'em out. He lay down in the coffin agen then, an' didn't say no more.

Soon after in come the young fellow. He didn't knock first: no need for him to do that, it seemed. The missis an' daughter was mighty pleased to see him; an' wi'out waiting more'n a minute or two off they all went upstairs together. At that the owld man sat up very sharp. 'I knowed it,' he says; 'I knowed they was carrying on wi' him.' An' he jumped out'n the coffin, an' away he went after 'em. He'd hardly got to the top'n the stairs but what there was a loud crack of a gun going off. Presently he came back agen. 'I've settled that,' he says, 'for good an' all.'

He turned on me now. He would have no tales towld about this business, he said, an' was wondering what manner o' death to put me to. I dropped on my two bended knees, an' begged an' implored him to spare my life. I'd done nowt to harm him, I said, an' I wouldn't: I was noways to blame, I said, for what had happened. But no; he meant to kill me. So he got a biscuit tin, an' shoved me into that, an' fastened it up safe so as I couldn't get out. Then he hoisted me onto his showlder, an' took me to the top'n one o' the great big mountains thereabouts. Here he chucked me on the ground, an' set me off rowling down the mountain side. Faster an' faster I went, bumpety, bumpety, bump, bump, bump. After a bit I begun to feel at myself. Pretty nigh every bone into my body was broken, an' I was as good as churned into a pudding by what I could mek out. Still I was rowling on, though not so fast now. Then plop, splash I went an' come to a standstill. I'd landed into a big pool a' water – a tarn as they say up there – which lies at the foot'n the mountain. Very like you'll know the place: it's to the left hand as you come down for Kendal.

After a while some cows come to drink at the pool. So I took my pocket-knife, an' cut a hole in the tin big enough to get a finger out. I caught howld'n one o' the cows' tails, an' twisted the end of it round an' round this finger. Then I pulled an' pulled till the fleshy part'n the tail was just through the hole in the tin, when I bit into it as hard as I could. Away the owld cow went, the tin at its tail, an' me hanging on for dear life by my teeth an' one finger. It galloped round an' round the field, bellowing like a mad thing. Some farm people making hay near by stopped working to watch, wondering what ailed the cow, an' what it could have at its tail. Round an' round it went, till at last it dropped down dead. The haymekers come over the wall now to see what was up; an' very soon they opened the tin an' let me out.

I'd lost my two horses, but in myself I was as right as rain, though a bit sore in places. I axed the farmer could he find me a job o' work, an' right away he took me on. I stopped wi' him till I'd enough money put by to get me an owld horse an' cart. Then I took to the roads agen. An' now here I am, sitting comfortable in my waggon, an' smoking my pipe, just as if all this hadn't happened to me.

Happy Boz'll

Source: Francis Hindes Groome, *In Gypsy Tents*, 1880, pp. 160–61.
Narrator: 'Leah Lovell', i.e. Esmerelda Lock.
Type: AT1889 'Munchhausen Tales'.

ONEST UPON A TIME there was a Romano, and his name was Happy Boz'll, and he had a German-silver grinding-barrow, and he used to put his wife and child on the top, and he used to go that quick along the road he'd beat all the coaches. Then he thought this grinding-barrow was too heavy and clumsy to take about, and he cut it up and made tent-rods of it. And then his dickey got away, and he didn't know where it was gone to; and one day he was going by the tent, and he said to himself, 'Bless my soul, wherever's that dickey got to?' And there was a tree close by, and the dickey shouted out and said, 'I'm here, my Happy, getting you a bit of stick to make a fire.' Well, the donkey come down with a lot of sticks, and he had been up the tree a week, getting firewood. Well then, Happy had a dog, and he went out one day; the dog one side the hedge, and him the other. And then he saw two hares. The dog ran after the two; and as he was going across the field, he cut himself right through with a scythe; and then one half ran after one hare, and the other after the other. Then the two halves of the dog catched the two hares; and then the dog smacked together again; and he said, 'Well, I've got 'em, my Happy'; and then the dog died. And Happy had a hole in the knee of his breeches, and he cut a piece of the dog's skin, after it was dead, and sewed it in the knee of his breeches. And that day twelve months his breeches-knee burst open, and barked at him. And so that's the end of Happy Boz'll.

In his *Gypsy Folk Tales* (1889), Groome writes, 'I believe it was largely this story . . . that led the great Lazarus Petulengro to remark once to Mr Sampson, "Isn't it wonderful, sir, that a real gentleman could have wrote such a thing – nothing but low language and povertiness, and not a word of grammar or high-learned talk in it from beginning to end."'

Groome was married to, and then separated from, the narrator of this story, Esmerelda Lock. She was previously married to Hubert Smith and is the heroine of his overblown account of *Tent Life with English Gypsies in Norway* (1874). A notebook in the T. W. Thompson manuscripts at the Brotherton Library contains her unpublished reminiscences.

Happy or Appy Boswell is the hero of many 'lying tales'. For further examples, see the Reverend George Hall's *The Gypsy's Parson* (pp. 258–60) and T. W. Thompson's 'English Gypsy Folk-Tales and Other Traditional Stories' in *JGLS* (new series, vol. 8, pp. 227–33).

Appy and the Conger Eel

Source: T. W. Thompson, 'Some New Appy Boswell Stories', *Journal of the Gypsy Lore Society*, 3rd series, vol. 5, pp. 122–4.
Narrator: Manivel Smith, Burton-on-Trent.
Type: AT 1889 'Munchhausen Tales'.

APPY HAD A CONGER eel. He bought it one day as he was going his rounds, and I can tell you who he had it off'n. He had it off'n a man as worked into a brewery at this very town. And that's a fact, that is. And when he gets it home he puts it in the wash-tub, Appy does; and then he goes and he fetches a bucket or two o' water for it to swim about it. 'There now,' he says – that's Appy to the eel – 'you should be nice and comfortable like for a bit.' Then he sits him down to his tea, him and the owld woman; and he doesn't think no more about it, not till the owld woman says as she's got a bit o' washing to do, and mun be making a start. 'But I got a conger eel in the wash-tub,' he says. 'A what?' she says. 'A conger eel,' he says. 'Well then,' she says, 'you mun just go and take it out.'

So Appy takes the eel out'n the wash-tub, and puts it into the inside pocket'n his coat. Then off he sets for the public. There was one not above three or four fields away from this place where he was a-stopping; and to be sure he was pretty well know'd there, being as he was fond o' company of an evening. Well, he calls for a pint o' beer, and has a pull at it. Then he sets it down aside him on the bench where he is sitting, and gets agate talking and joking. And when he comes to think'n it again what does he find but as his glass is empty. Somebody's bin playing him a trick, he thinks. But no; nobody will own to it. So after a bit of a to-do he has it filled up again. And again he takes a pull at it, and sets it down aside him, only this time he keeps his hand on to it.

He's talking and joking the same as he was afore, when he feels summat touch his hand – summat cowld and wet. He looks down, and if it wasn't the eel trying to get a drink of his beer: 'Oh!' he says, says Appy, 'so it was you, was it, as took my beer, you mischiefful monkey? Now get you back,' he says, 'into your own place.' And he hits it over the head, not to say to hurt it, and makes it get back into his pocket. But no sooner does he get talking afresh than it's at it again, and more retermined-like this time. And Appy, he gets right angry with it now; and he hits it hard three or fower times. 'I'll larn you', he says, 'to steal my beer.' But the eel, it gets angry too; and it bridles up at him. 'I bin used to having my glass o' beer same as any other man,' it says, 'and I'm not a-going to stand this.' 'Oh! ar'n't you?' says Appy, and he hits it again. Howsoever, the eel rears itsel' up at him. 'If this is the way you're a-going to treat me,' it says, 'then I'm a-going home, and you mun come back by yoursel' as best you can.' And wi' that it got up, and it walked out, as huffy as you please; walked straight out it did.

Well, come closing time Appy takes his way home. He's across the first field, and just a-going in the second, when he hears a noise o' summat coming up behind him. So he turns round; but he can't see nothing; only he can hear this thing, whatever it is, getting closer and closer. He's afear'd; terribly afear'd he is: being as he can't see nothing he thinks it mun be the devil hissel' come for him. And he takes to his heels, and runs for dear life, shouting and hollering blue murders. But it's no manner o' use: this thing, whatever it is, keeps gaining on him and gaining on him. It's close behind him now. He can hear it panting. 'Stop,' it says, 'stop.' And Appy stops: somehow he couldn't help hissel'. 'Why, it's only me, Appy,' it says; 'you needn't be afeard.' And so it was: it was the owld conger eel, puffing and blowing like a parpus. 'I thought as I'd wait for you after all, Appy,' it says; 'only I must ha' bin dozing or summat, as I never sin you, not till you'd gone past.' 'Well that was very kind of you now,' says Appy, 'so I shall give you a lift home.' Which he does. And right glad the owld conger was, I can tell you: it had run far enough for one night, being as it wasn't not to say used to it. And when he gets home Appy puts it in the wash-tub again, and gives it plenty o' water, the same as he'd done afore. He wouldn't like for it not to be comfortable like.

Next day Appy was busy, and he didn't bother no more about it not till after he'd had his tea. Then he goes to see how it's a-getting on. But it isn't there; and the owld woman, she doesn't know nothing about it; and sarch as he will he can't light on it nowheres. So he takes a stroll as far as the public, same as usual; and, believe me, there it is, as large as life, a-sitting up to a pint o' beer. 'Hello, my Appy,' it says; and it calls for another pint, and one for Appy. 'Very good,' says the landlord, and he fetches two pints. 'That'll be half a crown altogether, Mr Boswell,' he says. 'What?' says Appy. 'Half a crown, and beer threepence a pint!' 'Aye,' says the landlord; 'your friend here's had eight pints afore this, and he said as you'd pay when you come in.' 'Well now, did anyone ever hear the like o' that?' says Appy. 'Have you had 'em?' he says: he's a-speaking to the eel now. 'I have, my Appy,' it says, 'as true as I'm a-having this one.' 'Very well then,' says Appy; 'nobody shall ever say as Mr Boswell doesn't pay his debts.' And wi that he stumped up; for true enough Appy never could abide being in debt.

Well, to cut my story short, this conger eel come to die one day. And Appy had the skin tanned, and made into a pair o' braces. And after that every time he come to a public house these braces, they'd pull and pull at him, till at last he had to go in. There was nowt else for it, he said, not unless him and his breeches was to part company. And that's true, that is, every word of it; as true as Appy was Appy.

Thompson suspected that this story was 'intended to be a skit on the usual Appy Boswell story'. In his article 'English Gypsy Folk-Tales' he gives a trivial anecdote collected from Taimi Boswell called 'Appy Boswell and the Conger Eel':

Appy was fishing one day when he caught a great big conger eel. And it up an' run him across two fields. 'Aye s'help me God,' he says, 'it up an' run me across two fields.'

Hawks's Men at the Battle of Waterloo

Source: *Monthly Chronicle of North-Country Lore and Legend*, May 1887, p. 141.
Narrator: John Atlantic Stephenson.

MAN, AA FELL IN wi' Ned White the other day. Ye knaa Ned and other twenty-fower o' Haaks's cheps went oot te the Peninsular War, whor Wellin'ton was, ye knaa. Se, as we wor hevin' a gill tegithor, aa says te him, 'Ned, d'ye mind when ye wor in the Peninsular War?' 'Aa should think aa de,' says he. 'Did ye ever faall in wi' Wellin'ton?' says aa. 'Wellin'ton!' says he; 'wey, man, aa knaa'd him. Wey, just the day afore the Battle o' Watterloo he sent for me.' 'Ned,' he says, 'tyek yor twenty-fower men,' he says, 'an gan up and shift them Frenchmen off the top of yon hill.' 'Aall reet,' says aa, 'but it winnit tyek all the twenty-fower,' aa says. 'Ah! but it's Napoleon's crack regiment,' he says; 'ye'd bettor tyek plenty.' 'Aall reet,' aa says, 'we'll suen shift 'em.' Se doon aa cums te the lads, an' aa says: 'Noo, ma lads, Wellin'ton wants us te shift yon Frenchmen off the top of yon hill.' 'Aall reet,' they says. 'Heor, Bob Scott,' aa says, 'hoo mony Frenchmen are thor up yondor?' 'Aboot fower hundred,' he says. 'Hoo mony on us will it tyek te shift them?' aa axes. 'Oh! ten,' says Bob. 'Wey, we'll tyek fifteen,' aa says, 'just te humour the aad man.' 'Aall reet,' they says. Se off we set at the double alang the lonnen: but just as we torned the corner at the foot of the hill who should we meet but Bonnipart hissel on a lily-white horse, wi' a cocked hat on. 'Whor are ye off te, Ned?' says he. 'Wey, te shift yon Frenchmen off yon hill!' 'Whaat!' he says; 'wey, that's my crack regiment,' he says. 'Nivvor mind that,' aa says; 'Wellin'ton says we hev te shift 'em, and shifted they'll be, noo!' 'Ye're coddin',' says he. 'Ne coddin' aboot it,' aa says; 'we'll suen shift them off.' Aa says, 'Cum by!' 'Had on!' he says, and he gallops reet up the hill te them and shoots oot, 'Gan back, ma lads, gan back! Heor's Ned White from Haaks's and his twenty-fower lads comin' up te shift ye. Ye hevvent a hap-porth of chance!' And back they went. Did aa ivvor see Wellin'ton? Wey, man, ye shud think shyem!'

The Austwick Carles

Source: S. O. Addy, *Household Tales with Other Traditional Remains*, 1895, pp. 112–13.

Narrator: Unknown, District of Austwick, near Settle, West Yorkshire.

Type: (I) AT1213 'The Pent Cuckoo', (II) AT1245 'Sunlight Carried in a Bag into the Windowless House', (III) AT1297 'Jumping into the River after their Comrades', (IV) AT1278 'Under the Cloud' (type suggested by Katharine Briggs).

I

At Austwick, near Settle, in the West Riding, the villagers had noticed that when the cuckoo was about the weather was generally fine. So they thought that if they could always keep the cuckoo they would always have fine weather. One season when it rained very hard, and they could not get their hay in, instructions were given that when a cuckoo had been seen in one of the small 'plantins', or woods, in the neighbourhood the village should be warned. So when the cuckoo appeared warning was given, and the morning after the warning all the villagers turned out to build a wall round the wood where the cuckoo was. The work was heavy, but by dinner-time they had got the wall up to the height of six or seven feet. But whilst they were eating their dinners the cuckoo, to the great astonishment of all, was seen to fly from the trees towards the wall, and just managed to get over the top. And it was always said that if they had only built the wall one round of stones higher the bird could never have got out.

II

Season after season a farmer in this village had been very unlucky with his crops. He cut his grass at the usual time, and one day the sun dried it, and another day the rain came and wet it. So he thought the best thing would be to take the grass into the barn as soon as it was cut, and then bring the sunshine into the barn. So one day they found him busy with his cart. First he took the cart out into the sunshine, and let the sun shine on it for a few minutes, and then he began to tie the sunshine on with ropes. After he had done this he led the horses and cart into the barn, took the rope off the cart, and kicked the sunshine on to the grass.

III

There was a deep, dark pool at Austwick, whose banks were a favourite resort of men and boys. One day a man fell into the pool, and did not come up again, but presently a number of bubbles came up, making a strange noise, which seemed to the rest to take the form of words, and to say, 'T' b-b-b-best 's at t' b-b-bottom.' So they all jumped in one after another, to see what this good thing was. And hence comes the local proverb 'T' best 's at t' bottom, as the Astic carles say.'

IV

Many centuries ago there was only one knife in the village, and it, for the sake of convenience, was kept in a large hollow tree in or near the village. If anybody wanted the knife, and it was not there, he let all the villagers know by shouting 'T' whittle to t' tree, t' whittle to t' tree,' and then the man who had the knife had to produce it, or account for its absence. One day, a number of men who were going to cut ling on the fells, borrowed the whittle for that purpose. As they intended to cut ling on the following day, they thought it was no use taking the whittle home again if they could find a safe place to put it in. After some search they found a large dark patch on the moor, which could be seen from a long distance. And so they put the whittle in one corner of the patch, and covered it over with a lump of ling. Next morning not a trace of the dark patch could be found, and the whittle was irretrievably lost. Long afterwards they found that they had laid the whittle in the corner of a shadow caused by a passing cloud.

Village-numskull tales are among the most popular folktales, along with the local taunts known as *blasons populaires*. The best-known stories are those of the 'Wise Men of Gotham' in Nottinghamshire, but villages throughout England are regarded as centres of well-meaning stupidity. Katharine Briggs gives a list of forty-seven villages 'supposed to be inhabited by simpletons' (*Dictionary*, Part A, vol. 2, p. 5), to which can be added: Lamberhead Green, Lancashire; Madeley, Salop; Ruiton, West Midlands; and no doubt many others. Inhabitants of any of these places are liable to be asked embarrassing questions such as, 'Who put the pig on the wall to watch the band go by?' A correspondence on this matter in the *Daily Mirror*'s 'Live Letters' column during November 1984 showed traditional local ridicule very much alive and well.

The Three Big Sillies

Source: Charlotte S. Burne, 'Variant of the Three Noodles', *Folk-Lore Journal*, 2, 1884, pp. 40–43.

Narrator: A nursemaid, then aged sixteen, from Houghton, near Stafford, 1862 and after.

Type: AT1 384 'The Husband Hunts Three Persons as Stupid as His Wife'.

ONCE UPON A TIME there was a farmer and his wife who had one only daughter, and she was courted by a gentleman. Every evening he used to come and see her, and stop to supper at the farmhouse, and the daughter used to be sent down into the cellar to draw the beer for supper. So one evening she was gone down to draw the beer, and she happened to look up at the ceiling while she was drawing, and she saw an axe stuck into one of the beams. It must have been there a long, long time, but somehow or other she had never noticed it before, and she began a-thinking. And she thought it was very dangerous to have that axe there, for she said to herself, 'Suppose him and me was to be married, and we was to have a son, and he was to grow up to be a man, and come down into the cellar to draw the beer, like as I'm doing now, and the axe was to fall on his head and kill him, what a dreadful thing it would be!' And she put down the candle and the jug, and sat herself down and began a-crying.

Well, they began to wonder upstairs how it was that she was so long drawing the beer, and her mother went down to see after her, and she found her sitting on the setluss crying, and the beer running over the floor. 'Why, whatever is the matter?' said her mother. 'Oh, mother!' says she, 'look at that horrid axe! Suppose we was to be married, and was to have a son, and he was to grow up, and was to come down into the cellar to draw the beer, and the axe was to fall on his head and kill him, what a dreadful thing it would be!' 'Dear, dear! what a dreadful thing it would be!' said the mother, and she sat her down a-side of the daughter and started a-crying too.

Then, after a bit, the father began to wonder that they didn't come back, and he went down into the cellar to look after them himself, and there they two sat a-crying, and the beer running all over the floor. 'Whatever is the matter?'

says he. 'Why,' says the mother, 'look at that horrid axe. Just suppose, if our daughter and her sweetheart was to be married, and was to have a son, and he was to grow up, and was to come down into the cellar to draw the beer, and the axe was to fall on his head and kill him, what a dreadful thing it would be!' 'Dear, dear, dear! so it would!' said the father, and he sat himself down aside of the other two, and started a-crying.

Now the gentleman got tired of stopping up in the kitchen by himself, and at last he went down into the cellar too to see what they were after; and there they three sat a-crying side by side, and the beer running all over the floor. And he ran straight and turned the tap. Then he said, 'Whatever are you three doing, sitting there crying, and letting the beer run all over the floor?' 'Oh!' says the father, 'look at that horrid axe! Suppose you and our daughter was to be married, and was to have a son, and he was to grow up, and was to come down into the cellar to draw the beer, and the axe was to fall on his head and kill him!' And then they all started a-crying worse than before. But the gentleman burst out a-laughing, and reached up and pulled out the axe, and then he said, 'I've travelled many miles, and I never met three such big sillies as you three before; and now I shall start out on my travels again, and when I can find three bigger sillies than you three then I'll come back and marry your daughter.' So he wished them goodbye, and started off on his travels, and left them all crying because the girl had lost her sweetheart.

Well, he set out, and he travelled a long way, and at last he came to an old woman's cottage that had some grass growing on the roof. And the old woman was trying to get her cow to go up a ladder to the grass, and the poor thing durstn't go. So the gentleman asked the old woman what she was doing. 'Why, lookye,' she said, 'look at all that beautiful grass. I'm going to get the cow on to the roof to eat it. She'll be quite safe, for I shall tie a string round her neck, and pass it down the chimney, and tie it to my wrist as I go about the house, so she can't fall off without my knowing it.' 'Oh, you poor old silly!' said the gentleman, 'you should cut the grass and throw it down to the cow!' But the old woman thought it was easier to get the cow up the ladder than to get the grass down, so she pushed her and coaxed her and got her up, and tied a string round her neck, and passed it down the chimney, and fastened it to her own wrist. And the gentleman went on his way, but he hadn't gone far when the cow tumbled off the roof, and hung by the string tied round her neck, and it strangled her. And the weight of the cow tied to her wrist pulled the old woman up the chimney, and she stuck fast halfway and was smothered in the soot.

Well, that was one big silly.

And the gentleman went on and on, and he went to an inn to stop the night, and they were so full at the inn that they had to put him in a double-bedded room, and another traveller was to sleep in the other bed. The other man was a very pleasant fellow, and they got very friendly together; but in the morning, when they were both getting up, the gentleman was surprised to see the other hang his trousers on the knobs of the chest of drawers and run across the room and try to jump into them, and he tried over and over again and couldn't manage it, and the gentleman wondered whatever he was doing it for. At last he stopped and wiped his face with his handkerchief. 'Oh dear!' he says, 'I do think trousers are the most awkwardest kind of clothes that ever were. I can't think who could have invented such things. It takes me the best part of an hour to get into mine every morning, and I get so hot! How do you manage yours?' So the gentleman burst out a-laughing, and showed him how to put them on, and he was very much obliged to him, and said he never should have thought of doing it that way.

So that was another big silly.

Then the gentleman went on his travels again: and he came to a village, and outside the village there was a pond, and round the pond was a crowd of people. And they had got rakes, and brooms, and pickels [pitchforks] reaching into the pond, and the gentleman asked what was the matter. 'Why,' they says, 'matter enough! moon's tumbled into the pond, and we can't get her out anyhow!' So the gentleman burst out a-laughing, and told them to look up into the sky, and that it was only the shadow in the water. But they wouldn't listen to him, and abused him shamefully, and he got away as quick as he could.

So there was a whole lot of sillies bigger than them all, and the gentleman turned back home again and married the farmer's daughter.

A perennially popular tale, the component parts of which can also be found as independent noodle tales (see W. A. Clouston, *The Book of Noodles*, 1888). There are half a dozen English versions.

The Miser and His Wife

Source: J. O. Halliwell, *Popular Rhymes and Nursery Tales of England*, 1849,
pp. 31–2.
Narrator: Unknown.
Type: AT1541 'For the Long Winter'.

ONCE UPON A TIME there was an old miser, who lived with his wife near a great town, and used to put by every bit of money he could lay his hands on. His wife was a simple woman, and they lived together without quarrelling, but she was obliged to put up with very hard fare. Now, sometimes, when there was a sixpence she thought might be spared for a comfortable dinner or supper, she used to ask the miser for it, but he would say, 'No, wife, it must be put by for Good Fortune.' It was the same with every penny he could get hold of, and notwithstanding all she could say, almost every coin that came into the house was put by 'for Good Fortune'.

The miser said this so often, that some of his neighbours heard him, and one of them thought of a trick by which he might get the money. So the first day that the old chuff was away from home, he dressed himself like a wayfaring man, and knocked at the door. 'Who are you?' said the wife. He answered, 'I am Good Fortune, and I am come for the money which your husband has laid by for me.' So this simple woman, not suspecting any trickery, readily gave it to him, and, when her good man came home, told him very pleasantly that Good Fortune had called for the money which had been kept so long for him.

Baring-Gould contributed a version of this tale, 'Jack Hannaford', to Henderson's *Folk-Lore of the Northern Counties*, Joseph Jacobs prints another, 'Hereafterthis', from an unidentified correspondent, in *More English Fairy Tales*. He also had a manuscript variant, 'The Bob-tailed Mare', which failing discovery of his manuscripts we must assume to be lost. Halliwell quotes Ben Jonson:

> Say we are robb'd,
> If any come to borrow a spoon or so;
> I will not have Good Fortune or God's Blessing
> Let in, while I am busy.

A nice reversal of the traditional tale is told of the impressively bearded novelist T. H. White by Francois Gallix in his introduction to *T. H. White: Letters to a Friend* (1984):

a young American . . . had knocked at his door in Alderney announcing to White that he was a Jehovah's Witness. White grabbed the collecting-box and replied: 'And *I* am Jehovah! Hand over the takings!'

Stupid's Mistaken Cries

Source: Professor Dr George Stephens, F.S.A., 'Two English Folk-Tales', *Folk-Lore Record*, 3, 1880–81, pp. 153–6.
Narrator: Unknown, 'told in Essex about the year 1800'.
Type: AT1696 'What Should I have Said (Done)?'

THERE WAS ONCE A little boy, and his mother sent him to buy a sheep's head and pluck; afraid he should forget it, the lad kept saying all the way along –

> Sheep's head and pluck!
> Sheep's head and pluck!

Trudging along, he came to a stile; but in getting over he fell and hurt himself, and, beginning to blubber, forgot what he was sent for. So he stood a little while to consider; at last he thought he recollected it, and began to repeat –

> Liver and lights and gall and all!
> Liver and lights and gall and all!

Away he went again, and came to where a man was sick, bawling out –

> Liver and lights and gall and all!
> Liver and lights and gall and all!

Whereon the man laid hold of him and beat him, bidding him say -

> Pray God send no more up!
> Pray God send no more up!

The youngster strode along, uttering these words, till he reached a field where a hind was sowing wheat –

> Pray God send no more up!
> Pray God send no more up!

This was all his cry. So the sower began to thrash him, and charged him to repeat –

> Pray God send plenty more!
> Pray God send plenty more!

Off the child scampered with these words in his mouth till he reached a churchyard and met a funeral, but he went on with his –

> Pray God send plenty more!
> Pray God send plenty more!

The chief mourner seized and punished him, and bade him repeat –

> Pray God send the soul to heaven!
> Pray God send the soul to heaven!

Away went the boy, and met a dog and a bitch going to be hung, but his cry rang out –

> Pray God send the soul to heaven!
> Pray God send the soul to heaven!

The good folk nearly were furious, seized and struck him, charging him to say –

> A dog and a bitch a-going to be hung!
> A dog and a bitch a-going to be hung!

This the poor fellow did, till he overtook a man and a woman going to be married. 'Oh! oh!' he shouted –

> A dog and a bitch a-going to be hung!
> A dog and a bitch a-going to be hung!

The man was enraged, as we may well think, gave him many a thump, and ordered him to repeat –

> I wish you much joy!
> I wish you much joy!

This he did, jogging along, till he came to two labourers who had fallen into a ditch. The lad kept bawling out –

> I wish you much joy!
> I wish you much joy!

This vexed one of the folk so sorely that he used all his strength, scrambled out, beat the crier, and told him to say –

> The one is out, I wish the other was!
> The one is out, I wish the other was!

On went young 'un till he found a fellow with only one eye; but he kept up his song –

> The one is out, I wish the other was!
> The one is out, I wish the other was!

This was too much for Master One-eye, who grabbed him and chastised him, bidding him call –

> The one side gives good light, I wish the other did!
> The one side gives good light, I wish the other did!

So he did, to be sure, till he came to a house, one side of which was on fire. The people here thought it was he who had set the place a-blazing, and straightway put him in prison. The end was, the judge put on his black cap and condemned him to die.

Professor Stephens' two tales (the other is 'The Three Noodles') were presumably remembered from the telling of his nursemaid. See 'Lazy Jack' (p. 25) for a variant. The *Journal of American Folklore* (3, 1890) contains a version sent by Sylvans Howard, whose grandmother heard it during her childhood at North Bridgewater, near Brockton, in Shropshire. It restores, in an American idiom, some of the colloquial verve missing from Professor Stephens' text:

> By and by he came across a man puking. He took him and gave him a whipping, and said, 'You want I should puke up my heart, liver and lights and all, do you?'

The Doctor's Pestle

Source: George Bourne (pseudonym of George Sturt), *A Farmer's Life*, 1927,
p. 135.
Narrator: John Smith, farmer, Farnborough, Surrey, *c.* 1800.

THE TALE WENT THAT this doctor was making up pills with pestle and mortar, while his man – who couldn't read but was to deliver the pills – waited and watched. At last they were put into their boxes and handed to the man, whereupon he began straightway to name the patients they were for. 'This box', he said, 'is for Lady Gray, at the Grange; and this other for old Dame Russell at the workhouse.'

The doctor stared. 'That's all right,' he said, 'but how the devil did you know?'

'Why,' the man explained, 'when you was making up Lady Gray's I heard the pestle saying in the mortar, "Linger along, linger along." But presently it begun to say, "Die and be damned, die and be damned," and then I knew 'twas for poor old Mother Russell.'

Bourne has an interesting discussion of this kind of 'folk-anecdote' in an appendix to *A Farmer's Life*. A good many folktales turn sounds into words, in much the same way as rustic naturalists have turned birds' calls into recognizable phrases. In the chapter 'Old-fashioned Times' in *The Heart of England*, Edward Thomas tells of a man who in the prime of life heard the coach-horses' hooves proudly rapping out his name, 'Peter Durrant! Peter Durrant', but now, in his old age, 'there is not a pair of horses that does not clatter: "Poor pluck today! Poor pluck today!".' Tennyson's 'Northern Farmer – New Style', heard the horses' hooves pound 'Propputy, propputy, propputy'.

The Landlord and the Farmer's Boy

Source: Alfred Williams, *Round About the Upper Thames*, 1922, pp. 216–17.
Narrator: Unknown.
Type: AT921 'The King and the Peasant's Son'.

THIS LANDLORD, AS NO rent was forthcoming for several quarters, determined to take a ride round and look up his long-winded tenants. He accordingly mounted his nag and trotted from farm to farm, but could not meet with anyone for some time. At last he came up with a boy, the son of one of the defaulting farmers, and addressed him. 'Where's thi father?' said he.

'Oh! He's gone to make a bad matter wuss,' the boy replied.

'How's that, gone to make a bad matter wuss?'

'He went to market yesterday wi' a cow, best cow we'd a got. Was in want o' money, an' a means to bide ther' till 'is all gone.'

'Is thi mother at home?'

'Yes. Very busy bakin' the bread we ate yesterday.' 'How's that, bakin' the bread you ate yesterday?' 'Why! 'er's bakin' some more in the place on't, to be sure.' 'Thee's got a sister. Wher's she?'

'Upstairs, cryin' for want o' calico to make her a milkin' smock.'

'Well!' says the landlord, 'if thee can'st come to my house neither daylight nor dark, neither a foot nor a hossback, neither naked nor clothed, I'll forgive thi father the rent.'

When the squire had gone, the boy considered and eventually thought out a way to do it. He waited till the sun had set behind the wood, then took off his clothes, wrapped a calf net around him, jumped upon the donkey, rode up to the front door of the manor-house and challenged the landlord.

'Well! well! You've beat me. There! There! Go on about thi business and tell thi father there's no more rent due now till Christmas,' said he good-humouredly.

See also 'The History of the Four Kings' (p. 39). This story of native wit conquering assertive wealth or power has – with a variety of clever answers – proved lastingly popular in both written and oral tradition.

The Lad who was Never Hungry

Source: E. M. Wilson, 'Some Humorous English Folk Tales: Part One', *Folk-Lore*, 49, 1938, pp. 185–6.

Narrator: Mrs Emily Harrison, Crosthwaite, Westmorland, September 1937.

Type: AT1561 'The Lazy Boy Eats Breakfast, Dinner and Supper One After the Other'.

THE FARMER WAS TALKING to the lad at the hiring fair. T' farmer asked him if he was a good getter up. 'O, aye,' he said, he was a good gitter up, he says: 'Ye kna I's nivver tired, ah's nivver hungry an' ah's nivver dry.'

'Oh!' he says, 'tha's just t'reet fella for me.'

So when he lands up to t'place, whatever's set before him he eats it, whatever he has to drink he drinks it all and whenever he went to bed he always went in good time – nine o'clock prompt. So it went on for a few days, so t'boss said to him:

'I thowt thou was nivver hungry, nivver dry an' nivver tired.'

'Nay,' he said. 'It's o' this way. I it afoor I's hungry, I sup before I's dry, and ah ga to bed afoor I's tired.'

E. M. Wilson's splendid three-part essay on English comic tales (*Folk-Lore*, 49, pp. 182–92, 277–86; and *Folk-Lore*, 54, pp. 258–61) offers the best collection of rural jokes such as this, which was told to Mrs Harrison by an old farmer from Preston, when she was hired at Ulverston Fair as a young girl. Wilson notes, 'the farmer told the story as having occurred to himself with a new farm lad.'

Bad Meat

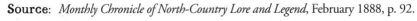

Source: *Monthly Chronicle of North-Country Lore and Legend*, February 1888, p. 92.
Narrator: Unknown.

'ARE YE IN WANT of a lad, sor?' said a young farm labourer to a farmer at a Newcastle hiring. 'I am not,' replied the latter, 'but why are you leaving Farmer N.? I'm sure he is a good master?' 'The maistor is all reet,' said the lad, 'it's the meat that's bad. Six months sin', we had an aad coo deed, an we eat hor. Then the aad soo deed, and we eat hor. Yesterday the maistor's mother deed, and aa runn'd away!'

***

This mordant comment on farmworkers' living conditions may have been fashioned out of a song such as 'Mutton Pie' (Roy Palmer, *Everyman's Book of English Country Songs*).

The Doctor and the Trapper

Source: William Wood, *A Sussex Farmer*, 1938, p. 108.
Narrator: Unknown, West Sussex.

I HEARD A STORY about another of these old trappers, rather a gruesome one, from an old friend of mine in West Sussex, who knew both the parties concerned who lived in his own parish. One was a rat- and rabbit-catcher of the usual type, the other a sporting doctor, who joined him, whenever he could, ferreting rabbits. They were both remarkably well made, big men, each of them over six feet high. One day the doctor said: 'Jim, I don't suppose you care much what happens to your body when you die; you are a fine specimen of a man, I wish you would agree to allow your body to be at the service of the College of Surgeons for dissection.' Jim said: 'Well, I don't mind, but let's have an understanding about this. If I die first, let the "Sawbones" see what I am made of; and if you die first, then I am to have your body for my ferrets. Can't have it all your way.'

And the doctor agreed. My old friend told me that the doctor died first, and Jim wheeled a hand truck up to his house to get the contract carried out, but it did not come off.

Not So Bad After All

Source: W. Rye, *Songs, Stories and Sayings of Norfolk*, 1897, pp. 145–6.
Narrator: 'My old skipper Tungate', Norfolk Broads.

ANOTHER OF HIS TALES was how a well-known yachting man, of whose boat he was the skipper, and who was very fond of a good meal, had his boat invaded by several friends just about lunchtime one day, when he had only a small piece of salt beef on board, just enough for himself and Tungate.

So he went below and stuck it all over with dry rice, and when they sat down to feed, and the beef was brought in, it seemed to be full of maggots with their heads just shewing. 'So he hallered out,' said Tungate, '"well, them as like jumpers can hev 'em, I don't, so take that stuff away, Tungate,"' and the visitors had to make their meal off bread and cheese; and when they went away, he said, 'I don't think that beef was so bad arter all, so bring it back again, Tungate.'

This is one of Tungate's 'inexhaustible mine' of tales, a number of which Rye recorded.

The Wrong Train

Source: *The Monthly Chronicle of North-Country Lore and Legend*, March 1886, p. 44.
Narrator: Unknown.

A FEW YEARS AGO a pitman went to the Central Station, Newcastle, with a return ticket for Seghill. He presented himself at the first platform, and got into the south train. Before starting, the guard inquired at the door 'All for the south?' Geordie exclaimed, 'Aa's for Seghill.' The guard consequently told him to come out. Geordie sallied off, and then got into the Sunderland train, with the same result. Next time he strolled to the opposite end of the station, and got into the Carlisle train. He now, quite bewildered, inquired of a porter, and then found that he had got to the wrong station. He at last arrived at the Blyth and Tyne terminus, and got all right. Seating himself beside some acquaintances, he, with a volume of strong oaths, detailed to them his misfortunes, to the evident annoyance of a minister, who accosted Geordie with, 'My good man, do you know where you are going to?' 'Ay,' says Geordie, 'aa's gan te Seghill.' 'No, my good man, you are going to hell!' says the minister. 'Whaat!' cries Geordie; 'in the wrang train agyen!' and thereupon jumped out, when the train started and left him to find his road to Seghill on foot.

In a version of this joke given in Briscoe's *Stories About the Midlands* (1883–8), the story is set during a Moody and Sankey crusade, and the sanctimonious clergyman is identified as Moody.

The New Church Organ

Source: Edward Boys Ellman, *Recollections of a Sussex Parson*, 1912, p. 196.
Narrator: Unknown, Jevington, Sussex.

JEVINGTON WAS NOT IN our Rural Deanery, being the other side of the Cuckmere Valley. As a village, it always prided itself upon being very musical. For about a hundred years it had the reputation of being the most musical village in the neighbourhood. Some time about the thirties, before railroad days, the good people of Jevington decided to have an organ, of the kind that could be played by simply winding up a handle. A farmer's wife – as a waggon had to go to London to fetch the organ – decided to take advantage of the waggon and have a washing-machine down from London at the same time.

Saturday night came, and with it the waggon. It was late, and by some mistake the box washing-machine was put in church, and the organ left at the farm. However, early next morning the mistake was discovered, and an exchange made in good time for service. The man who was to manage the organ studied it, and was certain that he knew how to manage it. A large congregation assembled. When the Psalm was given out, the organ was wound up, and went beautifully, and the singing was most hearty. At the end of the Psalm, about four or six verses, the congregation left off singing, but the organ went on. It was necessary to stop it. In his flurry the poor man forgot exactly what he had to turn or push in – he however did something, and the Psalm tune changed into 'Drops of Brandy'. He made fresh attempts, and the tune changed into 'Go to the Devil and Shake Yourself'. Playing this air, the organ was carried out of church, and put down in the churchyard, where it by degrees played itself out. For the truth of this story I cannot vouch, but it was told me as a fact when I first came to Berwick. These grinding organs usually had three psalm tunes (one long, one common, and one short metre), and the remainder of the tunes were secular.

Stories about untoward disturbances in church were, and still are, widely told.

Moved by the Spirit

Source: Edward Boys Ellman, *Recollections of a Sussex Parson*, 1912, pp. 112–13.

Narrator: Unknown, Portsmouth.

ON PASSING A QUAKERS' meeting-house on our return, one of our party related to us an anecdote of two middies passing the Quakers' meeting-house one day when a meeting was going on. One midshipman remarked that he had often looked in and waited to hear someone speak, but that he had never done so, as unfortunately the Spirit would not move them; whereupon his companion made him a bet that he would go into the chapel and before he had been there two minutes the Spirit would move some of them. The bet was accepted, and so they walked in. The second middy pulled a handful of nuts out of his pocket, saying. 'Here, my friends, here is a scramble for you.' Two or three Quakers immediately jumped up and began to reprove him, whereupon he quietly walked out, saying to his companion, 'I have won my bet.'

Jokes about religious sects are of course still common. It is worth noting that both this and the preceding story are told with relish by an Anglican clergyman.

Abraham's Bosom

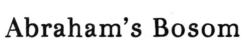

Source: Richard Blakeborough, *Wit, Character, Folklore and Customs of the North Riding of Yorkshire*, 1898, p. 63.
Narrator: Unknown.

OLD SALLY WAS DYING. On being asked by the vicar if she felt quite happy, the old lady said, with great unction, 'Oh yes, Ah s'all seean be iv Jacob's bosom.' 'Abraham's bosom, Sally,' corrected the vicar. 'Aye, well, mebbe it is, bud if you'd been unmarried for sixty-fahve year, leyke what Ah 'ev, ya wudn't be particular wheeas bosom it war, seea lang ez ya gat inti sumbody's.'

There is a whole section in the Aarne–Thompson index (AT1475–1499) for 'jokes about old maids'.

The Maid who
Wanted to Marry

Source: S. O. Addy, *Household Tales*, 1895, p. 30.
Narrator: Unknown, Eckington, Derby.
Type: AT1467a 'Prayer to Christ Child's Mother'.

A YOUNG IRISH GIRL wanted to marry a young Irishman, so she went to Spinkhill to pray. When she had got very near to the church she knelt down behind a hedge and said: 'O, holy mother, can I have Patrick?' An old man, who was behind the hedge, heard her question and said, 'No, thou can'st not.' But the girl said, 'Thee be quiet, little Jesus, and let thy mother speak.'

This is one of those trivial anecdotes which appears in all sorts of odd places. A version in *Notes and Queries* (III, 1867; Briggs, *Dictionary*, Part A, vol. 2, p. 204) has the line 'Hol' thee noise, little Jesus, an' let thee mother speak!', and the wonderful punch-line, 'owt but a tailor, but a tailor rather than nowt, good Lord'. An undated jest-book entitled *New Joe Miller: or, The Tickler* contains, as jest No. 121, a more blasphemous version: a woman who has sworn to remain celibate in widowhood prays to the Virgin to be released from the vow. A hidden man says 'No', whereupon she says, 'Hold your tongue, you bastard; I am speaking to your mother.'

The Wife's Request

Source: *Monthly Chronicle of North-Country Lore and Legend*, May 1887, p. 142.
Narrator: Unknown.

A NEWCASTLE MAN, TROUBLED with a drunken wife, thought he would cure her of her bad habits by terror. When she was one day in a helpless state of intoxication he procured a coffin, placed her in it, and screwed the lid partially down. Waking up, but being unable to release herself, the wife demanded to know where she was. The husband informed her through the half-closed lid that she was in the regions of his Satanic Majesty. 'And is thoo thor tee?' she asked. 'Ay.' 'And hoo lang hes thoo been thor?' 'Six months.' 'And hoo lang hev aa been thor?' 'Three months.' 'Had away, then,' said the thirsty wife, 'and get's a gill o' whisky: thoo knaas the plyace bettor than aa de!'

The Parsons' Meeting

Source: Edward M. Wilson, 'Some Humorous English Folk Tales: Part Three', *Folk-Lore*, 54, 1943, pp. 259–60.

Narrator: Mrs Joseph Haddow, Crosthwaite, Westmorland, September 1940.

Type: AT1738 'The Dream: All Parsons in Hell'.

IT WAS, LIKE, A parsons' meeting and they were all sitting round t'fire, waiting of this one to come in. And when he arrived he just looked round 'em all an' smiled. And t'main parson (what do you call him?), t'bishop, he just stood up an' asked him where he'd been.

'Wha!' he says, 'I've been to Hell.'

'And what was it like there?'

'Why it was summat similar till it is here.'

'And what's that?'

'Why, ye couldn't git round t'fire fer parsons.'

The Penzance Solicitor

Source: M. A. Courtney, *Cornish Feasts and Folklore*, 1890, p. 84.
Narrator: A Penzance butcher.
Type: AT1589 'The Lawyer's Dog Steals Meat'.

A SOLICITOR IN PENZANCE had a very large dog that was in the habit of coming into their market and stealing joints of meat from the stalls. One day one of them went to the lawyer, and said – 'Please sir, could I sue the owner of a dog for a leg of mutton stolen from my stall?' 'Certainly, my good man.' 'Then, please sir, the dog is yours, and the price of the mutton is 4s. 6d.' The money was paid, and the man was going way in triumph, when he was called back by these words: 'Stay a moment, my good man, a lawyer's consultation is 6s. 8d., you owe me the difference': which sum the discomfited butcher had to pay.

This is described as 'a favourite story handed down amongst the butchers [of Penzance market] from father to son'. The Elizabethan lawyer Plowden is reputed (Burne & Jackson, *Shropshire Folk-Lore*, 1883, p. 591) to have coined the proverbial phrase 'the case is altered' in similar circumstances. W. M. Dickinson's *Cumbriana, or, Fragments of Cumbrian Life* (1875, p. 95) has the following anecdote:

> An eccentric attorney met a country client in Main-street, Cockermouth, who stopped him and said, 'O, Mister Nicholson, can ye tell me if this sebben shillin' piece is a good an?' 'Yes,' replied the lawyer, putting it into his pocket and giving him fourpence change – it is perfectly good, and I'm obliged to you.'

The same story is told in Briscoe's *Stories About the Midlands* (1853, pp. 57–8) about a Nottingham solicitor, George Hopkinson, known as Lawyer Brassey, who died *c.* 1836; Clement Freud gives a similar story in the *Sunday Times*

(10 January 1988) as a 'joke *c.* 1936'. Six shillings and eightpence was the standard lawyer's fee. Seven shilling gold pieces were first issued in 1797.

Solicitors, like clergymen and doctors, are a perennial target for popular wit, though as with all professions most solicitor jokes are perpetrated by solicitors themselves. My own solicitor, Christopher Findley, asked me in 1989 if I had 'heard the one about the rich solicitor and the two poor solicitors?':

> They were walking down the road, when suddenly the rich solicitor looked round and the two poor solicitors had vanished. They were figments of his imagination.

But then, old solicitors never die, they say: they just lose their appeal.

By Line and Rule

Source: G. F. Northall, *English Folk-Rhymes*, 1892, p. 547.
Narrator: Unknown.

A CERTAIN LADY RENOWNED for her wit, but not for her virtue, observing a mason carefully working said, 'By line and rule, works many a fool, good morning, Mr Stonemason,' to which the man readily responded, 'In silk and scarlet walks many a harlot, good morning, madam.'

The Hedge Priest

Source: S. O. Addy, *Household Tales with Other Traditional Remains: Collected in the Counties of York, Lincoln, Derby and Nottingham*, 1895, p. 22.

Narrator: Unknown, from North Derbyshire

AN IRISH PARSON WAS walking in Derbyshire one day when a heavy storm came on, and he had to take shelter under a tree. Two young gentlemen and two young ladies were also taking shelter under this tree. The parson saw that they all looked very sad, and he asked them what made them look so miserable. They said, 'We are all on our way to get married, but the storm has hindered us, and we are afraid it is now too late.'

'If that is all,' said the parson, 'I can marry you.'

They gladly agreed, so the parson took his prayer-book out of his pocket and married them at once. After he had said his marriage service, he repeated these lines over each couple:

> Under a tree in stormy weather
> I married this man and maid together;
> Let him alone who rules the thunder
> Put this man and maid asunder.

Addy notes that James Orchard Halliwell gives 'hedge marriage' as northern English for 'a secret, clandestine marriage.' A 'hedge priest' is defined in Jonathan Green, *The Cassell Dictionary of Slang*, as 'a priest, or a beggar who poses as such, who works in rural areas, ministering to other beggars and the local peasantry; the implication is that such clergy were not true priests.' Hedge priests appear to have often been Irish.

The Socialist Convert

Source: Richard Blakeborough, *Wit, Character, Folklore and Customs of the North Riding of Yorkshire*, 1898, pp. 7–8.
Narrator: Unknown.

IT SEEMS THAT SOME socialist won one man over to his views, and this man met a friend of his. 'Whya, noo then,' began the friend; 'what tha tell ma 'at thoo's to'n'd ti be a socialist, is 't reet?' 'Aye, it's reet; an' it's a gran thing an' all. Thoo owt ti join uz.' 'Owt Ah? What is't 'at ya're after?' 'Whya, thoo knaws it's lyke this; ther's a lot o' fau'k living i' gert hooses, an' tha're eating an' drinking all t' daay lang an' guzzling t' neet thruff, sum on 'em, an' it's gahin ti be stopped. Ivverthing's gahin ti be shared up, an' all on uz get what's wer awn; neeabody nowt na mair 'an onnybody else, dizn't ta see.' 'Whya, nut fur sartin,' said his friend. 'Diz ta meean 'at thoo'll share up an' all?' 'Aye, ivverybody will.' 'What, is 't gahin to be a soart o' brotherly luv? Ivverybody wi' nowt neea mair na onnybody else.' 'Aye, that's it; brotherly luv'. Ivverybody all t' seeam, neeabody nowt neea different neeawaays ti neeabody i' neea road.' 'It soonds grand; bud diz ta meean ti saay if thoo 'ed tweea hosses an' Ah 'edn't a hoss 'at thoo'd gi'e ma yan?' 'Iv a mink Ah wad. If Ah'd tweea an' thoo 'edn't yan Ah s'u'd gi'e tha yan leyke all that,' said he, slapping his friend on the back. 'Aye, an' if ta 'ed tweea coos, an' Ah wanted a coo, wad ta gi'e uz a coo?' 'Just t' seeam. If thoo 'edn't a coo, an' Ah 'ed tweea, Ah s'u'd tell tha ti tak yan awaay wi tha. Noo thoo understands what wa're after.' 'An' if thoo'd tweea pigs, an' Ah 'edn't a pig, an' Ah ass'd tha fur a pig, wad ta gi'e ma yan?' 'Naay noo,' said the socialist; 'thoo's cumin' teea clooase hand noo; thoo knaws 'at Ah 'ev tweea pigs.'

This joke can also be found as story No. 31 on page 29 of B. Knyvet Wilson's *More Norfolk Tales* (1931). It was used by Richmal Crompton as the basis for one of her 'William' stories.

The Railway Ticket

Source: William Wood, *A Sussex Farmer*, 1938, p. 49.
Narrator: Unknown.

WE WERE COMING BACK from a game of cricket one evening, the whole eleven being in one compartment, and when somewhere between Falmer and London Road Station where tickets were collected it was noticed that one of the party was asleep, his railway ticket visible in his waistcoat pocket. Someone took it out, then woke him up and told him to get his ticket ready as we were near London Road. He soon found he had lost it, so he was advised to get under the seat, which he did and we shrouded him with cricket bags. When the tickets were collected the man counted them, looked round and said, 'I've got eleven tickets, there are only ten of you, how's that?' 'Oh,' our joker said, 'the other man is under the seat, he always rides there when he can.'

Wood tells this as a true story, in a passage relating practical jokes. I heard it at school in the 1960s told as a joke; Katharine Briggs includes a version, 'The Lost Ticket', heard by herself in a train in May 1967, in her *Dictionary* (Part A, vol. 2, p. 158).

Box About

Source: John Aubrey, *Brief Lives* (1813), ed. Oliver Dick, 1949.
Narrator: James Harrington, from Sir Benjamin Ruddyer.
Type: AT1557 'Box on the Ear Returned'.

MY OLD FRIEND JAMES Harrington, Esq, was well acquainted with Sir Benjamin Ruddyer, who was an acquaintance of Sir Walter Raleigh's. He told Mr J. H. that Sir Walter Raleigh, being invited to dinner with some great person, where his son was to goe with him: He sayd to his Son, Thou art such a quarrelsome, affronting creature that I am ashamed to have such a Beare in my Company. Mr Walt humbled himselfe to his Father, and promised he would behave himselfe mightily mannerly. So away they went, and Sir Benjamin, I thinke, with them. He sate next to his Father and was very demure at least halfe dinner time. Then sayd he, I this morning, not having the feare of God before my eies, but by the instigation of the devill, went to a Whore. I was very eager of her, kissed and embraced her, and went to enjoy her, but she thrust me from her, and vowed I should not, *For your father lay with me but an hower ago.* Sir Walt, being so strangely supprized and putt out of his countenance at so great a Table, gives his son a damned blow over the face; his son, as rude as he was, would not strike his father, but strikes over the face of the Gentleman that sate next to him, and sayed, *Box about, 'twill come to my Father anon.* 'Tis now a common used Proverb.

Aubrey's life of Sir Walter Raleigh is among his most irreverent and amusing, notable especially for this anecdote and for another which informs us that:

> He loved a wench well; and one time getting up one of the Mayds of Honour up against a tree in a Wood ('twas his first Lady) who seemed at first boarding to be something fearfull of her Honour, and modest, she

cryed, sweet Sir Walter, what doe you me ask; Will you undoe me? Nay, sweet Sir Walter! Sweet Sir Walter! Sir Walter! At last, as the danger and the pleasure at the same time grew higher, she cryed in the extasey, Swisser Swatter Swisser Swatter.

A later version of AT1557 follows.

His Highness's Joke

Source: Augustus Hare, *The Story of My Life*, 1900, vol. 6, p. 359.
Narrator: Augusta, 1894.
Type: AT1557 'Box on the Ear Returned'.

GEORGE IV, AS PRINCE Regent, was very charming when he was not drunk, but he generally *was*. Do you remember how he asked Curran to dinner to amuse him – only for that? Curran was up to it, and sat silent all through dinner. This irritated the Prince, and at last, after dinner, when he had had a good deal too much, he filled a glass with wine and threw it in Curran's face, with 'Say something funny, can't you!' Curran, without moving a muscle, threw his own glass of wine in his neighbour's face, saying, 'Pass his Royal Highness's joke.'

The Turnip and the Horse

Source: Edward Boys Ellman, *Recollections of a Sussex Parson*, 1912, p. 93.
Narrator: Unknown, Brighton.
Type: This is motif J.2415.1 *The Two Presents to the King: Beet and Horse*.

A POOR MAN NEAR Brighton grew a huge turnip and sent it to the King. The King graciously accepted and sent the man a guinea. Hearing this an individual (whose descendants are living, so I leave out the name) bought and sent King William a beautiful valuable horse. The King accepted, and immediately sent the huge turnip in return, saying the horse was so fine that he must give something in return that was equally fine of its kind. The man who had expected a valuable gift was not pleased.

Here we find a story popular in medieval jestbooks, which is told as true and attached to a nineteenth-century monarch. The *Daily Mirror* (19 November 1984, p. 7) printed a photograph of gardener Steven Hobday and his giant, 75lb pumpkin. He says, 'I wrote to Buckingham Palace offering it . . . I was told that the Queen would be delighted to receive it and that it would definitely be cooked for her.' Halliwell's *Jokes of the Cambridge Coffee-houses in the Seventeenth Century* (1842) includes a jest of this type told of James I, 'A Gift for a Gift', reprinted from *Cambridge Jests* of 1674.

The Miller with the
Golden Thumb

Source: W. Carew Hazlitt, *Shakespeare Jest-Books: Reprints of the Early and Very Rare Jest-Books Supposed to have been Used by Shakespeare*, 1864, p. 23.

Narrator: Unknown.

Type: AT1620 'The King's New Clothes'.

A MARCHANT THAT THOUGHT to deride a mylner seyd vnto the mylner syttynge amonge company: sir, I haue harde say that euery trew mylner that tollyth trewlye hathe a gylden thombe. The mylner answeryd and sayde it was true. Than quod the marchant: I pray the let me se thy thombe; and when the mylner shewyd hys thombe the marchant sayd: I can not perceyue that thy thombe is gylt; but it is as all other mens thombes be. To whome the mylner answered and sayde: syr, treuthe it is that my thombe is gylt; but ye haue no power to se it: for there is a properte euer incydent *vnto it*, that he that is a cockolde shall neuer haue power to se it.

This is No. 10 of the *Hundred Merry Tales* to which Beatrice refers in *Much Ado About Nothing* (II, i). Hazlitt notes the Somersetshire saying, 'An honest miller hath a golden thumb . . . none but a cuckold can see it'.

Four Jests of
Sir Nicholas le Strange

Source: H. P. Lippincott, *'Merry Passages and Jeasts': A Manuscript Jestbook of Sir Nicholas le Strange (1603–55)*, 1974, pp. 18, 20, 102, 120.
Narrator: (I and II) His mother, (III) his cousin, Dorothy Gourny, (IV) Lady Spring.

I

Sir Henry Sidny dranke one time to an old woman that was exceeding deafe and satt at the lower end of the Table, in a glasse of sacke, but with the annexion of this Phrase, that I be your bedfellow this night; she seeing the sacke (her eyes being better then her eares) replyde, I thanke your good worshipp, with all my Hart, Sir you know whats good for an old woman.

II

A Fellow-commoner in Cambridge comming late to Saint Maries, thrust into a Towne-Pue, where he was repulst by an handsome wench, (that was scarse so chast as faire) so he left the seate, and amongst other foule tearmes calld her whore, whereupon she complaind to the Vice-chancellor, (who was her inward fr[i]end) and he enjoynd him this Penance, to aske her forgivenesse in her Pue the next Sunday openly; so he came to her and Recanted thus; I once calld you whore, tis true, and I confesse it; I now say you are an honest woman, I have done you wrong; and am sorry for it.

III

The Bury Ladyes that usd Hawking and Hunting, were once in a great vaine of wearing Breeches; and some of them being at dinner one day at Sir Edward Lewkenors, there was one Mr Zephory, a very precise and a silenc't Minister, (who frequented that house much) and discourse being offerd of fashions, he fell upon this and declaimd much against it; Rob: Heighem a Jouviall blade being there, he undertooke to vindicate the Ladyes, and their fashion, as decent and such as might cover their shame: for sayes he, if an Horse throwes them, or by any mischance they gett a fall, had you not better see them in their Breeches then Naked? sayes the over-zealous man, in detestation of Breeches, O no, by no meanes: By my Troth Parson, sayes Rob: Heighem, and I commend the for't, for I am of thy mind too.

IV

A woman was speechlesse and had lost her Tongue, and her Husband was advised to goe to a famous Physitian that had done Notable Cures of many kinds; He went, and consulted; and was directed to goe to a certaine wodde, and in such a corner of it, he should find a long Leafe, which being layde on her Tongue, would recover her speech againe; He did so, found it, and apply'de it, and immediatly she came to that volubilitie of speech, as her Tongue was a perpetuall Motion, and the poore Man began now to be more tormented with the Cure, then ever he was with the Disease, having exchangd Silence for Clamour; well, away he goes to his Doctor, informes of all, and beggs something of him, if it were possible, to make his Wifes Tongue lye still; Friend sayes he, God helpe the now for I cannot; A woman that hath lost her speech, thou see'st may be recovered; but if once her Tongue setts a running, all the Divells in Hell cannot make it lye still.

These four jokes come from a manuscript compiled apparently for the private pleasure of the author. It was plundered over the years by jest-book compilers (notably W. Carew Hazlitt), but never published in full on account of the bawdy nature of many of the stories. Le Strange was careful to record who had told him each joke, and it is interesting to note that the narrators of all four given above were women. The book, admirably edited by Lippincott, is a valuable record, as he says, of 'the sort of jests which circulated among the gentry in Norfolk in the mid seventeenth century' – and presumably in other counties too. It is much more readable than most of the literary jest-books, preserving as it does the rhythms of real speech.

The first jest is No. 6 in le Strange's original, and occurs again as No. 554, with the woman identified as 'Mrs Thurlow'. Jest II is No. 16 in le Strange, and in the final sentence 'have done you wrong' is replaced by 'belyed you' in a different hand. Jest III is No. 354 in le Strange and Jest IV is No. 431, of which there is an English ballad on the same theme, 'The Dumb Wife' (Holloway and Black, *Later English Broadside Ballads*, vol. 2, 1979, p. 73); another prose jest-book version, also called 'The Dumb Wife', can be found in the Briggs *Dictionary* (Part A, vol. 2, pp. 65–6).

The Bishop and the Doorbell

Source: Augustus Hare, *The Story of My Life*, 1900, vol. 6, p. 385.
Narrator: Miss R., 1895.

THE BISHOP OF WINCHESTER and the Dean of Windsor were walking together down the street of Windsor, when they saw a little boy struggling to reach a bell. 'Why, you're not tall enough, my little man; let me ring the bell for you,' said the Bishop. 'Yes, if you please, sir,' said the boy modestly. So the Bishop gave the bell a good pull. 'Now then, sir, run like the devil,' shrieked the boy, as he made off as hard as he could.

The Independent Bishop

Source: Ella Mary Leather, *The Folklore of Herefordshire*, 1912, pp. 177–8.
Narrator: A mason, at Longtown, 1909.
Type: AT922 'The Shepherd Substituting for the Priest Answers the King's Questions'.

ONCE KING GEORGE CAME to Worcester, and went to see the Bishop. Now he was a very independent man and would give way to nobody, therefore he had fixed to his door a brass plate, and on it was this: 'The Independent Bishop of Worcester'. When King George saw this he stared. 'I like this,' he says, 'this won't do at all; I'll give him independent indeed.' So he walked in. When the Bishop came in, he said: 'I see you call yourself the Independent Bishop of Worcester?' 'Yes,' said the Bishop, 'so I am; I am afraid of no man,' says he. 'Well,' says King George, 'you must come to me in the Tower of London in three weeks' time, and you must answer three questions. If you can answer truly you can keep that plate on the door; if not, off it comes, and you shall not call yourself the independent Bishop any more. You shall tell me first how soon I can travel all round the world; secondly, to a farthing what I am worth; thirdly, what I think at the moment we are speaking.' 'Very well, your Majesty,' said the Bishop. And the King went off to London. Next morning the Bishop was up very early; he had not slept a wink, and he kept walking up and down, up and down the walk in his garden. His old gardener asked him what the trouble was. 'Nothing at all, nothing at all,' said the Bishop. But he walked up and down faster and faster, and the gardener, an old servant, ventured to ask him again what was the matter. 'Well,' said the Bishop, 'I'll tell you; you've served me well these many years.' 'Is that all?' said the gardener, when the Bishop had finished. Then he thought a bit. 'Does the King know you well?' he asked. 'No,' said the Bishop, 'he saw me yesterday for the first time.' 'They say I am a bit like your lordship,' says the gardener, 'give me a suit o' your clothes and I'll answer those questions in the Tower o' London for you.' It was agreed, and when the day came the King, with the courtiers all round, asked the first question: 'Well, how soon can I travel all round the world?' 'You must go with the sun,' said the gardener, 'then it will take you exactly twenty-four hours.' 'Well done,' said the King, and all the courtiers said, 'There, that's one for the Bishop.' 'Ah,' said the King, 'but you must tell me what I am worth?' 'Nothing at all; only one man in the world has ever been worth anything, and that was our Saviour; he was sold for thirty silver pieces, and you therefore cannot be worth one farthing.' 'True again,' said the King. 'Another to the Bishop!' they all shouted, 'another to the Bishop!' 'But you cannot tell me what I think?' said King George. 'You think I am the Independent Bishop of Worcester, but I am his gardener and his servant come to answer for him,' said he. The King laughed, and they all said 'The Independent Bishop, another for the Bishop!' So the gardener took good news home to his master, who was independent still, and he kept that plate on his door as long as he was Bishop of Worcester.

This is a version of the ballad 'King John and the Abbot' (F. J. Child, *The English and Scottish Popular Ballads*, No. 45). Walter Anderson's *Kaiser und Abt* (1923) is a thorough study of this tale type.

The Miller at the Professor's Examination

Source: *Folk-Lore Record*, 2, 1879, pp. 173–6.
Narrator: Unknown.
Type: AT924b 'The Language of Signs Misunderstood'.

THERE ONCE CAME TO England a famous foreign professor, and before he came he gave notice that he would examine the students of all the colleges in England. After a time he had visited all but Cambridge, and he was on his road thither to examine publicly the whole university. Great was the bustle in Cambridge to prepare for the reception of the professor, and great also were the fears of the students, who dreaded the time when they must prove their acquirements before one so famous for his learning. As the period of his arrival approached their fears increased, and at last they determined to try some expedient which might avert the impending trial, and for this purpose several of the students were disguised in the habits of common labourers, and distributed in groups of two or three at convenient distances from each other along the road by which the professor was expected.

He had in his carriage arrived at the distance of a few miles from Cambridge when he met the first of these groups of labourers, and the coachman drew up his horses to inquire of them the distance. The professor was astonished to hear them answer in Latin. He proceeded on his way, and after driving about half a mile, met with another group of labourers at work on the road, to whom a similar question was put by the coachman. The professor was still more astonished to hear them give answer in Greek. 'Ah,' thought he, 'they must be good scholars at Cambridge, when even the common labourers on the roads talk Latin and Greek. It won't do to examine them in the same way as other people.' So all the rest of the way he was musing on the mode of examination he should adopt, and just as he reached the outskirts of the town, he came to the determination that he would examine them by signs. As soon, therefore, as he had alighted from his carriage, he lost no time in making known this novel method of examination.

Now the students had never calculated on such a result as this from their stratagem, and they were, as might well be expected, sadly disappointed. There was one student in particular who had been studying very hard, and who was expected by everybody to gain the prize at the examination, and, as the idlest student in the university had the same chance of guessing the signs of the professor as himself, he was in very low spirits about it. When the day of examination arrived, instead of attending it, he was walking sadly and mournfully by the banks of the river, near the mill, and it happened that the miller, who was a merry fellow, and used to talk with this student as he passed the mill in his walks, saw him, and asked him what was the matter with him. Then the student told him all about it, and how the great professor was going to examine by signs, and how he was afraid that he should not get through the examination. 'Oh! if that's all,' said the miller, 'don't be low about the matter. Did you never hear that a clown may sometimes teach a scholar wisdom? Only let me put on your clothes, with your cap and gown, and I'll go to the examination instead of you; and if I succeed you shall have the credit of it, and if I fail I will tell them who I am.' 'But,' said the student, 'everybody knows that I have but one eye.' 'Never mind that,' said the miller; 'I can easily put a black patch over one of mine.' So they changed clothes, and the miller went to the professor's examination in the student's cap and gown, with a patch on his eye.

Well, just as the miller entered the lecture-room, the professor had tried all the other students, and nobody could guess the meaning of his signs or answer his questions. So the miller stood up, and the professor, putting his hand in his coat pocket, drew out an apple, and held it up towards him. The miller likewise put his hand in his pocket and drew out a crust of bread, which he in like manner held out towards the professor. Then the professor put the apple in his pocket and pointed at the miller with one finger: the miller in return pointed at him with two: the professor pointed with three; and the miller held out his clenched fist. 'Right!' said the professor; and he adjudged the prize to the miller.

The miller made all haste to communicate these good tidings to his friend the student, who was waiting at the mill; and the student, having resumed his own clothes, hastened back to hear the prize given out to him. When he arrived at the lecture-room the professor was on his legs explaining to the assembled students the meaning of the signs which himself and the student who had gained the prize made use of.

'First,' said he, 'I held out an apple, signifying thereby the fall of mankind through Adam's sin, and he very properly held up a piece of bread, which signified that by Christ, the bread of life, mankind was regenerated. Then I held out one finger, which meant that there is one God in the Trinity; he held out two fingers, signifying that there are two; I held out three fingers, meaning that there are three; and he held out his clenched fist, which was as much as to say that the three are one.'

Well, the student who got the prize was sadly puzzled to think how the miller knew all this, and as soon as the ceremony of publishing the name of the successful candidate was over he hastened to the mill, and told him all the professor had said. 'Ah!' said the miller, 'I'll tell you how it was. When I went in the professor looked mighty fierce, and he put his hand in his pocket, and fumbled about for some time, and at last he pulled out an apple, and he held it out as though he would throw it at me. Then I put my hand in my pocket, and could find nothing but an old crust of bread, and so I held it out in the same way, meaning that if he threw the apple at me I would throw the crust at him. Then he looked still more fiercely, and held out his one finger, as much as to say he would poke my one eye out, and I held two fingers, meaning that if he poked out my one eye I would poke out his two, and then he held out three of his fingers, as though he would scratch my face, and I clenched my fist and shook it at him, meaning that if he did I would knock him down. And then he said I deserved the prize.'

The Building of the Wrekin

Source: Charlotte S. Burne (ed.), from the collections of Georgina F. Jackson, *Shropshire Folk-Lore: A Sheaf of Gleanings*, 1883, p. 2.
Narrator: Unknown.

LONG, LONG AGO, IN the days when there were giants in the land, two of them were turned out by the rest and forced to go and live by themselves, so they set to work to build themselves a hill to live in. In a very short time they had dug out the earth from the bed of the Severn, which runs in the trench they made to the present time, and with it they piled up the Wrekin, intending to make it their home. Those bare patches on the turf, between the Bladderstone and the top of the hill, are the marks of their feet, where from that day to this the grass has never grown. But they had not been there long before they quarrelled, and one of them struck at the other with his spade, but failed to hit him, and the spade descending to the ground cleft the solid rock and made the 'Needle's Eye'. Then they began to fight, and the giant with the spade (for they seem to have had only one between them – perhaps that was what they quarrelled about!) was getting the best of it at first, but a raven flew up and pecked at his eyes, and the pain made him shed such a mighty tear that it hollowed out the little basin in the rock which we call the Raven's Bowl, or sometimes the Cuckoo's Cup, which has never been dry since, but is always full of water even in the hottest summers. And now you may suppose that it was very easy for the other giant to master the one who had the spade, and when he had done so, he determined to put him where he could never trouble anyone again. So he very quickly built up the Ercall Hill beside the Wrekin, and imprisoned his fallen foe within it. There the poor blind giant remains until this day, and in the dead of night you may sometimes hear him groaning.

Georgina Jackson's extensive collection of Shropshire folklore is one of the fullest and most trustworthy of English local surveys. These quarrelsome giants may be compared with their brothers in Cornish and Yorkshire tradition. The notion of the 'poor blind giant' still to be heard groaning beneath his hill recalls the 'moans and groans' of the townsfolk buried by the giant Addleback (see the introduction, p. xxvi).

A second account of the origin of the Wrekin, from the same source, follows.

How Far is it to Shrewsbury?

Source: Charlotte S. Burne (ed.), from the collections of Georgina F. Jackson,
Shropshire Folk-Lore: A Sheaf of Gleanings, 1883, pp. 2–3.
Narrator: Unknown.

ONCE UPON A TIME there was a wicked old giant in Wales, who, for
some reason or other, had a very great spite against the Mayor of Shrewsbury
and all his people, and he made up his mind to dam up the Severn, and by
that means cause such a flood that the town would be drowned. So off he
set, carrying a spadeful of earth, and tramped along mile after mile trying to
find the way to Shrewsbury. And how he missed it I cannot tell, but he must
have gone wrong somewhere, for at last he got close to Wellington, and by
that time he was puffing and blowing under his heavy load, and wishing he
was at the end of his journey. By-and-bye there came a cobbler along the road
with a sack of old boots and shoes on his back, for he lived at Wellington,
and went once a fortnight to Shrewsbury to collect his customers' old boots
and shoes, and take them home with him to mend. And the giant called out
to him. 'I say,' he said, 'how far is it to Shrewsbury?' 'Shrewsbury!' said the
cobbler; 'what do you want at Shrewsbury?' 'Why,' said the giant, 'to fill up
the Severn with this lump of earth I've got here. I've an old grudge against
the Mayor and the folks at Shrewsbury, and now I mean to drown them
out and get rid of them all at once.' 'My word!' thought the cobbler, 'this'll
never do! I can't afford to lose my customers!' and he spoke up again. 'Eh!'
he said, 'you'll never get to Shrewsbury, not today, *nor* tomorrow. Why,
look at me! *I'm* just come from Shrewsbury, and I've had time to wear out
all these old boots and shoes on the road since I started.' And he showed
him his sack. 'Oh!' said the giant, with a great groan, 'then it's no use! I'm
fairly tired out already, and I can't carry this load of mine any farther. I shall
just drop it here and go back home.' So he dropped the earth on the ground
just where he stood, and scraped his boots on the spade, and off he went
home again to Wales, and nobody ever heard anything of him in Shropshire
after. But where he put down his load there stands the Wrekin to this day,

and even the earth he scraped off his boots was such a pile that it made the little Ercall by the Wrekin's side.

___◌◖◗◌___

Edward Thomas made use of this lively aetiological legend in his poem in celebration of the stubborn and wily virtues of the English countryman, 'Lob':

> And while he was a little cobbler's boy
> He tricked the giant coming to destroy
> Shrewsbury by flood. 'And how far is it yet?'
> The giant asked in passing. 'I forget;
> But see these shoes I've worn out on the road
> And we're not there yet.' He emptied out his load
> Of shoes for mending. The giant let fall from his spade
> The earth for damming Severn, and thus made
> The Wrekin hill; and little Ercall hill
> Rose where the giant scraped his boots.

For a story from Kidderminster in which the thwarted character is the Devil, and not, as here, a giant, see 'The Devil's Spittleful' (Briggs, *Dictionary*, Part B, vol. 1, p. 92). Devizes was similarly saved from the Devil's wrath by a man who claimed, 'I started for Devizes when my beard was black, and now it's grey, and I haven't got there yet,' so the Devil threw down his load in disgust, creating Cley Hill near Warminster (J. U. Powell, 'Folklore Notes from South Wilts', pp. 78–9).

Carn Galva, and the Giant of the Carn

Source: William Bottrell, *Traditions and Hearthside Stories of West Cornwall*, 2nd series, 1870, pp. 43–5.

Narrator: Unknown, West Cornwall, mid nineteenth century.

ONE CAN'T FAIL TO pass a pleasant time, should the weather be fine, among the rocks and glades of Carn Galva. Above all, if we ramble hither through the ferns, heath, and furze, in the whortleberry season, we may pick the rich fruit, roll in the shade, or bask in the sun, on the beautiful green patches of turf, as soft as velvet, to be found everywhere; or one may ramble in and out, and all around, playing hide-and-seek, through the crellas between the carns, whence the good old Giant of the Carn often sallied forth to protect his Morvah people and their cattle against the incursions of the giants of other carns and hills. Those of Trink and Trecrobben were the most troublesome, because they lived near, in castles strong and high.

Now, they say that when the Trecrobben giant once got the cattle, or tin, into his stronghold, he would defy all the other giants in the country. By the traditions, still preserved in Morvah, the Giant of Carn Galva was more playful than warlike. Though the old works of the giant now stand desolate, we may still see, or get up and rock ourselves upon, the logan-stone which this dear old giant placed on the most westerly carn of the range, that he might log himself to sleep when he saw the sun dip into the waves and the sea-birds fly to their homes in the cleaves. Near the giant's rocking-seat, one may still see a pile of cubical rocks, which are almost as regular and shapely now as when the giant used to amuse himself in building them up, and kicking them down again, for exercise or play, when alone and he had nothing else to do. The people of the northern hills have always had a loving regard for the memory of this giant, because he appears to have passed all his life at the carn in single blessedness, merely to protect his beloved people of Morvah and Zennor from the depredations of the less honest Titans who then dwelt on Lelant hills. Carn

Galva giant never killed but one of the Morvah people in his life, and that happened all through loving play.

The giant was very fond of a fine young fellow, of Choon, who used to take a turn over to the carn, every now and then, just to see how the old giant was getting on, to cheer him up a bit, to play a game of bob, or anything else to help him to pass his lonely time away. One afternoon the giant was so well pleased with the good play they had together that, when the young fellow of Choon threw down his quoit to go away home, the giant, in a good-natured way, tapped his playfellow on the head with the tips of his fingers. At the same time he said, 'Be sure to come again tomorrow, my son, and we will have a capital game of bob.' Before the word 'bob' was well out of the giant's mouth, the young man dropped at his feet – the giant's fingers had gone right through his playmate's skull. When, at last, the giant became sensible of the damage he had done to the brain-pan of the young man, he did his best to put the inside workings of his mate's head to rights and plugged up his finger-holes, but all to no purpose; for the young man was stone dead, long before the giant ceased doctoring his head.

When the poor giant found it was all over with his playmate, he took the body in his arms, and sitting down on the large square rock at the foot of the carn, he rocked himself to and fro; pressing the lifeless body to his bosom, he wailed and moaned over him, bellowing and crying louder than the booming billows breaking on the rocks in Permoina.

'Oh, my son, my son, why didn't they make the shell of thy noddle stronger? A es as plum [soft] as a pie-crust, dough-baked, and made too thin by the half! How shall I ever pass the time without thee to play bob and mop-and-heede [hide-and-seek]?'

The giant of Carn Galva never rejoiced any more, but, in seven years or so, he pined away and died of a broken heart.

So the Morvah people say – and that one may judge of the size of their giant very well, as he placed his logan-rock at such a height that, when seated on it, to rock himself, he could rest his feet comfortably on the green turf below.

Some, also, say that he gathered together the heap of square blocks, near his favourite resting-place, that he might have them at hand to defend his Morvah people against the giants of Trecrobben and Trink, with whom he fought many a hard battle. Yet when they were all on good terms they would pass weeks on a stretch in playing together, and the quoits which served them to play bob, as well as the rocks they hurled at each other when vexed, may still be seen scattered all over this hilly region.

Bottrell writes, 'We have often heard the high-country folks relate this legend of their giant in a much more circumstantial manner than we can attempt, because we do not, like the good Morvah folk, give implicit credence to all the traditions of Carn Galva.' Cornwall seems to have been particularly rich in giant legends, with giants especially associated with any notable rocks.

The Giant of Dalton Mill

Source: Contributed by Sabine Baring-Gould to William Henderson, *Notes on the Folklore of the Northern Counties of England and the Borders*, 2nd edn, 1879, p. 195.

Narrator: Unknown, Yorkshire.

Type: AT1137 'The Ogre Blinded (Polyphemus)'.

AT DALTON, NEAR THIRSK, in Yorkshire, is a mill. It has quite recently been rebuilt, but when I was at Dalton, six years ago, the old building stood. In front of the house was a long mound, which went by the name of 'the giant's grave', and in the mill was shown a long blade of iron something like a scythe-blade, but not curved, which was said to have been the giant's knife. A curious story was told of this knife. There lived a giant at this mill, and he ground men's bones to make his bread. One day he captured a lad on Pilmoor, and instead of grinding him in the mill he kept him as his servant and never let him get away. Jack served the giant many years and never was allowed a holiday. At last he could bear it no longer. Topcliffe fair was coming on, and the lad entreated that he might be allowed to go there to see the lasses and buy some spice. The giant surlily refused leave; Jack resolved to take it.

The day was hot, and after dinner the giant lay down in the mill with his head on a sack and dozed. He had been eating in the mill and had laid down a great loaf of bone bread by his side, and the knife was in his hand, but his fingers relaxed their hold of it in sleep. Jack seized the moment, drew the knife away, and holding it with both his hands drove the blade into the single eye of the giant, who woke with a howl of agony, and starting up barred the door. Jack was again in difficulties, but he soon found a way out of them. The giant had a favourite dog which had also been sleeping when his master was blinded. Jack killed the dog, skinned it, and throwing the hide over his back ran on all fours barking between the legs of the giant, and so escaped.

The incident of the blinded ogre, familiar from the *Odyssey*, is widely found as an independent folktale. For a fairy-lore version which includes the *Odyssey*'s 'No man' motif, see 'My Ainsell' (p. 270).

Tommy Lindrum

Source: Ethel Rudkin, *Lincolnshire Folklore*, 1936, pp. 63–4.
Narrator: A native of Wroot, Lincolnshire, 1931.
Type: ML7061 'The Unfinished Bridge' (Katharine Briggs suggested type).

TOMMY LINDRUM WAS A won'erful chap, they sa-ay. When 'e was a lad 'is father set 'im ter tent sparrers offen corn, whiles 'is father went ter Wroot Feast – that would be i' July. Tom was mad at 'avin' ter stop 'ome, so 'e wayited while sparrers flew in barn, then 'e puts an 'arrow over the pigeon-'oles, an' shuts barn door, an' off 'e goes ter Wroot Feast! 'Is father was that mad when 'e met the lad, an' axed 'im wot 'e meant by le-avin' the corn ter the sparrers? Tom said as 'e'd shut all the sparrers in the barn. Anyways, in the mornin', when 'is father went to the barn, sparrers flew out – leastways, them as flew out was white wi' fright, but there was lots of others in the barn but they was dee-ad. An' the odd part of it is, that not over thirty years back there *was* a white sparrer in Wroot! I know there was, 'cos I seed it mesen.

Then Tom was in lea-gue wi' the Devil, an' sold 'im 'is soul. Now, it was very wet goin', i' them da-ays, 'twixt Wroot an' Lindrum, so Tom said as 'e'd build a proper causey a-tween the two – an' the Devil reckoned to do it as fast as a man on an 'oss could gallop – but the man looked back, an' 'e gie'd over doin' it; an' the odd part of *that* is, that there *is* the beginnin's of a cobbled roo-ad there now – I've seed it – well! 'ow did it get there if Tommy didn't maa-ke it?

An' they do sa-ay that Tommy threw the old stoo-an in the gress field up agen the village there, right from Lindrum; but no ones da-ares so much as ter touch the stoo-an, or ter ra-ise it noo, though its nearly gressed o'er. If ever it *should* get gressed o'er, then, th' earth'll be covered wi' blood! No moss'll grow on t' stoo-an, for stoo-an eats it off as fast as it grows. Years agoo, when yon field was plooghed, stoo-an war i' the roo'ad for plooghin', so the farmer wot 'ad the land then, reckoned 'e'd shift it. So 'e yocked 'is 'osses ter the stoo-an, an' they tugged an' pulled at it, but th' 'osses dropped doown an' deed. After that no-one dares touch it.

In an ole box i' the granary at Lindrum, they've gotten Tommy's bones, fur I've seed 'em.

When it come ter be time, 'e buried 'is sen under 'is 'earth-stoo-an. 'E dug a gra-ave, got inside, an' let stoo-an doown a-top on 'im.

But wot I'm thinkin' is, that if Tommy really *was* somebody, why isn't theere a book aboot 'im? Why cant we re-ad aboot 'im an' 'is doin's? An' its 'cos theere is none o' these things writ doown as ma-akes me think that 'e niver *was* anybody. But then – theere's 'is stoo-ans, an' 'is roo-ad, an' if 'e didn't put 'em theere, 'oo did? I dunno wot ter think.

They sa-ay the stoo-an i' the gress clo-ose up yonder is sha-aped like a 'oose, but yer can't see it, fer its sunk i' the groound wi' its own weight.

For more stories of William of Lindholme, see Gutch and Peacock, *Examples of Printed Folk-Lore Concerning Lincolnshire* (*County Folk-Lore*, V, 1908, p. 322). They supply an essential element of 'The Unfinished Bridge' story:

> 'He undertook to do it as fast as a man could gallop a horse, on condition that the rider should not look behind him.' When the person had proceeded a few yards he heard such a noise and confusion that his fears got the better of his resolution; he looked back and saw stones and gravel flying in all directions and William in the midst of hundreds of little demons, not in blue but in red jackets, macadamizing as fast as possible. The terrified horseman exclaimed, 'God speed your work,' which, as is usual in all these stories, put a stop to the whole business.

The significance of Tommy Lindrum burying himself is to cheat the Devil of his due. Ethel Rudkin notes that in 1727 a hermit's grave was excavated on Lindholme by men intrigued by the legends then current about the great 'stone-thrower'. Beneath a large freestone slab they found human bones 'all of a very large size, also a piece of beaten copper and a peck of hempseed'.

Jack o' Kent

Source: Ella Mary Leather, *The Folklore of Herefordshire*, 1912, pp. 163–6.

Narrators: Various. 'Jack and the Mince Pie' told at Grosmont, 1908. 'The Christmas Block' told by Mrs M—, of Orcop, aged eighty-six in 1909. 'Jack and the Pigs' told at Ashperton, also at Weobley. 'Jack as Thresherman' told at Weobley by W. Colcombe, 1908 (narrator of 'Jack the Giant Killer', p. 10)

Type: (The Bridge at Kentchurch) AT1191 'The Dog on the Bridge', (Jack and the Pigs) AT1036 'Hogs with Curly Tails', (Jack as Thresherman) AT1089 'Threshing Contest', (The Tops and the Butts) AT1030 'The Crop Division'.

Jack o' Kent's Funeral

Jack was a wizard in league with the Devil, and when still a boy he sold his body and soul to the 'old un' in exchange for supernatural power in this world, whether he were buried in the church or out of the church, that was the bargain. He was therefore buried at Kentchurch, or some say at Grosmont, in the wall of the church, so that he should be 'neither in nor out'. This part of the story is very generally known in Herefordshire, but an aged woman at Wigmore (1908), added that her mother used to relate how during the funeral ceremony a voice was heard saying –

> False David Sir Ivan,
> False alive, false dead.

She could not explain the name 'David Sir Ivan', but supposed it was a Welsh name for the renowned Jack o' Kent.

The Crows in the Barn

Jack was sent by his master to mind the crows from the wheat, while he was away at Hereford fair. Later in the day, the farmer was much surprised and annoyed to meet Jack in the fair, and asked him sharply why he had left his work. 'Ay, ay,' said Jack, 'ay ay maister, the crows be all right, they be all in the barn.' When the farmer reached home, there were the crows as Jack had said, sitting in an old barn with no roof on it. Their master, the 'old un', was sitting on a cross-beam keeping them in order till Jack came back. 'He was like a big old crow, was their master, and every now and then he said "crawk, crawk".'

The Bridge at Kentchurch

Jack and the Devil built the bridge over the Monnow between Kentchurch and Grosmont in a single night. What they built by night fell down by day, as long as the bridge remained incomplete; hence the need for haste. The first passenger to pass over the bridge was to belong to the Devil, so Jack threw a bone across and a poor dog ran after it. That dog was all the Devil had for his pains.

The White Rocks, Garway

The Devil was helping Jack to stop up the weir, at Orcop Hill, in order to flood the valley, and make a fishpool. But as the Devil was coming over Garway Hill his apron strings broke, and down fell all the stones he was carrying. Then the cock crew, and he had to go home, so there are the stones to this day.

That is an Orcop version; but an old inhabitant of Grosmont said, 'Jacky was the Devil's master. When they were breaking stone up at Garway, the old un said he wouldn't leave off till cock-crow. But that made no difference to Jack, him could make the cocks crow when he liked, him could!'

Jack and the Mince Pie

Jack once went from Kentchurch to London with a mince pie for the King. He started at daybreak, and was there in time for breakfast; the pie was still quite hot. He lost a garter on the way: it was found on the top of a church spire, having caught in the weathercock as he flew over.

The Christmas Block

Once Jack was going to put a Christmas block [a Yule-log] on the fire. It was a very large one, and folks said that he would never get it into the house. 'Wait a bit,' said Jack. He went and fetched four goslings, and fastened them to the log; at his bidding they drew it into the house as easily as if they had been horses.

Jack and the Pigs

Jack and the Devil agreed that Jack should go to the market and buy some pigs. 'Which will you have,' said Jack, 'the curly tailed pigs, or the straight-tailed pigs?' 'Straight tails,' said the Devil. So on the way home Jack gave them all a feed of beans, and their tails all curled, every one of them; they were as curly as pigs' tails could be. Next time Jack went to the market, the Devil said he would have all the curly-tailed pigs. That time Jack drove them through a pool of water, by the roadside, on the way home; all their tails became straight then, because they were so wet and cold.

Jack as Thresherman

The Devil was always putting Jack to do hard tasks, trying to find something he couldn't do, but he never succeeded. Once he had to thresh a bay of corn in the barn in a day, and this is how he managed it. He took off his boot, and put it on the top of the stack of corn, and it threw down the sheaves to him, of itself, one by one. He took his flail and set it on the floor, and it threshed the corn by itself, while he sat down and just played his fiddle, repeating continually –

> Nobble, stick, nobble,
> Play, fiddle, play!

So he went on, over and over, and the hay was threshed long before the day was out. 'But when Jack was doing anything like that he always took out his little black stick as he carried, hollow at one end. In the hollow was a thing like a fly; one o' the Devil's imps it was. He would lay the stick down near him, and then he could do anythink, like.'

The Tops and the Butts

One day, Jack took the Devil into a field of wheat, when it was springing up. He said, 'Which will you have, the tops or the butts?' There was not much top to be seen, so the Devil said he'd have the butts. At harvest time, Jack accordingly had the wheat, the Devil the straw; naturally he grumbled a good deal over such a bad bargain. Next year the field was sown with turnip seed, and Jack said 'You shall have tops this time'; the Devil agreed to this, and in due time Jack had the turnips, leaving for his partner the green tops. After that they went to mow a field of grass, each one to have all the hay he could cut: they were to begin together in the morning. Jack got up in the night and put harrow tynes in the grass, on the side of the meadow where the Devil was to mow. In the morning these notched and blunted the scythe, which was continually catching in them; but the 'old un', thinking they were only burdocks, kept muttering, 'Burdock, Jack! Burdock, Jack!' Jack took no notice, and moving away diligently, secured nearly all the crop for himself once more. Then they went to threshing; Jack was to have bottoms this time, so he got the barn floor, and the Devil went on top; he put up a hurdle for the Devil to thresh on, and as he battered away Jack collected the corn on the floor.

The Dove and the Raven

On his death-bed Jack commanded that his 'liver and lights' should be placed on three iron spikes which projected from the church tower. Some say the church was Kentchurch, but at Grosmont they show the iron spikes still *in situ.* Jack prophesied that a dove and a raven would come and fight over his remains if thus exposed, and that, if his soul were saved, and the Devil successfully cheated, the dove would be victorious. This is the usual version, but some say that the dove's victory was only an omen, a sign of a good harvest. Another variant states that if birds came and devoured the remains, Jack would be proved indeed a wizard; if they remained untouched he was not. My informant could not remember what the result of the experiment was supposed to have been.

The Pecked Stone, Trelleck (Monmouthshire)

From Monmouthshire come further accounts of Jack's wonderful exploits. 'Why, one day he jumped off the Sugar Loaf mountain right on to the Skirrid, and there's his heel-mark to this day, an' when he got there he began playing quoits, he pecked [threw] three stones as far as Trelleck, great big ones, as tall as three men (and there they still stand in a field), and he threw another but that did not go quite far enough, and it lay on the Trelleck road, just behind the five trees, till a little while ago, when it was moved so as the field might be ploughed, and this stone, in memory of Jack, was always called the Pecked Stone.

A cellar is still shown at Kentchurch Court, which is said to have been Jack's stable, wherein he kept horses that traversed the air with the speed of Lapland witches. There one may see also Jack o' Kent's bedroom, a panelled room five hundred years old, in which a mysterious ghostly figure has been seen to issue from a recess in the wall on stormy nights. 'As great as the Devil and Jack o' Kent' is still a proverb in Kentchurch.

Readers will recognize various motifs from these legends, such as the wizard cheating the Devil of his due by artful burial, and the magical confinement of crows in the barn, from the stories of 'Tommy Lindrum' (p. 252). John Kent (Sion Cent) was Vicar of Kentchurch in the reign of Henry V. Stories of this magician were told on both sides of the Welsh border, centring on Kentchurch and Grosmont. Ella Mary Leather notes of 'Tops and Butts' that 'This story of Jack is most common of all in the county.' Variants of this legend were well-known throughout the English countryside (see 'The Devil and the Farmer', p. 343).

Legends of Sir Francis Drake

Source: Anna Eliza Bray, *A Description of the Parts of Devonshire Bordering on the Tamar and the Tavy*, 1836, vol. 2, pp. 170–75.

Narrator: Unknown, Devon.

Type: III ML8005 'The Soldier's Return'.

I

One day whilst Sir Francis Drake was playing at the game of Kales on the Hoe at Plymouth, it was announced to him that a foreign fleet (the Armada, I suppose) was sailing into the harbour close by. He showed no alarm at the intelligence, but persisted in playing out his game. When this was concluded, he ordered a large block of timber and a hatchet to be brought to him. He bared his arms, took the axe in hand and manfully chopped up the wood into sundry smaller blocks. These he hurled into the sea, while, at his command, every block arose a fire-ship; and, within a short space of time, a general destruction of the enemy's fleet took place in consequence of the irresistible strength of those vessels he had called up to 'flame amazement' on the foes of Elizabeth and of England.

II

The people of Plymouth were so destitute of water in the reign of Queen Elizabeth, that they were obliged to send their clothes to Plympton to be washed in fresh water. Sir Francis Drake resolved to rid them of this inconvenience. So he called for his horse, mounted, rode to Dartmoor, and hunted about till he found a very fine spring. Having fixed on one that would suit his purpose, he gave a smart lash to his horse's side, pronouncing as he did so some magical words, when off went the animal as fast as he could gallop, and the stream followed his heels all the way into the town.

III

The good people here say that whilst the 'old warrior' was abroad, his lady, not hearing from him for seven years, considered he must be dead, and that she was free to marry again. Her choice was made – the nuptial day fixed, and the parties had assembled in the church. Now it so happened that at this very hour

Sir Francis Drake was at the antipodes of Devonshire, and one of his spirits, who let him know from time to time how things went on in England, whispered in his ear in what manner he was about to lose his wife. Sir Francis rose up in haste, charged one of his great guns, and sent off a cannon ball so truly aimed that it shot up right through the globe, forced its way into the church, and fell with a loud explosion between the lady and her intended bride-groom.

IV

The story says that whilst he was once sailing in foreign seas he had on board the vessel a boy of uncommonly quick parts. In order to put them to the proof, Sir Francis questioned the youth and bade him tell what might be their antipodes at that moment. The boy without hesitation told him Barton Place (for so Buck-land Abbey was then called), the Admiral's own mansion in his native county. After the ship had made some further progress Sir Francis repeated his question, and the answer he received was, that they were then at the antipodes of London Bridge. Drake, surprised at the accuracy of the boy's knowledge, exclaimed 'Hast thou, too, a devil? If I let thee live, there will be one a greater man than I am in the world'; and, so saying, he threw the lad overboard into the sea, where he perished.

Anna Bray's survey of Devon lore, couched as a series of letters to Robert Southey, is one of the first and fullest of such local investigations, though marred by the author's somewhat high-flown style. These anecdotes of Drake as necromancer show romantic legend accreting to an heroic figure. Mrs Bray quotes Southey's response to her letter on Drake, in which he gives a slightly different account of the interrupted wedding. In this Sir Francis returns as a beggar to ask alms from his wife, but is recognized by his smile: an incident, as Southey notes, 'borrowed from Guy, Earl of Warwick . . . and other romances'. Southey quotes Lope de Vega as saying that he had heard of Drake's dealings with the Devil while serving in the Armada, from soldiers who had been prisoners in England. Among other legends touched on by Mrs Bray is one that Drake offered to make his home town of Tavistock, which is fourteen miles inland, into a sea-port, in return for a coveted estate. Further legends of Drake can be found in J. R. W. Coxhead's *The Devil in Devon* (1967, p. 9) and Briggs and Tongue's *Folktales of England* (1965, p. 94).

Biard's Leap

Source: W. H. Jones and L. L. Kropf, *The Folk-Tales of the Magyars*, 1889, pp. 392–3.
Narrator: Unknown, Boston, Lincolnshire.

NEAR LINCOLN IS A place called Biard's Leap; near there an old witch lived in a cave, who enticed people in and ate them. One day a man offered to go and kill her. He had his choice of a dozen horses, so he took them all to a pond, where he threw a stone into the water, and then led the horses to have a drink, and the one which lifted its head first he chose. It was blind. He got on its back, and, taking his sword, set off. When he got to the cave's mouth, he shouted to the witch to come out.

> Wait till I've buckled my shoe,
> And suckled my cubs,

cried the witch. She then rushed out, and jumping on to the horse stuck her claws into its rump, which made it jump over thirty feet (the so-called Biard's leap). The man struck behind him with his sword, which entered the old woman's left breast, and killed her.

This story exists in a number of variants, with the hero sometimes a knight, as in the version in Gutch and Peacock's *County Folklore V: Lincolnshire* (pp. 81–7), and sometimes a farmer, as in 'Byard's Leap', collected in Nottinghamshire, in Addy's *Household Tales* (pp. 25–6). Another story in Addy, 'The Witch and the Ploughman' (pp. 45–6), is substantially the same; it lacks the motif L.210 *Modest choice best* but contains, as Addy's first text does not, the witch's rhyme: 'Wait till I have suckled my cubs and buckled my shoes, and then I will be with thee.' A gypsy version, perhaps rather elaborated, is given by George Hall in *The Gypsy's Parson: His Experiences and Adventures* (1915, pp. 140–1). In this, the witch was once a beautiful girl, 'who sold her blood to the *Beng* [Devil], and that's how she got her powers'; the shepherd who rides blind Bayard is her former sweetheart.

The Prophecy

Source: Contributed by Sabine Baring-Gould to William Henderson, *Notes on the Folk-Lore of the Northern Counties of England and the Borders*, 1866, p. 336.

Narrator: Unknown, Yorkshire.

Type: AT934a 'Predestined Death'.

THERE WAS ONCE A rich man, and he had brass: that he had. One day he was riding out of t' town, and he saw an old witch, and her child had fallen intut mire, and she axed rich man to hug him out, but he wouldn't do nowt o't sort. Eh! she were angry.

She said to him, 'Tha must have a son, and he shall dee afore he be turned twenty-one.'

Well, he had a son, and he was flayed lest what she said should come true.

So he built a tower all round, and there was no door, no but a window high up. And he put bairn in there. And he put an old man i't tower to fend for bairn, and he sent him food and clothes and all he wanted by a rope up intut chamber. Well, when t' lad was one and twenty, ont' very day, it was cold, and t' lad was right starved, so he said tut old man that he'd fain have a fire, and they let down rope and they pulled up a bundle of wood. T' lad hugged bundle, and cast it in t' fire, and as he cast it a snake came out from t' bundle in which it had been hidden, and it bit t' lad, and he died.

She wor a bad un wor that witch!

The Spotted Dog

Source: M. A. Courtney, *Cornish Feasts and Folklore*, 1890, p. 207.
Narrator: 'A girl whose grandmother was the friend mentioned', Cornwall.

IN THE LAST CENTURY there lived in Trezelah (a hamlet in the parish of Gulval, near Penzance), a widow who had been deprived of her rights. Walking one day in the fields near her home she saw a strange spotted dog who seemed to know her; she met it a second time, and decided when she next went out to take a friend with her. Again she saw it (her friend did not), and said 'In the Name of the Lord, speak to me.' It changed into her husband, who told her to be ready at a certain time, when he would fetch her. Soon after, her friend being in the house, the woman, who was giving her children their supper, said 'The time is come, I must be gone'; she then put on her sun-bonnet and went out. She was away about an hour, when she suddenly appeared with a great noise, as if someone had hurled her in through the door. Her story was that her husband had taken her up in his arms and carried her over the tree-tops as far as Ludgvan Church, where he deposited her on the Church-stile, from whence she saw a great many spirits, some good and some bad. The latter wanted her to join them, but her husband bade her remain where she was. What they told her was never known; but by their aid she got back her rights. Then her husband bore her home again by the way they had come; but before he parted from her said 'I must take something from you; either your eyesight, or your hearing.' She preferred losing the latter, and from that hour could never hear a word. One of her shoes that in her flight through the air had caught on a tree-top, seven years after was placed on her window-sill.

The Witch Wife

Source: Alfred Williams, *Round About the Upper Thames*, 1922, pp. 126–7.
Narrator: 'Angel'.

THEN ANGEL MUST RELATE what he had heard from his mother concerning a farm labourer who wedded a beautiful young woman, of whom he was very proud, and who proved to be a witch. Before they had long been married the husband discovered that his bride arose from bed at midnight and left him alone in the darkness. Not knowing how to account for her disappearance, he determined to say nothing but to watch her movements. Accordingly, when night came, he lay very still and pretended to be asleep. A little before midnight his wife arose and dressed, and was going downstairs. Then the husband sprang out of bed, seized her by the arm, and demanded an explanation of her conduct. As she insisted upon going out he announced his intention of accompanying her, to which she agreed, on condition that he should by no means utter a word, for if he did evil would certainly follow, said she.

Then, without another syllable, like young Hermes, she slipped through the keyhole of the door and drew her husband after her. Two milk-white calves were waiting outside. These they mounted and then flew off in the darkness, unimpeded by any obstacles. The husband thought it was an extraordinary adventure, but he said nothing till they came to the river, dimly seen in the starlight. Surely, thought he, the calves would not leap over that. They did so, however, with a mighty bound, and were just coming to earth on the other side when the bridegroom, who was a cowman, amazed at the feat, lost his self-possession and cried: 'That's a good jump for a calf to make!' A moment afterwards the calf shot from under him and he found himself in water up to his waist and alone in the stillness, for the others had vanished. His wife, however, with loving kindness, called for him on her way back and took him out with her on the white calves many times afterwards, but he had the good sense to observe her injunctions and never to break the silence with any incautious remark.

The Witch Hare

Source: J. C. Atkinson, *Forty Years in a Moorland Parish*, 1891, pp. 91–2.
Narrator: Unknown, Cleveland, Yorkshire.
Type: ML3055 'The Witch that was Hurt' (Katharine Briggs suggested type).

IN GLAISDALE HEAD THE trees in a young plantation were continually eaten off. If replaced, still the same fate awaited their successors. It was easy to say there was nothing new in having young sapling trees gnawed completely off by hares and rabbits; or, if of larger size, barked by the latter if not by the former. But there were circumstances in this case which showed – so it was said – that no mere ordinary hare was the cause of the damage complained of. 'Hares might have been seen in the nursery [plantation], leastwise, one particular hare, a bit off the common to look at: but common hares did not cut the tops of the young trees off, ommost as gin they had been cut wiv a whittle, and leave 'em liggin' about just as they were cut, as if nobbut for mischeef. Hares was reasonable creatur's eneugh, and i' lang ho'dding-storms, when ivvery thing was deep happed wi' snow, and they could na get a bite ov owght else, they'd sneap t' young trees, and offens dee a canny bit ov ill. But they did not come, storm or nae storm, and just knipe off tweea or three score o' young saplings, any soort o' weather, as if for gam' or mischeef.' So the usual consultation was held, and with the issue that watch was to be kept by the owner concerned, with a gun loaded with silver shot – which, by the way, was procured as in the last case – and the moment he saw the suspicious hare beginning its nefarious practices, he was to take steady aim and shoot. The watch was set, and at the 'witching hour of night' of course, the hare put in an appearance – 'a great, foul au'd ram-cat ov a heear t' leuk at – and began knepping here and knepping there as if 't wur stoodying how best t' deea maist ill i' lahtlest tahm. Sae t' chap at wur watching, he oop wi's gun, and aiming steady he lat drive [discharged his gun]. My wo'd! but there was a flaysome skrike! An' t' heear, sair ho't [badly wounded], gat hersel' a soort o' croppen out o' t' no'ssery, and ho'ppled [hirpled, limped, hobbled] away as weel 's she could, an' won heeam at last at Au'd Maggie's house-end, in a bit o' scroggs at grows on t' bank theear.' Inquiries, however, were made next day, not among the brushwood on the bank, but at the cottage of the old woman called 'Au'd Maggie'; and unluckily for her reputation, already more than sufficiently shaky in the witch connection, she was found in her bed 'sair ho't in many spots', she said with splinters of a broken bottle she had fallen down upon; but her visitors thought 'mair lik'ly wi' shot-coorns o' some soort'.

This is probably the most widespread single witch story. The Briggs *Dictionary* has thirteen further examples.

Watching for the Milk-Stealer

Source: J. C. Atkinson, *Forty Years in a Moorland Parish*, 1891, pp. 88–90.
Narrator: Unknown, Cleveland, Yorkshire.

THE SCENE WAS LAID in Commondale, part of which valley lies in this parish and part in the parish of Guisborough. A farmer there was perpetually finding that his cows gave very much less milk to the milker's fingers than they ought; and the loss became so considerable that it was deemed necessary to try and put a stop to the cause of it. There were witches *galore* in the neighbourhood, and their well-known nefarious practices in the way of diverting the flow of milk from the right channel were also only too well known. But how to discover if this were the right explanation of the loss complained of, and, if it were, how to obviate its continuance, were both matters the solution of which was not unattended with difficulty. In the issue it was settled that the best and most feasible plan would be to watch the field in which the cows were turned out to pasture during the night, and to take further means or measures according to the result of the watching process. Accordingly the farmer set a trusty hand to keep the necessary watch. An uneventful night, a second, a third passed. The sentinel declared nothing had passed into the field, the cows had never been approached by a soul, and least of all by crone or maid with pail and stool complete. And yet the morning meal of milk was as deficient as ever, there being nothing in the condition of the cows, or in the circumstances of the pasture, or what not, to account for the vexatious fact. At last one of the neighbours, 'mair skeely 'an t'ithers', or perhaps, like the Westerdale yeoman, a little more suspicious, on cross-examining the watcher, elicited the fact that it was not quite accurate to say that nothing whatever had gone into the field where the cows were pasturing, for that each night he had noticed a hare that came in through a gapway in the dike, and that seemed to be feeding about, and mostly right in amongst the cows where they were feeding or standing the closest together. Asked whether the hare always came from the same side, and entered the field through the same broken way, he answered, 'Ay, for seear [sure], and wherefore not? Hares allays gaed the seeam gate, as a' folks kenned.' But the said gap happened to be on the side that was handiest of access to a certain 'Au'd Mally', who had an uncanny reputation, and the 'skeely' [or perhaps suspicious] neighbour suggested that 'Au'd Mally might lik'ly ken whilk weea t' milk gaed.' Hereupon followed another deliberation, the upshot of which was that the farmer himself should watch the next night armed, and with his gun loaded – not with leaden pellets, but – with silver slugs; and as it was not easy to come by silver slugs in an out-of-the-way place like Commondale – and besides that, it was highly expedient to keep their plans as quiet as possible, which could not be if they went to a town to buy such ammunition – it was resolved to cut up an old silver button or two, and charge the gun with the pieces. Well, all was duly done according to programme; the farmer, with his 'hand-gun' charged according to rule, took up his position near the gap aforesaid, and in such a place that, while he was well concealed himself, he could have a good sight of the hare as she entered, and also of the pasturing cows; for he did not want to 'ware' [expend] his costly charge on a mere ordinary long-eared pussy, but wished to catch 'Au'd Mally' – if it were she – *flagrante delicto*, and shoot at her in the very act. Midnight passed and nothing came; but as the small hours drew on the hare was seen approaching with stealthy step, and sitting up on her haunches every minute or two to listen for suspicious sounds, as natural as life. With sheer expectancy the farmer's heart began to beat much faster than usual, and the palpitation did not decrease when, just at the verge of the gap, it stood up again and glowered at the very spot where he lay concealed. Apparently reassured by the stillness, pussy resumed her leisurely advance, and entered the enclosure; but instead of approaching the feeding cows, she came deliberately on with direct course to the farmer's ambush, her eyes getting bigger and bigger with each lope she took, until almost upon the startled watcher, when she reared herself up, growing taller and taller, and 'wiv her een glooring and widening while they war as big as saucers', and with their glare directed full upon the terrified skulker the form stalked straight up to him! With a scream of utter, horrified terror, he sprang from his hiding-place, flung his gun far from him, and rushed headlong away, 'rinning what he could', and never halting even to draw breath until he had got himself safely within his own door, and doubly locked and bolted it. And so ended that attempt to bring the milk-stealing witch to book; and certainly hardly either to her complete discomfiture, or even to her complete conviction.

The Hart Hall Hob

Source: J. C. Atkinson, *Forty Years in a Moorland Parish*, 1891, pp. 54–5.
Narrator: Old woman, Cleveland, Yorkshire.
Type: ML7015 'The New Suit'.

I BEGAN TO ASK her if in her youth she had had any knowledge of the Hart Hall 'Hob'. On this topic she was herself again. 'Why, when she was a bit of a lass, everybody knew about Hart Hall in Glaisdale, and t' Hob there, and the work that he did, and how he came to leave, and all about it.' Had she ever seen him, or any of the work he had done? 'Seen him, saidst 'ee? Neea, naebody had ever seen him, leastwise, mair nor yance. And that was how he coomed to flit.' – 'How was that?' I asked. 'Wheea, everybody kenned at sikan a mak' o' creatur as yon never tholed being spied efter.' – 'And did they spy upon him?' I inquired. 'Ay, marry, that did they. Yah moonleeght neeght, when they heared his swipple [the striking part of the flail] gannan' wiv a strange quick bat [stroke] o' t' lathe fleear [on the barn floor] – ye ken he wad dee mair i' yah neeght than a' t' men o' t' farm cou'd dee iv a deea – yan o' t' lads gat hissel' croppen oop close anenst lathe-deear, an' leeak'd in thruff a lahtle hole i' t' boards, an' he seen a lahtle brown man, a' covered wi' hair, spangin' about wiv fleeal lahk yan wud [striking around with the flail as if he was beside himself]. He'd getten a haill dess o' shaffs [a whole layer of sheaves] doon o' t' fleear, and my wo'd! ommost afore ye cou'd tell ten, he had tonned [turned] oot t' strae, an' sided away t' coorn, and was rife for another dess. He had nae claes on to speak of, and t' lad, he cou'd na see at he had any mak' or mander o' duds by an au'd ragg'd soort ov a sark.' And she went on to tell how the lad crept away as quietly as he had gone on his expedition of espial, and on getting indoors, undiscovered by the unconscious Hob, had related what he had seen, and described the marvellous energy of 't' lahtle hairy man, amaist as nakt as when he wur boorn'. But the winter nights were cold, and the Hart Hall folks thought he must get strange and warm working 'sikan a bat as yon, an' it wad be sair an' cau'd for him, gannan' oot iv lathe wiv nobbut thae au'd rags. Seear, they'd mak' him something to hap hissel' wiv.' And so they did. They made it as near like what the boy had described him as wearing – a sort of a coarse sark, or shirt, with a belt or girdle to confine it round his middle. And when it was done, it was taken before nightfall and laid in the barn, 'gay and handy for t' lahtle chap to notish' when next he came to resume his nocturnal labours. In due course he came, espied the garment, turned it round and round, and – contrary to the usual termination of such legends, which represents the uncanny, albeit efficient, worker as displeased at the espionage practised upon him – Hart Hall Hob, more mercenary than punctilious as to considerations of privacy, broke out with the following couplet –

> Gin Hob mun hae nowght but a hardin' hamp,
> He'll coom nae mair, nowther to berry nor stamp.

'Berry' in the Hart Hall Hob's rhyme means 'thresh'. Reginald Scot's *The Discoverie of Witchcraft* of 1584 tells us that Robin Goodfellow 'would chafe exceedingly, if the maid or good-wife of the house, having compassion for his nakednes, laid anie clothes for him, beesides his messe of white bread and milke, which was his standing fee. For in that case he saith, "What have we here? Hemton, hamten, here will I never more tread nor stampen."'

The best-known English tale of this type is probably that of 'The Cauld Lad of Hilton'. The Cauld Lad is a restless ghost, not a hob or boggart. His song is truly haunting:

> Wae's me, wae's me,
> The acorn's not yet
> Fallen from the tree
> That's to grow the wood,
> That's to make the cradle,
> That's to rock the bairn,
> That's to grow to a man,
> That's to lay me.

My Ainsell

Source: Anon., 'North-Country Fairies', *North-Country Lore and Legend*, December 1889, pp. 549–50.
Narrator: Unknown, Northumberland.
Type: AT1137 'The Ogre Blinded (Polyphemus)'.

A WIDOW AND HER son, a wilful little fellow, in or near Rothley, in the parish of Hartburn, famed in the days of border 'raids', were sitting alone in their solitary cottage, one winter evening, when the child refused to go to bed, because, as he averred, he was not sleepy. His mother told him that, if he would not go, the fairies would come to take him away. He laughed, however, and sat still by the fire, while his mother retired to rest. Soon a beautiful little figure, about the size of a child's doll, came down the wide chimney and alighted on the hearth. 'What do they ca' thou?' asked the astonished boy. 'My Ainsell,' was the reply, 'and what do they ca' thou?' 'My Ainsell,' retorted he, and no more questions were asked. Shortly they began to play together, like brother and sister. At length the fire grew dim. The boy took up the poker to stir it, but in doing so a hot cinder accidentally fell on the foot of his strange playmate. The girl set up a terrific roar, and the boy flung down the tongs and bolted off to bed. Immediately the voice of the fairy mother was heard, asking 'Who's done it?' 'Oh, it was My Ainsell,' screamed the girl. 'Why, then,' said the mother, 'what's all the noise about? There's nyen to blame.'

See 'The Giant of Dalton Mill' (p. 250) for a fuller version of this tale type. Marie Clothilde Balfour supplied Joseph Jacobs with a somewhat literary story for his *More English Fairy Tales* under the title 'Me A'an Sel', anglicized by him to 'My Own Self'. She had heard it from 'Mrs W., a native of North Sunderland'; Jacobs notes that the story is 'widely spread in the North Country'.

The Fairy Bairn

Source: J. C. Atkinson, *Forty Years in a Moorland Parish*, 1891, p. 54.
Narrator: Old woman, North York Moors.
Type: ML5085 'The Changeling'.

SHE HAD KNOWN A lass quite well, who one day, when raking in the hayfield, had raked over a fairy bairn. 'It was liggin' in a swathe of the halfmade hay, as bonny a lahtle thing as ever yan seen. But it was a fairy bairn, it was quite good to tell. But it did not stay lang wi' t' lass at fun' [found] it. It a soort o' dwinied away, and she aimed [supposed] the fairy-mother couldn't deea wivout it any langer.'

———

This chance finding of a fairy child is unlike the common run of changeling stories; the next tale, 'The Fairy Changeling', is much more typical.

The Fairy Changeling

Source: Ella Mary Leather, *The Folklore of Herefordshire*, 1912.
Narrator: Jane Probert of Kington, told in the Homme hop-yard at Weobley,
September 1908.
Type: ML5085 'The Changeling'.

A WOMAN HAD A baby that never grew; it was always hungry, and never satisfied, but it lay in its cradle year after year, never walking, and nothing seemed to do it good. Its face was hairy and strange-looking. One day, the woman's elder son, a soldier, came home from the war, and was surprised to see his brother still in the cradle. But when he looked in, he said, 'That's not my brother, Mother.' 'It is indeed,' said the Mother.

'We'll see about that,' he said. So he obtained, first, a fresh egg, and blew out the contents, filling the shell with malt and hops. Then he began to brew over the fire. At this, a laugh came from the cradle. 'I am old, old, ever so old,' said the changeling, 'but I never saw a soldier brewing beer in an eggshell before.' Then he gave a terrible shriek, for the soldier went for him with a whip, chasing him round and round the room, what had never left his cradle! At last he vanished through the door, and when the soldier went out after him, he met on the threshold his long-lost brother. He was a man, twenty-four years of age, fine and healthy. The fairies had kept him in a beautiful palace under the rocks, and fed him on the best of everything! He should never be so well off again, he said, but when his mother called him, he had to come home.

———

The narrator believed this story to be true. Nineteenth-century newspapers record tragic instances of mothers whose children did not thrive, cruelly misusing them in the belief that the fairies, having previously swapped babies with her, would reclaim the 'changeling' and bring back her own healthy child.

Robert Hunt notes in his *Popular Romances of the West of England* that it has been my fortune, some thirty or forty years since, to have seen several children of whom it had been whispered amongst the peasantry that they were changelings. In every case they have been sad examples of the influence of mesenteric disease.

Skillywidden

Source: William Bottrell, *Traditions and Hearthside Stories of West Cornwall*, 2nd series, 1870, pp. 72–4.

Narrator: 'Capt. Mathy', but told to Bottrell by Jack Tregear, 'an aged tinner of Lelant'.

Type: ML6010 'The Capture of a Fairy'.

'I WISH WE COULD but catch a spriggan, a piskey, or a knacker,' says Capt. Mathy one night, 'ef one can but lay hands on any of the smale people unawares before they vanish, or turn into muryans [ants], they may be made to tell where the goold es buried.'

'Ded 'e ever hear of anybody who ever catched one?' Jack asked.

'Why ess, and knowed his son too; he was my near neighbour, and lived in Trevidga: he told me all about et. One day Uncle Billy, his father, was over in the craft, Zennor church-town side of the hill, cuttan away down in the bottom, where the furze was as high as his head, with bare places here and there, among the brakes all grown over with three-leaved grass [white clover], hurt-trees [whortleberry plants], and griglans [heath]. Uncle Billy was cuttan an openan into one of these places, thinkan to touch pipe there, eat his fuggan [heavy cake], and have a smoke. As he opened the furze, to come to work his hook handy, he spied the prettiest little creature of a smale body one ever seed, sleepan away on a bank of wild thyme all in blossom. The little creature wasn't bigger than a cat, yet every inch like a man, dressed in a green coat, sky-blue breeches and stockings, with diamond-buckled shoes; his little three-cocked hat was drawn over his face to shade en from the sun while he slept. Uncle Billy stopped and looked at am more than a minute, langan to carry an home some way or other. "Ef I could but keep am," thought he, "we should soon be rich enow to ride in a coach." Then he put down the furze-hook easy, took off the cuff from his arm, and slipped the little gentleman into the cuff, feet foremost, before he waked up. The little fellow then opened his pretty brown eyes and said, "Mammy! where are 'e, mammy and daddy! and where am I? And who are you? You are a fine great bucca sure enough; what are 'e caled, an?" says he to Uncle Billy. "I want my mammy! can 'e find her for me?" "I don't know whereabouts she do put up," says Uncle Billy; "come, you shall go home with me, ef you will, and live with our people till your mother do come for 'e." "Very well," says the spriggan, "I dearly love to ride the kids over the rocks, and to have milk and blackberries for supper; will 'e give me some?" "Ess, my son, and bread and honey too," says the old man Uncle Billy, as he took the small body up in his arms and carried him home.

'When the little chap was took out of the furze-cuff and placed upon the hearth-stone, he begun to play with the children as if he had lived with them all his lifetime. The old man and woman were delighted. The children crowed for joy to see the pretty little man jumpan about, and they called am Bobby Griglans. Twice a day a little chayne cup of milk, fresh from the cow, was given to Bobby. He was very nice in his diet, and didn't care for anything but a drop of milk, and a few blackberries, hurts, or hoggans [haws] for a change.

'In the mornings, when the work was going on, he would perch himself up on the furze and ferns in the top of the wood-corner, to be out of the smut and dirt. There he would sing and chirrup away like a robin redbreast. When the hearth was swept, the turfy fire made up, and the old woman fixed on the chimney stool, to knit for the afternoon, Bobby would dance for hours together on the hearth-stone, before her; the faster the knitting-needles clicked, the quicker Bobby would spin round and round. Uncle Billy and An Mary wouldn't leave Bobby go out to play, for fear he might be seen, or run away, before the next good moonlight nights, when he promised to show the old couple the exact spot, on Rosewall Hill, where there was lots of money buried, and another place on the hill where there was a good lode of tin.

'Three days after Bobby Griglans was catched and carried up to Trevidga, half-a-score or more of the neighbours came, with their horses and leaders, to help Uncle Billy get home his furze from the hill, in trusses, and to help him make the rick for winter, as the custom was before wheel-roads were made and wains came into use. The old man didn't like for the spriggan to be seen, so he shut him and the youngest children up in the barn and put a padlock on the door. The smale people had been getting scarcer and scarcer, as so much laming and love of unpoetical facts came into fashan, until they were nearly all frightened away. However, Uncle Billy would keep his out of sight for the time, because you see it was become such a rare thing to see a spriggan or piskey that the folks would be coming about in troops to have a look at Bobby, who didn't like to be gazed at and made to show all his parts to strangers. "Now, stay in the barn and play like good children, but ef one of 'e cry, or try to get out, you will get your breeches warmed with a good wallopan," says Uncle Billy.

'The children were sometimes heard laughan and sometimes cryan. Bobby passed the time dancean on the barn-boards and peepan through the cracks in the door at the furze-carriers; but, as soon as ever the men went in to dinner, up jumped Bob, unbarred the winder, called to the children, "Come along, come, quick; now for a game of mop-and-heede" [hide-and-seek]. Bob and the children jumped out and away, to play among the trusses of furze dropped all round the stem of the rick. In turnan a corner they saw a little man and woman no bigger than Bob. The little man was dressed just like an, only he wore high ridan boots with little silver spurs. The little woman's green gound was spangled all over with silver stars; diamond buckles shone in her high-heeled shoes; and her little steeple-crowned blue hat, perched on a pile of golden curls, was wreathed round with griglan blossoms. The pretty little soul was wringan her hands and cryan, "Oh! my dear and tender Skillywidden; wherever can'st a be gone to? Shall I never cast eyes on thee any more, my only joy?" "Now go'e back, do," says Bob to the children, "my dad and mam are come here too!" On the same breath he called out, "Here I am, mammy." By the time he said "Here I am," the little man and woman, with their precious Skillywidden, were no more to be seen, and they have never been seen there since.

'The children got a good threshan for leavan Skillywidden get away, and serve them right, for ef they had kept an in tell night, he would have shown their daddy where plenty of crocks of gold are buried, and all of them would be gentry now.'

———— ⚜ ————

Robert Hunt, under the title 'A Fairy Caught', prints verbatim in *Popular Romances of the West of England* a letter almost certainly from Bottrell relating this tale as 'heard last week'; this shorter, sparser text offers an interesting comparison with the story as worked-up for publication. According to Bottrell, 'The spoken parts of the story are, for the most part, given in the tinner's words, to serve as an example of the every-day speech of the old country folk.'

Nursing a Fairy

Source: Robert Hunt, *Popular Romances of the West of England*, 3rd edn, 1881, pp. 83–5.

Narrator: Unknown, Cornwall.

Type: ML5070 'Midwife to the Fairies'.

A THRIFTY HOUSEWIFE LIVED on one of the hills between Zennor Church-town and St Ives. One night a gentleman came to her cottage, and told her he had marked her cleanliness and her care: that he had a child whom he desired to have brought up with much tenderness, and he had fixed on her. She should be very handsomely rewarded for her trouble, and he showed her a considerable quantity of golden coin. Well, she agreed, and away she went with the gentleman to fetch this child. When they came to the side of Zennor hill, the gentleman told the woman he must blindfold her, and she, good, easy soul, having heard of such things, fancied this was some rich man's child, and that the residence of its mother was not to be known, so she gave herself great credit for cunning in quietly submitting. They walked on some considerable distance. When they stopped the handkerchief was taken from her eyes, and she found herself in a magnificent room, with a table spread with the most expensive luxuries, in the way of game, fruits, and wines. She was told to eat, and she did so with some awkwardness, and not a little trembling. She was surprised that so large a feast should have been spread for so small a party – only herself and the master. At last, having enjoyed luxuries such as she never tasted before or since, a silver bell was rung, and a troop of servants came in, bearing a cot covered with satin, in which was sleeping the most beautiful babe that human eyes ever gazed on. She was told this child was to be committed to her charge; she should not want for anything; but she was to obey certain laws. She was not to teach the child the Lord's Prayer; she was not to wash it after sundown: she was to bathe it every morning in water, which she would find in a white ewer placed in the child's room: this was not to be touched by any one but herself, and she was to be careful not to wash her own face in this water. In all other respects she was to treat the child as one of her own children. The woman was blinded again, and the child having been placed in her arms, away she trudged, guided by the mysterious father. When out on the road, the bandage was removed from her eyes, and she found she had a small baby in her arms, not remarkably good-looking, with very sharp, piercing eyes, and but ordinarily dressed. However, a bargain is a bargain; so she resolved to make the best of it, and she presented the babe to her husband, telling him so much of the story as she thought it prudent to trust him with. For years the child was with this couple. They never wanted for anything; meat, and even wines, were provided – as most people thought – by wishing for them; clothes, ready-made, were on the child's bed when required; and the charmed water was always in the magic ewer. The little boy grew active and strong. He was remarkably wild, yet very tractable, and he appeared to have a real regard for his 'big mammy', as he called the woman. Sometimes she thought the child was mad. He would run, and leap, and scream, as though he were playing with scores of boys, when no soul was near him. The woman had never seen the father since the child had been with them; but ever and anon, money was conveyed to them in some mysterious manner. One morning, when washing the boy, this good woman, who had often observed how bright the water made the face of the child, was tempted to try if it would improve her own beauty. So directing the boy's attention to some birds singing on a tree outside the window, she splashed some of the water up into her face. Most of it went into her eye. She closed it instinctively, and upon opening it, she saw a number of little people gathered round her and playing with the boy. She said not a word, though her fear was great; and she continued to see the world of small people surrounding the world of ordinary men and women, being with them, but not of them. She now knew who the boy's playmates were, and she often wished to speak to the beautiful creatures of the invisible world who were his real companions; but she was discreet, and kept silence.

Curious robberies had been from time to time committed in St Ives Market, and although the most careful watch had been kept, the things disappeared, and no thief detected. One day our good housewife was at the market, and to her surprise she saw the father of her nursling. Without ceremony she ran up to him – at a moment when he was putting some choice fruit by stealth into his pocket – and spoke to him. 'So, thou seest me, dost thou?' 'To be sure I do, and know 'ee too,' replied the woman. 'Shut this eye,' putting his finger on her left eye. 'Canst see me now?' 'Yes, I tell 'ee, and know 'ee too,' again said the woman.

> Water for elf, not water for self;
> You've lost your eye, your child, and yourself,

said the gentleman. From that hour she was blind in the right eye. When she got home the boy was gone. She grieved sadly, but she never saw him more, and this once happy couple became poor and wretched.

The Adventure of Cherry of Zennor

Source: Robert Hunt, *Popular Romances of the West of England*, 3rd edn, 1881, pp. 120–6.
Narrator: Unknown, Cornwall.
Type: ML5071 'The Fairy Master'.

OLD HONEY LIVED WITH his wife and family in a little hut of two rooms and a 'talfat' [a half-floor at one end of a cottage on which a bed is placed], on the cliff side of Trereen in Zennor. The old couple had half-a-score of children, who were all reared in this place. They lived as they best could on the produce of a few acres of ground, which were too poor to keep even a goat in good heart. The heaps of crogans [limpet-shells] about the hut, led one to believe that their chief food was limpets and gweans [periwinkles]. They had, however, fish and potatoes most days, and pork and broth now and then of a Sunday. At Christmas and the Feast they had white bread. There was not a healthier nor a handsomer family in the parish than Old Honey's. We are, however, only concerned with one of them – his daughter Cherry. Cherry could run as fast as a hare, and was ever full of frolic and mischief.

Whenever the miller's boy came into the 'town', tied his horse to the furze-rick and called in to see if any one desired to send corn to the mill, Cherry would jump on to its back and gallop off to the cliff. When the miller's boy gave chase, and she could ride no further over the edge of that rocky coast, she would take to the cairns, and the swiftest dog could not catch her, much less the miller's boy.

Soon after Cherry got into her teens she became very discontented, because year after year her mother had been promising her a new frock that she might go off as smart as the rest, 'three on one horse to Morva Fair'. As certain as the time came round the money was wanting, so Cherry had nothing decent. She could neither go to fair, nor to church, nor to meeting.

Cherry was sixteen. One of her playmates had a new dress smartly trimmed with ribbons, and she told Cherry how she had been to Nancledry to the preaching, and how she had ever so many sweethearts who brought her home. This put the volatile Cherry in a fever of desire. She declared to her mother she would go off to the 'low countries' [valleys] to seek for service, that she might get some clothes like other girls.

Her mother wished her to go to Towednack, that she might have the chance of seeing her now and then of a Sunday.

'No, no!' said Cherry, 'I'll never go to live in the parish where the cow ate the bell-rope, and where they have fish and taties [potatoes] every day, and conger-pie of a Sunday for a change.'

One fine morning Cherry tied up a few things in a bundle and prepared to start. She promised her father that she would get service as near home as she could, and come home at the earliest opportunity. The old man said she was bewitched, charged her to take care she wasn't carried away by either the sailors or pirates, and allowed her to depart. Cherry took the road leading to Ludgvan and Gulval. When she lost sight of the chimneys of Trereen, she go out of heart, and had a great mind to go home again. But she went on.

At length she came to the four cross roads on the Lady Downs, sat herself down on a stone by the roadside, and cried to think of her home, which she might never see again.

Her crying at last came to an end, and she resolved to go home and make the best of it.

When she dried her eyes and held up her head she was surprised to see a gentleman coming towards her – for she couldn't think where he came from; no one was to be seen on the Downs a few minutes before.

The gentleman wished her 'Good morning', inquired the road to Towednack, and asked Cherry where she was going.

Cherry told the gentleman that she had left home that morning to look for service, but that her heart had failed her, and she was going back over the hills to Zennor again.

'I never expected to meet with such luck as this,' said the gentleman. 'I left home this morning to seek for a nice clean girl to keep house for me, and here you are.'

He then told Cherry that he had been recently left a widower, and that he had one dear little boy, of whom Cherry might have charge. Cherry was the very girl that would suit him. She was handsome and cleanly. He could see that her clothes were so mended that the first piece could not be discovered; yet she was as sweet as a rose, and all the water in the sea could not make her cleaner. Poor Cherry said 'Yes, sir,' to everything, yet she did not understand one quarter part of what the gentleman said. Her mother had instructed her to say 'Yes, sir,' to the parson, or any gentleman, when, like herself, she did not understand them. The gentleman told her he lived but a short way off, down in the low countries; that she would have very little to do but milk the cow and look after the baby; so Cherry consented to go with him.

Away they went, he talking so kindly that Cherry had no notion how time was moving, and she quite forgot the distance she had walked.

At length they were in lanes, so shaded with trees that a checker of sunshine scarcely gleamed on the road. As far as she could see, all was trees and flowers. Sweetbriars and honeysuckles perfumed the air, and the reddest of ripe apples hung from the trees over the lane.

Then they came to a stream of water as clear as crystal, which ran across the lane. It was, however, very dark, and Cherry paused to see how she should cross the river. The gentleman put his arm around her waist and carried her over, so that she did not wet her feet.

The lane was getting darker and darker, and narrower and narrower, and they seemed to be going rapidly down hill. Cherry took firm hold of the gentleman's arm, and thought, as he had been so kind to her, she could go with him to the world's end.

After walking a little farther, the gentleman opened a gate which led into a beautiful garden, and said, 'Cherry, my dear, this is the place we live in.'

Cherry could scarcely believe her eyes. She had never seen anything approaching this place for beauty. Flowers of every dye were around her; fruits of all kinds hung above her; and the birds, sweeter of song than any she had ever heard, burst out into a chorus of rejoicing. She had heard granny tell of enchanted places. Could this be one of them? No. The gentleman was as big as the parson; and now a little boy came running down the garden-walk shouting, 'Papa, papa.'

The child appeared, from his size, to be about two or three years of age; but there was a singular look of age about him. His eyes were brilliant and piercing, and he had a crafty expression. As Cherry said, 'He could look anybody down.'

Before Cherry could speak to the child, a very old, dry-boned, ugly-looking woman made her appearance, and seizing the child by the arm, dragged him into the house, mumbling and scolding. Before, however, she was lost sight of, the old hag cast one look at Cherry, which shot through her heart 'like a gimblet'.

Seeing Cherry somewhat disconcerted, the master explained that the old woman was his late wife's grandmother; that she would remain with them until

Cherry knew her work, and no longer, for she was old and ill-tempered, and must go. At length, having feasted her eyes on the garden, Cherry was taken into the house, and this was yet more beautiful. Flowers of every kind grew everywhere, and the sun seemed to shine everywhere, and yet she did not see the sun.

Aunt Prudence – so was the old woman named – spread a table in a moment with a great variety of nice things, and Cherry made a hearty supper. She was now directed to go to bed, in a chamber at the top of the house, in which the child was to sleep also. Prudence directed Cherry to keep her eyes closed, whether she could sleep or not, as she might, perchance, see things which she would not like. She was not to speak to the child all night. She was to rise at break of day; then take the boy to a spring in the garden, wash him, and anoint his eyes with an ointment, which she would find in a crystal box in a cleft of the rock, but she was not, on any account, to touch her own eyes with it. Then Cherry was to call the cow: and having taken a bucket full of milk, to draw a bowl of the last milk for the boy's breakfast. Cherry was dying with curiosity. She several times began to question the child, but he always stopped her with, 'I'll tell Aunt Prudence.' According to her orders, Cherry was up in the morning early. The little boy conducted the girl to the spring, which flowed in crystal purity from a granite rock, which was covered with ivy and beautiful mosses. The child was duly washed, and his eyes duly anointed. Cherry saw no cow, but her little charge said she must call the cow.

'Pruit! pruit! pruit!' called Cherry, just as she would call the cows at home; when, lo! a beautiful great cow came from amongst the trees, and stood on the bank beside Cherry.

Cherry had no sooner placed her hands on the cow's teats than four streams of milk flowed down and soon filled the bucket. The boy's bowl was then filled, and he drank it. This being done, the cow quietly walked away, and Cherry returned to the house to be instructed in her daily work.

The old woman, Prudence, gave Cherry a capital breakfast, and then informed her that she must keep to the kitchen, and attend to her work there – to scald the milk, make the butter, and clean all the platters and bowls with water and gard [gravel sand]. Cherry was charged to avoid curiosity. She was not to go into any other part of the house; she was not to try and open any locked doors.

After her ordinary work was done on the second day, her master required Cherry to help him in the garden, to pick the apples and pears, and to weed the leeks and onions.

Glad was Cherry to get out of the old woman's sight. Aunt Prudence always sat with one eye on her knitting, and the other boring through poor Cherry.

Now and then she'd grumble, 'I knew Robin would bring down some fool from Zennor – better for both that she had tarried away.'

Cherry and her master got on famously, and whenever Cherry had finished weeding a bed, her master would give her a kiss to show her how pleased he was.

After a few days, old Aunt Prudence took Cherry into those parts of the house which she had never seen. They passed through a long dark passage. Cherry was then made to take off her shoes; and they entered a room, the floor of which was like glass, and all round, perched on the shelves, and on the floor, were people, big and small, turned to stone. Of some, there were only the head and shoulders, the arms being cut off; others were perfect. Cherry told the old woman she 'wouldn't cum ony furder for the wurld'. She thought from the first she was got into a land of Small People underground, only master was like other men; but now she know'd she was with the conjurors, who had turned all these people to stone. She had heard talk on 'em up in Zennor, and she knew they might at any moment wake up and eat her.

Old Prudence laughed at Cherry, and drove her on, insisted upon her rubbing up a box, 'like a coffin on six legs', until she could see her face in it. Well, Cherry did not want for courage, so she began to rub with a will; the old woman standing by, knitting all the time, calling out every now and then, 'Rub! rub! rub! harder and faster!' At length Cherry got desperate, and giving a violent rub at one of the corners, she nearly upset the box. When, O Lor! it gave out such a doleful, unearthly sound, that Cherry thought all the stone-people were coming to life, and with her fright she fell down in a fit. The master heard all this noise, and came in to inquire into the cause of the hubbub. He was in great wrath, kicked old Prudence out of the house for taking Cherry into that shut-up room, carried Cherry into the kitchen, and soon, with some cordial, recovered her senses. Cherry could not remember what had happened; but she knew there was something fearful in the other part of the house. But Cherry was mistress now – old Aunt Prudence was gone. Her master was so kind and loving that a year passed by like a summer day. Occasionally her master left home for a season; then he would return and spend much time in the enchanted apartments, and Cherry was certain she had heard him talking to the stone-people. Cherry had everything the human heart could desire, but she was not happy; she would know more of the place and the people. Cherry had discovered that the ointment made the little boy's eyes bright and strange, and she thought often that he saw more than she did; she would try; yes, she would!

Well, next morning the child was washed, his eyes anointed, and the cow milked; she sent the boy to gather her some flowers in the garden, and taking a 'crum' of ointment, she put it into her eye. Oh, her eye would be burned out of her head! Cherry ran to the pool beneath the rock to wash her burning eye; when lo! she saw at the bottom of the water, hundreds of little people, mostly ladies, playing – and there was her master, as small as the others, playing with them. Everything now looked different about the place. Small people were everywhere, hiding in the flowers sparkling with diamonds, swinging in the trees, and running and leaping under and over the blades of grass. The master never showed himself above the water all day; but at night he rode up to the house like the handsome gentleman she had seen before. He went to the enchanted chamber and Cherry soon heard the most beautiful music.

In the morning, her master was off, dressed as if to follow the hounds. He returned at night, left Cherry to herself, and proceeded at once to his private apartments. Thus it was day after day, until Cherry could stand it no longer. So she peeped through the keyhole, and saw her master with lots of ladies, singing; while one dressed like a queen was playing on the coffin. Oh, how madly jealous Cherry became when she saw her master kiss this lovely lady! However, the next day, the master remained at home to gather fruit. Cherry was to help him, and when, as usual, he looked to kiss her, she slapped his face, and told him to kiss the Small People, like himself, with whom he played under the water. So he found out that Cherry had used the ointment. With much sorrow he told her she must go home – that he would have no spy on his actions, and that Aunt Prudence must come back. Long before day, Cherry was called by her master. He gave her lots of clothes and other things – took her bundle in one hand, and a lantern in the other, and bade her follow him. They went on for miles on miles, all the time going up hill, through lanes, and narrow passages. When they came at last on level ground, it was near daybreak. He kissed Cherry, told her she was punished for her idle curiosity; but that he would, if she behaved well, come sometimes on the Lady Downs to see her. Saying this, he disappeared. The sun rose, and there was Cherry seated on a granite stone, without a soul within miles of her – a desolate moor having taken the place of a smiling garden. Long, long did Cherry sit in sorrow, but at last she thought she would go home.

Her parents had supposed her dead, and when they saw her, they believed her to be her own ghost. Cherry told her story, which every one doubted, but Cherry never varied her tale, and at last every one believed it. They say Cherry was never afterwards right in her head, and on moonlight nights, until she died, she would wander on to the Lady Downs to look for her master.

Fairies Down the Lane

Source: T. W. Thompson, 'Two Tales of Experience', *Journal of the Gypsy Lore Society*, 22, 1943, pp. 47–51.
Narrator: Taimi Boswell, Oswaldtwistle, 1915.

ONCE, A MANY YEARS ago, we was stopping into a owld green lane betwixt Blackburn an' Chorley, an' being as it was a fine day, an' I wa'n't not to say partic'lar busy, I thought as I'd have me a walk down dis lane, farther on nor where my tent was. Well, I hadn't gone not so very far, not half a mile it wouldn't be, when I sin another tent. I didn't know as dere was annybody else stopping into de lane, but den I'd only come in de night afore, an' getting late at dat. It was a dotty little tent, not above two foot high; one o' dem double tents it was, like what owld-fashioned Gypsies used to build in dose days. Outside a stick fire was burning; an' standing agen de tent was a dotty little man happen about eighteen inches to two foot high: hardly as tall as what it was, he wa'n't. He'd knee-breeches on, an' top-boots; an' a red waistcoat he had, an' a green an' yellow hankisher round his neck. It was into de summer time, an' he'd ta'en his jacket off being as it was a bit warm. His missis was at home an' all, not having gone out wid her basket dat day. She was wearing a red dress, a bit owld-fashioned even for dem times, but good an' expensival; an' her hair was done all into ringlets hanging down over her showlders. Jet black it was: in fact dey was both 'n 'em very dark.

'Good day, brother,' I says, 'an' sister as well.' 'Good day to you, brother,' dey answers me very civil-like. So I axed 'em had dey bin dere long, an' did dey of'en stop into dis lane. Yes, dey said, dey was of'en into it, but dey'd not bin dere long dis time. As was only but likely, dey axed me de same. I towld 'em as I'd not come in till de night afore, but as I knowed de lane pretty well, being as I stopped dere for a few days every summer.

Seems dey must ha' drawed in about de 'dentical time what I did, an' me not know it, though I couldn't think how I should ha' missed 'em. Den I axed de man about his horses, an' if he hadn't some as I could trade wid him for; an' I towld him what I'd got, an' which I'd be willing to part wid, eether swap or sell, if he'd a mind to do a deal. But he didn't seem as if he wanted to. So after dat we got a-gate talking more general, first one thing an' den another; an' to tell you de truth I was dat ta'en up wid him I forgot all about de time till I sin it was coming nightfall. De little man sat opposite to me, cross-legged onto de ground like what I was, smoking away at his teeny pipe, an' all de while talking an' answering of me as nice an' natural-like as could be. An' every now an' agen his missis would come an' put in a word or two, though mostly she was busying herself wid cooking de vittles an' dat.

You may be sure I thanked 'em for deir company; an' come deir turn dey said as I was right welcome, an' thanked me for mine. I must be going den, I said; 'but afore I do,' I says, 'dere's one thing as I'd like to ax of yous, if I may mek so bowld.' What was dat, dey axed. It was de little box, I said, lying onto de ground by de tent-opening; a dear little box it was, about six or eight inches long, wid de prettiest doll you ever sin in your life laid into it. I'd a-looked at it, I said, time an' agen while we was talking, which was de dear God's truth; an' if dey'd let me, I said, I'd very much like for to buy it off'n 'em. I wanted it for my little girl, I said, an' would pay good money for it; though, mind you, I hadn't no children at de time, an' it was for myself as I wanted it, being as I'd ta'en a real proper fancy to it. But de bitty man, he says as he's very sorry but he can't sell it, not at no price. 'My little girl', I says, 'would so like it to play wid, an' as she's de only one I have,' I says, 'I'd give annythink in reason to get it for her.' 'Well den,' he says, de bitty man does, 'seeing as you wants it dat bad I'll give it to you. I can do dat,' he says, 'but not sell it: it wouldn't do for me to sell it,' he says, though he didn't give no reason. 'I don't want to rob you,' I says, 'an' I'd sooner you let me pay for it.' An' so I wou'd. But he won't hear on it; so at de finish I ta'en it for nothink.

I put it into my jacket pocket, an' was just starting off when de bitty woman called me back. She give me another little box what she'd fatched from de tent; a square one dis time – de one I had was oblong. 'As you'm having dat,' she says, 'you must tek dis an' all.' 'No, no,' I says; 'I can't think on it. I didn't come begging,' I says, 'an' I won't tek nothink more off'n yous.' 'But it's no use to me wi'out de tother one,' she says, 'an' you must have it.' An' at dat she opened it, an' showed me what was inside. It was all full o' little doll's clothes med out'n silk an' lace an' dat; an' dere was a teeny pair o' slippers an' all. Nothink would satisfy her but as I must tek dis little box along wid de tother; so at last I did, being as I didn't see how I could help it.

I put it into my tother jacket pocket, an' off I set agen, but agen de bitty woman called me back. She had a little weeny tin into her hand wid bread an' milk into it, an' a dotty little spoon to eat it wid. I must have dese as well, she said, for I'd be sure to want 'em. 'No, no,' I says; 'my missis'll see to annythink what's needful into dis line, an' be only too glad to,' I says. 'Besides,' I says, 'I can't tek annythink more off'n yous, or you'll be thinking,' I says, 'as I'd come on parpose for to beg.' But she won't rest, de little woman won't, not till I've ta'en dese things as well. I was fair ashamed, I can tell you, at having so much off'n 'em; an' dem perfect strangers to me not above a few hours afore.

I started off a third time, an' now I did manage to get away. It was near dark, an' I knowed as my missis would ha' bin back from calling a many hours since, so you may be sure I was in a hurry to get home. Howsoever, afore I'd gone very far I noticed as dere was a weeny little girl walking by my side; keeping up wid me an' all she was, though I was going extra fast. 'Hello, my little dear,' I says; 'an' where have you come from?' 'Oh!' she says, 'I'm de little girl what was into de box you axed my daddy for.' I felt into de pocket where I'd put dis box, an' sure enough it was gone. I felt into my tother pocket where I'd put de little box o' clothes. It was gone an' all. So was de little tin an' spoon. All gone dey was; all clean banished away. Den I looked down on de tother side 'n me, an' if dere wa'n't another weeny little girl dere! 'An' who might you be, my little dear?' I says, 'an' where have you come from?' 'Oh!' she says, 'I've come to keep my sister company.' I was fair ta'en aback at dis; an' so'd annybody ha' bin if it had happened to dem. 'Well, my dears,' I says, 'you'd best be going back now, de both'n yous.' Dey didn't tek no heed'n dis. 'Come,' I says, 'run away wid yous now.' But dey wouldn't go: say what I will, I can't get rid'n 'em.

What was I to do den? I darsn't go home for fear of what my missis would say. She'd think, very likely, as I'd bin wid some other woman afore I knowed her, an' as dese was my children by dis tother woman. No, it wouldn't never do for me to tek 'em home. So I laid myself down under de hedge, meaning to stay dere for de night. An' when I did dis, de two weeny girls come an' nestled close up agen me; an' dere we slept till morning.

Come daylight I did everythink I could to try an' persuade 'em to go back to deir parents; but no matter what I said, or threatened 'em wid, dey defused to go. I must get rid'n 'em: dat was a certain fact. But how was I to do it? Well, I couldn't think of nothink better but what I should drown de poor little dears. Dere was a pond only but a field or two away; so I med straight for dat; an' depend on it dey followed me. It was all covered over wid big flat water-lily leaves, dis pond was. I went right up to de edge. Den I got howld'n one o' de weeny girls to throw her in, but she grasped my leg an' clung on to it, an' try as I would I couldn't shift her off of it, though she wa'n't no bigger'n a squir'l, if as big as dat. It was just de same wid de tother sister: she stuck to my tother leg, an' I couldn't pull her off neether, though I used all my strength. At dat I got right angry, an' I cursed an' swore; den, when I looked down agen, dey was gone; clean banished away dey was. How dey went I don't know; nor whether it was through my cursing an' swearing so. But, annyways, dey was gone; an' I was mighty glad, I can tell you, to be rid on 'em.

It was breakfast time when I got home. Of course my missis wanted to know where I'd bin, an' what I'd bin doing wid myself. 'Oh!' I says, 'I bin to see about a horse,' I says, 'an' I couldn't get back no sooner.' 'You'm lying,' she says; an' she stuck to it as I was; so in de end I towld her all what had happened to me, de same as what I've towld you. 'Dat's all lies agen,' she says; 'nothink but lies from start to finish. I never heeard'n such things', she says, 'happening to annybody else. You bin wid another woman,' she says; 'dat's where you bin; you can't receive me wid your lies.' Women's al'ays jealous like dat: deir minds runs on such things. I towld her I'd kiss de book onto it; onto dis what I'd said about being wid de little people, an' about de two weeny girls. But no; she won't believe me still. So I sets to an' has my breakfast, which I was in want of I can tell you, as I hadn't had a bite since de morning afore.

Later on dat same day I went to de farm close by to where we was. 'So you've got some more travellers into de lane,' I says to de man. 'Dere's none besides yous,' he says, 'not as I'm deware on; not', he says, 'unless dey come in very late last night.' 'De people I'm meaning on', I says, 'was into de lane yesterday'; an' I towld him where I'd sin 'em. 'Well, dat's queer,' he says. 'I was past de place a two three times yesterday,' he says, 'being as I've some fields dat way on where we're working just now; but I never sin nobody dere,' he says, 'nor yet de day afore,' he says, 'nor anny day lately.'

When my missis come home from calling, an' we'd had us teas, I says to her: 'Let's have a walk down de lane as far as de tother people.' She said as she'd come. I'd ta'en partic'lar note just where dey was stopping: it was by an owld ash tree near half a mile farther on. But when we got there we couldn't see nothink; not a sign on 'em annywheres; not a trace as anny-body'd bin stopping dere at all. She called me for all de liars, my missis did, an' started off agen about my being wid some other woman de night afore. She was more sure on it 'an ever now, she said.

After dat I didn't say no more about my meeting wid de bitty people not for three or fower days, not in fact till we was moving out'n de lane. Den, when I come to tek de tent down, I sin as I'd gone an' pitched it right on top'n a fairies' ring. It was getting dark when I'd put it up, an' I hadn't noticed dis ring afore. But dere it was, plain to be seen in de daylight. So I called my missis. 'What's dat,' I says, 'where de tent's bin?' 'It must be a fairies' ring,' she says. 'It is,' I says. 'An' now,' I says, 'maybe you'll believe me – what I towld you about meeting wid de bitty people, an' about de two weeny girls; an' 'll stop blackguarding of me,' I says, 'about dat tother woman you was so sure I'd bin wid.'

All de while, even when 'pearances was most agen me, I knowed as I'd spoken nothink but de truth. An' here was de proof – finding dis fairies' ring under de tent. No getting over dat, for eyes can't lie if tongues can.

The Pisky Ring

Source: R. S. Hawker, *The Prose Works*, 1843, pp. 186–7.
Narrator: 'Old Trevarten', Morwenstow, Cornwall.

'WHY, SIR, YOU SEE the case was this. I'd a bin to Simon Jude fair, and I stayed rather latish settling with the jobber Brown for some sheep, and so it wor past twelve o'clock at night before I come through Stowe wood; and just as I crossed Combe Water, sure enough I yeerd the piskies. I know'd very well where their ring was close by the gate, and so I stopped my horse and got off. Well, on I croped afoot till there was nothing but a gap between me and the pisky ring, and I could hear every word they said. One had got the crowder, and he was working away his elbow to the tune of "Green Slieves" bravely, and the rest wor dauncing and singing and merrymaking like a stage-play. It made me just 'mazed in my head to look at 'em. Well, I thort to myself, if I could but catch one of these chaps to carry home. I've yeerd that there's nothing so lucky in a house as a tame pisky. So I stooped down and I picked up a stone, oh, as big as my two fistes, and I swinged my arm and I scrashed the stone right into the ring. What a screech there was! Such a yell! and one in pertickler I yeerd screaming and hopping with a leg a-brok like a drashel. That one I was pretty sure of. But still, as it was very late, and my wife would be looking for me home, and it was dark also, so I thout I might as well come down and fetch my pisky in the morning by daylight. Well, sure enough, soon as I rose, I took one of these baskets with a cover that the women have invented – a ridicule they call it – and down I goes to the ring. And do you know, sir, they'd a be so cunning – they'd a had the art for to carry their comrade clear off, and there wasn't so much as a screed of one left! But, however,' said my venerable friend, seeing that I did not look quite satisfied with the evidence – 'however, there the stone was that I drashed in amongst mun!'

Hawker, the eccentric parson of Morwenstow, expressed a wish to 'Old Trevarten' to see a fairy, and was told, 'I dare say I can oblige you one day. It is not a month agone that I'd all but catched one.' Trevarten claimed, 'I've yeerd mun at their rollicking night-times frayquently, but I can't say that I ever seed their faytures, so as to know 'em again next time.'

The Merry-Maid

Source: R. S. Hawker, *The Prose Works*, 1843, pp. 166–7.
Narrator: 'Uncle Tony', Morwenstow, Cornwall.

OH, SIR, MY OLD father seen her twice! He was out once by night for wreck (my father watched the coast like most of the old people formerly), and it came to pass that he was down by the duck-pool on the sand at low-water tide, and all at once he heard music in the sea. Well, he croped on behind a rock, like a coastguard-man watching a boat, and got very near the noise. He couldn't make out the words, but the sound was exactly like Bill Martin's voice, that singed second counter in church. At last he got very near, and there was the merry-maid very plain to be seen, swimming about upon the waves like a woman bathing – and singing away. But my father said it was very sad and solemn to hear – more like the tune of a funeral hymn than a Christmas carol by far – but it was so sweet that it was as much as he could do to hold back from plunging into the tide after her. And he an old man of sixty-seven, with a wife and a houseful of children at home! The second time was down here by Holacombe Pits. He had been looking out for spars: there was a ship breaking up in the Channel, and he saw some one move just at half-tide mark. So he went on very softly, step and step, till he got nigh the place, and there was the merry-maid sitting on a rock, the bootifullest merry-maid that eye could behold, and she was twisting about her long hair, and dressing it just like one of our girls getting ready for her sweetheart on the Sabbath-day. The old man made sure he should greep hold of her before ever she found him out, and he had got so near that a couple of paces more and he would have caught her by the hair as sure as tithe or tax, when, lo and behold! she looked back and glimpsed him. So in one moment she dived head-foremost off the rock, and then tumbled herself topsy-turvy about in the waters, and cast a look at my poor father, and grinned like a seal!

Droll of the Mermaid

Source: William Bottrell, *Traditions and Hearthside Stories of West Cornwall*,
2nd series, 1870, pp. 61–7.
Narrator: Uncle Anthony James.
Type: ML4080 'The Seal Woman'.

HUNDREDS OF YEARS AGO, there lived somewhere near the Lizard
Point a man called Lutey or Luty, who farmed a few acres of ground near the
seashore, and followed fishing and smuggling as well, when it suited the time.
One summer's evening, seeing from the cliff, where he had just finished his
day's work of cutting turf, that the tide was far out, he sauntered down over
the sands, near his dwelling, in search of any wreck which might have been
cast ashore by the flood; at the same time he was cursing the bad luck, and
murmuring because a godsend worth securing hadn't been sent to the Lizard
cliffs for a long while.

Finding nothing on the sands worth picking up, Lutey turned to go home,
when he heard a plaintive sound, like the wailing of a woman or the crying
of a child, which seemed to come from seaward; going in the direction of the
cry, he came near some rocks which were covered by the sea at high water,
but now, about half ebb and being spring tides, the waves were a furlong or
more distant from them. Passing round to the seaward side of these rocks, he
saw what appeared to him a fairer woman than he had ever beheld before.
As yet, he perceived little more than her head and shoulders, because all the
lower part of her figure was hidden by the ore-weed [sea-weed] which grew
out from the rocks, and spread around the fair one in the pullan [pool] of
sea-water that yet remained in a hollow at the foot of the rocks. Her golden-
coloured hair, falling over her shoulders and floating on the water, shone
like the sunbeams on the sea. The little he saw of her skin showed that it was
smooth and clear as a polished shell. As the comely creature, still making a
mournful wail, looked intently on the distant and ebbing sea, Lutey remained
some minutes, admiring her unperceived. He longed to assuage her grief, but,
not knowing how to comfort her, and afraid of frightening her into fits by

coming too suddenly on her, he coughed and ahem'd to call her attention before he approached any nearer.

Looking round and catching a glimpse of the man, she uttered a more unearthly yell than ever, and then gliding down from the ledge, on which she reclined, into the pullan, all but her beautiful head and swan-like neck was hidden under the water and the ore-weed.

'My dear creature,' says Lutey, 'don't 'e be afraid of me, for I'm a sober and staid married man, near thirty years of age. Have 'e lost your clothes? I don't see any, anywhere! Now, what shall I do to comfort 'e? My turtle-dove, I wouldn't hurt 'e for the world,' says Lutey, as he edged a little nearer. He couldn't take his eyes from the beautiful creature for the life of him. The fair one, too, on hearing his soothing words, stayed her crying, and, when she looked on him, her eyes shone like the brightest of stars on a dark night. Lutey drew near the edge of the pullan and, looking into the water, he discovered the fan of a fish's tail quivering and shaking amongst the floating ore-weed: then, he knew that the fair one was a mermaid. He never had so near a view of one before, though he had often seen them, and heard them singing, of moonlight nights, at a distance, over the water.

'Now my lovely maid of the waves,' said he, 'what shall I do for 'e? Speak but the word; or give me a sign, if you don't know our Cornish tongue.'

'Kind good man,' she replied, 'we people of the ocean understand all sorts of tongues; as we visit the shores of every country, and all the tribes of earth pass over our domain; besides, our hearing is so good that we catch what is said on the land when we are miles away over the flood. You may be scared, perhaps,' she continued, 'to see me simply dressed, like naked truth, because your females are always covered with such things as would sadly hinder our sporting in the waves.'

'No, my darling, I am'at the least bit frightened to see 'e without your dress and petticoats on,' Lutey replied, as he still drew nearer, and continued as kindly as possible to say, 'now, my dear, dont 'e hide your handsome figure in the pullan any longer, but sit up and tell me what makes 'e grieve so?'

The mermaid rose out of the water, seated herself on a ledge of the rock, combed back her golden ringlets from her face, and then Lutey observed that her hair was so abundant that it fell around and covered her figure like an ample robe of glittering gold. When this simple toilette was settled, she sighed and said, 'Oh! unlucky mermaid that I am; know, good man, that only three hours ago I left my husband soundly sleeping on a bed of soft and sweet sea-flowers, with our children sporting round him. I charged the eldest to be sure and keep away the shrimps and sea-fleas, that they mightn't get into their daddy's ears and nose to disturb his rest. "Now take care," I told them, "that the crabs don't pinch your dad's tail and wake him up, whilst I'm away to get 'e something nice for supper, and if you be good children I'll bring 'e home some pretty young dolphins and sea-devils for 'e to play with. Yet noble youth of the land," she went on to say, 'with all my care I very much fear my merman may wake up and want something to eat before I get home. I ought to know when the tide leaves every rock on the coast, yet I was so stupid as to remain here looking at myself in the pullan as I combed the broken ore-weed, shrimps, crabs, and sea-fleas out of my hair, without observing, till a few minutes since, that the sea had gone out so far as to leave a bar of dry sand between me and the waves.'

'Yet why should 'e be in such trouble, my heart's own dear?' Lutey asked. 'Can't 'e wait here, and I'll bear ye company till the tide comes in, when you may swim away home at your ease?'

'Oh, no, I want to get back before the turn of the tide; because, then, my husband and all the rest of the mermen are sure to wake up hungry and look for their suppers; and, can 'e believe it of my monster (he looks a monster indeed compared with you), that if I am not then at hand with half-a-dozen fine mullets, a few scores of mackerel, or something else equally nice to suit his dainty stomach, when he awakes with the appetite of a shark, he's sure to eat some of our pretty children. Mermen and maidens would be as plenty in the sea as herrings if their gluttons of fathers didn't gobble up the tender babes. Scores of my dear ones have gone through his ugly jaws, never to come out alive.'

'I'm very sorry for your sad bereavements,' said Lutey. 'Yet why don't the young fry start off on their own hook?'

'Ah! my dear,' said she, 'they love their pa, and don't think, poor simple innocents, when they hear him whistling a lively tune, that it's only to decoy them around him, and they, so fond of music, get close about his face, rest their ears on his lips, then he opens his great mouth like a cod's, and into the trap they go. If you have the natural feelings of a tender parent you can understand,' she said, after sobbing as if her heart were ready to burst, 'that, for my dear children's sakes, I'm anxious to get home in an hour or so, by which time it will be near low water; else, I should be delighted to stay here all night, and have a chat with you, for I have often wished, and wished in vain, that the powers had made for me a husband, with two tails, like you, or with a tail split into what you call your legs; they are so handy for passing over dry land! Ah,' she sighed, 'what wouldn't I give to have a pair of tails like unto you, that I might come on the land and examine, at my ease, all the strange and beautiful creatures which we view from the waves. If you will', she continued, 'but serve me now, for ten minutes only, by taking me over the sands to the sea, I'll grant to you and yours any three wishes you may desire; but there's no time to spare – no, not a minute,' said she, in taking from her hair a golden comb in a handle of pearl, which she gave to Lutey, saying, 'Here, my dear, keep this as a token of my faith; I'd give 'e my glass, too, had I not left that at home to make my monster think that I didn't intend to swim far away. Now mind,' she said, as Lutey put the comb into his pocket, 'whenever you wish me to direct you, in any difficulty, you have only to pass that comb through the sea three times, calling me as often, and I'll come to ye on the next flood tide. My name is Morvenna, which, in the language of this part of the world, at the time I was named, meant sea-woman. You can't forget it, because you have still many names much like it among ye.'

Lutey was so charmed with the dulcet melody of the mermaid's voice that he remained listening to her flutelike tones, and, looking into her languishing sea-green eyes till he was like one enchanted, and ready to do everything she desired; so, stooping down, he took the mermaid in his arms, that he might carry her out to sea.

Lutey being a powerful fellow, he bore the mermaid easily on his left arm, she encircling his neck with her right. They proceeded thus, over the sands, some minutes before he made up his mind what to wish for. He had heard of a man who, meeting with similar luck, wished that all he touched might turn to gold, and knew the fatal result of his thoughtless wish, and of the bad luck which happened to several others whose selfish desires were gratified. As all the wishes he could remember ended badly, he puzzled his head to think of something new, and, long before he came to any conclusion, the mermaid said,

'Come, my good man, lose no more time, but tell me for what three things do ye wish? Will you have long life, strength, and riches?'

'No,' says he, 'I only wish for the power to do good to my neighbours – first that I may be able to break the spells of witchcraft; secondly that I may have such power over familiar spirits as to compel them to inform me of all I desire to know for the benefit of others; thirdly, that these good gifts may continue in my family for ever.'

The mermaid promised that he and his should ever possess these rare endowments, and that, for the sake of his unselfish desires, none of his posterity should ever come to want. They had still a long way to go before they reached the sea. As they went slowly along, the mermaid told him of their beautiful dwellings, and of the pleasant life they led beneath the flood. 'In our cool caverns we have everything one needs,' said she, 'and much more. The walls of our abodes are encrusted with coral and amber, entwined with sea-flowers of every hue, and their floors are all strewn with pearls. The roof sparkles with diamonds, and other gems of such brightness that their rays make our deep grots in the ocean hillsides, as light as day.' Then, embracing Lutey with both her arms round his neck, she continued, 'Come with me, love, and see the beauty of the mermaid's dwellings. Yet the ornaments, with which we take the most delight to embellish our halls and chambers, are the noble sons and fair daughters of earth, whom the wind and waves send in foundered ships to our abodes. Come, I will show you thousands of handsome bodies so embalmed, in a way only known to ourselves, with choice salts and rare spices, that they look more beautiful than when they breathed, as you will say when you see them reposing on beds of amber, coral, and pearl, decked with rich stuffs, and surrounded by heaps of silver and gold for which they ventured to traverse our domain. Aye, and when you see their limbs all adorned with glistening gems, move gracefully to and fro with the motion of the waves, you will think they still live.'

'Perhaps I should think them all very fine,' Lutey replied, 'yet faix [faith] I'd rather find in your dwellings, a few of the puncheons of rum that must often come down to ye in the holds of sunken ships, and one would think you'd be glad to get them in such a cold wet place as you live in! What may 'e do with all the good liquor, tobacco, and other nice things that find their way down below?'

'Yes indeed,' she answered, 'it would do your heart good to see the casks of brandy, kegs of Hollands, pipes of wine, and puncheons of rum that come to our territory. We take a shellful now and then to warm our stomachs, but there's any quantity below for you, so come along, come.'

'I would like to go very well,' says Lutey, 'but surely I should be drowned, or smothered, under the water.'

'Don't 'e believe it,' said she, 'you know that we women of the sea can do wonders. I can fashion 'e a pair of gills; yes, in less than five minutes I'll make you such a pair as will enable 'e to live in the water as much at your ease as a cod or a conger. The beauty of your handsome face will not be injured, because your beard and whiskers will hide the small slits required to be made under your chin. Besides, when you have seen all you would like to see, or get tired of my company and life in the water, you can return to land and bring back with you as much of our treasures as you like, so come along, love.'

'To be sure,' said Lutey, 'your company, the liquor, and riches below are very tempting; yet I can't quite make up my mind.'

The time passed in this kind of talk till Lutey, wading through the sea (now above his knees), brought her near the breakers, and he felt so charmed with the mermaid's beauty and enchanted by the music of her voice that he was inclined to plunge with her into the waves. One can't, now, tell the half of what she said to allure the man to her home beneath the flood. The mermaid's sea-green eyes sparkled as she saw the man was all but in her power. Then, just in the nick of time, his dog, which had followed unnoticed, barked and howled so loud, that the charmed man looked round, and, when he saw the smoke curling up from his chimney, the cows in the fields, and everything looking so beautiful on the green land, the spell of the mermaid's song was broken. He tried long in vain to free himself from her close embrace, for he now looked with loathing on her fishy tail, scaly body, and sea-green eyes, till he roared out in agony, 'Good Lord deliver me from this devil of a fish!' Then, rousing from his stupor, with his right hand he snatched his knife from his girdle, and, flashing the bright steel before the mermaid's eyes, 'By God,' said he, 'I'll cut your throat and rip out your heart if you don't unclasp your arms from my neck, and uncoil your conger-tail from my legs.'

Lutey's prayer was heard, and the sight of the bright steel (which, they say, has power against enchantments and over evil beings) made the mermaid drop from his neck into the sea. Still looking towards him, she swam away, singing in her plaintive tone, 'Farewell my sweet, for nine long years, then I'll come for thee my love.'

Lutey had barely the strength to wade out of the sea, and reach, before dark, a sown [cavern] in the cliff, where he usually kept a few tubs of liquor, buried in the sand, under any lumber of wreck, secured there above high-water mark. The weary and bewildered man took a gimlet from his pocket, spiled an anker of brandy, fixed a quill in the hole, and sucked a little of the liquor to refresh himself; then lay down among some old sails and was soon asleep.

In the meantime, dame Lutey passed rather an anxious time, because her husband hadn't been home to supper, which the good man never missed, though he often remained out all night on the sands to look after wreck, or with smugglers or customers in the 'sown' and on the water. So, as there was neither sight nor sign of him when breakfast was ready, she went down to the 'sown' and there she found her man fast asleep.

'Come! wake up,' said she; 'and what made thee stay down here without thy supper? Thee hast had a drop too much, I expect!'

'No by gambers,' said he, rising up and staring round, 'but am I here in the "sown" or am I in a cavern at the bottom of the sea? And are you my dear Morvenna? Ef you are, give me a hornful of rum, do: but you don't look like her.'

'No indeed,' said the wife, 'they cale me An Betty Lutey, and, what's more, I never heard tell of the lass thee art dreaman about before.'

'Well then, ef thee art my old oman, thee hast had a narrow escape, I can tell thee, of being left as bad as a widow and the poor children orphans, this very night.'

Then on the way home, he related how he found a stranded mermaid; that for taking her out to sea, she had promised to grant his three wishes, and given him the comb (which he showed his wife) as a token; 'but,' said he, 'if it hadn't been for the howling of our dog Venture, to rouse me out of the trance, and make me see how far I was from land, as sure as a gun I should now be with the mermaidens drinkan rum or huntan sharks at the bottom of the sea.'

When Lutey had related all particulars, he charged his wife not to say anything about it to the neighbours, as some of them, perhaps, wouldn't credit his strange adventure; but she, unable to rest with such a burthen on her mind, as soon as her husband went away to his work, she trotted round half the parish to tell the story, as a great secret, to all the courseying old women she could find, and showed them what Lutey gave her as the mermaid's comb, to make the story good. The wonder (always told by the old gossips as a great secret) was talked of far and near in the course of a few weeks, and very soon folks, who were bewitched or otherwise afflicted, came in crowds to be helped by the new pellar or conjuror. Although Lutey had parted from the mermaid in a very ungracious manner, yet he found that she was true to her promise. It was also soon discovered that he was endowed with far more than the ordinary white-witch's skill. Yet the pellar dearly purchased the sea-woman's favours. Nine years after, to the day on which Lutey bore her to the waters, he and a comrade were out fishing one clear moonlight night; though the weather was calm and the water smooth as a glass, about midnight the sea suddenly arose around their boat, and in the foam of the curling waves they saw a mermaid approach them, with all her body, above the waist, out of the water, and her golden hair floating far behind and around her.

'My hour is come,' said Lutey, the moment he saw her; and, rising like one distraught, he plunged into the sea, swam with the mermaid a little way, then they both sunk, and the sea became as smooth as ever.

Lutey's body was never found, and, in spite of every precaution, once in nine years, some of his descendants find a grave in the sea.

Here ends the droll-teller's story.

Bottrell names this as the favourite story of one of the last of the wandering droll-tellers of Cornwall, blind Uncle Anthony James, who tramped the Lizard in the early years of the nineteenth century with his dog and a boy to guide him and sing to his fiddle. He writes:

> In all the farmhouses, where this old wanderer rested on his journey, he and his companions received a hearty welcome, for the sake of his music and above all for his stories, the substance of most of which every one knew by heart, yet they liked to hear these old legends again and again, because he, or some of his audience, had always something new to add, by way of fashioning out the droll, or to display their inventive powers.

In his introduction to *Popular Romances of the West of England* Robert Hunt quotes at length a letter almost certainly from Bottrell giving further information about Uncle Anthony; Hunt's 'The Old Man of Cury' offers an alternative version of the tale.

Johnny Reed! Johnny Reed!

Source: Anon., 'North-Country Fairies', *Monthly Chronicle of North-Country Lore and Legend*, December 1889, p. 549.

Narrator: Unknown, Co. Durham.

Type: ML6070b 'The King of the Cats'.

A STAINDROP FARMER WAS crossing a bridge at night, when a cat jumped out, stood right before him, looked him in the face earnestly, and at last, opening its mouth like Balaam's ass, said in articulate vernacular North-country speech –

> Johnny Reed! Johnny Reed!
> Tell Madam Mumfort
> 'At Mally Dixen's deed.

The farmer came home and told his wife what he had seen and heard, when up sprang their old black cat, which had been sitting cosily beside the fire, and, exclaiming, 'Is she! Then aa mun off!' bolted out at the door and disappeared for ever.

A Shropshire version, 'The King of the Cats'; contributed by Charlotte S. Burne to the *Folk-Lore Journal* (2, pp. 22–3), ends more conventionally than this one, with the cat disappearing up the chimney with the cry, 'By Jove! old Peter's dead! and I'm the King o' the cats!' William Brockie's *Legends and Superstitions of the County of Durham* (1886, pp. 8–10) gives another version of 'Johnny Reed!' and a variant in which the dead cat's name is 'Catherine Curley'.

Jahn Tergagle the Steward

Source: Robert Hunt, *Popular Romances of the West of England*, 3rd edn, 1881, pp. 138–40.

Narrator: Remembered by J. C. H. from the narration years before of the sexton of the parish church of St Breock, where a John Tregeagle is buried.

THEESS JAHN TERGAGLE, I'VE a heerd mun tell, sir, he was a steward to a lord. And a man came fore to the court and paid az rent: and Jahn Tergagle didn't put no cross to az name in the books.

And after that Tergagle daied: and the lord came down to look after az rents: and when he zeed the books, he zeed this man's name that there wasn't no cross to ut.

And he zent for the man, and axed'n for az rent: and the man zaid he'd apaid az rent: and the lord said he hadn't, there warn't no cross to az name in the books, and he tould'n that he'd have the law for'n if he didn't pay.

And the man, he didn't know what to do: and he went vore to the minister of Simonward; and the minister axed'n if he'd a got faith: and the man, he hadn't got faith, and he was obliged for to come homewards again.

And after that the 'Zaizes was coming naigh, and he was becoming afeerd, sure enough: and he went vore to the minister again, and tould'n he'd a got faith; the minister might do whatever a laiked.

And the minister draed a ring out on the floor: and he caaled out dree times, Jahn Tergagle, Jahn Tergagle, Jahn Tergagle! and (I've a heerd the ould men tell ut, sir) theess Jahn Tergagle stood before mun in the middle of the ring.

And he went vore wi' mun to the Ezaizes, and gave az evidence and tould how this man had a paid az rent; and the lord he was cast.

And after that they was come back to their own house, theess Jahn Tergagle he gave mun a brave deal of trouble; he was knackin' about the place, and wouldn't laive mun alone at all.

And they went vore to the minister, and axed he for to lay un.

And the minister zaid, thicky was their look-out; they'd a brought'n up, and they was to gett'n down again the best way they could. And I've a heerd the ould men tell ut, sir. The minister he got dree hunderd pound for a layin' of un again.

And first, a was bound to the old epping-stock up to Church-town; and after that a was bound to the ould oven in T'evurder; James Wyatt down to Wadebridge, he was there when they did open ut.

And after that a was bound to Dozmary Pool; and they do say that there he ez now emptying of it out with a lampet-shell, with a hole in the bottom of ut.

***

Hunt devotes an entire section of his book to 'Romances of Tregeagle', and there is a book about him, *John Tregeagle of Trevorden: Man and Ghost* (1935), by Barbara C. Spooner.

The Roaring Bull of Bagbury

Source: Charlotte S. Burne (ed.), from the collections of Georgina F. Jackson, *Shropshire Folk-Lore: A Sheaf of Gleanings*, 1883, pp. 108–9.
Narrator: An old farmer named Hayward, 1881.
Type: ML4020 'The Unforgiven Dead'.

THERE WAS A VERY bad man lived at Bagbury Farm, and when he died it was said that he had never done but two good things in his life, and the one was to give a waistcoat to a poor old man, and the other was to give a piece of bread and cheese to a poor boy, and when this man died he made a sort of confession of this. But when he was dead his ghost would not rest, and he would get in the buildings in the shape of a bull, and roar till the boards and the shutters and the tiles would fly off the building, and it was impossible for any one to live near him. He never come till about nine or ten at night, but he got so rude at last that he would come about seven or eight at night, and he was so troublesome that they sent for twelve parsons to lay him. And the parsons came, and they got him under, but they could not lay him; but they got him, in the shape of a bull all the time, up into Hyssington Church. And when they got him into the church, they all had candles, and one old blind parson, who knowed him, and knowed what a rush he would make, he carried his candle in his top boot. And he made a great rush, and all the candles went out, all but the blind parson's, and he said, 'You light your candles by mine.' And while they were in the church, before they laid him, the bull made such a burst that he cracked the wall of the church from the top to the bottom, and the crack was left as it was for years, till the church was done up; it was left on purpose for people to see. I've seen it hundreds of times.

Well, they got the bull down at last, into a snuff-box, and he asked them to lay him under Bagbury Bridge, and that every mare that passed over should lose her foal, and every woman her child; but they would not do this, and they laid him in the Red Sea for a thousand years.

I remember the old clerk at Hyssington. He was an old man then, sixty years ago, and he told me he could remember the old blind parson well.

Burne and Jackson give several variants of this legend, from William Hughes, John Thomas, John Clark, Susan Jones and others. In one, the ghost is referred to in grisly terms as 'the flayed bull o' Bagbury'. John Thomas added that despite the banishment to the Red Sea (the standard destination of such troublesome spirits), 'folk were always frightened to go over Bagbury Bridge. I've bin over it myself many a time with horses, and I always got off the horse and made him go quietly, and went pit-pat, ever so softly, like this, for fear of *him* hearing me and coming out.'

The Owl was a Baker's Daughter

Source: Contributed by Douce to Malone's *Variorum Shakespeare*, 1821, vol. 7, p. 426.

Narrator: Unknown, Gloucestershire.

Type: AT751 'The Greedy Peasant Woman'.

OUR SAVIOUR WENT INTO a baker's shop where they were baking, and asked for some bread to eat. The mistress of the shop immediately put a piece of dough into the oven to bake for him: but was reprimanded by her daughter, who, insisting that the piece of dough was too large, reduced it to a very small size. The dough, however, immediately afterwards began to swell, and presently became of a most enormous size. Whereupon, the baker's daughter cried out, 'Heugh, heugh, heugh', which owl-like noise probably induced our Saviour for her wickedness to transform her into that bird.

There is a longer Herefordshire version in Halliwell's *Nursery Rhymes of England*, in which the punishment is inflicted by a fairy, not Christ. Some version of the tale was known to Shakespeare: 'They say the owl was a baker's daughter' (Hamlet, IV, v).

The Curse of the Shoemaker

Source: William Henderson, *Notes on the Folklore of the Northern Counties of England and the Borders*, 2nd edn, 1879, p. 82.

Narrator: A Devonshire shoemaker.

Type: AT777 (variant) 'The Wandering Jew'.

WE SHOEMAKERS ARE A poor slobbering race, and so have been ever since the curse that Jesus Christ laid on us . . . when they were carrying Him to the cross, they passed a shoemaker's bench, and the man looked up and spat at Him; and the Lord turned and said: 'A poor slobbering fellow shalt thou be, and all shoemakers after thee, for what thou hast done to me.'

The First Smith

Source: G. E. C. Webb, *Gypsies: The Secret People*, 1960, pp. 139–41.
Narrator: Homi Smith.

'THIS IS MY STORY, the story of Homi Smith, which was told to me by my old mam. Yes, told me by my old mother, it was. And she was told it by her mam, and she was told it by her mam, and so like that ever since our fambly began.

'A very, very long time ago, there was a Great King. And this Great King, he ordered for to be built for 'im, a great palace. Everythink there was to be the bestest that could be 'ad, and the men what was got to build it was the cleverest that could be 'ad. And it took a very long time for to build this great palace, 'cause it was so big, and 'cause it 'ad to be so good, but at last, there came the day when it was finished.

'And the Great King, he called together all the men what 'ad worked to build it for 'im, so as there could be a great eatin' and drinkin' – a feast as the story goes.

'Well, they all comes to this great feast, and there was much good food all on gold plates and dishes, and there was much strong drink all in gold cups. And they all sat and ate and drank for a long time. And when they was all full up and couldn't eat nor drink no more, all the men what was there, started arguin' who was the bestest one among 'em. First, up spoke the man what 'ad told 'em the right shape, and all that, for to build each little part of the palace. "Without me," he says, "there wouldn't 'ave been no palace, so I reckons as 'ow I must be the bestest man of all."

'Then up spoke the man what 'ad laid all the bricks and built the walls. "Without me," he says, "there wouldn't 'ave been no building of the walls. And without walls, there couldn't 'ave been no palace. So I reckon as 'ow I must be the bestest man of all."

'Then up spoke the carpenter, what 'ad made all the doors and different things out of wood. "Without me," he says, "there wouldn't 'ave been no doors, nor no furniture. And without all those things; there wouldn't 'ave been no palace."

'Then up spoke the man what 'ad put all the glass in the windows. "Without me," he says, "there wouldn't 'ave been no windows. I've fixed glass in a thousand windows, else the wind and the rain would all 'ave blowed in. Without windows, there wouldn't 'ave been no palace."

'And after that, one and another all stands up one by one, and tells of the different things what they'd done, and each one says 'ow there wouldn't 'ave been no palace if it 'adn't been for 'im.

'And all the time, the Great King, 'e just sits, and 'e don't say nothing. Only 'e listens very careful to 'em all. Then at last, they suddenly spies a dark man, standin' apart from all the others, just inside the door.

'"Come inside and tell us who you might be," says the Great King. So the dark man, 'e steps right inside the great hall. "I am the smith," he says, in a loud voice so as all could 'ear 'im. And then they all sees as 'ow his face is all black from the forge, and he's still got 'is leather apron on, where he 'as come straight from 'is work.

'Then one or two of 'em there (them as was dressed up all in fine clothes, and looks down at the *petulengro* – yes, looks down at the smith, they does), they starts a-sayin' to one another, "What right 'as that man in 'ere? He ain't done nothing towards building this 'ere great palace for the Great King." So at last, the Great King, he turns to the smith and 'e says, "Now answer. What right 'ave you in 'ere? Can you say as 'ow you done anything towards building this 'ere great palace?"

'And the smith, 'e smiles, and 'e speaks up and 'e says, "We've heard the window maker; we've heard the carpenter; we've heard the brick-layer; and we've heard all the other men what reckons they was the most important men of all. But I says that not one of 'em could 'ave done anythink without their tools. And who was it made their tools?"

'And the man stopped and looked all round while they all thought about it. Then he speaks up again: "Yes," he says. "Yes. None of 'em could 'ave done anythink without their tools. And who was it made all their tools? Why, it was me, the *petulengro*, the smith! And now," he says, a-drawin' of his-self up, for 'e was a tall man. "And now," he says, "I'll ask the Great King his-self to tell us who he thinks is the most important man of all."

'So then the Great King, 'e stands up and 'e says, "You 'ave all 'eard what the smith says. And it is a great truth that not one of you could 'ave done any work at all, without the tools what the smith made. Therefore," he says, "Therefore, I says as 'ow the smith is the most importantest man of all."

'And then the Great King 'as a place made for the smith by 'is right 'and. And the smith, 'e sits down there all in 'is workin' clothes, with 'is apron on and 'is face all black from the forge. And the Great King give 'im food to eat and drink in 'is gold cup, with 'is own 'and.'

Homi paused for a moment and leaned back a little.

'And that Smith what I've been a-telling about, 'e was the first *petulengro* – yes, the very first Smith what started all our fambly, long ago.'

Homi Smith was the wife of Amos Smith, a horse dealer, but was also a Smith by birth. She told her tale 'in a low voice' to Webb, Amos and 'old Ben', a tramp she was nursing. She was sitting on the lowest step of her wagon, hands folded in her lap.

The Haunted Widower

Source: Robert Hunt, *Popular Romances of the West of England*, 3rd edn, 1881, p. 233.

Narrator: Unknown.

A LABOURING MAN, VERY shortly after his wife's death, sent to a servant girl, living at the time in a small shipping port, requesting her to come to the inn to him. The girl went, and over a 'ha' pint' she agreed to accept him as her husband.

All went on pleasantly enough for a time. One evening the man met the girl. He was silent for some time and sorrowful, but at length he told her his wife had come back.

'What do'st mean?' asked the girl; 'have 'e seen hur?'

'Naw, I han't seed her.'

'Why, how do'st knaw it is her then?'

The poor man explained to her, that at night, when in bed, she would come to the side of it, and 'flop' his face; and there was no mistaking her 'flop'.

'So you knawed her flop, did 'e?' asked the girl.

'Ay, it couldn't be mistook.'

'If she do hunt thee,' said the girl, 'she'll hunt me; and if she do flop 'e, she'll flop me – so it must be off atween us.'

The unfortunate flop of the dead wife prevented the man from securing a living one.

The Waff

Source: Mrs Gutch, *Examples of Printed Folk-Lore Concerning the North Riding of Yorkshire, York and the Ainsty* (*Country Folk-Lore, 2*), 1901, p. 83.
Narrator: Unknown.

NOT VERY MANY YEARS have gone by since a man of Guisborough entering a shop in this old fishy town [Whitby] saw his own wraith standing there unoccupied. He called it a 'waff'. Now it is unlucky in the highest degree to meet one's own double; in fact, it is commonly regarded as a sign of early death. There is but one path of safety; you must address it boldly.

The Guisborough man was well aware of this and went up without hesitation to the waff. 'What's thou doing here?' he said roughly. 'What's thou doing here? Thou's after no good, I'll go to bail. Get thy ways yom, wi' thee, get thy ways yom.' Whereupon the waff slunk off abashed and the evil design with which it came there was brought happily to nought.

The Pilot's Ghost Story

Source: Robert Hunt, *Popular Romances of the West of England*, 3rd edn, 1881,
p. 357.
Narrator: Unknown.

JUST SEVENTEEN YEARS SINCE, I went down on the wharf from my house one night about twelve and one in the morning, to see whether there was any 'hobble', and found a sloop, the *Sally* of St Ives (the *Sally* was wrecked at St Ives one Saturday afternoon in the spring of 1862), in the bay, bound for Hayle. When I got by the White Hart public-house, I saw a man leaning against a post on the wharf – I spoke to him, wished him good morning, and asked him what o'clock it was, but to no purpose. I was not to be easily frightened, for I didn't believe in ghosts; and finding I got no answer to my repeated inquiries, I approached close to him and said, 'Thee'rt a queer sort of fellow, not to speak; I'd speak to the devil, if he were to speak to me. Who art a at all? thee'st needn't think to frighten me; that thee wasn't do, if thou wert twice so ugly; who art a at all?' He turned his great ugly face on me, glared abroad his great eyes, opened his mouth, and it was a mouth sure nuff. Then I saw pieces of sea-weed and bits of sticks in his whiskers; the flesh of his face and hands were parboiled, just like a woman's hands after a good day's washing. Well, I did not like his looks a bit, and sheered off; but he followed close by my side, and I could hear the water squashing in his shoes every step he took. Well, I stopped a bit, and thought to be a little bit civil to him, and spoke to him again, but no answer. I then thought I would go to seek for another of our crew, and knock him up to get the vessel, and had got about fifty or sixty yards, when I turned to see if he was following me, but saw him where I left him. Fearing he would come after, I ran for my life the few steps that I had to go. But when I got to the door, to my horror there stood the man in the door grinning horribly. I shook like an aspen-leaf; my hat lifted from my head; the sweat boiled out of me. What to do I didn't know, and in the house there was such a row, as if everybody was breaking up everything. After a bit I went in, for the door was 'on the latch' – that is, not locked – and called the captain of the boat, and got light, but everything was all right, nor had he heard any noise. We went out aboard of the *Sally*, and I put her into Hayle, but I felt ill enough to be in bed. I left the vessel to come home as soon as I could, but it took me four hours to walk two miles, and I had to lie down in the road, and was taken home to St Ives in a cart; as far as the Terrace from there I was carried home by my brothers, and put to bed. Three days afterwards all my hair fell off as if I had had my head shaved. The roots, and for about half an inch from the roots, being quite white. I was ill six months, and the doctor's bill was £4, 17s. 6d. for attendance and medicine. So you see I have reason to believe in the existence of spirits as much as Mr Wesley had. My hair grew again, and twelve months after I had as good a head of dark-brown hair as ever.

This vivid ghost story was sent to Hunt by 'C.F.S.' (possibly the postman-poet C. Taylor Stephens). Hunt says that he gives it 'in the words in which it was communicated', and it retains the robust flavour of oral narration to an unusual degree. C.F.S. added that, 'the man has still a good thick head of hair'.

The Man-Monkey

Source: Charlotte S. Burne (ed.), from the collections of Georgina F. Jackson, *Shropshire Folk-Lore: A Sheaf of Gleanings*, 1883, pp. 106–7.
Narrator: Unknown.

A VERY WEIRD STORY of an encounter with an animal ghost arose of late years within my own knowledge. On the 21st of January, 1879, a labouring man was employed to take a cart of luggage from Ranton in Staffordshire to Woodcote, beyond Newport, in Shropshire, for the use of a party of visitors who were going from one house to the other. He was late in coming back; his horse was tired, and could only crawl along at a foot's pace, so that it was ten o'clock at night when he arrived at the place where the highroad crosses the Birmingham and Liverpool Canal. Just before he reached the canal bridge, a strange black creature with great white eyes sprang out of the plantation by the road-side and alighted on his horse's back. He tried to push it off with his whip, but to his horror the whip went *through* the Thing, and he dropped it to the ground in his fright. The poor tired horse broke into a canter, and rushed onwards at full speed with the ghost still clinging to its back. How the creature at length vanished the man hardly knew. He told his tale in the village of Woodseaves, a mile further on, and so effectually frightened the hearers that one man actually stayed with his friends there all night, rather than cross the terrible bridge which lay between him and his home. The ghost-seer reached home at length, still in a state of excessive terror (but, as his master assured me, perfectly sober), and it was some days before he was able to leave his bed, so much was he prostrated by his fright. The whip was searched for next day, and found just at the place where he said he had dropped it.

Now comes the curious part of the story. The adventure, as was natural, was much talked of in the neighbourhood, and of course with all sorts of variations. Some days later the man's master (Mr B— of L—d) was surprised by a visit from a policeman, who came to request him to give information of his having been stopped and robbed on the Big Bridge on the night of the 21st January!

Mr B——, much amused, denied having been robbed, either on the canal bridge or anywhere else, and told the policeman the story just related. 'Oh, was that all, sir?' said the disappointed policeman. 'Oh, I know what *that* was. That was the Man-Monkey, sir, as *does* come again at that bridge ever since the man was drowned in the Cut!'

Billy B—'s Adventure

Source: William Hone, *The Table Book*, vol. 2, 1827, p. 655.
Narrator: Billy B—y, Grassington in Craven, Yorkshire, 1827.

'YOU SEE, SIR, AS how I'd been a clock-dressing at Gurston [Grassington], and I'd staid rather lat, and may be gitten a lile sup o' spirit, but I war far from being drunk, and knowed every thing that passed. It was about eleven o'clock when I left, and it war at back end o' t' year, and a most admirable [beautiful] neet it war. The moon war varra breet, and I nivver seed Rylstone-fell plainer in a' my life. Now, you see, sir, I war passin down t' mill loine, and I heerd summut come past me – brush, brush, brush, wi' chains rattling a' the while; but I seed nothing; und thowt I to mysel, now this is a most mortal queer thing. And I then stuid still, and luik'd about me, but I seed nothing at aw, nobbut the two stane wa's on each side o' t' mill loine. Then I heerd again this brush, brush, brush, wi' the chains; for you see, sir, when I stuid still it stopped; and then, thowt I, this mun be a Bargest, that sae much is said about: and I hurried on towards t' wood brig, for they say as how this Bargest cannot cross a watter; but lord, sir, when I gat o'er t' brig, I heerd this same thing again; so it mud either hev crossed t' watter, *or gane round by t' spring heed!* [About thirty miles!] And then I became a valiant man, for I war a bit freeten'd afore; and thinks I, I'll turn and hev a peep at this thing; so I went up Greet Bank towards Linton, and heerd this brush, brush, brush, wi' the chains a' the way, but I see nothing; then it ceased all of a sudden. So I turned back to go hame, but I'd hardly reach'd t' door, when I heerd again this brush, brush, brush, and the chains going down towards t'Holin House, and I followed it, and the moon there shone varra breet, and *I seed its tail!* Then, thowt I, thou owd thing! I can say Ise seen thee now, so I'll away hame. When I gat to t' door, there war a girt thing like a sheep, but it war larger, ligging across t' threshold of t' door, and it war woolly like; and says I, 'git up', and it wouldn't git up – then says I, 'stir thysel', and it wouldn't stir itsel! And I grew valiant, and I rais'd t' stick to baste it wi', and then it luik'd at me, and sich oies! [eyes] they did glower, and war as big as saucers, and like a cruelled ball; first there war a red ring, then a blue one, then a white one; and these rings grew less and less *till they cam to a dot!* Now I war nane feer'd on it, tho' it girn'd at me fearfully, and I kept on saying 'git up', and 'stir thysel', and t' wife heerd as how I war at t' door, and she cam to oppen it; and then this thing gat up and walked off, *for it war mare feer'd o' t' wife than it war o' me!* and I told t' wife, and she said it war Bargest; but I nivver seed it since, and that's a true story!'

——— ⚜ ———

The shape-changing demon dog known as the Bargest is one of the most fearsome of English apparitions. Legends of threatening and protective black dogs are common in the English countryside, and have been studied by Theo Brown in her essay 'The Black Dog' (*Folk-Lore*, September 1958). The Briggs *Dictionary* (Part 6, vol. 1) has a good selection of black-dog stories. This one was sent to William Hone by T.Q.M. on 6 November 1827, who writes:

> The spectre hound is *Bargest*. Of this mysterious personage I am able to give a very particular account, having only a few days ago seen Billy B——y, who had once a full view of it. I give the narrative in his own words; it would detract from its merit to alter the language.

The Ghostly Woolpack

Source: Florence Emily Hardy, *The Life of Thomas Hardy: 1840–1928*, 1962, p. 314.

Narrator: Thomas Hardy, diary entry dated 20 April 1902.

VAGG HOLLOW, ON THE way to Load Bridge (Somerset) is a place where 'things' used to be seen – usually taking the form of a woolpack in the middle of the road. Teams and other horses always stopped on the brow of the hollow, and could only be made to go on by whipping. A waggoner once cut at the pack with his whip: it opened in two, and smoke and a hoofed figure rose out of it.

The Haunted Barn

Source: Thomas Hardy, *The Personal Notebooks of Thomas Hardy*, ed. Richard
H. Taylor, 1979, p. 14.

Narrator: Thomas Hardy, 1873.

AT MELBURY OSMOND THERE was a haunted barn. A man coming
home drunk entered the barn and fell asleep in a cow's crib that stood within.
He awoke at twelve, and saw a lady riding round and round on a buck, holding
the horns as reins. She was in a white riding-habit, and the wind of her speed
blew so strong upon him that he sneezed, when she vanished.

The Shepherd and the Crows

Source: Ella Mary Leather, *The Folklore of Herefordshire*, 1912, p. 168.
Narrator: W. Parry, shepherd, of Walterstone, aged eighty, a native of Longtown, May 1903.
Type: AT960a 'The Cranes of Ibycus'.

YEARS AGO, ON THE Black Mountain above Longtown, there lived a hired shepherd, who managed a little farm for his master. There were on either side of this farm two brothers, farming for their father. I can remember, in my time, there was terrible jealousy and animosity between the shepherds on the mountain, where the sheep all run together. I could always tell my sheep; if I whistled they would all come running to me, every one, while the strangers took no notice. A good shepherd knows his sheep and they know him. Well, it was worse nor ever for this man, because the brothers were together, and they hated him. He stuck to his master, and they to their father. At last, one day, they got him alone on the mountain, and caught him and said they would murder him. They told him there was no one about, and it would never be known. 'If you kill me,' he said, 'the very crows will cry out and speak it.' Yet they murdered and buried him. The body was found, after some time, but there was no evidence to show who the murderers were. Well, not long after, the crows took to come whirling round the heads of those two brothers, 'crawk, crawk, crawk', there they were, all day long – when they were together, when they were apart. At last they could scarcely bear it, and one said to the other, 'Brother, do you remember when we killed the poor shepherd on the mountain top there, he said that the very crows would cry out against us?' These words were overheard by a man in the next field, and the matter was looked into, so that in the end the brothers were both hanged for the murder.

Bodmin Assizes

Source: Augustus Hare, *The Story of My Life*, 1900, vol. 5, pp. 278–9.
Narrator: Miss Farrer, 17 June 1880, at the house of Lady Airlie.

HER BROTHER KNEW WELL a shopkeeper in Plymouth, who felt one day, he could not tell why, that he must go to Bodmin. To get there, it was necessary that he should cross a ferry. It was late at night, and he expected to have great difficulty in getting across, but, to his amazement, he found the boat ready for him. The ferryman said, 'I am ready, because you called me an hour ago.'

When the shopkeeper reached Bodmin, the town was full of crowds and confusion; the assizes were going on. He made his way to the court. A man was being tried for murder, and likely to be condemned. He protested his innocence in vain, and in an agony was just saying, 'I was in Plymouth at the time, if I could only prove it.' The shopkeeper was just in time to hear him, and exclaim, 'I can prove it, my Lord; I remember the prisoner perfectly: he came into my shop at the very time in question.' And it saved the man's life.

Hare notes that this was 'a story I have often heard before'.

The Girl in the Train

Source: Augustus Hare, *The Story of My Life*, 1900, vol. 5, pp. 184–8.
Narrator: Mrs T., 29 April 1879, London.

SIR THOMAS WATSON, BETTER known as Dr Watson, was a well-known physician. During the last years of his life he was in failing health, and only saw patients at his own house, but till then he went about in England wherever he was sent for. One day he was summoned to attend an urgent case at Oxenholme in Cumberland. There was only one carriage in the train which went through to Oxenholme, and in a compartment of that carriage he took his seat. He tipped the guard, and said he should be glad to be alone if he could.

The train at Euston was already in motion, when a young lady came running down the platform, with a porter laden with her hand-bags and cloaks. The man just contrived to open the carriage door, push the young lady in, throw in her things after her, and the train was off. The young lady, a very pretty, pleasing young lady, took the seat opposite Dr Watson. Being a polite, gallant old gentleman, very soon Dr Watson began to make himself agreeable: 'What beautiful effects of cloud there were. How picturesque Harrow church steeple looked through the morning haze,' &c. &c, and the young lady responded pleasantly. At last, as their acquaintance advanced, Dr Watson said, 'And are you travelling far?' 'Oh yes,' said the young lady, 'very far, I am going to Oxenholme in Cumberland.' 'How singular,' said Dr Watson, 'for that is just where I am going myself. I wonder if you happen to know Lady D. who lives near Oxenholme.' 'Yes,' said the young lady, 'I know Lady D. very well.' 'And Mrs P. and her daughters?' said Dr W. 'Oh yes, I know them too.' 'And Mr Y.?' There was a moment's pause, and then the young lady very naïvely and ingenuously said, 'Yes, I do know Mr Y. very well; and perhaps I had better tell you something. I am going to be *married* to him tomorrow. My own parents are in India, and I am going to be married from his father's house. Since I have been engaged to him, I have made the acquaintance of many of his friends and neighbours, and that is how I know so many people near Oxenholme, though I have never been there before.'

Dr Watson was charmed with the simple candour of the young lady. They went on talking, and they became quite friends. The train arrived at Rugby, and they both got out and had their bun in the refreshment-room. They were in the carriage again, and the train was already moving, when, in great excitement, the young lady called out: 'Oh stop, stop the train, don't you see how he's urging me to get out. There! that young man in the brown ulster, that's the young man I'm going to be married to.' Of course it was impossible to get out, and the young lady was greatly distressed, and though Dr Watson assured her most positively that there was no one standing where she described, she would not and could not believe him.

Then Dr Watson said, 'Now, my dear young lady, you're very young and I'm very old. I am a doctor. I am very well known, and from what you have been seeing I am quite sure, as a physician, that you are not at all well. Now, I have my medicine chest with me, and you had better let me give you a little dose.' And he did give her a little dose.

The train arrived at Stafford, and exactly the same thing occurred. 'There, there! don't you see him! *that* young man with the light beard, in the brown ulster, don't you see how he's urging me to get out.' And again Dr Watson assured her there was no one there, and said, 'I think you had better let me give you another little dose'; and he gave her another little dose.

But Dr Watson naturally felt that he could not go on giving her a dose at every station all the way to Oxenholme, so he decided within himself that if the same thing happened at Crewe, the young lady's state indicated one of two things: either that there was some intentional vision from Providence, with which he ought not to interfere; or that the young lady was certainly not in a state of health or brain which should allow of her being married next day. So he determined to act accordingly.

And at Crewe just the same thing happened. 'There, there! don't you see him! he's urging me more than ever to get out,' cried the young lady. 'Very well,' said Dr Watson, 'we will get out and go after him', and, with the young lady, he pursued the imaginary figure, and of course did not find him. But Dr Watson had often been at Crewe station before, and he went to the hotel, which opens on the platform, and said to the matron, 'Here is this young lady, who is not at all well, and should have a very quiet room; unfortunately I am not able to remain now to look after her, but I will leave her in your care, and tomorrow I shall be returning this way and will come to see how she is.' And he slipped a five-pound note into the woman's hand to guarantee expenses.

Dr Watson returned to the railway carriage. There was another young lady there, sitting in the place which the first young lady had occupied – a passenger who had arrived by one of the many lines which converge at Crewe. With the new young lady he did not make acquaintance, he moved his things to the other side of the carriage and devoted himself to his book.

Three stations farther on came the shock of a frightful accident. There was a collision. The train was telescoped, and many passengers were terribly hurt. The heavy case of instruments, which was in the rack above the place where Dr Watson had first been sitting, was thrown violently to the other side of the carriage, hit the young lady upon the forehead and killed her on the spot.

It was long before the line could be sufficiently cleared for the train to pass which was sent to pick up the surviving passengers. Many hours late, in the middle of the night, Dr Watson arrived at Oxenholme. There, waiting upon the platform, stood the young man with the light beard, in the brown ulster, exactly as he had been described. He had heard that the only young lady in the through carriage from London had been killed, and was only waiting for the worst to be confirmed. And Dr Watson was the person who went up to him and said: 'Unfortunately it is too true that a young lady has been killed, but it is not your young lady. Your young lady is safe in the station hotel at Crewe.'

Hare notes, 'I have again heard the curious story of Sir T. Watson from Mrs T., to whom he told it himself, so will write it down.'

The Ghost at the Dance

Source: Augustus Hare, *The Story of My Life*, 1900, vol. 5, p. 387.
Narrator: Mrs Thompson Hankey, 2 July 1883.

TWO BEAUTIFUL BUT PENNILESS sisters were taken out in London by an aunt. A young gentleman from the north, of very good family and fortune, fell in love with one of them, and proposed to her, but she was with difficulty persuaded to accept him, and afterwards could never be induced to fix a date for their marriage. The young man, who was very much in love, urged and urged, but, on one excuse or another, he was always put off. Whilst things were in this unsettled state, the young lady was invited to a ball. Her lover implored her not to go to it, and when she insisted, he made her promise not to dance any round dances, saying that if she did, he should believe she had ceased to care for him.

The young lady went to the ball, and, as usual, all the young men gathered round her, trying to persuade her to dance. She refused any but square dances. At last, however, as a delightful valse was being played, and she was standing looking longingly on, she suddenly felt herself seized round the waist, and hurried into the dance. Not till she reached the end of the room, very angry, did she succeed in seeing with whom she had been forced to dance: it was with her own betrothed. Furious, she said she should never forgive him. But, as she spoke, he disappeared. She begged several young men to look for him, but he could not be found anywhere, and, to her astonishment, every one denied altogether having seen him. On reaching home, she found a telegram telling her of his death, and when the hours were compared, he was found to have died at the very moment when he had seized her for the dance.

The Tell-Tale Sword

Source: Augustus Hare, *The Story of My Life*, 1900, vol. 6, pp. 363–4.
Narrator: Mrs Hall Dare, 16 November 1894, Gurdons, Suffolk.

MRS HALL DARE HAD told of a young girl friend of hers. She was with a number of other girls, foolish and frivolous, who went to consult an old woman who had the reputation of being a witch, and who was supposed to have the power of making them see their future husbands. She said they must say their prayers backwards, perform certain incantations with water, lock their doors when they went to bed, and then they would see whom they were to marry, but they would find their doors locked in the morning.

The girl followed all the witch's directions. Then she locked her door, went to bed, and waited. Gradually, by the firelight, a young man seemed to come in – to come straight through the locked door – a young man in uniform; she saw him distinctly.

He went to the end of the room and returned. As he passed the bed his sword caught in the curtain and fell upon the floor. Then he seemed to pass out. The girl fainted.

In the morning at first she thought it was a dream, but there, though her door was still locked, lay the actual sword upon the floor! Greatly aghast, she told no one, but put it away and kept it hidden. It was a terrible possession to her.

The following year, at a country house, she met the very young man she had seen. They fell violently in love and were married. For one year they were intensely – perfectly – happy.

Then her husband's regiment had to change its quarters. As she was packing up, with horror which was an instinct, she came upon the sword put away among her things. Just then, before she could hide it, her husband came in. He saw the sword, turned deadly pale, and in a stern voice said, 'How did you come by that?' She confessed the whole truth.

He was rigid. He said, 'I can never forgive it; I can never see you again'; and nothing she could say or do could move him. 'Do you know where I passed that terrible night?' he said; 'I passed it *in hell!*' He has given up three-quarters of his income to her, but she has never seen him since.

―⊷⊶―

There is an Irish version of this story, 'The Charm of the Knife', in Michael J. Murphy's *My Man Jack: Bawdy Tales from Irish Folklore* (1989).

Mr Akroyd's Adventure

Source: Augustus Hare, *The Story of My Life*, 1900, vol.5, pp. 71–3.
Narrator: Mrs Pole-Carew, 13 April 1878.

AT MY TABLE WERE two young men, one of them a Mr Akroyd. He began to talk of a place he knew in one of the Midland counties, and how a particular adventure always befell him at a certain gate there.

'Yes,' said the other young man, 'your horse always shies and turns down a particular lane.'

'Yes,' exclaimed Mr Akroyd, 'but how do you know anything about it?'

'Oh, because I know the place very well, and the same thing always happens to me.'

'And then I come to a gateway,' said Mr Akroyd.

'Yes, exactly so,' said the other young man.

'And then on one occasion I drove through it and came to a house.'

'Ah! well, *there* I do not follow you,' said the other young man.

'It was very long ago,' continued Mr Akroyd, 'and I was a boy with my father. When we drove down that lane it was very late, quite dark, and we lost our way. When we reached the gateway, we saw within a great house standing on one side of a courtyard, brilliantly lighted up. There was evidently a banquet inside, and through the large windows we saw figures moving to and fro, but all were in medieval dress: we thought it was a masquerade.

'We drove up to the house to inquire our way, and the owner came out to speak to us. He was in a medieval dress. He said he was entertaining his friends, and he entreated us, as chance had brought us there that night, to come in and partake of his hospitality. We pleaded that we were obliged to go on, and that to stay was impossible. He was excessively civil, and said that if we must really go on, we must allow him to send a footman to guide us back into the right road. My father gave the footman half-a-crown. When we had gone some distance I said, "Father, did you see what happened to that half-crown?" – "Yes, my boy, I *did*," said my father. It had fallen *through* the footman's hand on to the snow.

'The gateway really exists in the lane. There is no house, but there was one once, inhabited by very wicked people who were guilty of horrible blasphemies – a brother and sister, who danced upon the altar in the chapel, &c.'

Mrs Pole-Carew heard this story from Dr Benson, Bishop of Truro, afterwards Archbishop of Canterbury.

In a Haunted House

Source: T. W. Thompson mss, Bodleian Library, Eng. misc., c 765, pp. 134–40.
Narrator: Taimi Boswell, Oswaldtwistle, 9 January 1915.

AT DE TIME WHAT I'm speaking of we was stopping by Bolton. It was into de afternoon, an' I was letting de horses eat down a lane along wid owld Jim Charlotte. We'd bin dere a tidy while when a man came along dis lane. He was de first person as we'd sin since we'd bin dere, but I don't think we'd ha' ta'en much notice on him if he hadn't come up to us an' started talking. He said as nobody ever come down dis lane after it was dark, an' he'd advise us, he said, to go home afore it got dusk. We axed him for why, an' he towld us as dere was a big empty house at de end'n de lane what was haanted, an' after dark people was afrit'n de ghost, as sometimes it come out an' walked up an' down de lane.

Dis house, he said, had belonged to a gentleman in a big way o' business in de cotton trade as lived by hisself, an' was well knowed to be a owld miser. He went to the mill every day reg'lar, never once missed, though he'd money enough to ha' stopped at home if he'd wanted to. So one day, when he didn't land up dere, dey all thought as summat must be up; an' dat night dey went to see, some on 'em did. De doors was all locked an' de windows fastened, an' dey had to brek in. He was dead into his bed; an' after, when dey sarched de house, dey fun gowld coins under de mattresses, onto ledges, under de carpets, in fact everywheres where annybody could think of hiding of 'em. Nobody knowed how he died, an' dey never fun out. Another thing: de money wa'n't left same as it should ha' bin; dere wa'n't no will to be found. Ever since den, 'cording to dis man we sin in de lane, de house had bin locked up, an' de owld miser's spirit had haanted it.

I axed him was dere such things as spirits an' ghostes. Certainly dere was, he said. Dere was two parts to a man, his body an' his spirit, he said, an' it was only his body as was buried. His spirit was anloosed, he said, an' if dere was nothink as shouldn't ha' bin it wandered up an' down in de air, which was full o' spirits, he said, as never hurted nor molested nobody. (He called hisself a spirtualess, dis man did.) But if, he said, de dead man had bin done away wid, or had bin

– 332 –

over fond'n his money an' hadn't willed it to nobody, den, he said, his spirit was bad an' violent an' vicious. It haanted de place where he'd lived and died, he said, an' was like to hurt, an' may be to kill, annybody as come nigh it, or anterfered wid it at all.

Well, when me an' Jim Charlotte got back wid de horses we had 'casion to see Joe Bunk, a dealing sort'n a man; an' we towld him about dis house at de end'n de lane. I'd go, I said, if dey two would, an' brek into it to see if dere really was a ghost inhabiting of it; an' being as dey regreed, we fixed as we'd go dat very night at ten o'clock. So I went to a shop an' bought me a pound o' candles, a nounce o' 'bacca – I couldn't do wi'out dat – an' a pen'orth o' matches. Den a bit afore ten I goes an' axes Jim Charlotte is he ready, but he makes some excuse for not coming. An' it's de same wid Joe Bunk; he won't come neether. It would be flying in de face o' providence, he said, to go on a errand like dis what I was bent on. So in de finish I had to go by myself.

De doors 'n de house was all locked, an' de bottom windows had thick iron bars to 'em same so what prison windows has. I didn't see how I was going to get in, but annyways I started on de front door. It was a heavy massy door like what you'll see to a church, an' had nails all over it wid heads to 'em as big 'n your fist. I started kicking it, an' I kicked away at it till my shoes was pretty near to bits, but it didn't give not a inch. Den I threw bricks at it, an' some great stones I fun in de garden, but dat was anuseless an' all. So den I run at it wid my head; butted it I did, for all de world like a owld tup when it's angered. I tried dis three or fower times at de least, teking a mighty big run an' all; but it was no manner o' good; I was no nearer to bursting it open 'an I'd bin at de start. So now I tried one 'n de windows instead, hammering away at de bars wid big stones. I managed to bend some 'n 'em a bit, but not enough to let me get through. Howsoever, I at 'em agen, an' I kept on till at last one 'n 'em gives way: it come loose from its socket at de bottom. Dat seemed to put fresh strength into me, an' it wa'n't so very long afore I did de next one de same way. Den, thinking as I'd room to squeedge through, I throwed two a three stones through de windows to brek anny glass as was left.

I climbed up now, an' sat a-straddle de window ledge, one leg into de room, de tother hanging down outside. I got my owld pipe going; after which I lighted a candle an' had a good look all about de room. De furniture 'd bin knocked about a bit, an' de fireplace had bin pulled out an' throwed onto de floor. Dere wa'n't a sound to be heeard nowheres: de house was still as death. Well, I bided where I was a bit; den I got down into de room, an' seated myself in de armchair by where de fireplace should ha' bin. I sat dere puffing away at my pipe, waiting for de ghost to repear. Now an' agen I'd think I heeard summat stirring, an' I'd go to see if it was it. 'Come out,' I'd say, 'if so be you'm dere. Come out,' I'd say; 'no need to be afrit 'n me, as all I wants is to have a look at you. Come out, you —, come out.' But it never did; an' me wanting so to see it 'at I'd ha' gi'en £5 for it to repear. Dere's a owld saying though, what generations has had proof on, as 'dem as wants, can't'; an' it looked as if dis was to be de case wid me an' dis ghost what I'd set my mind on seeing.

Howsoever, I wa'n't going to fail for want o' trying, so after when I'd waited a bit longer into dis first room I thought as I'd try de tothers. De next as I come to had a hole into one wall big enough for a man to walk through wi'out drooping his head, an' dere was bricks an' mortar all about de floor; but I couldn't see not a sign 'n de ghost, nor yet catch a sound on it. It was de same into all de tother downstairs rooms: dey'd all bin knocked about above a bit, but as for dis violent an' vicious spirit I'd come for to see, well it wa'n't dere.

Nothink for it den but to try upstairs; so upstairs I went, my candle into my hand; an' I should say as all de while I was looking up in front'n me, watching if I could see annythink. I got very near to de top 'n de stairs when all at once I stum'led, an' come falling bumpety bump right down to de bottom agen. My candle was knocked out'n my hand, an' being as I was now in de pitch dark I couldn't find it agen, though I went scrawling after it for a tidy while. But I had a plenty left yet, so I lighted another one, an' started off upstairs agen. I retermined as I'd be more careful dis time, an' watch where I was putting my feet. Well, I got to de place where I'd stum'led afore. Dere should ha' bin six steps more, but dey'd bin rived out, an' all dere was was a great hole; an' I thought to myself what a wonder an' a mercy I hadn't bin killed, as I might easy ha' bin if I'd fell through it. I'd a hard job to get over dis hole, but I wa'n't going to be beaten, an' after a while I managed somehow to get to de top'n de stairs.

It's a good thing I was minding now where I stepped, as de whole floor upstairs had bin rooted up, an' dere was great heaps o' stuff lying all about de place. Looks as if de ghost had bin sarching for money what de owld miser had hid, though what it wanted it for is more 'n I can tell you. Well, I sat me down for a bit an' waited, but nothink come. So den I med my way through every room upstairs, same as I'd done downstairs; an' every now an' agen I called out to dis vicious spirit to come out. 'Come out,' I called, 'if so be as you'm dere. Come out,' I called; 'no need to be afrit'n me, as all I want is to have a look at you. Come out, you —, come out.' But for all my calling it never showed up, any more 'n it had done afore.

I waited an' waited, till at last I got tired o' waiting an' went downstairs agen, back to de room I'd landed into at de first, back to de armchair I'd sat in dere. I had another pipe or two, an' time to time I kept calling for de ghost to come out; but it's not a bit o' use, none whatsumever; it don't come. By now it would be past 2 o'clock in de morning. I thought p'r'aps if I put my candle out dat will help. So I did; an' den I climbed back onto de window ledge what I'd come in by. Dere I sat, puffing away at my pipe, waiting an' watching for dis ghost; but it never repeared. An' being as it was come light now, dere was nothing left for me to do but to go home.

I'd ha' gi'en £5 just for to see dis spirit, gladly I would. I expecks as if I hadn't ha' minded so much I'd ha' sin it right enough. Dat's where I was wrong; no doubt about it. 'Dem as wants, can't'; dat is, dem as wants annythink mighty badly can't never have it. Dat's a owld saying, an' a true un: dere's generations, I tell you, has had proof on it, owld ancient people long since dead an' done, an' dere's generations as is to come yet what will find out, as I did, as it's de 'stantial truth. It was de way o' things into de beginning; an' it al'ays will be long as dere 's people onto de earth. You can put your trust into dat, for, no mistake, it's de God's truth.

This story, in which the hero challenges a ghost to appear and is disappointed when it does not, offers a kind of reverse image of the tale type AT326a 'Soul Released from Torment'. See 'The Golden Ball' (p. 118) and 'The Dauntless Girl' (p. 336).

The Dauntless Girl

Source: W. Rye, *Recreations of a Norfolk Antiquary*, 1920, pp. 22–6.
Narrator: Unknown.
Type: AT326 'The Youth Who Wanted to Learn What Fear Is', AT326a 'Soul Released from Torment'.

SHE LIVED FIRST WITH a farmer, and he and his friends were a-drinking one night and they ran out of liquor. So the farmer he up and say, 'Never you mind, my girl will go down to the public and bring us up another bottle.' But the night was very dark, so his friends they say, 'Surelie she'll be afeared to go out such a dark night by herself all alone.' But he say, 'No she won't, for she's afeared of nothing that's alive nor dead.' So she went and she brought 'em back their licker, and his friends they say it was a wery funny thing she shewd be so bold. But the farmer he say, 'That's nuthin at all, for she'd go anywhere day or night for she ain't afeared of nothing that's alive or dead.' And he offered to bet a golden guinea that none of 'em could name a thing she would not dew. So one of 'em agreed to take the bet and they were to meet the same day as it might be next week and he was to set her her task. Meanwhile he goes to the old parson and he borrows the key of the Church and then he goes to the old sexton and right-sided it with him for half the guinea to go into the church and hide himself in the dead house so that he was to frighten the Dauntless Girl when she came.

So when they all met together at the farmer's he say, '*This* is what the Dauntless Girl *won't* dew – she won't go into the Church alone at midnight and go into the dead house and bring back a skull bone.' But she made no trouble about it and up and went down to the church all along of herself and she opened the door of the dead house and she picked up a skull bone.

Then the old sexton behind the door he muffled out, 'Let that be, that's my mother's skull bone.' So she put it down and picked up another. Then the old sexton he muffled out again, 'Let that be, that's my father's skull bone.' So she put that down tew, and took up still another and she say out loud, for she'd lost her temper, 'Father or mother, sister or brother, I *must* hev a skull bone and that's my last word', and so she up and walked out with it, and she locked the door of the dead house behind her and she come home, and she put the skull bone on the table and she say, 'There's your skull bone, master,' and she was for going back to her work.

But him as had made the bet he up and say, 'Didn't yew hear nothing, Mary?' 'Yes,' she say, 'some fule of a ghost called out to me, "Let be, that's my father's skull bone, and let be, that's my mother's skull bone", but I told him right straight that father or mother, sister or brother, I *must* hev a skull bone, so I tuk it and here't be, and then as I was goin' away arter I had locked the door, I heard the old ghost a-hallering and shrieking like mad.'

Then him as had made the bet was rarely upset, for he guessed it was the old sexton a-hallerin' about for fear of being locked up all alone in the dead house. And so it was, for when they ran down to let him out they found him lying stone dead on his face a dead-o-fright.

And it sarved him right to try and terrify a poor mawther. But her master he gave her the golden guinea he had won.

A little while after down in Suffolk there was a squire and his mother, a very old lady and she died and was buried. But she would *not* rest and kept on coming into the house 'specially at meals'. Sometimes you could see all of her, sometimes not all, but you'd see a knife and fork get up off the table, and play about where her hands should be. Now this upset the servants so much that they would *not* stop, and the Squire was sadly put to, to know what he should do. One day he heard of the Dauntless Girl, tree villages off, who was feared at nowt. So he rode over, and told her all about it, and asked her if she would come as servant, and she said she paid no regard to ghosts so she would come, but that it ought to be considered in her wages. And so it was and she went back with the Squire. First thing she did was to alius lay a place regular for the ghost at meals, and took great care not to put the knife and fork criss-cross way. And she used to hand her the vegetables and the rest just as if she were real. And would say, 'Peppaw, mum', or 'Salt, mum', as it might be. This fared to pleased the old ghost, but nothing come of it, till Squire had to go up to London on some law business.

Next day, the Dauntless Girl was down on her knees a-cleaning the parlour grate when she noticed a thin thing push in through the door, which was just ajar and open out wide when it got into the room, till she turned out to be the old ghost.

Then the ghost she up and spoke for the first time and she say, 'Mary, are you afeared of me?' and the girl say, 'No, mum, I've no call to be afeared of yew, for *yew* are dead, and *I'm* alive', which fairly flummoxed the old ghost, but she went on and say, 'Mary, will yew come down into the cellar along o' me – yew musent bring a light but I'll shine enow to light you.' So they went down the cellar steps, and she shone like an old lantern, and when they got down she pointed out to some loose tiles and said, 'Pick yew up those tiles.' So she did, and there were tew bags of gold, one a big 'un, and one a little 'un, and she said, 'Mary, that big bag's for your master, and that little bag's for yew, for you are a dauntless girl, and desarve it.' Then off went the old ghost and never was seen no more and the Dauntless Girl she had a main o' trouble to find her way up in the dark out of the cellar.

Then in tree days' time, back there came the Squire and he said, 'Morning, Mary, hae yew seen anything of my mother since I've been away?' and she said, 'Iss, sir, that I hev, and if yew ain't afraid of coming down into the cellar, along o' me, I'll show yew something.' And he larfed, and said *he* wornt afraid if *she* wornt, for the Dauntless Girl wor a very pretty girl.

So they lit a candle and went down and she opened up the tiles and she say, 'There are the tew bags of gold, the *little* one is for yew, and the big 'un is for *me*.' And he say, 'Lor!' for he thought his mother might have given *him* the big one (and so she had), but he took what he could. And the Dauntless Girl she ollus afterwards crossed the knives and forks, to keep the ghost from telling what she had done. But after a while the Squire thort it all over, and he married the Dauntless Girl so arter all he got both bags of gold, and he used to stick-lick her whensoever he got drunk. And I think she desarved it, for deceiving the old ghost.

Dowser and Sam

Source: W. H. Barrett, *Tales from the Tens*, 1963, pp. 38–42.
Narrator: W. H. Barrett, from the narration of Chafer Legge.

SEVERAL YEARS AGO THERE was a small farmer, named Dowser, living in a very lonely house down Hockwold Fen. I don't suppose that he or his wife came out of the fen twice in twelve months. He worked the place himself and the pair of them never mixed with other people if they could help it. Both of them were a little bit weak up top and folk never went to their house unless they were obliged to. Old Dowser and his wife must have found it pretty hard to keep going because the land was very poor, and, as time went on, things got worse. First he had to sell his only horse, then his cow and, one day, a chap down that way saw him trying to plough by making his wife pull the plough while he pushed. Two farmers, who lived close by, offered to lend a horse each, but Dowser said he didn't want them as he and his old woman were quite able to look after themselves and they didn't want other people poking their noses in where they weren't wanted. So after that folks left them alone.

As time went on, those who ran into Dowser by chance, noticed that he was getting worse in the head and they used to keep as far away from him as they could as they didn't like the look in his eyes. Then, one night, Jim Pendles, whose house was the nearest place to Dowser's, was woken up by a loud banging on the door and when he went down he found Dowser outside. He said he was looking for his wife who'd gone off in a temper when he'd told her he was going to open up a butcher's shop as he was fed up with farming and with looking after live meat when he could make more out of dead.

Pendle told him to cut off home and he'd find his wife asleep in bed when he got there. You see, he was a bit scared of Dowser coming at that time of night; so he didn't go back to bed but waited till it was daylight, then looked out of the door. He could see Dowser walking across the fen towards his home, but no one saw him alive after that. Then, one Saturday night, some of the men in the pub began talking about Dowser and saying they hadn't seen him about for some time, so in the end four of them said they'd go down next morning and see if everything was all right.

They met at the Anchor and, after a pint or two, went into the fen and up to Dowser's house, and knocked on the door. When no one came they tried to open it but it was bolted, so at last they burst their way in and then stood staring in horror at what they saw. The table and the floor were covered with blood and so were two big knives and a chopper; hanging from the ham and bacon hooks in the beam were big lumps of flesh. In the pig-scalding trough they found a woman's head and bones. From the biggest hook Dowser was hanging; he'd climbed up a short pair of steps, put his throat on the hook and swung there till he was dead.

Well, no one would live in the house after that and it was left to fall to bits. It wasn't long, either, before people began saying they'd seen Dowser's ghost moving across the fen, looking for his wife. I saw something myself when I was out there one night, but I couldn't swear to it that it was him as I took care not to be out that way again, after dark.

Then, some years after all this, the family who'd owned all the fen since it was drained, died out and the whole lot was sold to old Billy Luddington's father who turned out all the farmers and farmed the land himself. Where Dowser's house had stood he built a big bullock yard and he used to thresh out there, after harvest, as they couldn't get the portable engine and tackle down there after the rains had set in. There would be six or seven great big straw stacks, ready for the seventy or eighty bullocks to tread into muck. He paid a half-witted old man to feed and look after the bullocks; his name was Sam and if he had another name, no one ever knew it. Sam built himself a hut of thatched hurdles to sleep in and he treated those beasts like children, giving them all a name; and they knew it too. He used to go down to the Anchor for his grub – he lived on bread, cheese and cold fat pork – but on Sundays the landlord gave him a good hot dinner, though he had to eat it in the tap-room because he was lousy. Of course, Sam was the butt of everyone, but even teasing couldn't take the silly grin off his face. He liked a pint, but he never took more than he could carry.

One night, the men in the Anchor started teasing Sam about Dowser's ghost, but he only grinned and said no ghost could upset him or his bullocks. So then they tried to frighten him by telling him tales of what ghosts could do, but they got no change out of him. So at last, just before closing time, six of the chaps borrowed a steel and a carving knife from the landlord and slipped out of the pub before Sam left and went down to the bullocks, hoping to get a bit of fun out of them before the old chap arrived.

It wasn't long before Sam came up; he'd run the last half mile down the drove because he could hear his bullocks blaring when they should have been lying down asleep. One of the chaps had nipped over the gate and had spent ten minutes whacking the beasts with a big cudgel. As the yard was crowded, the bullocks couldn't get out of each other's way and so they were pushing each other and making a frightful din, as they weren't used to such treatment. The more the man whacked the more his five mates, who'd climbed up on to a cut in one of the straw stacks, roared with laughter, and they kept shouting to him to keep on till Sam came. One or two of the biggest bullocks kept giving the man a hint that they could use their horns all right and, once, when he slipped in the soft muck, they soon turned and would have had him if the cudgel hadn't kept giving them some nasty clouts.

When the chap thought he'd done enough another of his mates took his place, just before Sam got to the yard gate. The old man peered into the yard and could see a man moving about among the bullocks and sharpening a knife on a steel.

'What's frightening you, my beauties?' asked Sam.

'I'm Dowser's ghost,' said the man. 'I've come back from hell to carve your old bullocks up.'

'Oh, you have, have you?' says Sam. 'And what sort of a place is it you come from?'

'All frying pans and toasting forks; and we want some big slabs of beefsteak to cook. But I can't waste a lot of time talking. I've orders to take you back with me for supper.'

'Who gave you the orders?' asked Sam.

'Why, the devil of course; he told me to make sure I brought you back so he could grill the biggest fool on earth at the end of a pitchfork.'

'Well, you go back and tell him,' said Sam, 'that I'm too full of beer tonight to be grilled, and tell him, too, to keep away from my old bullocks as they're a bit too strong for him as they've been all winter on swedes and turnips.'

'Oh, he won't mind that,' said the man, and he gave the nearest bullock a prick with the knife, which made the beast jump a yard or two towards the gate. In the half-light Sam could see blood running down its flanks.

'Out of the way, my beauty,' he shouted, 'and I'll let Dowser and all his mates in hell know they aren't coming up here upsetting my bullocks.'

Then, grabbing a pitchfork, he opened the gate and the bullocks made way for him; and before the chap could get away Sam had stuck him through twice and he left the fork sticking him to the muck.

'You can keep the fork,' he told him, 'and take it back with you; it'll be handy down there. And you can tell the devil that no ghosts, or devils either, are going to upset my beasts when I'm paid to look after them.'

Then Sam went out of the yard and stood leaning on the gate, looking on; and so did those five chaps lying on the stack. The chap in the yard was no sooner on the ground than those bullocks were on him, tossing him on their horns, kneeling on him and trampling him with their hooves. All the rest of the night Sam stood and watched and the other chaps lay on the straw, too frightened to move. Then, when it was daylight, Sam went into the yard and pulled bits of shirt and coat from the bullocks' horns, then fetched forkfuls of straw to cover up the night's work. And when the five on the stack saw him coming with the fork to get the straw, they jumped down and ran off home as fast as their legs could go.

When the bullocks were turned out of the yard the muck was carted out and laid on the muckle for a few months before it was taken into the field and spread. One day, after this had been done, the farmer was walking across a field with two of his dogs and he saw one of them pick up a bone in its mouth. Going to have a look, he saw a watch and chain on the ground, so he took them along to Sam and asked if they belonged to him.

'No,' said Sam, 'they're not mine. I reckon they belong to the chap who lost these things I found here the other morning,' and he handed the farmer a knife and a steel.

⟞⟞☙⟝⟝

Barrett notes, 'The events in this story, told by Chafer Legge, took place in Feltwell Fen, Norfolk, c. 1865. Because of its macabre nature the tale was very popular in the public houses of Southery on dark, winter nights.' Chafer Legge, 'the last of the old Fen tigers', was the source of many of W. H. Barrett's best stories.

The Devil and the Farmer

Source: J. Salisbury, *A Glossary of Words and Phrases Used in South-East Worcestershire*, 1893, pp. 72–5.

Narrator: 'Related by a thresher man while at work in a barn'.

Type: AT1090 'Contest between Man and Ogre: Mowing Contest', AT1175 'Straightening the Curly Hair'.

THE DEVIL ONCE CALLED on a farmer and exed 'im if he could give him a job. 'What con'st do?' said the farmer. 'Oh! enything about a farm,' said the devil. 'Well, I wans a mon to 'elp mu to thresh a mow o' whate,' sez the farmer. 'All right,' sez the devil, 'I'm yer mon.' When they got to the barn, the farmer said to the devil, 'Which oot thee do, thresh or thraow down?' 'Thresh,' said the devil. So the farmer got o' top o' the mow and begun to thraow down the shuvs of whate on to the barn flur, but as fast as 'e cud thraow 'em down the devil ooth one stroke uv 'is nile, knocked all carn out on um, un send the shuvs flying out o' the barn dooer. The farmer thought he had got a queer sart uv a threshermon; un as 'e couldn't thraow down fast enough far 'im, 'e sez to 'im, '*Thee* come un thraow down oot?' 'All right,' sez the devil. So the farmer gets down off the mow by the ladther, but the devil 'e just gives a lep up from the barn flur to the top o' the mow, athout waiting to goo up the ladther. 'Be yu ready?' sez the devil. 'Iss [yes]', sez the farmer. Ooth that the devil sticks 'is shuppick into as many shuvs as ood kiver the barn flur, an thraows um down. 'That'll do fur a bit,' sez the farmer, so the devil sat down un waited t'll the farmer 'ud threshed that lot, un when a was ready agyun, 'e thraow'd down another flur full; un afore night they'd finished threshin' the whole o' the mow o' whate. The farmer couldn't 'elp thinkin' a good dyull about 'is new mon, fur 'e'd never sin sich a one afore. ('E didn't knaow it was the devil, thu knaowst, 'cos he took keer nat to let the farmer see 'is cloven fut.) So in the marnin' 'e got up yarly un went un spoke to a cunnin mon about it. The cunnin' mon said it must be the devil as 'ad come to 'im, un as 'e 'ad exed 'im in, 'e couldn't get shut on 'im athout 'e could give 'im a job as 'a couldn't do. Soon atter the farmer got wum agyun, 'is new mon (the devil) wanted to knaow what he wus to do that day, and the farmer thought 'e'd give 'im a 'tazer; so he sez, 'Goo into the barn look, un count the number o' carns there be in that yup o' whate as we threshed out istaday.' 'All right,' sez Old Nick, un off a went. In a faow minutes 'e comes back and sez, 'Master, there be so many' (namin' ever so many thousan' or millions un odd, Id'na 'ow many). 'Bist sure thee'st counted un all?' sez the farmer. 'Every carn,' sez Satan. Then the farmer ardered 'im to goo un fill a 'ogshead borrel full a water ooth a sieve. So off 'e shuts agyun, but soon comes back un tells the farmer e'd done it; un sure anough 'a 'ad; un every job the farmer set 'im to do was the same. The poor farmer didn't know what to make on it, fur thaough 'e wus a gettin' 'is work done up so quick, 'e didn't like 'is new mon's company. 'Owever, the farmer thought he'd 'ave another try to trick 'im, un teld the devil 'e wanted 'im to goo ooth 'im a mowin' next marnin'. 'All right,' sez the old un, 'I'll be there, master.' But as soon as it was night the farmer went to the fild, un in the part the devil was to mow, 'e druv a lot o'horrow tynes into the ground amongst the grass. In the marnin' they got to the fild in smartish time, un begun to mow; the farmer 'e took 'is side, and teld the devil to begin o' the tother, where 'e'd stuck in the horrow tynes thu knaowst. Well, at it went the devil, who but 'e, un soon got in among the stuck up horrow tynes; but thay made no odds, 'is scythe went thraough 'em all, un the only notice on 'em e' took was to say to the farmer, every time 'e'd cut one on um thraough, 'A burdock, master'; un kep on just the same. The poor farmer 'e got so frightened at last, 'e thraough'd down 'is scythe un left the devil to finish the fild. As luck ood 'ave it, soon atter 'a got wum, a gipsy ooman called at the farm 'ouse, and seein' the farmer was in trouble exed 'im what was the matter; so 'e up un tell'd 'er all abour it. 'Ah, master,' 'er sez to 'im, when 'e 'ad tell'd 'er all about it; 'you 'a got the devil in your 'ouse sure enough, un you can only get shut on 'im by givin' 'im summut to do as 'a caunt manage.' 'Well, ooman,' sez the farmer, 'what's the use o' telling mu that? I a tried every thing I con think on, but darned uf I cun find 'im eny job as 'a caunt do.' 'I'll tell you what to do,' sez the gipsy ooman: 'when 'a comes wum, you get the missis to give 'im one uv 'er curly 'airs; un then send 'im to the blacksmith's shap, to straighten 'im on the blacksmith's anvil. 'E'll find 'a caunt do that, un 'e'll get so wild over it as 'e'll never come back to yu agyun.' The farmer was very thenkful to the gipsy ooman, and said 'e'd try 'er plan. So bye 'n bye in comes the aowd fella, un sez, 'I a finished the mowin', master; what else a you got far mu to do?' 'Well, I caunt think uv another job just now,' sez the farmer, 'but I thinks thee missis a got a little job for thu.' So 'e called the missis, un 'er gan the devil a curly 'air lapped up in a bit o' paper, un tell'd 'im to goo to the blacksmith's shap, un 'ommer that there 'air straight; un when 'a was straight to bring 'im back to 'er. 'All right, missis,' sez the devil, un off a shut. When 'a got to the blacksmith's shap, 'e 'ommer'd un 'ommer'd at that there 'air on the anvil, but the moore 'e 'ommered, the cruckeder the 'air got; so at last 'e thraowed down the 'ommer and the 'air un baowted, un never went back to the farmer agyun.

Salisbury heard this story as a boy. He writes, 'the delight (slightly spiced with awe) with which it was listened to by the present narrator is not forgotten to this day.' A story in Thomas Sternberg's *The Dialect and Folk-Lore of Northamptonshire* (pp. 140–41) combines the mowing contest with type AT1030 'The Crop Division' (see 'Jack o' Kent', p. 254). As in this story, the farmer plants the Bogie's half of the field with iron bars:

> 'Mortal hard docks these!' said he; 'Nation hard docks!' His blunted blade soon brings him to a stand-still; and as, in such cases, it is not allowable for one to sharpen without the other, he turns to his antagonist, now far ahead, and in a tone of despair inquires – 'When d'ye wiffle waffle [whet], mate?' 'Waffle!' said the farmer, with a well-feigned stare of amazement, 'Oh, about noon, mebby.' 'Then,' said the despairing Bogie, 'I've lost my land!'

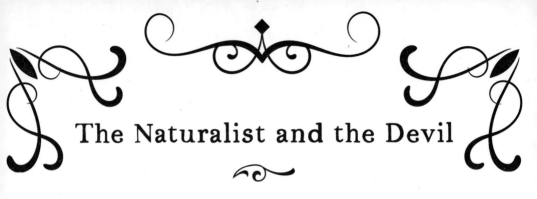

The Naturalist and the Devil

Source: Augustus Hare, *The Story of My Life*, 1900, vol. 6, p. 363.
Narrator: Unknown, Gurdons, Suffolk, 16 November 1894.

SOME YOUNG MEN ONCE determined to frighten the famous naturalist Cuvier. One of them got horns, hoofs, and a tail, and appeared by Cuvier's bedside. 'I am the devil,' he said, 'and I am come to eat you.' Cuvier looked at him. 'Carnivorous! horns – hoofs – impossible! Good-night'; and he turned over and went to sleep.

How the Hedgehog Ran the Devil to Death

Source: Ella Mary Leather, *Folk-Lore*, 23, 1912, p. 357.

Narrator: The Reverend T. H. Philpott, Hedge End, Botley, learned from his mother in Worcestershire.

Type: AT1074 'Race Won by Deception: Relative Helpers'.

A HEDGEHOG MADE A wager with the Devil to run him a race, the hedgehog to have the choice of time and place. He chose to run up and down a ditch at night. When the time came the hedgehog rolled himself up at one end of the ditch, and got a friend to roll himself up at the other; then he started the Devil off. At the other end of the ditch, the friend said to the Devil – 'Now we go off again.' Each hedgehog kept repeating this formula at his own end of the ditch, while the Devil ran up and down between them, until they ran him to death. This story would be introduced by the remark, 'Now we go off again, as the Hedgehog said to the Devil.'

Kentsham Bell

Source: Charlotte S. Burne, *Folk-Lore Journal*, 2, 1884, pp. 21–2.
Narrator: The daughter of a Herefordshire squire who told the story *c.* 1845–6,
remembering it in turn from the narration of his nursemaid.
Type: ML7070 'Legends about Church Bells'.

GREAT TOM OF KENTSHAM was the greatest bell ever brought to
England, but it never reached Kentsham safely, nor hung in any English tower.
Where Kentsham is I cannot tell you, but long, long ago the good folk of the
place determined to have a larger and finer bell in their steeple than any other
parish could boast. At that time there was a famous bell-foundry abroad, where
all the greatest bells were cast, and thither the Kentsham people sent to order
their famous bell, and thither too sent many others who wanted greater bells
than could be cast in England. And so it came to pass at length that Great Tom
of Lincoln, and Great Tom of York, and Great Tom of Christchurch, and Great
Tom of Kentsham, were all founded at the same time, and all embarked on
board the same vessel, and carried safely to the shore of dear old England. Then
they set about landing them, and this was anxious work, but little by little it
was done, and Tom of Lincoln, Tom of York, Tom of Christchurch, were safely
laid on English ground. And then came the turn of Tom of Kentsham, which
was the greatest Tom of all. Little by little they raised him, and prepared to
draw him to the shore; but just in the midst of the work the captain grew so
anxious and excited that he swore an oath. That very moment the ropes which
held the bell snapped in two, and Great Tom of Kentsham slid over the ship's
side into the water, and rolled away to the bottom of the sea.

Then the people went to the cunning man and asked him what they should
do. And he said, 'Take six yoke of white milch-kine, which have never borne
the yoke, and take fresh withy bands which have never been used before, and
let no man speak a word either good or bad till the bell is at the top of the hill.'

So they took six yoke of white milch-kine, which had never borne the yoke,
and harnessed them with fresh withy-bands which had never been used, and
bound these to the bell as it lay in the shallow water, and long it was ere they

could move it. But still the kine struggled and pulled, and the withy-bands held firm, and at last the bell was on dry ground. Slowly, slowly they drew it up the hill, moaning and groaning with unearthly sounds as it went; slowly, slowly, and no one spoke, and they nearly reached the top of the hill. Now the captain had been wild with grief when he saw that he had caused his precious freight to be lost in the waters just as they had reached the shore; and, when he beheld it recovered again and so nearly placed in safety, he could not contain his joy, but sang out merrily,

> In spite of all the devils in hell
> We have got to land old Kentsham Bell.

Instantly the withy bands broke in the midst, and the bell bounded back again down the sloping hillside, rolling over and over, faster and faster, with unearthly clanging, till it sank far away in the very depths of the sea. And no man has ever seen it since, but many have heard it tolling beneath the waves, and if you go there you may hear it too.

***

Charlotte Burne was sent this story in 1882. Repeating the story in *The Folk-Lore of Herefordshire*, Ella Mary Leather gives a similar legend from Marden, where an ancient bronze bell, now in the Hereford Museum, was discovered in a pond in 1848. She notes that there is no place called Kentsham in Herefordshire, and suggests Kinsham or Kentchurch as possible locations. In his *A Shepherd's Life*, W. H. Hudson records a similar story from 'Caleb Bawcombe', heard during his brief period as head-shepherd at a farm in Dorset, just across the border from his native Wiltshire:

> It was a foreign country, and the ways of the people were strange to him, and it was a land of very strange things. One of the strangest was an old ruined church in the neighbourhood of the farm where he was shepherd. It was roofless, more than half fallen down, and all the standing portion, with the tower, overgrown with old ivy; the building itself stood in the centre of a huge round earth-work and trench, with large barrows on the ground outside the circle. Concerning this church he had a wonderful story: its decay and ruin had come about after the great bell in the tower had mysteriously disappeared, stolen one stormy night, it was believed, by the Devil himself. The stolen bell, it was discovered, had been flung

into a small river at a distance of some miles from the church, and there in summertime, when the water was low, it could be distinctly seen lying half buried in the mud at the bottom. But all the king's horses and all the king's men couldn't pull it out; the Devil, who pulled the other way, was strongest. Eventually some wise person said that a team of white oxen would be able to pull it out, and after much seeking the white oxen were obtained, and thick ropes were tied to the sunken bell, and the cattle were goaded and yelled at, and tugged and strained until the bell came up and was finally drawn right up to the top of the steep, cliff-like bank of the stream. Then one of the teamsters shouted in triumph, 'Now we've got out the bell, in spite of all the devils in hell', and no sooner had he spoken the bold words than the ropes parted, and back tumbled the bell to its old place at the bottom of the river, where it remains to this day. Caleb had once met a man in those parts who assured him that he had seen the bell with his own eyes, lying nearly buried in mud at the bottom of the stream.

The Master and His Pupil

Source: Contributed by Sabine Baring-Gould to William Henderson, *Notes on the Folk-Lore of the Northern Counties of England and the Borders*, 1866, pp. 343–4.
Narrator: Unknown, Yorkshire.
Type: ML3020 'Inexperienced Use of the Black Book'.

THERE WAS ONCE A very learned man in the north-country who knew all the languages under the sun, and who was acquainted with all the mysteries of creation. He had one big book bound in black calf and clasped with iron and with iron corners, and chained to a table which was made fast to the floor; and when he read out of this book, he unlocked it with an iron key, and none but he read from it, for it contained all the secrets of the spiritual world. It told how many angels there were in heaven, and how they marched in their ranks, and sang in their quires, and what were their several functions, and what was the name of each great angel of might. And it told of the devils of hell, how many of them there were, and what were their several powers, and their labours, and their names, and how they might be summoned, and how tasks might be imposed on them, and how they might be chained to be as slaves to man.

Now the master had a pupil who was but a foolish lad, and he acted as servant to the great master, but never was he suffered to look into the black book, hardly to enter the private room.

One day the master was out, and then the lad, impelled by curiosity, hurried to the chamber where his master kept his wondrous apparatus for changing copper into gold, and lead into silver, and where was his mirror in which he could see all that was passing in the world, and where was the shell which when held to the ear whispered all the words that were being spoken by anyone the master desired to know about. The lad tried in vain with the crucibles to turn copper and lead into gold and silver – he looked long and vainly into the mirror; smoke and clouds fleeted over it, but he saw nothing plain, and the shell to his ear produced only indistinct mutterings, like the breaking of distant seas on an unknown shore. 'I can do nothing,' he said: 'as I know not the right words to utter, and they are locked up in yon book.' He looked round, and, see! the book was unfastened: the master had forgotten to lock it before he went out. The boy rushed to it, and unclosed the volume. It was written with red and black ink, and much therein he could not understand; but he put his finger on a line, and spelled it through.

At once the room was darkened, and the house trembled: a clap of thunder rolled through the passage of the old mansion, and there stood before the terrified youth a horrible form, breathing fire, and with eyes like burning lamps. It was the Evil One, Beelzebub, whom he had called up to serve him.

'Set me a task!' said a voice, like the roaring of an iron furnace.

The boy only trembled, and his hair stood up. 'Set me a task, or I shall strangle thee!'

But the lad could not speak. Then the evil spirit stepped towards him, and putting forth his hands touched his throat. The fingers burned his flesh. 'Set me a task.'

'Water yon flower,' cried the boy in despair, pointing to a geranium which stood in a pot on the floor.

Instantly the spirit left the room, but in another instant he returned with a barrel on his back, and poured its contents over the flower; and again and again he went and came, and poured more and more water, till the floor of the room was ankle-deep.

'Enough, enough!' gasped the lad; but the Evil One heeded him not: the lad knew not the words by which to dismiss him, and still he fetched water.

It rose to the boy's knees, and still more water was poured. It mounted to his waist, and Beelzebub ceased not bringing barrels full. It rose to his armpits, and he scrambled to the table-top. And now the water stood up to the window and washed against the glass, and swirled around his feet on the table. It still rose: it reached his breast. In vain he cried: the evil spirit would not be dismissed, and to this day he would have been pouring water, and would have drowned all Yorkshire, had not the master remembered on his journey that he had not locked his book, and had therefore returned, and at the moment when the water was bubbling about the pupil's chin, spoken the words which cast Beelzebub back into his fiery home.

Chips

Source: Charles Dickens, 'Nurse's Stories', *The Uncommercial Traveller*, 1860
(first published in *All the Year Round*).
Narrator: Charles Dickens, remembering the narration of Mary Weller.

THERE WAS ONCE A shipwright, and he wrought in a Government Yard, and his name was Chips. And his father's name before him was Chips, and *his* father's name before *him* was Chips, and they were all Chipses. And Chips the father had sold himself to the Devil for an iron pot and a bushel of tenpenny nails and half a ton of copper and a rat that could speak; and Chips the grandfather had sold himself to the Devil for an iron pot and a bushel of tenpenny nails and half a ton of copper and a rat that could speak; and Chips the great-grandfather had disposed of himself in the same direction on the same terms; and the bargain had run in the family for a long long time. So, one day, when young Chips was at work in the Dock Slip all alone, down in the dark hold of an old Seventy-four that was haled up for repairs, the Devil presented himself, and remarked:

> A Lemon has pips,
> And a Yard has ships,
> And *I*'ll have Chips!

(I don't know why, but this fact of the Devil's expressing himself in rhyme was peculiarly trying to me.) Chips looked up when he heard the words, and there he saw the Devil with saucer eyes that squinted on a terrible great scale, and that struck out sparks of blue fire continually. And whenever he winked his eyes, showers of blue sparks came out, and his eyelashes made a clattering like flints and steels striking lights. And hanging over one of his arms by the handle was an iron pot, and under that arm was a bushel of tenpenny nails, and under his other arm was half a ton of copper, and sitting on one of his shoulders was a rat that could speak. So, the Devil said again:

> A Lemon has pips,
> And a Yard has ships,
> And *I*'ll have Chips!

(The invariable effect of this alarming tautology on the part of the Evil Spirit was to deprive me of my senses for some moments.) So, Chips answered never a word, but went on with his work. 'What are you doing, Chips?' said the rat that could speak. 'I am putting in new planks where you and your gang have eaten the old away,' said Chips. 'But we'll eat them too,' said the rat that could speak; 'and we'll let in the water and drown the crew, and we'll eat them too.' Chips, being only a shipwright, and not a Man-of-war's man, said, 'You are welcome to it.' But he couldn't keep his eyes off the half a ton of copper or the bushel of tenpenny nails; for nails and copper are a shipwright's sweethearts, and shipwrights will run away with them whenever they can. So, the Devil said, 'I see what you are looking at, Chips. You had better strike the bargain. You know the terms. Your father before you was well acquainted with them, and so were your grandfather and great-grandfather before him.' Says Chips, 'I like the copper, and I like the nails, and I don't mind the pot, but I don't like the rat.' Says the Devil, fiercely, 'You can't have the metal without him – and *he's* a curiosity. I'm going.' Chips, afraid of losing the half a ton of copper and the bushel of nails, then said, 'Give us hold!' So, he got the copper and the nails and the pot and the rat that could speak, and the Devil vanished. Chips sold the copper, and he sold the nails, and he would have sold the pot; but whenever he offered it for sale, the rat was in it, and the dealers dropped it, and would have nothing to say to the bargain. So, Chips resolved to kill the rat, and, being at work in the Yard one day with a great kettle of hot pitch on one side of him and the iron pot with the rat in it on the other, he turned the scalding pitch into the pot, and filled it full. Then, he kept his eye upon it till it cooled and hardened, and then he let it stand for twenty days, and then he heated the pitch again and turned it back into the kettle, and then he sank the pot in water for twenty days more, and then he got the smelters to put it in the furnace for twenty days more, and then they gave it him out, red hot, and looking like red-hot glass instead of iron – yet there was the rat in it, just the same as ever! And the moment it caught his eye, it said with a jeer:

> A Lemon has pips,
> And a Yard has ships,
> And *I*'ll have Chips!

(For this Refrain I had waited since its last appearance, with inexpressible horror, which now culminated.) Chips now felt certain in his own mind that the rat would stick to him; the rat, answering his thought, said, 'I will – like pitch!'

Now, as the rat leaped out of the pot when it had spoken, and made off, Chips began to hope that it wouldn't keep its word. But, a terrible thing happened next day. For, when dinner-time came, and the Dock-bell rang to strike work, he put his rule into the long pocket at the side of his trousers, and there he found a rat – not that rat, but another rat. And in his hat, he found another; and in his pocket-handkerchief, another; and in the sleeves of his coat, when he pulled it on to go to dinner, two more. And from that time he found himself so frightfully intimate with all the rats in the Yard, that they climbed up his legs when he was at work, and sat on his tools while he used them. And they could all speak to one another, and he understood what they said. And they got into his lodging, and into his bed, and into his teapot, and into his beer, and into his boots. And he was going to be married to a corn-chandler's daughter; and when he gave her a work-box he had himself made for her, a rat jumped out of it; and when he put his arm round her waist, a rat clung about her; so the marriage was broken off, though the banns were already twice put up – which the parish clerk well remembers, for, as he handed the book to the clergyman for the second time of asking, a large fat rat ran over the leaf. (By this time a special cascade of rats was rolling down my back, and the whole of my small listening person was overrun with them. At intervals ever since, I have been morbidly afraid of my own pocket, lest my exploring hand should find a specimen or two of those vermin in it.)

You may believe that all this was very terrible to Chips; but even all this was not the worst. He knew besides, what the rats were doing, wherever they were. So, sometimes he would cry aloud, when he was at his club at night, 'Oh! Keep the rats out of the convicts' burying ground! Don't let them do that!' Or, 'There's one of them at the cheese down-stairs!' Or, 'There's two of them smelling at the baby in the garret!' Or, other things of that sort. At last, he was voted mad, and lost his work in the Yard, and could get no other work. But, King George wanted men, so before very long he got pressed for a sailor. And so he was taken off in a boat one evening to his ship, lying at Spithead, ready to sail. And so the first thing he made out in her as he got near her, was the figure-head of the old Seventy-four, where he had seen the Devil. She was called the Argonaut, and they rowed right under the bowsprit where the figure-head of the Argonaut, with a sheepskin in his hand and a blue gown on, was looking out to sea; and sitting staring on his forehead was the rat who could speak, and his exact words were these: 'Chips ahoy! Old boy! We've pretty well eat them too, and we'll drown the crew, and will eat them too!' (Here I always became exceedingly faint, and would have asked for water, but that I was speechless.)

The ship was bound for the Indies; and if you don't know where that is, you ought to, and angels will never love you. (Here I felt myself an outcast from a future state.) The ship set sail that very night, and she sailed, and sailed, and sailed. Chips's feelings were dreadful. Nothing ever equalled his terrors. No wonder. At last, one day he asked leave to speak to the Admiral. The Admiral giv' leave. Chips went down on his knees in the Great State Cabin. 'Your Honour, unless your Honour, without a moment's loss of time makes sail for the nearest shore, this is a doomed ship, and her name is the Coffin!' 'Young man, your words are a madman's words.' 'Your Honour, no; they are nibbling us away.' 'They?' 'Your honour, them dreadful rats. Dust and hollowness where solid oak ought to be! Rats nibbling a grave for every man on board! Oh! Does your Honour love your Lady and your pretty children?' 'Yes, my man, to be sure.' 'Then, for God's sake, make for the nearest shore, for at this present moment the rats are all stopping in their work, and are all looking straight towards you with bare teeth, and are all saying to one another that you shall never, never, never, never, see your Lady and your children more.' 'My poor fellow, you are a case for the doctor. Sentry, take care of this man!'

So, he was bled and he was blistered, and he was this and that, for six whole days and nights. So, then he again asked leave to speak to the Admiral. The Admiral giv' leave. He went down on his knees in the Great State Cabin. 'Now, Admiral, you must die! You took no warning; you must die! The rats are never wrong in their calculations, and they make out that they'll be through, at twelve tonight. So, you must die! – With me and all the rest!' And so at twelve o'clock there was a great leak reported in the ship, and a torrent of water rushed in and nothing could stop it, and they all went down, every living soul. And what the rats – being water-rats – left of Chips, at last floated to shore, and sitting on him was an immense overgrown rat, laughing, that dived when the corpse touched the beach and never came up. And there was a deal of seaweed on the remains. And if you get thirteen bits of seaweed, and dry them and burn them in the fire, they will go off like in these thirteen words as plain as plain can be:

> A Lemon has pips,
> And a Yard has ships,
> And *I*'ve got Chips!

See the note to 'Captain Murderer' (p. 162) for more information on Mary Weller. There are many folktales in which men promised to the Devil, evaded him, either by becoming a priest, or being buried neither inside nor outside a church (see 'Jack o' Kent', p. 254), or spending the night in church, or setting the devil some impossible riddle or endless task, or some other trickery. This one is unusual in that poor Chips has no escape from his family's tradition of Satanic service.

The Candle

Source: Sabine Baring-Gould, *A Book of Folk-Lore*, 1912, pp. 138–9.

Narrator: An old woman in the parish of Luffincott in North Devon, 'in her own words'.

Type: AT1187 'Meleager'.

THERE WAS AN OLD woman lived in Bridgerule parish, and she had a very handsome daughter. One evening a carriage and four drove to the door, and a gentleman stepped out. He was a fine-looking man, and he made some excuse to stay in the cottage talking, and he made love to the maiden, and she was rather taken with him. Then he drove away, but next evening he came again, and it was just the same thing; and he axed the maid if on the third night she would go in the coach with him, and be married. She said Yes; and he made her swear that she would.

Well, the old mother did not think that all was quite right, so she went to the pars'n of Bridgerule and axed he about it. 'My dear,' said he, 'I reckon it's the Old Un. Now, look y' here. Take this 'ere candle, and ax that gen'leman next time he comes to let your Polly alone till this 'ere candle be burnt out. Then take it, blow it out, and rin along on all your legs to me.'

So the old woman took the candle.

Next night the gen'leman came in his carriage and four, and he went into the cottage and axed the maid to come wi' he, as she'd sworn and promised. She said, 'I will, but you must give me a bit o' time to dress myself.' He said, 'I'll give you till thickey candle be burnt out.'

Now, when he had said this, the old woman blew the candle out and rinned away as fast as she could, right on end to Bridge-rule, and the pars'n he tooked the can'l and walled it up in the side o' the church; you can see where it be to this day (it is the rood loft staircase upper door, now walled up). Well, when the gen'leman saw he was done, he got into his carriage and drove away, and he drove till he comed to Affaland Moor, and then all to wance down went the carriage and horses and all into a sort o' bog there, and blue flames came up all round where they went down.

The Green Mist

Source: M. C. Balfour, 'Legends of the Lincolnshire Cars: Part 2', *Folk-Lore*, 2, 1891, pp. 259–64.
Narrator: Unknown man, Lindsey, Lincolnshire.
Type: AT1187 'Meleager'.

So THOU 'ST HEERD tell o' th' boggarts an' all the horrid things o' th' au'd toimes? Ay; they wor mischancy, onpleasant sort o' bodies to do wi', an' a 'm main glad as they wor all go'an afore ma da'ays. I ha' niver seed nowt o' that sort; cep' mappen a bogle or so – nuthin wu'th tellin' of. But if thou likes them sort o' ta'ales, a can tell 'ee some as ma au'd gran'ther tould us when a wor nobbut a tiddy brat. He wor main au'd, nigh a hunner year, fo'ak said; an' a wor ma fa'ather's gran'ther reetly speakin', so thou can b'leeve as a knowed a lot 'bout th' au'd toimes. Mind, a wunnut say as ahl th' ta'ales be tre-ue; but ma gran'ther said as they wor, and a b'leeved un ahl hissel. Anny-ways a 'll tell um as a heerd um; and that's ahl as a can do.

Wa'al, i' they toimes fo'ak mun ha' bin geyan unloike to now. 'Stead o' doin' their work o' da'ays, 'n smokin' ther pipes o' Sundays, i' pe'ace 'n comfort, tha wor alius botherin' ther he'ads 'bout summat 'r other – or the cho'ch wor doin' it for 'um. Th' priests wor alius at 'un 'bout thur sowls; an', what wi' hell an' th' boggarts, ther moinds wor niver aisy. An' ther wor things as didn't 'long to th' cho'ch, an' yit – a can't reetly 'splain to 'ee; but th' fo'ak had idees o' ther o'an, an' wa'ays o' ther o'an, as 'ad kep' oop years 'n years, 'n *hunnerds* o' years, since th' toime when ther worn't no cho'ch, leastwise no cho'ch o' that sort; but tha gi'n things to th' bogles 'n sich, to ke'p un friendly. Ma gran'ther said's how the bogles'd wanst bin thowt a deal more on, an' at da'arklins ivery noight th' fo'ak 'd bear loights i ther han's roon' ther ha'ouses, sa'ain' wo'ds to ke'p 'um off; an' a'd smear blo'od o' th' door-sil' to skeer awa'ay th' horrors; an' a'd put bre'ad and salt o' th' flat stouns set oop by th' la'ane side to get a good ha'arvest; an' a'd spill watter i' th' fower co'ners o' th' fields, when a wanted ra'in; an' they thowt a deal on th' sun, fur tha reckoned as a ma'ade th' yarth, an' brout th' good an' ill chances an' a do'ant know what ahl. A can't tell 'ee reetly what they b'leeved;

fur 'twor afore ma gran'ther's toime, ahl that; an' that's more'na hunnerd 'n fifty years agone, seest-tha; but a reckon tha made nigh iverythin' as they seed 'n heerd into sort o' gre'at bogles; an' tha wor alius gi'un 'um things, or sa'ayin' so't o' prayers loike, to keep um fro' doin' th' fo'ak anny evil.

Wa'al that was a long toime agone, as a said afore, an' twor no'on so bad i' ma gran'ther's da'ay; but, natheless, 'twon't furgot, an' some o' th' foak b'leeved it ahl still, an' said ther au'd prayers or spells-loike, o' th' sly. So ther wor, so to sa'ay, two cho'ches; th'wan wi' priests an' candles, an' a' that; th' other jist a lot o' au'd wa'ays, kep 'oop ahl onbeknown an' hidden-loike, mid th' fo'ak thersels; an' they thowt a deal more, ma gran'ther said, on th' au'd spells, 's on th' sarvice i' th' cho'ch itsel.' But 's toime want on tha two got so't o' mixed oop; an' some o' tha fo'aks cudn't ha' tould thee, ef 'twor fur won or t' other as tha done th' things.

To Yule, i th' cho'ches, thur wor gran' sarvices, wi' candles an' flags an' what not; an' i' th' cottages thur wor candles 'n ca'akes 'n gran' doin's; but tha priests niver knowed as mony o' th' foak wor on'y wakin' th' dyin' year, an' 'at tha wine teemed upo' that door-sil to first cock-crow wor to bring good luck in th' new year. An a' reckon some o' th' fo'ak thersells 'd do th' au'd heathen wa'ays 'n sing hymns meantime, wi' neer a thowt of tha stra'angeness o't.

Still, thur wor many 's kep' to th' au'd wa'ays ahl togither, thoff tha done it hidden loike; an' a'm goin' to tell ee of wan fam'bly as ma gran'ther knowed fine, and how they waked th' spring wan year.

As a said afore, a can't, even ef a wud, tell'ee ahl th' things as tha useter do; but theer wos wan toime o'th year 's they p'rtic'larly want in fur ther spells 'n prayers, an' that wor th' yarly spring. Tha thout as th' yarth wor sleepin' ahl th' winter; an' at th' bogles – ca'all urn what ee wull – 'd nobbut to do but mischief, fur they'd nowt to see to i' tha fields; so they wor feared on th' long da'ark winter days 'n noights, i' tha mid' o ahl so'ts o unseen fearsome things, ready 'n waitin' fur a chance to pla'ay un evil tricks. But as tha winter want by they thout as 'twor toime to wake th' yarth fro 'ts sleepin' 'n set the bogles to wo'k, care'n' fur th' growin' things 'n bringin' th' harvest. Efter that th' yarth wor toired, an' wor sinkin' to sleep agean; an' tha useter sing hushieby songs i' tha fields o' th' A'tum evens. But i' th' spring, tha want – tha fo'ak did as b'leeved in th' au'd wa'ays – to every field in to'n, 'n lifted a spud o' yarth fro' th' mools; an' tha said stra'ange 'n quare wo'ds, as tha cudn't sca'arce unnerstan' thersel's; but th' same as' 'd bin said for hunnerds o' ye'ars. An' ivery mornin' at th' first dawn, tha stood o' th' door-sil, wi' salt an' bread i' ther han's, watchin' in waitin' for th' green mist 's rose fro th' fields 'n tould at th' yarth wor awake agean; an' th' life wor comin' to th' trees an' the pla'ants, an' th' seeds wor bustin' wi' th' beginning o' th' spring.

Wa'al ther wor wan fam'bly as 'd done ahl that, year arter year, fro's long as they knowd of, jest's ther gran'thers 'd done it afore un; an' wan winter e'n, nigh on a hunnerd n' thutty year gone to now, tha wor makin' ready for wakin' the spring. Th' 'ad had a lot o' trooble thruff th' winter, sickness 'n what not'd bin bad i' th' pla'ace; an' th' darter, a rampin' young maid, wor grow'd whoite 'n wafflin' loike a bag o' bo'ans, stead o' bein' th' purtiest lass i' th' village as a'd bin afore. Day arter da'ay a growed whiter 'n sillier, till a cudn't stan upo's feet more 'n a new born babby, an' a cud on'y lay at th' winder watchin' an' watchin' th' winter crep' awa'ay. An' 'Oh mother,' a'd kep sa'ayin' ower 'n ower agin; 'ef a cud on'y wake th' spring with 'ee agin, mebbe th' Green Mist 'd mek ma strong 'n well, loike th' trees an' th' flowers an' th' co'n i' th' fields.'

An' tha mother 'd comfort her loike, 'n promise 'at she'd coom wi' em agean to th' wakin', an' grow 's strong 'n straight 's iver. But da'ay arter da'ay a got whiter 'n wanner, till a looked, ma gran'ther said, loike a snow-flake fadin' i' th' sun; an' day arter da'ay' th' winter crep by, an' th' wakin' o' th' spring wor amost theer. Th' pore maid watched 'n waited for th' toime fur goin' to th' fields; but a'd got so weak 'n sick 'at a knowed a cudn't git ther wi' th' rest. But a wudn't gi'n oop fur ahl that; an' 's mother mun sweer 'at she 'd lift th' lass to th' door-sil, at th' comin' o' the Green Mist, so 's a mowt toss oot th' bread 'n salt o' th' yarth her o'an sel' an' wi' her o'an pore thin han's.

An' still th' da'ays went by, an' th' foak wor goin' o' yarly morns, to lift the spud i' th' fields; an' th' comin' o' th' Green Mist wor lookit for ivery dawning.

An wan even th' lass, as 'd bin layin', wi 's eyne fixed o' th' little gy'arden said to 's mother:

'Ef tha Green Mist don't come i' tha morn's dawnin' – a'll not can wait fur't longer. Th' mools is ca'allin' ma, an tha seeds is brustin' as'll bloom ower ma he'ad; a know't wa'al, mother – 'n yit, if a cud on'y see th' spring wake wanst agin! – mother – a sweer a'd axe no more 'n to live's long's wan o' them cowslips as coom ivery year by th' ga'ate, an' to die wi' th' fust on 'em when tha summer's in.'

The mother whisht tha maid in fear; fur tha bogles 'n things as they b'leeved in wor alius gainhand, an' cud hear owt as wor said. They wor niver sa'afe, niver aloan, the pore fo'ak to than, wi' th' things as tha cudn't see, an' cudn't he'ar, alius roon 'em. But th' dawn o' th' nex' da'ay browt th' Green Mist. A comed fro' th' mools, an' happed asel' roon' iverythin', green 's th' grass i' summer sunshine, 'n sweet-smellin 's th' yarbs o' th' spring; an' th' lass wor carried to th' door-sil, wheer a croom'led th' bread 'n salt on to th' yarth wi' 's o'an han's an' said the stra'ange au'd wo'ds o' welcoming to th' new spring. An a lookit to the ga'ate, wheer th' cowslips growed, an' than wor took ba'ack to 's bed by th' winder, when a slep loike a babby, an' dreamt o' summer an' flowers an' happiness. Fur fither 'twor th' Green Mist as done it, a can't tell 'ee more 'n ma gran'ther said, but fro' that da'ay a growed stronger 'n prettier nor iver, an' by th' toime th' cowslips wor buddin' a wor runnin' aboot, an' laughin' loike a very sunbeam i' th' au'd cottage. But ma gran'ther tould's as a wor alius so white 'n wan, while a lookit loike a will-o-th'-wyke flittin' aboot; an' o th' could da'ays a'd sit shakin' ower th' foire, an' 'd look nigh de'ad, but whan th' sun'd coom oot, a'd da'ance an' sing i' th' loight, 'n stretch oot 's arms to 't 'sif a on'y lived i' th' warmness o' t. An' by 'n by th' cowslips brust ther buds, an' coom i' flower, an' th' maid wor growed so stra'ange an' beautiful 'at they wor nigh feared on her – an' ivery mornin' a'd kneel by th' cowslips 'n watter 'n tend 'em 'n da'ance to 'em i th' sunshine, while th' mother 'd stan' beggin' her to leave 'em, 'n cried 'at she'd have 'em pu'd oop by th' roots 'n throwed awe'ay. But th' lass 'd on'y look stra'ange at a, 'n sa'ay – soft 'n low loike:

'Ef thee are'nt tired o' ma, mother – niver pick wan o' them flowers; they'll fade o' ther sel's soon enuff – ay, soon enuff – thou knows!' An' tha mother'd go'a back to th' cottage 'n greet ower th' wo'k; but a niver said nowt of her trooble to th' neebors – not till arter'ds. But wan da'ay a lad o' th' village stopped at th' ga'ate to chat wi 'em, an' by-'n-by, whiles a wor gossipin' a picked a cowslip 'n pla'ayed wi 't. Th' lass didn't see what a'd done; but as he said goodbye, a seed th' flower as 'd fa'allen to th' yarth at's feet. 'Did thee pull that cowslip?' a said – lookin' stra'ange 'n white wi' wan han' laid ower her he'art.

'Ay' said he – 'n liftin' 't oop, a gi'n it to her smilin' loike, 'n thinkin' what 'n 'a pretty maid it wor.

She looked at th' flower an' at th' lad, an' ahl roon' aboot her; at th' green trees, an' th' sproutin' grass, an' th' yaller blossoms; an' oop at th' gowlden shinin' sun itsel'; an' ahl to wanst, shrinkin' 's if th' light a'd loved so mooch wor brennin' her, a ran into th' hoose, wi' oot a spoken wo'd, on'y a so't o' cry, loike a dumb beast i' pain, an' th' cowslip catched close agin her bre'ast.

An' then – b'leeve it or not as 'ee wull – a niver spo'ak agin, but la'ay on th' bed, starin' at th' flower in's han' an' fadin' as it faded ahl thruff th' da'ay. An' at th' dawnin' ther wor on'y layin' o' th' bed a wrinkled, whoite, shrunken dead thing, wi'in 's han' a shrivelled cowslip; an' th' mother covered 't ower wi' th' clo's an' thowt o' th' beautiful joyful maid da'ancin' loike a bird i' th' sunshine by th' gowden noddin' blossoms, on'y th' da'ay go'an by. Th' bogles 'd heerd a an' a'd gi'n 's wish; a'd bloomed wi' th' cowslips an' a'd fa'ded wi' th' first on 'em! and ma gran'ther said as 'twor ahl's treue's de'ath!

See the note to 'The Flyin' Childer' (p. 130) for my reservations about the authenticity of both the content and the dialect of Mrs Balfour's Lincolnshire tales. This is, however, assignable to a tale type, in which the heroine usually lives for as long as the brand burning on the fire lasts. For a variant, see 'The Candle' (p. 358).

Assuming authenticity, the 'strange and queer words' used to wake the earth from sleep might have been a jumbled recollection of an Anglo-Saxon charm such as the 'Remedy for Cultivated Land' that starts 'Erce, Erce, Erce, eorþan, motor'.

The writer Alan Garner has used this story as the basis of a striking and powerful dance-drama, *The Green Mist*, the text of which is available in *Labrys* (7, November 1981, pp. 27–47).

The closest English comparison to this story I can find is that given in chapter 11, 'Hampshire – An Umbrella Man', of Edward Thomas's *The South Country* (1909). The speaker, 'John Clark', is vividly described, and given a specific birth date: 21 June 1831, in Sussex. Thomas says he had been on the road for forty years. However, such chance-met figures in Thomas's prose seem to have been as much dream-extensions of himself as actual characters. 'John Clark' says:

I remember how it was my little girl died – my little girl, says I, but she would have been a big handsome woman now, forty-eight years old on the first of May that is gone. She was lying in bed with a little bit of a cough, and she was gone as white as a lily, and I went in to her when I came home from reaping. I saw she looked bad and quiet-like – like a fish in a hedge – and something came over me, and I caught hold of both her hands in both of mine and held them tight, and put my head close up to hers and said, 'Now look here, Polly, you've got to get well. Your mother and me can't stand losing you. And you aren't meant to die; such a one as you be for a lark.' And I squeezed her little hands, and all my nature seemed to rise up and try to make her get well. Polly she looked whiter than ever and afraid; I suppose I was a bit rough and dirty and sunburnt, for 'twas a hot harvest and 'twas the end of the second week of it, and I was that fierce I felt I ought to have had my way . . . All that night I thought I had done a wrong thing trying to keep her from dying that way, and I tell you I cried in case I had done any harm by it . . . That very night she died without our knowing it. She was a bonny maid, that fond of flowers. The night she was taken ill she was coming home with me from the Thirteen Acre, where I'd been hoeing the mangolds, and she had picked a rose for her mother. All of a sudden she looks at it and says, 'It's gone, it's broke, it's gone, it's gone, gone, gone', and she kept on, 'It's broke, it's gone, it's gone', and when she got home she ran up to her mother, crying, 'The wild rose is broke, mother; broke, gone, gone.'

The girl's cries were made 'in a high finical voice more like that of a bird than a child'.

The Pale Rider

Source: W. H. Jones and L. L. Kropf, *The Folk-Tales of the Magyars*, 1889, p. 417.
Narrator: An old woman (nearly eighty) in Lincolnshire.

ONE FINE FROSTY NIGHT, as the Winterton carrier was going along the road, he met a pale man on horseback, who said, 'It's a hard winter, and there's going to be a hard time: twenty years' disease amongst vegetables, twenty years' disease amongst cattle, and twenty years' disease amongst men, and this will happen as surely as you have a dead man in your cart.' The carrier angrily declared that there was no dead man in his cart. 'But there is,' said the horseman. Then the carrier went and looked, and found that a man he had taken up to give a ride was dead. Turning round he found the horseman had disappeared. The potato disease, cattle disease, and cholera followed.

The Wizard of Alderley Edge

Source: W. E. Axon, *Cheshire Gleanings*, 1884, pp. 56–8.
Narrator: Unknown.
Type: AT766 'The Seven Sleepers'.

ONCE UPON A TIME a farmer from Mobberley, mounted on a milk-white horse, was crossing the Edge on his way to Macclesfield to sell the animal. He had reached a spot known as the Thieves' Hole, and, as he slowly rode along thinking of the profitable bargain which he hoped to make, was startled by the sudden appearance of an old man, tall and strangely clad in a deep flowing garment. The old man ordered him to stop, told him that he knew the errand upon which the rider was bent, and offered a sum of money for the horse. The farmer, however, refused the offer, not thinking it sufficient. 'Go, then, to Macclesfield,' said the old man, 'but mark my words, you will *not* sell the horse. Should you find my words come true, meet me this evening, and I will buy your horse.' The farmer laughed at such a prophecy, and went on his way. To his great surprise, and greater disappointment, nobody would buy, though all admired his beautiful horse. He was, therefore, compelled to return. On approaching the Edge he saw the old man again. Checking his horse's pace, he began to consider how far it might be prudent to deal with a perfect stranger in so lonely a place. However, while he was considering what to do, the old man commanded him, 'Follow me!' Silently the old man led him by the Seven Firs, the Golden Stone, by Stormy Point, and Saddle Boll. Just as the farmer was beginning to think he had gone far enough he fancied that he heard a horse neighing underground. Again he heard it. Stretching forth his arm the old man touched a rock with a wand, and immediately the farmer saw a ponderous pair of iron gates, which, with a sound like thunder, flew open. The horse reared bolt upright, and the terrified farmer fell on his knees praying that his life might be spared. 'Fear nothing,' spoke the Wizard, 'and behold a sight which no mortal eye has ever looked upon.' They went into the cave. In a long succession of caverns the farmer saw a countless number of men and horses, the latter milk-white, and all fast asleep. In the innermost cavern heaps of treasure were piled up on the ground. From these glittering heaps the old man bade the farmer take the price he desired for his horse, and thus addressed him: 'You see these men and horses; the number was not complete. Your horse was wanted to make it complete. Remember my words, there will come a day when these men and these horses, awakening from their enchanted slumber, will descend into the plain, decide the fate of a great battle, and save their country. This shall be when George the son of George shall reign. Go home in safety. Leave your horse with me. No harm will befall you; but henceforward no mortal eye will ever look upon the iron gates. Begone!' The farmer lost no time in obeying. He heard the iron gates close with the same fearful sounds with which they were opened, and made the best of his way to Mobberley.

Although King Arthur is not specifically mentioned in this story, it was locally accepted, at least by the twentieth century, that it was Arthur and his knights who lay asleep under Alderley Edge. W. E. Axon notes that, 'The antiquity of the tradition is not easily ascertainable, the story used to be told by Parson Shrigley, and he placed the meeting of the Mobberley Farmer and the Enchanter at about eighty years before his time. Shrigley was curate of Alderley in 1753. He died in 1776.' The legend first entered print in the *Manchester Mail* in 1805, in a version told by Thomas Broadhurst, 'Old Daddy', a servant of the Stanleys of Alderley.

The legend of the sleeping hero who will return is one of the most persistent of all beliefs. It has a number of British expressions, mostly connected with legends of King Arthur. A farmer at Sewingshields in Northumberland is supposed to have penetrated King Arthur's hall, where the king lies with his knights in an enchanted sleep from which he will be woken by the man who draws his sword, cuts a garter and then blows a bugle-horn. The farmer drew the sword, at which the sleepers opened their eyes and sat up, and cut the garter, but failed to blow the horn. As he sheathed the sword, the once and future king succumbed once more to sleep, with the cry:

> O woe betide that evil day,
>> On which the witless wight was born,
> Who drew the sword – the garter cut,
>> But never drew the bugle-horn.

Potter Thompson had a similar experience under Richmond Castle, and was told:

> Potter, Potter Thompson.
> If thou hadst either drawn
>   The sword or blown that horn
> Thou'd been the luckiest man
>   That ever was born.

The Dead Moon

Source: M. C. Balfour, 'Legends of the Lincolnshire Cars: Part 1', *Folk-Lore*, 2, 1891, pp. 156–64.
Narrator: A nine-year old girl, 'Fanny (Agnes) Brattan', Lindsey, Lincolnshire.

LONG AGONE, I' MA gran's toime, th' Car-lan's doun by wor a' in bogs, as thee's heerd tell, mebbe: gra'at pools o' black watter, an' creepin' trickles o' green watter, an' squishy mools as'd soock owt in, as stept on un.

Weel, my gran' used to sa'ay, how, long afwore her toime, tha moon's sel' wor towanst de'ad an' buried i' tha ma-ashes; an' if thee will, a'll tell thee aboot it as she used for to tell me.

Tha moon up yond', shone an' shone to than, jest as she do now, thoff thou moightn't ha' thowt it; an' whan she shone, she loighted oop a' tha bog-pads so's a body cu'd wa'alk aboot, most 's safe as o' days. But when she didna shine, then oot cam' a tha Things 'at dool i' tha Darkness, an' want aboot seekin' to do evil an' harm to all as worna safe beside ther ain he'arths. Harm an' mischance an' mischief: Bogles, an' de'ad Things, an' crawlin' Horrors: tha a' coomed oot o' noights when the moon didna shine.

Weel, it comed so, 'at tha Moon heerd tell on a' this; an' bein' kin' an' good – as she be, surely, a-shoinin' fur us a' noights, 'stead o' takin' her nat'ral rest; she wor main troubled to think o' what went on ahint her back, loike; an' says she: 'A'll see fur mysel, a wull; it mebbe, 'at its none so bad 's fo'ak mak' oot.'

So sewer 'nuff, come tha month end, doun she stept hapt oop wi' a black cloak, an' a black hood o'wer her yaller shinin' hair; an' straight she went to tha Bog edge, an' looked aboot her. Watter here, an' watter there; wavin' tussocks, an' trem'lin' mools, an' gra'at black snags a' twisted and bent; an' afwore her, a' dark – dark, but the glimmer o' tha stars on tha pools, an' tha loight as comed fro' 's 'ain white feet, stealin' oot o' s black clo'ak. On a went, fair into the mid' o' tha bogs; an' aye lookin' about her; an' 'twor a mortal quare soight as 'a looked on. Tha witches girned as tha rode past on ther gra'at black cats; an' tha evil Eye glowered fro' tha da'arkest corners – an' tha will-o'-tha-wykes danced a' aboot wi' ther lanterns swingin' o' ther backs. Than tha de'ad fo'ak rose i' tha

watter, an' lookit roon' 'em in white twisted fa'aces an' hell fire i' ther empty
een-holes; an' tha slimy drippin' De'ad Han's slithered aboot, beckonin' an'
p'intin', and makin' yer skin crawl wi' ther cowld wet feel.

Tha moon drew 's clo'ak faster aboot her, an' tremmelt; but a wouldna gaw
back, wi'oot seein' a' ther wor to be seen, so on she went, steppin' light as tha
win' in summer fro' tuft to tuft, atween tha greedy gurglin' watter ho'als; an'
jest as she comed nigh a big black pool, 's fut slipt, and a wor nigh toomlin'
in – an' a grabbed wi' bo'oth han's at a snag near by, to steady 'asel' wi'; but so
cum as she touched it, a twined itsel' round her wrists loike a pa'ir o' han'cuffs,
an' gript her so 's she culdna move. She pulled, an' twisted, an' fowt, but twor
no'on good: a wor fast, an' a mo'ost sta'ay fast; so a' lookit aboot, an' wunnerd
if help 'd coom by; but a saw nowt but shiftin' flurryin' evil Things, comin' an'
goin' here an' there busy wi' ther ain ill wark.

But presently, as a stood trem'lin' i' tha da'ark a heerd summat ca'allin' i' tha
distance – a voice 'at ca'alled an' ca'all'd, an' than de'ed away wi' a sob; an' then
began agean wi' a screech o' pain or fear, an' ca'd an' ca'd, till tha ma-ashes weer
full on tha pitiful cryin' voice; an' than a heerd steps floonderin' along, squishin'
i' tha muck, an' slippin' on' tha tufts; an' throff tha darkness, a saw han's catchin'
at the snags an' tha tussocks, an' a white face wi' gre'at feared eyen.

'Twor a man strayed i' tha bogs; an' a' roon' about un tha girnin' bogles, an'
tha de'ad fo'ak, an' tha creepin' Horrors crawled an' crooded; tha voices mocked
un, an' the De'ad Han's ploocked at un, an' ahead, tha will o' tha wykes dangelt
ther lanterns, an' shuk wi' evil glee as a led un furder 'n furder fro' tha reet track.
Ma-azed wi' fear an' loathin' for tha Things aboot un, a stroogled on t'ords tha
flick'rin' loights 'at looked loike he'p an' sa'afety.

'Thou yonder,' a'd shriek, 'Thou! – a'm catched i' tha bog-lan's! – dost hear?
– God an' Mary save 's fro' the Horrors – he'p, thou yonder!' An' then a'd stop
an' sob an' moan an' ca' on a' tha saints an' wise women an' God 'issel to fetch
un oot.

An' than 'a 'd break oot in a shriek age'an, as tha slimy slithery things crawled
round un, till a couldna even see the fause lights afwore un. An' than, 's if
'tworna bad aneugh a'ready, the horrors 'd tak a' sorts o' shapes; an' rampin'
lasses 'd keek at un wi' bright eyen, an' stretch oot soft he'pin' han's; but when
a'd try to catch hol' on un, a'd cha'ange in 's grip to slimy things an' shapeless
worms, an' tha wicked voices 'd mock un wi' foul glee. An a' tha evil thoughts
an' deeds o's life cam' an' whispet in 's ears, an' da'anced aboot an' shooted oot
tha secret things o's ain heart, till a shrieked an' sobbed wi' pain an' shame, an'
the Horrors crawled an' gibbered roon' aboot an' mocked un. An' when tha
poor Moon saw 'at he wor coomin' nigher an' nigher to the deep holes an' tha

deadly quicks, an' furder 'n furder fro' the pad, a wor so mad an' so sorry, 'at she stroogled an' fowt an' pulled, harder nor iver. An' thoff a couldna get loose, wi' a' her twistin' an' toogin', the black hood fell ba'ack off 'a shoinin' yaller hair, an' tha beautiful light as coomed fro't druv away tha darkness.

Ooh! but tha man grat wi' joy to see God's ain light age'an; an' towanst tha evil things fled ba'ack into tha da'ark corners; fur tha canna boide tha light. So tha left un, an' fled; an' a could see whur a wor, and whur tha pad wor, an' hoo a'd hev to gaw fur to get oot o' tha ma'ash. An' a wor in sich a ha-aste to get awa-ay fro' tha quicks an' tha boglan's, an' tha things 'at doolt thur, 'at a sca'arce lookit at tha bra'ave light 'at coomed fro' tha beautiful shinin' yaller hair streamin' oot o'er the black cloak, an' fallin' to the watter at's feet. An' tha Moon's sel wor so tuk oop wi' sa'avin' he, an' wi' rejoicin' 'at a wor ba'ack on tha reet pad, 'at a cle'an furgot 'at a needed he'p 'asel', an' 'at a wor held fast by the Black Snag.

So off a went; spent an' gaspin' an' stumblin', an' sobbin' wi' joy, fleein' fur's life oot o' tha tur'ble Bogs. Than it coom ower the Moon, 'at 'ad loike main to gaw wi' un; an' a gra'at fear coom to 'a; an' a pulled an' fowt 'sif a wor mad, till a fell on's knees, spent wi' toogin', at tha fut o' tha snag. An' as a la'ay thur, gaspin' fur bre'ath, tha bla'ack hood fell for'ard ower her he'ad; an' thoff she tried to throw un ba'ack, 'twor catched in her hair, an' wudna gaw. So oot want tha blessed light, an' back coomed tha darkness wi' a' its evil things, wi' a screech an' a howl. They cam croodin' round her, mockin' an' snatchin' an' beatin'; shriekin' wi' rage an' spite, an' swearin' wi' foul tongues, spittin' an' snarlin', fur tha kenned her fur ther au'd enemy, tha' bra'ave bright Moon, as druv 'em ba'ack into tha corners, an' kep'em fro' warkin' their wicked wills My – what a clapperdatch 'twor – an' tha poor Moon crooched tremblin' an' sick i'tha mid, an' won'erd when tha'd make an en' o't, an' o' she.

'Dom' tha!' yelled tha witch-bodies, 'thou'st spiled oor spells this year agone!'

'An' thou keeps us in wer stra'ight coffins o' noights!' mo'aned tha de'id Fo'ak.

'An' us thou sen's to brood i' tha corners!' howled tha Bogles.

An' a' tha Things joined in wi' a gra'at 'Ho, ho!' till tha varry tussocks shuk, and tha watter gurgled. An' tha began age'an.

'Us'll poison her – poison her!' shrieked the witches. An' 'Ho, ho!' howled the Things age'an.

'Us'll smother her – smother her!' whispered the crawlin' Horrors, an' twined thersel's roon' her knees.

An' 'Ho, ho!' mocked the rest o'un.

'Us'll strangle her – strangle her!' screeched tha Dead Han's, an' ploocked at 'a throat wi' could fingers.

An' 'Ho, ho!' they yelled age'an.

But tha dead Fo'ak writhed an' girned about 'a, an' chuckled to thersel's.

'We'se bury thee, bury thee, doun wi' us i' tha black mools!'

An' age'an tha a' shouted wi' spite an' ill-will. An' tha poor Moon crooched doun, an' wished a wor de'ad, an' done wi'.

An' tha fowt an' squabbled what tha should do wi' her, till a pale gray light began to coom i' tha sky; an' it drew nigh the dawning. An' when tha saw that, tha wor feared lest tha shouldna hev toime to work ther wull; an' tha catched hol' on her, wi' horrid bony fingers, an' laid her deep i' tha watter at fut o' tha snag. An' tha dead fo'ak held her doun, while tha bogles fo't a stra'ange big sto'an an' rowled it o'top o' her, to keep her fro' rising. An' tha towld twae o' tha will o' tha wykes to ta'ake turns i' watchin', on tha black snag, to see 'at a lay safe an' still, an' couldna get oot to spoil ther sport wi' her loight, nor to he'p tha poor car-fo'ak to keep oot o' tha quicks an' ho'als o' nights. An' then, as tha grey light comed brighter i' tha sky, tha shapeless Things fled away to seek tha da'ark corners, an' tha dead fo'ak crept ba'ack into tha watter, or crammed thersel's into ther coffins, and tha witches went ho'am to ther ill-do'ins. An' tha green slimy watter shone i' tha dawnin' 'sif nae ill thing 'd aye coom nigh it.

An' thur lay tha poor moon, de'ad an' buried i' tha bog till sum 'un 'd set her loose; an' who'd ken whur to look fur a?

* * *

Weel, tha days pa'assed, an' 'twor tha toime fur tha new moon's coomin'; an' tha fo'ak put pennies i' ther pockets, and straws i' ther caps so's to be ready fur a, an lookit aboot onquietly, fur tha moon wor a good frien' to tha ma'ash fo'ak, an' tha wor main glad when tha da'ark toime wor ga'an, an' tha pads wor safe age'an, an' tha Evil Things wor druv back by the blessed Light into the darkness an' tha watter ho'als.

But days an' da'ays passed, an' tha new moon niver ca'ame, an' tha nights wor aye da'ark, an' th' Evil Things wor badder nor iver. Ther wor no'on a loaning safe to travel, an' tha boggarts crept an' wailed roon' tha hooses an' keekit in at the winders, an' sneepit at tha latches, till tha poor bodies mun ke'p lights a' night, else tha horrors 'd a coomed ower tha varry doorsils.

Aye so, tha bogles o' a' sorts seemed to ha' lost a' fearin'. Tha howled an' lafft an' screecht aroon', fit to wa'ake tha de'id thersel's, an' tha Car-fo'ak mun sit tremmlin' an' shakin' by tha foire, an' could nor sleep nor rast, nor pit fit across tha sil', a thae da'ark an' dreary nights.

An' still tha da'ays went on, an' tha new moon niver comed.

Nat'rally tha poor fo'ak were stra'ange feared and mazed, an' a lot o' un went to the wise woman wha doolt i' th' 'owd mill, an' axed ef so be 's tha could fin' oot wheer tha moon wor ga'an.

'Weel,' said she, arter lookin' i' tha brewpot, and i' tha mirror, an' i' tha Book, 'it be main quare, but a canna reetly tell ye what's hapt wi' her. It be dark, dark, an' a canna see nowt i' tha spells. Go'a slow, childer, a 'll think on it, an' mappen a 'll can he'p ye yet. If ye hear o' a'wthing, coom by 'n tell ma; 'n annyways pit a pinch o' salt, a stra'aw, an' a button on the door sil o' nights, an' tha Horrors 'll no can coom ower it, light or no light.'

So tha want ther wa'ays; an' as da'ays want by, an' niver a moon come, nat'rally tha talked – ma word! a reckon tha *did* ta'alk! ther tongues wagged like kenna what, at ho'am, an' at th' inn, an i' tha garth. But so come one da'ay, as tha sat on tha gra'at settle i' th' Inn, a man fro' tha fa'ar en' o' th' boglan's was smokin' an listenin', when all to wanst, a sat oop 'n slapt 's knee. 'Ma faicks!' sa'ays 'e, 'A 'd clean furgot, but a reckon a kens wheer tha moon be!' an' he telit 'em hoo a wor lost i' tha bogs, an' hoo when a wor nigh de'ad wi' fright, tha loight shone oot, an' a' tha Evil Things fled awa'ay, an' a fund tha pad 'n got ho'am safe.

'An' a wor so mazed wi' fear, loike,' says he, 'a didn't reetly look wheer the light comed fro'; but a mind fine 'twor saft an' white like tha moon's sel'. An 't comed fro' suthin' da'ark stannin' nigh a black snag i' tha watter. An' a didn't reetly look,' says he age'an, 'but a seem to mind a shinin' fa'ace an' yaller hair i' the mid' o' the dazzle, an' 't'ad a sort o' kin' look, loike th' aud moon 'asel aboon tha Cars o' nights.

So aff tha a' want to tha wise woman, an' tellt un aboot it, an' a looked lang i' the pot an' tha Book age'an, an' than a nodded 's head. Its da'ark still, childer, da'ark !' says she, 'an' a canna reetly see owt, but do 's a tell ye, an' ye'll fin' out for yersel's. Go'a all on ye, just afwore the night gathers, pit a sto'on i' yer gobs, an' tak' a hazel twig i' yer han's, an' say ne'er a word till yer safe ho'am age'an. Than wa'alk on an' fear nowt, fair into tha mid' o' tha ma'ash, till ye fin' a coffin, a can'lle, an' a cross. Than ye 'll no be far frae yer moon; look, and mappen ye 'll fin'.'

Tha lookit each at ither, an' scratched the'r heads.

'But wheer 'll us fin' her, mother?' says ane.

'An' hoo 'll us goa?' says t'other.

'An wull na' tha bogles fett us?' says another, an' so on.

'Houts!' said she, fratched loike. 'Passel o' fools! A can tell ye nae more; do as a tellt ee 'n fear nowt; 'n ef ye don't loike, than sta'ay by tha hoose, an' do wi' outen yer moon ef ye wull.'

So cum tha nex' night i' tha darklin's, oot tha want a' thegether, ivery man wi' a sto'on in's moath, an' a hazel-twig in's han', an' feelin', thou mayst reckon, main feared an' creepy. An' tha stummelt an' stottered along tha pads into the mid o' tha bogs; tha seed nowt, mirover, thoff tha heerd sighin's an' flust'rin's i' ther ears, an' felt cowld wet fingers techin' 'em; but on tha want, lookin' aroon' for tha coffin, tha can'le, an' tha cross, while tha comed nigh to the pool a side o' tha great snag, wheer the moon lay buried. An' a' towanst tha stopt, quakin' an' mazed an' skeery, fur theer wor tha gra'at sto'an, half in, half oot, o' tha watter, fur a' th' warl' loike a stra'ange big coffin; an' at tha he'ad wor tha black snag, stretchin' oot's twae arms in a dark grewsome cross; an' on it a tiddy light flickered, like a deein' can'le. An' tha a' knelt down i' tha muck, an' crossed thersel's, an' said, 'Our Lord', fu'st for'ard 'cause o' tha cross, an' then back'ard, to ke'p off tha Bogles; but wi'oot sp'akin' out, fur tha kenned as tha Evil Things 'd catch 'em, ef tha didna do as tha wise woman tellt 'em.

Than tha want nigher, an' tha took hol' on tha big sto'an, an' shoved un oop, an' arterwards tha said 'at fur wan tiddy minute, tha seed a stra'ange an' beautiful fa'ace lookin' oop at 'em glad loike oot o' tha black watter; but tha light coomed so quick 'an so white an' shinin', 'at tha stept ba'ack mazed wi' it, an' wi' tha gre'at angry wail as coomed fro' tha fleein' Horrors; an' tha varry nex' minute, when they could see age'an, theer wor tha full moon i' tha sky, bright an' beautiful an' kin' 's 'iver, shinin' an' smilin' doun at 'em, an' makin' tha bogs an' tha pads as clear as da'ay, an' stealin' into tha varry corners, as thoff she'd ha' druv tha darkness an' tha Bogles clean awa'ay ef a could.

So ho'am tha Car-fo'ak want, gladly and wi' light hearts; an' iver sence tha moon shines brighter 'n clearer ower tha Bogs than ither wheers; fur a mind's fine, 'at tha Horrors coom wi' tha da'ark, an' mischance an' mischief an' a' evil things, an' 'at tha Car-fo'ak sowt her an' found her, whan a wor de'ad an' buried i' tha Bog, an' ma'rk my wo'ds, it be a' true, fur ma gran 'asel a seed the snag wi' its twae arms, fur a' tha warl' loike a gre'at cross, an' tha green slimy watter at 's fut, wheer tha poor moon wor buried, an' the sto'an near by 'at kep' a doun, while tha wise woman sent 's Car-fo'ak to set a loose, an' pit a in's sky age'an.

Mrs Balfour states that this most unusual tale 'was obtained from a young girl of nine, a cripple, who stated that she had heard it from her "gran". But I think it was tinged by her own fancy, which seemed to lean to eerie things, and she certainly revelled in the gruesome descriptions, fairly making my flesh creep with her words and gestures. I have kept not only to the outline of her story, but in great part to her very words, which I think I could not have made more effective even if I had wished to do so.' The same girl told the story of 'Sam'l's Ghost'. Joseph Jacobs gives the surname of the narrator, 'Fanny', as Bratton; Maureen James has identified her as Agnes Brattan of Stoneham in Redbourne.

Some of the thick Fenland dialect in this text seems to have a Scots tinge to it, with 'Weel' and 'Houts', but I give it as printed. Retellings in standard English can be found in Jacobs, *More English Fairy Tales*, Crossley-Holland, *The Dead Moon*, and James, *Lincolnshire Folk Tales*.

Further Reading

THE ESSENTIAL COLLECTION OF English folktales can be found in the four volumes of Katharine Briggs's *A Dictionary of British Folk-Tales in the English Language: Incorporating the F. J. Norton Collection* (1970–71). I am deeply indebted both to Katharine Briggs's work and through it and independently to the manuscripts of F. J. Norton housed in the library of The Folklore Society at University College London. The Briggs *Dictionary* contains an extensive bibliography, which should be supplemented by that in Herbert Halpert's key 'Bibliographical Essay on the Folktale in Engish' in Halpert (ed.), *A Folklore Sampler from the Maritimes* (1982). Ernest W. Baughman's *Type and Motif Index of the Folk-Tales of England and North America* (1966) is an essential reference tool, supplemented for the medieval period by Gerald Bordman's *Motif-Index of the English Metrical Romances* (1963).

Representative collections of English folktales include Katharine Briggs's *British Folk Tales and Legends: A Sampler* (1977), selected from the *Dictionary*, and Katharine Briggs & Ruth Tongue's *Folktales of England* (1965). Sybil Marshall's *Everyman's Book of English Folk Tales* (1981) is retold by the author, as to a lesser extent are Kevin Crossley-Holland's *Folk-Tales of the British Isles* (1985) and *British Folk Tales: New Versions* (1987) and Alan Garner's *Book of British Fairy Tales* (1984) and *A Bag of Moonshine* (1986). The most important earlier surveys are James Orchard Halliwell's *Popular Rhymes and Nursery Tales of England* (1849; reissued 1970), E. S. Hartland's *English Fairy and Other Folk Tales* (1890) and Joseph Jacobs's *English Fairy Tales* (1890) and *More English Fairy Tales* (1894). The two Jacobs titles were reissued in one volume as *English Fairy Tales* (1968).

Individual collections of major importance include W. H. Barrett's *Tales from the Fens* (1963), *More Tales from the Fens* (1964) and *East Anglian Folklore and Other Tales* (with R. P. Garrod, 1976), Ruth Tongue's *Forgotten Folk-Tales of the English Counties* (1970) and Kingsley Palmer's *Oral Yolk-Tales of Wessex* (1973). Major earlier collections include Sidney Oldall Addy's *Household Tales with Other Traditional Remains: Collected in the Counties of York, Lincoln, Derby and Nottingham* (1895; reissued as *Folk Tales and Superstitions*, 1973), William Henderson's *Notes on the Folklore of the Northern Counties of England and the Borders* (1866; new edition 1879; reissued 1973), Robert Hunt's *Popular Romances of the West of England* (1865; 3rd edn 1881; reissued 1968) and Ella Mary Leather's *The Folk-Lore of Herefordshire* (1912; reissued 1973).

English legends are well surveyed in Jennifer Westwood's *Albion: A Guide to Legendary Britain* (1985). Individual categories of legend and belief can be pursued through such volumes as Katharine Briggs's *The Fairies in Tradition and Titerature* (1967), Theo Brown's *The Fate of the Dead* (1979), Leslie V. Grinsell's *Folklore of Prehistoric Sites in Britain* (1976) and Jacqueline Simpson's *British Dragons* (1980). John Aubrey's seminal *Miscellanies* and *Remaines of Gentilisme and Judaisme* are included in *Three Prose Works,* edited by John Buchanan-Brown (1972).

The best modern collection of traditional jests is E. M. Wilson's three-part 'Some Humorous English Folk Tales' printed in *Folk-Lore* (vols. 49 and 54, 1938 and 1943). For early material, see P. M. Zall (ed.), *A Hundred Merry Tales and Other English Jest Books of the Fifteenth and Sixteenth Centuries* (1963). Modern comic and macabre rumour legends are surveyed by Paul Smith in *The Book of Nasty Legends* (1983) and *The Book of Nastier Legends* (1986) and by Rodney Dale in *The Tumour in the Whale* (1978) and *It's True, It Happened to a Friend* (1984). Among many volumes of ghost stories, four volumes sent in by readers of the *Daily News* and edited by S. Louis Giraud in the 1920s as *True Ghost Stories, Warnings from Beyond, Uncanny Stories* and *Ghosts in the Great War and True Tales of Haunted Houses* should not be missed.

English folktales can be studied in their international context by use of Antti Aarne and Stith Thompson's *The Types of the Folktale: A Classification and Bibliography* (2nd revision, 1961), Stith Thompson's *Motif-Index of Folk Literature* (6 vols, 1955), Reidar Th. Christiansen's *The Migratory Legends* (1958), Jan Harold Brunvand's 'A Classification of Shaggy Dog Stories' in the *Journal of American Folklore* (vol. 76, 1963), Barbara A. Wood's *The Devil in Dog Form: A Partial Type-Index of Devil Legends* (1959), J. Bolte and G. Polivka's *Anmerkungen zu den Kinder – u. Hausmärchen der Brüder Grimm* (5 vols, 1913–32) and D. L. Ashliman's *A Guide to Folktales in the English Language* (1987). Stith Thompson's *The Folktale* (1946; reissued 1977) is still the best introduction to the world's folk literature. *The Classic Fairy Tales* by Iona and Peter Opie (1974) is incisive and authoritative. Richard Dorson's *The British Folklorists: A History* (1968) is an invaluable study, supplemented by two volumes of nineteeth-century debate, *Peasant Customs and Savage Myths* (1968).

The journals *Folklore* (previously *The Folk-Lore Record*, *The Folk-Lore Journal* and *Folk-Lore)*, the *Journal of the Gypsy Lore Society* and *Lore and Language* are repositories of much valuable unreprinted material, while the international cross-currents of folktale studies can be traced in the *Journal of American Folklore*, *Arv* and *Fabula*, among many folklore journals.

International scholarship on the folktale has of course proceeded in the three decades since the first edition of this book. The Aarne–Thompson tale-type index has been updated in three volumes by Hans-Jörg Uther as *The Types of International Folktales* (2004); luckily the AT numbers in this book will be the same as the new ATU numbers, though sometimes the titles of the tale types have been amended. There have also been a number of important works on the fairy tale in particular, notably Bengt Holbek, *Interpretation of Fairy Tales* (2nd edition 1998), Hilda Ellis Davidson and Anna Chaudhri, *A Companion to the Fairy Tale* (2003), Donald Haase, *The Greenwood Encyclopedia of Folktales and Fairy Tales* 2008), Jack Zipes, *The Oxford Companion to Fairy Tales* (2nd edition, 2015) and other works, Andrew Teverson, *The Fairy Tale World* (2019). For the non-specialist, two brief introductions to the fairy tale are Andrew Teverson, *Fairy Tale* (2013); Marina Warner, *Once Upon a Time* (2014). In regard to England I would like to draw attention to a particularly fine contribution to English folklore studies, *A Dictionary of English Folklore* by Jacqueline Simpson and Steve Roud (2000); and to Diane Purkiss, *Troublesome Things* (2000); Jennifer Westwood and Jacqueline Simpson, *The Lore of the Land* (2005); Carolyne Larrington, *The Land of the Green Man* (2015); Edward Parnell, *Ghostland* (2019); and Amy Jeffs, *Storyland* (2021). A book I missed from my original Further Reading is the multi-author *Folklore, Myths and Legends of Britain* (1973). So far as the English folktale itself is concerned, there have been notable contributions, standing at various angles to the source material, from Jem Roberts, *Tales of Britain* (2018); Kevin Crossley-Holland, *Between Worlds* (2019); Elizabeth Garner, *Lost and Found Stories* (2022); for ghost stories, Roger Clarke, *A Natural History of Ghosts* (2012), and for black dogs, Mark Norman, *Black Dog Folklore* (2016). The old county-by-county approach to English folklore has long been thought irredeemably old-fashioned, but in fact has produced some excellent books, such as Peter Tolhurst, *This Hollow Land: Aspects of Norfolk Folklore* (2018); Francis Young, *Suffolk Fairylore* (2019); and the too-many-to-list volumes in the History Press series mentioned in the Introduction. Lastly, there have been two major collections of oral storytelling: Michael Wilson, *Performance and Practice* (1997); and Herbert Halpert and J.D.A. Widdowson, *Folktales of Newfoundland* (1996).

Index